THE
WALKING
DEAD

Other Books in the Walking Dead Series

ROBERT KIRKMAN'S

THE WALKING DEAD

RETURN TO WOODBURY

JAY BONANSINGA

Thomas Dunne Books
St. Martin's Griffin
New York

THOMAS DUNNE BOOKS.
An imprint of St. Martin's Press.

ROBERT KIRKMAN'S THE WALKING DEAD: RETURN TO WOODBURY. Copyright © 2017 by Robert Kirkman LLC. All rights reserved. Printed in the United States of America. For information, address St. Martin's Press, 175 Fifth Avenue, New York, N.Y. 10010.

www.thomasdunnebooks.com
www.stmartins.com

The Library of Congress has cataloged the hardcover edition as follows:

Names: Bonansinga, Jay R., author.
Title: Robert Kirkman's The Walking Dead : return to Woodbury / Jay Bonansinga.
Other titles: Walking dead: Return to Woodbury | Return to Woodbury | Walking dead (Television program)
Description: First edition. | New York : Thomas Dunne Books/St. Martin's Press, 2017. | Series: The Walking Dead series ; 8
Identifiers: LCCN 2017027326 | ISBN 9781250058522 (hardcover) | ISBN 9781466862753 (ebook)
Subjects: LCSH: Zombies—Fiction. | GSAFD: Horror fiction.
Classification: LCC PS3552.O5927 R645 2017 | DDC 813/.54—dc23
LC record available at https://lccn.loc.gov/2017027326

ISBN 978-1-250-18170-1 (trade paperback)

Our books may be purchased in bulk for promotional, educational, or business use. Please contact your local bookseller or the Macmillan Corporate and Premium Sales Department at 1-800-221-7945, extension 5442, or by email at MacmillanSpecial Markets@macmillan.com.

First St. Martin's Griffin Edition: June 2018

10 9 8 7 6 5 4 3 2 1

To Walker Stalkers everywhere.

ACKNOWLEDGMENTS

Major thanks to the gentleman and scholar, Robert Kirkman, who started it all; also a huge gracias to Brendan Deneen, editor extraordinaire; Andy Cohen, the manager's manager; Sean Mackiewicz, the voice of reason; Susannah Noel for precision line editing; David Alpert, the rock of Gibraltar; the fabulous folks at Skybound; the badass WSC gangsters, James Frazier, Lee Ann Wyatt, Robin Justice, Jackie Prutsman, Monique Engh, and the amazing traveling staff and volunteers that pamper the celebs; Jon, Lou, Flynn, and all the folks at Forbidden Planet UK; and special shout-outs to Jeff Siegel, Mort Castle, Thomas Losey, Charles Robinson, Eagle Eye Books, Jim and Joe of Comix Revolution, and last but never, ever least, my moral compass, my soul mate, my everything bagel, the most beautiful girl in the room, my wife Jill Norton.

Los Dias Finales

Behold, evil is going forth from nation to nation. And a great storm is being stirred up from the remotest parts of the earth.

—Jeremiah 25:32

Twenty miles off the coast of Guantánamo, Cuba, on the small island of Ile de la Lumière, a man awakens early to a vague feeling that trouble is headed his way.

At first, the man has no idea what form this trouble will take, but it very likely will have something to do with the sky, a portion of which he can now see from the vantage point of his cot. Twenty feet above him, the corrugated tin roof of his prison dormitory—battered by recent storms—has lost a single rusty panel to the winds. Through the narrow gap, the man lying on the cot can now see the agitated heavens. Soupy gray clouds have blown in from the south. Something cold and sharp like a bullwhip intermittently lashes the side of the building, making an incessant rattle. An epic storm is brewing.

Rafael Rodrigo Machado sits up and stretches his weary joints. This morning marks his 1825th day in prison, and his emaciated limbs and sun-dried skin reflect his solitary confinement on this godforsaken spit of desolate beaches, rocky cliffs, and tangled, snake-infested rain forests. Over the last five years, every last guard, administrator, and fellow prisoner has either fled or swallowed the barrel of their 9 millimeter. The suicides—as far as Rafael can tell—have put these men to rest, their bodies left to rot in the unforgiving sun. Maybe they've gone to purgatory. Who knows? The only certainty for Rafael Machado now is that he has grown accustomed to being alone. But being alone is not the same as being lonely. Rafael is happy to keep to himself inside the hermetically sealed safety of this ramshackle prison, especially after what he has seen transpiring around him for the last four years or so.

He gets up and begins the same morning ritual that has comforted him for the last fifty-eight months, three weeks, and two days. He goes to the porcelain basin, washes up with rainwater, and harvests breakfast from his meager garden (he has subsisted on sweet potatoes and collards since being abandoned by the prison staff). At this stage of the ritual, he invariably takes a moment to peer through the slats of the prison walls in the futile hope that things on the island have changed.

Today, he gazes down the steep, rocky slope to the west and sees the same slumped roof pitches of Igreja do Sagrado Coração—the sad little chapel upon which he has gazed each morning for many months. He sees the same wind-damaged steeple, the cross hanging—ironically—upside down on its broken moorings. He sees the same thirteen parishioners aimlessly wandering the gated courtyard, snarling and spitting like animals, possessed by *os demonios do inferno*.

Rafael has seen so many fall prey to the Satan over the last couple of years. He has seen guards succumb to unclean spirits and attempt to eviscerate each other. He has seen fellow prisoners escape only to leap to their deaths off the cliffs to the east. He has seen distant columns of smoke rising off the rooftops of coastal villages, and he has heard the eerie choruses of the possessed at night like the singing of jackals. He believes he has witnessed the ushering in of *Los Dias Finales*—the End of Days—and for some reason *he* has remained unscathed in his little purgatory of tin, razor wire, mortar, and *Tipuana tipu* wood.

He wonders sometimes if he's one of those left behind, the orphans of the cosmos. Not that he's complaining. Since the coming of the End of Days, he has been blessed by the solitude of this crumbling prison, the embrace of these walls—once built to keep felons in, now repurposed to keep monsters out. He has plenty of food and water. He has enough room to take walks inside the periphery. And he has enough time to pray for forgiveness, to sketch on his bark, to play dominoes, and mostly to think. In fact, his routine has remained unchanged for many, many months . . . until this morning.

Now he sees the black sky approaching from the South Atlantic, the crackling light around the edges like tendrils of flame. He gapes at the sickly gray curtains of rain—still a few kilometers away but closing fast—and he notices with mounting horror the silver chaos of the sea, the tidal wave off in the distance like a mouth opening its maw. It's as if the entire ocean is possessed by the same eternal hunger as those poor souls down in the chapel.

He knows what all this means. As the wind curls around the feeble walls of the prison, shaking the bones of the place as a giant, petulant child might shake a toy building, Rafael swallows back his terror and slowly turns in a 360-degree circle of panic. He knows what he has to do. He just has to wait for the right moment, and he has to accomplish the task quickly . . . before the entire world collapses around him.

He doesn't have to wait long. At precisely 11:41 A.M. Cuba Daylight Time, the gale force winds take down the south wall adjacent to the garden. The timbers crack like pistol shots, and the entire section bows outward from a shockwave of air pressure while Rafael cowers behind a pillar.

Clad in a bright-yellow rain slicker from the deserted guards' quarters, boots that have been sealed with tape, a tactical knife on his hip, and a scarf tight around his lower face, he jerks at the earthshaking vibrations of the wall slamming down on the ground outside the cell block. Horizontal rain crashes into the yard with the force of a battering ram, vaporizing the garden and tossing into the ether anything that's not nailed down. Rafael gathers himself, takes a deep breath, and then plunges into the flickering pandemonium of the larger world.

Halfway down the slope, he slips and falls, careening on his ass nearly a hundred meters. He lands in a thicket of wild sumac, the rain lashing him, scourging his face. Already he is drenched and feels as though his lungs are filled with cement. The wind whistles like a runaway train. He wills himself to his feet and staggers the rest of the way down the hill to the rugged strip of sand lining the north end of the island.

The impound yard lies in the boiling gray mist half a kilometer away. Rafael lowers his head and charges as fast as he can toward the graveyard of confiscated vehicles, aircraft, weapons, and other accouterments of the drug trade. As a pilot for one of the largest cartels in South America, Rafael never sampled his product, never imbibed in his cargo. He always thought of himself as a professional. He loathed the messier aspects of the trafficking business, the blood feuds, the assassinations, the infighting, the spread of addiction among the poor and the young. Rafael considered himself above it all, a simple deliveryman. Now he prays that his old Bell Jet Ranger helicopter is still chained to its blocks out by the pier, the confiscated items still locked up in the shed next to it. He knows time is of the essence. He probably has less than half an hour before 90 percent of the island—including the impound yard—is underwater.

Through veils of rain and swirling vortexes of debris, the impound yard materializes a hundred meters away. At first, the ghostly outlines of rusted-out Humvees, motorbikes, and bullet-riddled wreckage appear almost as a mirage, an anachronism from days gone by, a time when gasoline and electricity and crooked politicians were plentiful. Now, Rafael struggles through the deluge and the rising winds, squinting into the mist as he scans the lot.

His heart pumps when he sees the old chopper chained to the far corner of the gravel apron, the shed next to it still intact and standing. His prayers turn to the Jet Ranger's fuel tank. He trudges through the storm, goes over to the shed, and kicks the padlocked door repeatedly until its rusted hinges snap. Inside, amid the cobwebs and dust motes, he finds the old arsenal, a cornucopia of firearms, all gauges and calibers, enough to equip an insurgency.

By this point, the wind has kicked up several degrees of intensity, and a gust smashes into the side of the shed, ripping the entire structure free of its foundation, and knocking it over with Rafael still inside. Guns and ammo cartons spill across the rain-lashed sands. Hyperventilating, Rafael gathers an armload, wrapping a nylon strap from one of the guns around it like bundling cordwood. He struggles to his feet. He has to cross only ten meters or so to get to the helicopter, but it's an excruciating ten meters. The wind blows the rain in his mouth and up his sinus cavities.

By the time he reaches the chopper, the tide has reached the edge of the impound lot. Somehow, with rain-slick, frozen fingers, Rafael gets a shell into a cut-down pistol grip shotgun. He aims the muzzle at the mooring chain and jacks the trigger. The gun roars. The blast sends the chain into oblivion.

Then, over the course of the next hundred seconds or so, Rafael Machado gets lucky. He pries open the chopper door and hurls the weapons and himself into the fuselage. The springs squeak under the seat as he sits down and frantically scans the gauges. Miraculously, the battery has some juice left, the intermittent tone beeping as Rafael flips the power switch. He reaches up and makes sure all the fuses are in, and then he sets the throttle to neutral.

Meanwhile, the flood tide has pummeled the beach, and now seawater rages under the Jet Ranger's belly, its skids starting to skate sideways. Rafael thumbs the Start button, and the turbine engine begins to sing. The craft pitches left as the floodwaters swirl under it. The rotor begins to turn, fighting the winds.

The tsunami hits.

It feels to Rafael as though his stomach has been yanked into his crotch as the water crashes against the Jet Ranger, tossing it sideward. Rafael twists the throttle, pulls back on the stick, and prays a little bit, as the currents take the aircraft backward down the beach. The chopper is sinking, sliding back toward the black void of the open sea.

"*Vamos!*" Rafael's voice is sandpaper rough, out of practice, speaking in the Portuguese patois of his native Brazil. "*VAMOS! VAMOS! VAMOS!*"

The Jet Ranger begins shaking convulsively up through its frame, feeling to Rafael as though it's about to pop its rivets.

He gives the throttle all he's got, and he feels the fulcrum of the rotors tugging, tugging, tugging . . . until finally, blessedly, mercifully, the contraption detaches from the waters and levitates upward into the dark, violent world of the storm.

At some point, somewhere over the northern coast of Haiti, tossed and whiplashed by the roller coaster of shifting winds, Rafael blacks out.

He knows this because one moment he's looking at the gauges, wrestling with the stick, trying to navigate through a gray wall of rain, and the next moment he's slumped over, staring at the floor between his legs.

Shaking off the disorientation and the pounding headache from banging the top of his head on the ceiling, he manages to pull out of the nosedive only seconds before crashing into the ocean. He gets back on course. He uses the instruments to nudge the Jet Ranger back on a northerly trajectory. He estimates that he is a little over three hundred miles from the coast of Florida.

The next hour is a horrendous battle to outrun the beast roaring across the Caribbean. The Jet Ranger fishtails, lurches, and slides sideways. It shudders, it rattles, and it bangs over turbulent patches. The passage of time crawls, Rafael's hands slick with blood from holding an iron grip on the stick for such a prolonged period. And to make matters worse, he sees that he has only enough fuel in his reserve tank to keep this speed up for another couple hundred miles. He's going to be cutting it close to the bone. Fortunately, it's the kind of calculated risk with which he is not completely unfamiliar.

Over the years, he has fled the authorities through impossible conditions. He has been in high-speed, high-altitude dogfights with heavily armed Federales. He has landed his aircraft on uncharted airfields in the middle of firefights. He has flown less than thirty feet above the rocky earth through mountain passes in Brazil. He has served the most brutal, ruthless, amoral cartel in South America for years, choosing a ten-year prison sentence over becoming an informant.

Somewhere west of the Bahamas, he gets blown off course. With his fuel down to fumes, his engine sputtering, he pulls his belt from his jeans and shackles his hand to the stick. The chopper groans and leans and starts losing altitude. The clouds begin to break, and through the wisps of vapor he sees the vast pale sea spreading out below him. He sees the whitecaps looming closer and closer.

He realizes he's going to die. But he can't stop staring down at those magnificent breakers rolling under him . . . which is when he remembers what waves and whitecaps mean when they appear in increasing profusion.

Way in the distance, on the unbroken horizon line, a green necklace of islands comes into view. He remembers the Florida Keys from his childhood, his grandmother taking him from São Paulo to Key West to visit his aunt Anita. The Jet Ranger coughs and shudders. The engine is running on fumes. Rafael can see the surface of the ocean less than twenty feet below him.

The rotors begin to fail. He sees the ashen sand of a deserted key two hundred meters away. His heart races. His hand is on fire, icy hot on the stick as he yanks it back to no avail. The Jet Ranger lists at a forty-five-degree angle, and then drifts, and finally goes down.

The impact slams him into the instrument panel as water rushes into the cabin. He kicks the hatch open. He grabs the bundle of weapons and two life preservers. The chopper starts sinking. He struggles to pull the bulky load and himself out the narrow hatchway.

The aircraft vanishes into the sea as Rafael starts dog-paddling madly toward the white sandy coastline less than a hundred meters in the distance. Something deep inside Rafael drives him on. It would be a shame to come this far, through all that he's been through, only to drown within sight of America.

The last twenty meters are pure agony. Rafael paddles and paddles, his lungs blazing with pain, his vision going haywire. When he finally reaches shallow water, he starts coughing and gasping. He has swallowed seawater. He knows enough of it can kill him. Then he feels the mushy sand beneath his feet, and he heaves the bundle of firearms onto high, dry land. Then he staggers onto the beach, collapses, and vomits milky, salty bile across the white sands.

He rolls onto his back. The world is spinning. Night is closing in. The dusky clouds hang low—the storm will reach these shores soon. But he feels thankful that he has made it to America.

America will be his savior. The Americans will know what to do. John Wayne, Tony Montana, Snoop Dogg, the Dallas Cheerleaders, Pam Grier, and General George S. Fucking Patton. Rafael finds these American icons from his childhood rattling around his brain as he stares at the sky. An American sky. Thank God, thank God, thank God. He made it. He is free, and safe, and in America, and he knows that the Americans will have the answers.

That night, the storm unfurls around him as he trudges inland. He finds an old deserted picnic shelter, builds a campfire under a thatched roof of cypress and banana leaves, rests, and dries out. Billowing curtains of rain envelop the shelter, making Rafael feel as though he's in a space capsule drifting alone in the black void of the universe.

The first creature makes itself known around dawn the next morning.

Rafael is dozing when the thing materializes in the rain, trundling out of the adjacent woods. Drawn by the glowing embers of the fire, it's a large male in tattered work clothes, maybe a former fisherman, apparently possessed by the same demons that gripped the poor souls inhabiting Rafael's island. This one is bloated and slimy-wet from exposure to the elements, and it smells of the abattoir.

Rafael has no time to be heartbroken—he had hoped America would be free of this inexplicable Satanic rule—as the thing lunges at him with its mouth working hungrily, chewing its ghastly cud, its eyes filmed in white. Rafael manages to get his hand around the grip of a Beretta .45 ACP semiauto and asks no questions. He fires three rounds into the thing's cranium, chunks of its skull flinging off on contrails of blood.

Science has its trial and error, its control groups and repeated experiments, and its close observation leading to general hypotheses. Rafael stands there for a moment, thunderstruck by the sight of the head-shot creature folding to the ground. The demon has been vanquished by . . . what? Brain death? The magical countermeasure of breaching the skull? Rafael remembers first observing the phenomena on Lumière, one of the guards ranting, *"Solo la cabeza!—SOLO LA CABEZA!* Only the head! *Only a shot to the head takes them!"*

Now Rafael watches the creature collapsing backward into the fire, tossing sparks into the air, ragged clothing catching, flames licking up its body, cocooning it in blazing light. *How odd,* Rafael muses silently, watching the abomination, *that flames alone do not vanquish the damned. Could it be that they are now creatures of hell?* Alas . . . Rafael has no time to make any further deductions. The savage, corrupted noises of the possessed rise above the rain all around the shelter.

As the shadowy figures converge on the oasis of light, Rafael quickly gathers his arsenal. By this point, he has fashioned a shoulder strap from a rope he found along the way, as well as a tarp to keep the guns dry. He hurriedly slings the bundle of weapons over his shoulder and secures them with his belt, then fires a few errant gunshots into the oncoming swarm.

He kicks the embers across the shelter, catching a few of the creatures on fire and causing enough of a diversion to slip away into the dawn.

Somewhere in the distant recesses of his memory, Rafael Machado remembers happier times. He recalls crossing the overseas highway that connects the hundred-mile chain of Florida Keys to the mainland. He remembers traveling the "All-American Road" in his aunt

Anita's battered Ford Galaxy, traversing dozens of bridges, feeling as if he were on a magic carpet, floating over the sun-spangled waters of the Gulf, singing joyous, off-key choruses of *"Se Essa Rua Fosse Minha"* ("If This Street Were Mine").

Now, the pitiful condition of the road weighs heavily on Rafael's heart as he slogs along the elevated highway in the rain with his mobile arsenal on his back. Weather-beaten wreckage litters the pavement, some of it appearing to have been there for so long the salt winds have rubbed the metal down to the primer. Many of the cars have been stripped, the tires gone, and the glass broken out—stalks of sea grass and weeds growing out of the cavities. Bodies lay strewn here and there, bleached by the sun into skeletons, some of the skulls petrified into black puddles of their own fluids now as hard and shiny as onyx.

It takes two days to make it to Marathon—the halfway point on the overseas highway—and by that time, Rafael has become dangerously dehydrated and pathologically weak. He hasn't eaten for seventy-two hours and has subsisted only on the occasional few drops of rainwater collected in bottles found along the way. He can barely walk as he circles around a former colony of luxury beach house condominiums, now infested with the possessed.

In his personal lexicon, Rafael has started thinking of these desecrated souls as Hunger Demons or *monstro da fome*—"Hungries," for short—and has chosen to avoid them whenever possible rather than wasting ammunition. He also has yet to see any other living human beings. Could Rafael be the last man on earth? The possibility chills him to the bone. But instead of dwelling on it, he focuses his efforts on a singular goal—*survival*. And right now, survival means finding water and food.

Marathon, Florida, turns out to be a ghost town. An atomic bomb could have been dropped here and it wouldn't make the place much more desolate than it already is. Trash blows through the corridors of once-grand resort hotels. Alligators wander the sidewalks outside boarded cafes. The air smells of decay—mold and dead flesh— punctuated by the ambient drone of mortified vocal cords.

Rafael is about to give up his search and keep heading north when he stumbles upon a storage unit behind one of the condos that appears to still be intact. Making as little noise as possible, he snaps the crumbling padlock and unearths a treasure trove.

"*Obrigado, Deus*—thank you—thank you, God," he mumbles almost reverently as he sorts through the contents of the unit. Most of the items are the useless and ephemeral trappings of resort life—long-ago-deflated beach balls, dusty Frisbees, disassembled patio tables, folded-up beach chairs, boogie boards, and various flotation toys. But there's also a pair of rucksacks with shoulder straps, a large jug of sealed bottled water, a picnic basket filled with dishes and utensils, a family-sized box of individually wrapped packs of Pringles potato chips (still shrink-wrapped), a plastic ten-gallon container marked GAS, and the pièce de résistance, a small all-terrain three-wheeler in showroom condition.

An hour later, Rafael departs Marathon, Florida, on his ATV, with a full fuel tank in back, his newly acquired provisions, and a belly full of stale processed potato product and tepid drinking water.

Over the next few days, as the rains descend upon the southern United States, Rafael averages just under two hundred miles per day. He uses the main highways whenever possible, skirting intermittent pockets of Hungries by taking rural access roads, and keeping a lookout for any sign of survivors. Along the way, he siphons gas from abandoned cars and finds extra ammunition on the floor of a tour bus. Around Orlando, near dusk one night, he sees lights burning in some of the buildings, perhaps powered by generators, but he decides to play it safe and keep moving. He has been in prison far too long to get trapped, ambushed, or cornered. Orlando doesn't feel right. The next day, around Gainesville, he sees a group of people on horseback along a highway overpass, and he waves, and they do not wave back, and that is the extent of the interaction. He keeps moving. The key to everything, he realizes now, is to keep moving.

At the end the third day, at precisely 7:13 P.M. Eastern Daylight

Time, he passes a bullet-riddled, sun-faded sign posted along the gravel shoulder:

Welcome
We're   Glad   Georgia's
On   Your   Mind
Site of the 1996
Olympic   Games

Rafael notices an almost instantaneous change in the terrain. The scrubby, sun-bleached orange groves of northern Florida soften and darken and plunge into the rolling patchwork hills of thick piney woods and leafy, kudzu-covered tobacco farms.

He stops for the night at a derelict rest area, the ruins of the restroom building now a burned-out shell of scorched timbers, crumbling plaster, and exposed rebar sticking up like bare bones. He sleeps out back under the cover of another picnic shelter, hidden from view of the highway, safe within a perimeter of makeshift trip wires and tin cans. He dreams of his old girlfriend, and his mother's death, and the execution-style murder of his friend Ramon, who was caught skimming off the cartel. He wakes up drenched in a cold sweat, the wind blowing intermittent rain across the shelter. Ironically, he feels invigorated. He has a weird feeling that fate brought him here. He has no idea why or how it will play out, but for the first time in his life, he feels as though he has a purpose.

Later that day, about seventy-five miles north of the state line, he begins to learn the specific nature of this purpose when the needle on the ATV's fuel gauge hits E, and he pulls off the two-lane to hunt for more gas.

For over an hour, he wanders the back roads like a ghostly revenant in his yellow rain slicker, searching for a stray abandoned vehicle or a gas station that hasn't been completely ransacked. He carries the bundle of firearms on his back, tucked into the rucksack, the muzzles sticking out the top like so many pieces of kindling. All the barns and farmhouses have been stripped of every last resource. The shells of old vehicles lie belly-up in the rain like the carcasses of dead animals tangled in vines and ironweed. All the tanks behind the feed and seed stores are as dry as flint. Adding to his misery is the fact that the woods are exceedingly rife with the pathetic spoor of Satan. Every five minutes or so, Rafael has to dodge another pack of them. He is tempted to open fire but he knows now the noise will draw more of them out of the shadows.

He is beginning to formulate an alternative course of action, maybe look for a horse to steal, when he hears the first signs of his destiny off in the trees to the north, near a small town called Thomaston.

Rafael slips into a stand of hardwoods and crouches down to listen. A single voice carries on the wind, barely audible under the droning white noise of the rain. It sounds male to Rafael, gravelly, taut with fear, maybe anger—it's hard to parse out the exact emotion at this distance.

Rafael has a modest understanding of the language—his aunt Anita taught him rudimentary English when he was a boy—and he has picked up a few of the more colorful expressions over the years from his dealings with North American drug lords. But there's something about this man's voice that sinks a hook into Rafael—something humane, intelligent, even friendly—which is ironic considering the fact that the man keeps hollering the word *stupid.* Rafael knows the meaning of the word, and it intrigues him enough to pull a sniper rifle from his pack and move closer.

It takes a few minutes to make his way up the adjacent wooded slope, the leaf-matted earth dangerously slick. The rains have turned the brick-red Georgia soil to the slimy consistency of axle grease. He reaches the apex of the ridge and sees movement down in a clearing below, about thirty yards away. He looks through the scope to get a better view and sees a solitary middle-aged man dressed in a shop-worn jacket, jeans, and hiking boots, surrounded on all sides by at least a dozen possessed souls. The man in the Windbreaker waves a makeshift torch—a thick pine bow, one end most likely dipped in some kind of accelerant—which now blazes and sputters and smokes in the rain, momentarily keeping the twelve or so Hungries at bay. In the narrow, magnified field of the scope's vision, Rafael sees that the hapless man in the jacket has gray hair swept off his forehead, eyes wet with emotion, and wounds on his face and neck that appear to be third-degree burns. His clothing also looks like it's been scorched and burned.

"Stupid—stupid!—STUPID!" the man keeps repeating, and Rafael realizes that the man is referring to *himself*. Rafael is not sure how he knows this but he just does. Either by the man's body language or the tone of voice or something inchoate about the whole scene unfolding now. The demonic souls press closer to the unfortunate man in the Windbreaker, their blackened mouths working, their eyes like those of barracudas. The torch has limited power over the damned, the fire merely a distraction, the heat having no effect on the monsters' deadened nervous systems.

All at once, a number of emotions and conclusions course through Rafael. He feels a tremendous wave of empathy for this man in the silk roadie jacket. But for the grace of God, Rafael could easily be down there, alone, surrounded, terrified, doomed. On top of that, the sardonic tone of voice and the way that the poor fool keeps repeating the word *stupid*—most likely a comment on his foolish mistakes that got him surrounded in the first place—resonate with Rafael. He gently puts his finger on the trigger pad and aims the crosshairs at the head of the closest possessed soul.

The first shot barks, the small spurt of blood mist visible in the scope, puffing off the skull of the first target. The possessed creature collapses. The man in the jacket jerks with a start, glancing over his shoulder for a second, but only for a second. He still can't safely take his eyes off his assailants for more than an instant. He waves the torch. A comet tail of sparks trail through the air as the rain douses the flame. Rafael injects another round into the breach with the cocking lever, aims at the second target, and fires.

Through the scope, the man reacts again with a start as the second attacker goes down, bewilderment and apprehension on the man's face. He throws another glance over his shoulder, and through the scope Rafael can sense the strange frisson of sudden eye contact with a man fifty yards away. It's possible that the Remington's barrel is visible glinting out of the foliage.

Rafael takes another breath and holds it, just as he learned in military school many years ago, and then proceeds to fire on the other assailants—one at a time, yanking the lever and injecting more shells in a rhythmic series of movements—systematically taking down the entire baker's dozen.

After the final shot is fired, and the man down in the clearing is the only one left standing, and the cloud of cordite and gun smoke engulfing Rafael clears, the man in the silk jacket looks up. He doesn't yell. He doesn't wave. He doesn't change his expression from utter vexation. He simply moves his lips, the words inaudible from Rafael's vantage point, but obvious to anyone who has a passing interest in reading lips. "What. The. Fuck."

Rafael ejects the last shell, the dull clatter of the hollow metal bouncing off the rocks at his feet reverberating through the air, faintly discernible above the monotonous thrum of rain. The noise seems to put a strange punctuation at the end of this—*what would Rafael call it? An act of mercy? An exorcism?*

The figure down in the clearing has not moved from his frozen tableau. He continues to gape up at the ridge, his expression unchanged. It remains fixed, seized up with awe. The silence stretches. The rain continues unabated, soaking the ground around the fallen monsters. Then the man in the jacket looks down at the human remains strewn across the clearing around him, the sad lumps of dead flesh now as inert and harmless as animal droppings. He tosses aside the makeshift torch, the flame already guttered and reduced to a dying ember.

Rafael lowers the scope and wipes his face, the hood of his rain slicker dripping profusely. He can't think of what to do or what to say. Should he withdraw and flee the scene? Does he trust this man? He waits. Exactly what he's waiting for he could not say. As he waits, he puts the optical cup back to his eye and takes a closer look at the man in the roadie jacket.

Through the crosshairs, upon further scrutiny, Rafael sees that the man is ruggedly handsome—or perhaps *was* handsome earlier in life—and has a spark of intelligence in his droopy eyes, despite the severe burns marring half his face. His neatly trimmed goatee is iron gray, and his hair, drenched and matted to his skull, is streaked with silver. The man also looks older than he first appeared, the crow's-feet around his eyes deep and prominent, the lines on his face abundant and etched into every corner.

At last the man in the clearing calls out, "If you think you're hiding from me, that yellow raincoat is about as subtle as a scream in the dark."

"*¿Habla inglés?*" the man in the silk jacket inquires after they've gotten out of the rain, keeping their distance at first, standing at opposite ends of a deserted covered pedestrian bridge two hundred yards north of the clearing.

The man waits patiently for an answer, wiping his face with a handkerchief.

"*Sí* . . . I mean . . . yes," Rafael replies, his hand resting on the grip of a pistol. "But I'm not Spanish."

"Oh yeah?" The other man's eyes glint with mild interest. "I thought I detected an accent."

"Brazilian."

"Ah, of course, my bad." Despite his injuries, the older man smiles. "In that case, I'm sure you speak better English than I do Portuguese."

Rafael shrugs. He shivers, his skin crawling with goose bumps. He can smell the sharp tang of decay all around him. The bridge—which once provided a quaint passageway for hikers, bicyclists, and nature buffs—spans a small creek, which has now flooded and risen to the point of saturating the adjacent woods and bubbling up through the cracks and seams of the bridge's warped flooring. The air inside the structure is fetid and moldy, and the unrelenting rain rings off the bridge's roof, so noisy it practically drowns the voices of the two men.

"Name's Stern," the man says above the drone. "First name David. Or Dave, if you prefer. Although the wife hates it when people call me Dave. Barbara says it reminds her of the Wendy's hamburger guy."

Rafael only comprehends about 50 percent of what David Stern is saying. "Rafael," he says finally. "My name . . . it is Rafael Machado."

"Nice to meet you, Rafael. I appreciate the save back there."

Rafael shrugs, not fully understanding.

David looks at him, then nods at the weapon. "You seem pretty handy with that sniper rifle."

"I was . . . soldier . . . long time ago." Rafael shrugs again. "I saw the Hungries had you. What is the word?" Shrug. "Surround? Surrounded . . . trapped?"

David Stern chuckles, then lets out a chortle of laughter. He wipes his eyes with the back of his hand. " 'Hungries' . . . I like that."

"They are possessed, no?"

David's laughter dies. "Wait . . . *what*? Possessed? Like by demons, you're talking about?"

"Demons, yes . . . *Diabo* . . . um . . . what you would call Satan, yes?"

David sighs. "First of all, I'm Jewish, so . . . there's really no such thing in my religion. Second of all, you mind if I ask you a personal question?"

Rafael chews the inside of his cheek, hesitating for a moment, comprehending most of the words. He's not sure how much he should tell this man. What if this is all an elaborate trick? What if this is a scheme of *o Diabo* to capture his soul? Finally, Rafael says, "I guess so."

"Where did you come from?"

"Here and there."

"Look . . . Rafael, is it?"

"Yes."

"You saved my life. You seem heavily armed. I'm hurting. I've been through some stuff. It doesn't matter. But maybe we can help each other. Whaddaya say?"

Rafael takes a deep breath, and for a brief instant, he envisions himself being alone in this apocalyptic world, living off scraps, surrounded mostly by unclean spirits dogging him at every turn. He flashes back on those lonely five years he survived solely on sweet potatoes, collards, rainwater, and a thin tissue of hope. He remembers those nights he hunkered in the dark, listening to the jackal calls, nearly losing his mind curled up in the corner of that tawdry outdoor pen, exposed, insane, completely alone. He looks up at the injured man in the jacket. "Yes, that would be good . . . we should help each other."

And then—for the first time in years—Rafael Rodrigo Machado proffers another human being a good, clean, sincere smile.

They pool their resources. David Stern has stashed away a horse and buggy about a mile from there, and they walk the distance side by side in the rain, keeping an eye on the periphery of the woods, getting to know each other, as well as keeping tabs on the shadowy nooks and crannies of the flooded landscape, watching for any errant Hungries.

On the way to the drop point, David explains that he respects all religions, but one thing he can assure Rafael is that the Hungries—or walkers, as David and many other Americans call them—are neither Satanic nor supernatural in any way. Nobody knows for sure what biological processes brought about such a bizarre plague upon humanity—specifically the dead reanimating and literally feeding off the living—but whatever catastrophic pathologies were involved, it is David Stern's unshakable belief that the gods have decided to sit this one out. Whatever caused this horrific outbreak, David can guarantee Rafael one thing: the living—in all their imperfect, lazy, narcissistic glory—started the domino that set off the chain of events.

"Here we go," David says, pausing behind the cover of an enormous tangle of deadfall logs and boulders. The rainwater bounces up and into the wind as David yanks a tarp off an old modified VW Beetle with the front end chopped off. The sound of a horse nickering and fidgeting nearby draws Rafael's attention over to movement behind a wall of foliage. There, in the shadows, an old gray spotted draft horse scrapes at the mud, obscured behind the limbs of an ancient live oak. "That's Shecky over there." David gestures. "I was out trying to find some vegetation to feed him when I got pinned down by those walkers in the clearing."

In the unyielding rain, which has now turned the earth to pudding, they mount up the horse. They stow the weapons and picnic basket full of provisions in the Bug's backseat area, and they climb in. They sit side by side in the makeshift horse-cart, and David snaps the reins, and old Shecky drags them out of the mire and onto a crumbling blacktop road that David is fond of calling a shit strip.

"May I ask you something?" Rafael says moments later, as David weaves though a row of overturned, fossilized wrecks still blocking the two-lane.

David keeps his eyes on the road, gripping the reins. "Of course."

"What is it that you were doing? Out here all by yourself?"

"Looking for my wife."

"Barbara?"

David gives him a look. "Very good. Yes. Barbara. She got kidnapped."

"When did this happen?"

David sighs. "Little over six months ago. Everything was going so well, too. We lived inside the walls of a sweet little town. Name of Woodbury. About two dozen survivors. All ages and types. Got along pretty well, too, considering. It was safe, sustainable, had solar cells, organic farming. But . . . I guess we were a target."

"A target?"

David shoots him a glance. "For a while it seemed like every meth-head, drifter, biker gang, and crazy within a hundred-mile radius who hadn't turned wanted to steal our shit, take over, fuck with us. And the ones that turned wanted to have us for lunch. But we fought back with everything we had, and we repelled most of them."

"Is this why your wife was kidnapped?"

David stares at the road, the horse clopping noisily, accentuating the pause. "To this day, I don't know why my wife was taken away from me. It happened one day when most of our people were out working in the fields." He looks down and takes a labored breath as though the very telling of the story is exhausting and toxic. "This paramilitary group invaded us and took every last child. I think Barbara was taken to keep the kids calm." His eyes well up. "Babs was always good with kids. Never had any of our own. She was the perennial favorite aunt."

Rafael frowns. "So they took children? Why would they do that?"

David wipes his eyes and shrugs. "That's a good goddamn question. Anyway, we all thought for sure they took Babs and kids north to Atlanta—it's about seventy miles away—and we sent out a rescue team. Gal named Lilly Caul led the group. She was the town leader, a badass, but she vanished as well. I've spent the last three months combing that town, and haven't found shit. Place is overrun with walkers and a small number of survivors you'd be better off avoiding . . . so searching for somebody is a losing proposition."

"How is it that you got burned? It looks . . . how would you say? *Recent?*"

David gives him a nod. "Happened last week, been on the run ever since." He takes a deep breath. "When I was looking for Babs in Atlanta, I realized I might be making the oldest mistake in the book."

Rafael struggles a bit with the phrase. "In the book? What book? I'm sorry I don't—"

"It's an expression, it just means I might be violating a classic axiom, a simple rule, an oldie but a goodie. When you and your loved ones have gotten separated, you don't go out looking for them. You just stay put. Let them find you. If you're both looking for each other, your paths might never cross. The point is, I got bogged down in Atlanta trying to find them and it hit me. They could be looking for *me*. I should get my ass back to Woodbury."

Rafael nods. "Okay . . . I understand. So how did you get burned?"

"Needless to say, when I got back to our little town, things were not as I expected them to be. While I was away, and the town was essentially deserted, a bunch of bottom feeders moved in. Half the town was infested with walkers, the other half with bandits. They had taken over our homes, our resources—most of these rascals barely old enough to buy liquor. They were feral, they were animals. Actually that's an insult to animals." He falls silent for a moment, giving one of the reins a snap and urging the horse around a tight turn crowded with wreckage.

A few walkers mill about the shoulder and reach for the buggy as it passes.

David's voice grows thicker, coarser with rage. "I saw one of those bastards wearing one of Barbara's scarves wrapped around his greasy head, I just lost it. I was hiding in the sticks, watching our little town go down for the last time, and I just couldn't take it anymore. I didn't know if I would ever see Babs or Lilly or the others again . . . and I just . . . I lost it."

He goes silent again, and the hiss of rain blends with the clopping of the horse's hooves. Rafael waits, then says, "What happened? What did you do?"

"I burned the place to the ground." David slumps in his seat, his head lolling. For a moment, it's hard to tell whether he's going to laugh, cry, or scream. Then the tears track down his cheeks. His shoulders tremble. He swallows the pain and guilt and shame, and he wipes his eyes with the back of his hand. "We had a row of old propane tanks that we found, and I snuck in, and I just opened them all up. Rolled them under the courthouse. Set fire to the feed store where the booze was kept and the methane in the alley out back was thick enough to cut with a knife."

Again his words dwindle into silence. Rafael sits there, thinking about it. "So you got burned by fires? That is how you got some wounds?"

David Stern looks up at the younger man, and his scarred features tighten into a crooked, demented smile. The taut skin makes his eyes look almost feline. "Not as much as those sons of bitches."

Rafael stares at him for a moment, then gazes out one of the open windows at the passing landscape of rotting woods and moving shadows. Rafael can't imagine the strings of the world's destiny not being operated by the Devil right now. He turns back to the older man. "Have you given up?"

David looks at him. "Given up on what?"

"For finding your wife? Finding Barbara?"

David lets out a pained, breathy sigh. "I'll never give up on that." He takes a deep breath and seems to shake off his doldrums. "I gotta believe they're out there somewhere . . . alive. Babs, Lilly, Tommy, Norma, Jinx, Miles, and those poor sweet little kids . . . they're out there . . . somewhere even better than Woodbury . . . where they have water and food, and they have a warm place to live . . . and they're secure, safe . . . comfortable. I truly believe this. I believe they're out there, and they're alive, and they've found a place to call home."

PART 1

Exodus

Let the groans of the prisoners come before you;
according to your great power, preserve those doomed to die.

—Psalm 79:11

ONE

At first glance, the figures now wandering through this grid of perfectly decorated interiors might be mistaken for masters of the manor, residents of some gracious old mansion strolling the confines of their burnished mahogany corridors and richly appointed parlors. They bump into each other occasionally, and sometimes they lift their pasty white faces to the ceiling to let out primordial, snarling yawps, but for the most part they look at home in these showrooms and alcoves arranged with such pristine taste. One of the denizens has now accidentally fallen backward onto a Scandinavian-designed divan, his ropy purple intestines spilling out of him in braided glistening strands. The former auto mechanic—still clad in a tattered work shirt with the needlepointed name FRED still visible on its breast pocket—slouches languidly there for a moment as if taking a break from his aimless meandering, his head drooping, his mouth oozing black tarry drool. A stark art deco lamp next to the creature—which is currently running off a generator—illuminates the scene with soft, diffuse, flickering light as delicate as moth wings. Other cadavers mill about a dining room sectioned off in onyx, lacquered dividers with Chinese calligraphy etched into the creamy surfaces. A tall Hepplewhite mirror framed in gleaming teak and cherrywood reflects a cluster of the dead scraping past walnut bookcases filled with artificial facades of book spines. These imitation books are stamped with the gilded titles of tomes nobody reads anymore because the reading of fictional strife has become such a luxury: *To Kill a Mockingbird*, *Treasure Island*, *War and Peace*, and *Tales of Mystery and Imagination*. Beyond the reflection, stretching in all directions, myriad variations of these high-quality, modestly priced rooms in all manner of styles and arrangements create a maze in which dozens more reanimated corpses now mill about and shuffle like slow-moving laboratory rats . . . until the first shot rings out.

It comes from the darkness beneath an emergency exit sign on the far side of the floor. It's a small-caliber blast—the report dampened by a noise suppressor—which makes a sound like a hammer striking metal. The walker on the divan whiplashes, a fountain of blood mist and fluids spraying out the back of its skull, creating an impromptu Jackson Pollock blot across the designer drapes behind it. The creature instantly slides down across the front of the cushions, collapsing onto the lovely handwoven Bjork-series throw rug.

More shots ring out from other directions—mostly .38-caliber and under—blowing tunnels through the heads of at least half a dozen more of the dead. Skulls burst open and bodies plunge to the floor en masse, defacing the sparkling furniture with the vandalism of cranial fluids, bile, and blood.

The commotion gets the attention of the remaining fifteen or so walkers, most of them slowly, drunkenly pivoting toward the noise and confusion of their brethren falling around them. Rancid mouths gape open, the creaky vocalizations like steam emanating from the dead concavities of their throats. Figures press in from the shadows behind the monsters, slipping through the gaps between austere oriental room dividers and glass-fronted knickknack shelves.

A stout black woman in a do-rag and dashiki drives a fireplace poker into the temple of the closest walker. An olive-skinned bodybuilder in a wifebeater and love beads closes in from the other side of the floor, swinging a machete in quick succession, shearing open the tops of three dead skulls with the efficiency of a gardener weeding a garden. Behind the bodybuilder, the woman who fired the first shot approaches. Thin, weathered, auburn hair in a tight ponytail, green eyes like a cat, dressed in a Georgia Tech T-shirt, with black cigarette jeans and combat boots, she grips her Ruger .22-caliber pistol in the classic Weaver position—Israeli commando style—her free hand cupped under the grip for stability. She has a full magazine in the firearm, ten rounds, one already gone, and she expertly picks off nine more creatures, one at a time, hardly pausing between blasts.

More humans appear on the periphery—an older, balding man in wire-rimmed eyeglasses, a beefy, bearded, potbellied man in denim, and a teenage boy with sun-freckled skin and an earnest face—each firing on the remaining few walkers with their handguns.

Within seconds, the unexpected infestation of walkers on the ground floor of the huge Atlanta Ikea is foiled in a haze of blue smoke, the ensuing silence as jarring as an earthquake. The store's inhabitants stand around for a moment, stunned by the abrupt absence of sound (other than a faint dripping noise), looking at each other expectantly. Eventually all eyes turn to the woman with the auburn ponytail—the leader—for further direction.

Lilly Caul slowly holsters her pistol. She can hear the faint evidence of intruders lurking nearby, their breathing barely audible above the dripping noises. Lilly puts her right index finger to her lips, shushing everybody and indicating that no one should relax quite yet. One last task remains to be performed. She points at Tommy, then at Boone, then at Stankowski, and then at Norma, gesturing for them to move behind the cover of the room dividers.

Then she motions to the bodybuilder, Musolino, to follow her.

The big olive-skinned man follows Lilly as she creeps around a row of tall armoires filled with faux glassware and fake mementos. Despite the fact that she spends most of her time on the third floor, in the cafeteria, and in the section of the store earmarked for bedroom sets, she knows practically every square inch of the first floor from studying the store map and walking the corridors, making notes, memorizing every nook and cranny, every potential resource to be cannibalized. Ironically, that's the best word for what she and the others have been doing—*cannibalizing* this massive home furnishings center on Atlanta's north side. Now she has to once again do the dirty work that ensures their safety inside the massive cathedral of consumerism.

In a series of silent hand gestures, she leads Musolino down a narrow service corridor. At the end of the corridor, an unmarked iron door is reinforced with a massive timber across its midsection. Lilly carefully lifts the timber out of its cradle, and then cautiously unbolts the door. She pushes the thing open a few inches.

The rain and wind greet her, the ruins of Atlanta rising in the distance like ancient Mayan temples petrified and blackened by time. The sky hangs low over Ikea's parking lot, which is littered with human remains and glittering particles of broken glass. The rain blows in great billowing sheets across the scabrous pavement. Musolino wants to build a barricade of razor wire around the ground level but Lilly has vetoed the idea, despite the fact that they've had to neutralize several assaults on the place over the last three months. Lilly still believes a barricade would merely draw attention to the treasures inside.

Right then, Lilly sees the broken planking lying around the base of the tall display windows on the south corner of the building. She can see the breach through which the walkers were let in.

She looks at Musolino, gives him a dour nod, and then ejects the spent magazine from the Ruger. She pulls a fresh mag from her belt and shoves it into the receiving port. "Let's go ahead and finish this thing," she says.

The two filthy, emaciated men, each dressed in blood-splattered rags, crouch behind a service door. They each have a .38-caliber revolver, each looking as though it was first used in World War II. They have the shakes and the hundred-yard stares of longtime junkies. The younger one, his eyes rimmed in dark circles from sleepless nights and unrelenting stress, whispers hoarsely, "What now? What the fuck are we supposed to do now?"

"You stupid fucking idiot," the older one hisses. "We were supposed to go in and fucking take them when the walkers had them distracted!"

"There were more of them than I thought. They had more firepower than I thought."

"Duh . . . ya *think*?"

"But Ollie said there was only—"

"What the fuck does Ollie know about it?! He's a fucking ice head."

"Should we get out of here?"

The older one starts to answer when he hears the telltale click of a hammer being drawn back behind him, in the shadows of the stockroom. "Oh fuck, oh Jesus," he says in a voice suddenly filled with remorse, sadness, and regret. He doesn't even have to turn around.

Lilly Caul stands behind the intruders. She holds the muzzle of the Ruger mere inches away from the back of the older one's head. "I'm gonna need both of you to drop those guns," she says. She speaks in a steady, even, flat tone. "Don't turn around, don't say anything, just do it."

The older one clears his throat. "Okay . . . got it. Don't shoot."

"Please don't waste us," the younger one implores in his tattered voice, which is already crumbling into tears. He looks down at the floor in front of him, a child caught with his hand in the till. "We ran out of everything. We have no food, no water . . . we just wanted to—"

"Excuse me." Lilly is strictly business. The men do not turn around. They look down, a lot of swallowing and licking of lips going on. Lilly does not raise her voice. "I asked you both to drop the guns, and I will not ask you again. Drop the fucking guns."

They do what she asks. The guns clatter to the tiles. The older one says, "Can I say something?"

Lilly squeezes off a single shot into the back of the older one's head.

The loud report—dampened by the noise suppressor—snaps like a firecracker in the enclosed space. The bullet exits out the man's left eye in a plume of blood mist, the impact sending him folding over and banging his skull on the doorjamb before sinking to the floor in a series of death-rattle twitches.

The younger one is in the process of whirling around when Lilly sends the second round into his temple. He convulses as the blood cloud spits out the other side and strikes the corridor wall in a sticky scarlet rosette three feet wide. The young man keels sideways, collapsing to the floor in a heap of soiled fabric and trembling flesh.

Musolino stands there, two-handing his 9-millimeter Glock, training the muzzle on the still-warm bodies as if they might sit back up or turn at any moment. At length, he relaxes and thumbs the hammer back down and lets out a thin, whispery breath of relief.

Lilly has not said another word. Ears ringing, she shoves the hot pistol down the back of her belt, kneels, and reaches down to the carotid pulse point on each man's neck. The older one has already expired. The younger one still has a feeble, birdlike pulse. Lilly waits until it fades away before murmuring, "Okay, we're good."

Musolino shoves the Glock back in its holster and kneels next to Lilly.

She picks up each of the .38 revolvers, snaps open their cylinders, and dumps the empties on the floor next to the dead bodies. She sorts through the rounds, plucking the useable ones up and stashing them in her back pocket. Then she gives one of the guns to Musolino and shoves the other one down the other side of her belt.

They drag the bodies back down the service corridor and out the exit.

The rain swirls around them as they pull the bodies across the concrete apron. There's a large dumpster on the other side of the loading dock, half-filled with the remains of walkers that have breached the building's weak spots. Lilly and Musolino drag the bodies over to the receptacle, lift the lid back, flinch at the smell, and heave the two corpses inside the enclosure.

The lid drops down with a resounding metallic bang as they head back inside.

Back on the third floor, after securing the damaged barricades and leaky doorways along the porous ground level and removing the walker remains from the maze of model living rooms, Lilly takes a few minutes to gather her bearings in the bathroom. She washes the blood stipple from her cheeks and arms and fingernails. She looks at her hand. She holds it up into the lantern light and notes how rock-steady it is. Not a single tremor of nervous tension. She wipes her wet hair with a towel and changes out of her rain-soaked sweats. She puts on an REM T-shirt and fresh jeans. She pauses.

Her reflection stares back at her from the mirror. The face is unfamiliar to her. This is not the face of a thirty-four-year-old woman. Nor is it the malnourished face of a frightened, cornered animal, which she has resembled in the recent past. Instead, what she sees gazing back at her now through the looking glass is an indigenous native of the apocalypse—cold, gaunt, deeply lined, cobra-calm, eyes sunken and fixed in their dark sockets. In fact, it takes a little searching to find the maternal spark behind her soft green irises, but it's there.

Being an accidental mother is what drives Lilly now; it's the hard carapace protecting her heart, the steel girders reinforcing her nerves, the source of her willingness to kill and her instinct to survive and her singular goal of protecting her children through any means necessary. And it's what makes her heart leap when she hears the little fist banging on the ladies' room door.

"Lilly?" The muffled and yet unmistakable voice of Bethany Dupree rings out behind the door. "You in there? They said to come get you."

Lilly finishes up at the sink, gives herself one last look, and then opens the door. "Hey there, Fluffer-Nutter! What are you, the sergeant at arms?"

"Huh?" The twelve-year-old has an old-soul face hardened by stress and contrasted by a profusion of freckles. Her pigtails are meticulously maintained by Lilly, and she wears a dirty cardigan sweater over her pinafore dress. "What's a surgeon in arms anyway?"

"Never mind—c'mere." Lilly pulls the girl into a hug. "Is everybody in the cafeteria?"

Bethany nods and wriggles out of the embrace. "C'mon, they're waiting for you."

Over the last three months, the inhabitants of the Ikea have made their individual territorial claims in different quadrants of the third floor. The adults have meticulously sectioned off portions of the luxury wing with its shag carpet and king-sized beds brimming with oversized pillows and lush thousand-thread-count linens. The young ones have each chosen their own domain in the children's area, making elaborate dividers and forts out of bookcases and fiberglass room organizers.

Norma Sutters has made her bedroom in one of the cafeteria back offices—most likely a former administrative area—from which she can have easy access to the kitchen. Norma has taken it upon herself to be the group's short-order cook, turning the sealed, freeze-dried packages of food stacked to the ceilings in the vast pantry area into improvised concoctions of savory soul food. She has taken great pride in her creations, some of them with names like Mac-Daddy Meatballs and Mama's Down-Home Muesli. The unspoiled Ikea restaurant has proven to be a godsend. Most of the fresh food left over after the great exodus out of the city had rotted into dust, but many items still in storage have been designed and packed for a long shelf life. And with the advent of generated power, Norma can heat, fry, bake, broil, or scramble anything the pantry has to offer.

They're all waiting for Lilly in the restaurant's main seating area.

As big as an airplane hangar, and outfitted with enough polished wooden booths to seat a small army, the dining room is bordered by gleaming stainless steel buffet stations from which weary patrons—their eyes glazed from merchandise overload—would sheepishly line up and order inexpensive dinners. In many ways, the old Ikeas operated in the manner of casinos. Food and drink were provided at either no cost or nominal fees in order to keep the gamblers gambling, and in this case, to keep the shoppers shopping. The convivial scent of coffee and cinnamon hangs in the air.

"Thanks, everybody," Lilly says a moment later, after the group has settled down and gathered around her. Even the kids have all paused from the games on the far side of the room and have taken seats on the floor in front of her as though expecting her to sing a ditty for them or teach them about adjectives and adverbs. "After tonight's little adventures on the first floor, I can't hold back something I've been wanting to say for a while now." She pauses. Swallows. Takes a breath. "We have to leave this place."

For the briefest instant, the room seems to seize up with thunderstruck silence. Around Lilly, on the floor, the faces of the children gawk up at her as though she'd just shat on their birthday cakes. To Lilly's immediate left, Musolino hops off his perch on the pass-through counter and silently begins to pace, hands in his pockets, a pensive look on his face. On the other side of the room, Norma Sutters comes around from behind the serving counter, wiping her plump hands on a dish towel. "You know . . . my hearing ain't too good anymore." She looks askance at Lilly as though smelling something bad. "I could have sworn I just heard you say 'leave this place.'"

Lilly smiles. "Okay, I know we've talked about this before. I realize how great this place is, we *all* do. We got all this luxury, supplies, food, generators. It's a place worth fighting for. I get that. But the city's just getting too dangerous."

Norma shakes her head. "Honey, it's always been dangerous."

"Our exposure here is just too great," Lilly persists. "We're going to be repelling attacks like the one today on an hourly basis, we don't leave."

Across the room, a middle-aged man in a Braves baseball cap sitting next to Tommy Dupree speaks up. "I don't mean to be the one who poops on your party, Lilly, but I'm willing to risk it." Potbellied, goateed, as beefy as a Mack truck, Burt Stankowski is a former long-haul trucker who was among the original six people who discovered the postplague Shangri-la of the Ikea. "We can build better barricades, countermeasures . . . we can camouflage the place better. There's a lot we can do."

Lilly looks at the man. "Much of which is only going to draw attention to the place."

"This is a big step you're talking about." The woman over by the steam table speaks with a clipped Jersey accent. Dark skinned, her raven-black hair perpetually done up in a bun, Eve Betts was a receptionist in a dental office before the Big Turn. "You sure you've weighed the pros and cons? I kind of agree with Burt."

"Look. We're sitting ducks here." Lilly's chest tightens with anger. She just killed two young men in cold blood, neither of whom truly deserved to die. "We've got targets on our backs. You really want to live like that? Constantly looking over your shoulder?"

Norma pipes up. "Correct me if I'm wrong, Lilly, but isn't it gonna be like that no matter where you live?"

"Norma, that's not what I'm—"

"May I ask a question?" The voice comes from a slender wisp of a woman perched on one of the adjacent serving counters. She holds a baby in her arms, one hand pressing a pacifier into the infant's mouth. The baby is a recent addition, rescued from the derelict Atlanta Medical Center by Lilly and Tommy. The baby—name and age unknown—has been dubbed "Doe" by Tommy, as in Jane Doe. The woman holding the child has become its ersatz nanny. With her long, thin, dishwater-blond hair, and her faded peasant dresses, Sophie Leland comes off as a refugee from Laurel Canyon in the 1970s. But beneath the surface of her dreamy Joni Mitchell exterior is a street-tough former prostitute from Athens, Georgia, who has survived the plague on sheer grit. Right now, though, she looks concerned. Not worried. Sophie Leland is not a worrier. She just looks a tad concerned. "Are you talking about leaving immediately or what? In weeks . . . months?"

Lilly sighs. "The sooner the better, Sophie, to be honest. We're running low on ammo, and we're drawing more and more walkers every time we stave off an attack. We're getting more vulnerable every day."

Tommy Dupree raises his hand as though he's in social studies class. The ruddy-complexioned fifteen-year-old doesn't look up, doesn't say anything, just keeps staring with a somber expression at the tabletop.

Lilly sees the young man's hand in the air and smiles sadly despite the tension in the room. "Tommy, this isn't Room 222. You don't have to raise your hand, you can just speak up."

The boy's hand goes down. He calmly looks up at the others and says, "I don't care what the rest of y'all do . . . I'm with Lilly a thousand percent." He turns and aims his intense brown eyes at Lilly Caul. "You want to bail on this place, Lilly, I'm right behind you. I'm with you. I got your back. End of story."

Lilly smiles at the boy and feels a tight, hot pinch of emotion in her belly. God bless this raggedy kid. Lilly Caul has wanted to be a mother from the time she was a teenager in Marietta, getting As in family and consumer sciences class and scrapbooking photos of babies. At the time, she idolized her social studies teacher, Mrs. Whitman, a woman who walked around the neighborhood with an infant on one hip, a cigarette dangling out of her mouth, and a Virginia Woolf novel in her free hand. In those days, a lot of women were talking about the myth of "having it all"—domestic bliss, career success, a flat tummy, and hot sex—but Lilly knew in her deepest heart of hearts that "having it all" meant the love of a child. It dwarfed all other considerations. Unfortunately for Lilly, life had gotten in the way. She had slogged through her twenties without ever enjoying a serious relationship that might have led to children.

And ironically, it was not until the world fell to a brutal, inexplicable pandemic that she finally began to scratch that powerful itch.

At the present moment, though—before Lilly can respond to the boy's poignant mission statement—Boone speaks up from a table near the window. "Lilly, I have to ask the obvious question." The former social worker from Jacksonville gazes intently at Lilly through his round, wire-rimmed eyeglasses. "I think I know the answer but I'll ask it anyway. Where exactly do you plan on going?"

Another long sigh escapes from deep within Lilly's lungs as she surrenders to the obvious. "Boone, you know exactly where I want to go. Why pretend?" She scans the cafeteria, looking at each person. "You all know good and well where I want to go. Might as well lay the cards on the table."

An awkward beat of silence ensues, the kids studying all the adult faces as if there were secrets being kept all of a sudden. At last, Musolino stops pacing and directs his attention to Lilly. "Okay, I'm sorry. I have to say it. You're obsessed with that place. The fact that you would even suggest going back there . . . after what we found last week? I don't get it."

Lilly looks down at the floor, formulating a response, even though she knows the big man has a point.

Located in the vast patchwork quilt of tobacco fields seventy miles south of Atlanta, the little railroad town of Woodbury, Georgia, has come to represent something so powerful and so important to Lilly that she would be hard-pressed to reduce it to words. It is a place of tragedy, violence, and heartbreak. It has been the home of horrible events and sinister people, such as the tyrannical Philip Blake, aka the Governor, the man who dragged Lilly into a quagmire of evil, ultimately turning her into a killer. But after Blake had been vanquished, and Lilly had become the pro tem leader of the town, something began to grow within her—a dream, a vision of the future. Deep down in her heart, Lilly Caul has begun to think of

Woodbury as a symbol of something deeper than a mere place on a map.

For Lilly, the town has come to represent the quest for a normal life.

Recent months, however, have not been kind to the dream. The town's once tightly knit group of inhabitants have been scattered to the winds. The man whom Lilly had chosen to stay behind and care for the fortified, walled-in village—David Stern—has vanished without a trace. Not a single one of the crank-powered two-way radios that once connected the network of neighboring settlements has survived the tumult of past months, and now Lilly prays that David survived the mysterious conflagration that was discovered by a small search party sent out eleven days ago.

Lilly will never forget what she saw as they rounded the corner of Highway 85 and Jones Mill Road. A low, black haze hung over the center of town, and steeples and roof pitches as far away as Riggins Ferry Road still smoldered like Dresden after the firestorms of World War II. Scorched wreckage and debris littered the deserted lots and fields, radiating outward from the embers of ground zero. The air smelled of brimstone and charred flesh, and it was impossible to distinguish between the remains of walkers and humans that lay scattered like ashy dead leaves across the outskirts of town. It looked as though someone had dropped a bomb on the place—many bombs, in fact—and it broke Lilly's heart.

But it did not break her will.

"Okay, fair enough," Lilly finally says in response to Musolino's rhetorical question. "Yeah, I'm obsessed . . . obsessed with building a permanent home, a place we can breathe . . . a place we can count on. Woodbury is our home. For better or for worse." She looks at the others. "No matter how great this place is, you can't deny it's only temporary. You mark my words. There's going to come a day, some-body launches an assault on this place that we can't stave off. Believe me, it's only a matter of time."

The others exchange skeptical glances, and Lilly can see she hasn't sold them on the idea. Boone has taken off his trademark John Lennon eyeglasses, and now he thoughtfully wipes them with a handkerchief, looking as though he's about to say something. Lilly watches him. "Go ahead, Boone," she says at last. "Speak up, speak your mind."

He puts his glasses back on. "Okay, for starters, the place is not even there anymore. Most of the main buildings have burned to the ground. There's nothing to return to. It's just a pile of smoldering ruins."

Before Lilly gets a chance to respond, Norma Sutters chimes in again. "Seems to me, it wouldn't matter if Woodbury was the damn Taj Mahal, it ain't ever gonna compare to the quality of life we got going in this place right here. Right?" She looks at the others as if she might ask for a hallelujah or launch into a gospel hymn at any moment. "Am I crazy? Why in God's name would we want to walk away from this place? Sure, we gotta deal with yahoos trying to steal it away from us, but I gotta think it's better than starting over someplace else with nothing."

Lilly swallows hard, pushing back her emotions, trying to stay calm. "I get what you're saying. I really do. But most of the brick buildings in Woodbury are still standing, and all those little cottages and ranch homes along Flat Shoals Road were untouched by the fires. It's still the perfect-sized place to settle down in. It's containable. It's manageable. We were almost there a few months ago. We had crops. We had solar cells. We just have to be more careful. That's all. Like Burt says, we just have to build better walls." She pauses, letting it sink in. She studies the faces. She softens. "I totally understand why you'd want to stay put here. But you have to trust me on this. We're living on the Titanic. It's gonna sink. Sooner or later. Believe me. It's going down."

Now the others sit mute, sullen, many of them staring at the floor. The muffled drone of incessant, unending rain on the roof accompanies the silence.

"Which brings me to the best part." Lilly says this with a touch of mania in her voice. She feels adrenaline crackling within her, a bracing surge of energy as brisk as a snort of smelling salts. "Yes, we have to leave this place." She looks at each of them with the fervor of an evangelist recruiting new souls. "But that doesn't mean we can't take it with us."

A long beat of silence follows, many of those present looking at Lilly as though she has finally lost her mind.

TWO

In the driving rain, they run for their lives: four of them, a family, racing through the curtains of mist, slipping and stumbling down the long muddy slope of a neglected soybean field, hounded by the twin headlight beams of a large flatbed truck a quarter mile behind them, gaining on them, the intermittent boom of a 12-gauge shotgun piercing the din of the rainstorm.

A bullet zips mere inches over the head of the father, a haggard, scrawny man in the rags of an old sport coat with a face stained dark by exposure. He ducks down and glances over his shoulder. He can see the menacing shafts of light slicing through the rain, quickly closing the distance, the dark figures of men riding on the flatbed with weapons poised, the engine screaming.

"This way—hurry!" The father grabs the mother's sleeve and urges her—as well as his two teenage daughters, each dressed in the rags of rural drifters—toward a dense wall of pines about a hundred yards away. The father knows if they can just make it to the woods, they can flee their pursuers. He has no idea what these men want, but he knows it will most likely be very unpleasant. People have been getting desperate lately, fighting for scraps, attacking each other, stealing each other's resources, raping, murdering, and plundering. These men in the flatbed came out of nowhere a mile or two back, just outside of Fayetteville, while the father and his family were searching for shelter in the barrens along Perry Creek.

Now the family reaches the bottom of the hill and are about to plunge into the safety of the thick trees when a bullet strikes the father between the shoulder blades, sending him careening to the ground and rolling another fifty feet through marshy weeds.

"*Daddy!*" one of the girls, the oldest sister—skin and bones in her cardigan and jeans—slips on the wet earth trying to lunge toward the spot at which her father now lies writhing in pain. The other girl, three years younger, helps her sister up.

The mother, her beleaguered face filling with terror, stumbles to a stop. "John! Oh my God!" She goes to the man's side, kneeling, cradling his head. Breathless, she strokes his wet, muddy face.

"I'm—I'm—I'm okay I think." Gasping for breath, the man on the ground is John Stack, a former insurance agent from Dothan who turned out to be more of a survivor than he thought. He had kept his family alive for this long, and he'd gotten this far on sheer stubbornness. But now he's certain it's over, he's gone, and he'll probably bleed out now in this relentless downpour that has made life even more miserable than usual for the Stacks.

Jennifer Stack frantically turns the man over, looking for the entrance wound. "I don't see any blood, John! There's no blood!"

The rain billows and curtains them, cold and miserable, as the magnesium-bright beams of light loom closer and closer, the rig roaring up to the edge of the forest preserve. John Stack lies back, looking up at the flickering heavens, trying to get a breath into his lungs, as the rest of his family hover over him. He looks up into the faces of his girls, Kayla and Kourtney, his faithful wife of twenty-one years, sweet Jen, and he manages to blurt, "Go!"

Jennifer Stack shakes her head, wiping rain and tears from her face. She has the damaged, run-down beauty of a matriarch who will not let go without a fight. "No way."

"Get outta here!" John Stack croaks, his upper cervical vertebrae blazing with pain. "I'm not kidding. Run, now—GO!"

Both daughters shake their heads at him. "No, Daddy, I don't think so." The older one, Kayla, mutters this softly, her voice nearly drowned by the noise of the rain and the roar of a huge diesel truck engine. Next to her, the one named Kourtney tries to push her tears back down her throat but it's not working very well. She cries convulsively, the moisture from the rain mingling with the snot and the tears on her dirty face.

The big truck has pulled up on the gravel apron thirty feet away from them, scraping to a stop. The sound of doors clanging open, male voices, and shotgun breaches snapping shut penetrate the white noise of the downpour. The shadows of big men approach through the rainy haze.

"Damn it, I'm begging you," John Stack says with a groan. "Please get the fuck out of here! Now! I'm serious—please go! NOW!"

A deep, whiskey-cured voice draws everybody's attention over to the truck. "Let's everybody just take a deep breath and relax."

Through his bleary, watery vision, John sees a tall, middle-aged man standing on the running board of the big Mack stake truck. Clad in a bulky camouflaged rain parka, with a lavish cowboy hat and shoulders as broad as bridge trestles, the man radiates quiet authority over the half a dozen or so gunmen now surrounding the family in the rain. The big man hops off the running board and ambles over to the muddy patch in which the Stack family now huddles.

The man takes off his hat in a gesture of Old World manners as he looks down at John Stack. "Howdy, folks. My name is Spencer-Lee Dryden, and this is not as it appears. Last thing in the world we want to do is hurt you or make you uncomfortable in any way. Trust me on that. We're here to help."

John Stack just stares, nonplussed, the rain enveloping him in its chill.

It turns out that the bullets being used are nonlethal. In fact, the most recently fired projectile, which only a moment ago struck the homeless patriarch between the shoulder blades, is made of rubber, fired from an old 12-gauge riot gun that Spencer-Lee had procured from an Atlanta precinct house. The former city council member is a born politician, and when he was in office, years ago, he had a skeleton key that fit just about every door to every agency office, precinct house, and government building on Atlanta's south side. Now he escorts his new guests to the rear of the flatbed truck with the bouncy enthusiasm of a Boy Scout den father. Any day Spencer-Lee Dryden has an opportunity to serve his fellow citizens is a good day in his book.

"It's murder out there for a solitary family this day and age," he is saying as he ushers the shell-shocked family around the rear of the flatbed.

Two men in long waterproof dusters and ammo belts are standing on the edge of the truck bed, waiting for the family. The men are holding blankets and thermoses of coffee. As the family approaches, the men proffer courteous smiles that would impress a hotel concierge.

"I promise you, you ain't never gonna be hanging out to dry all by your lonesome ever again," Spencer-Lee adds as the men help the father and mother board the truck. "From now on, you're gonna be safe and sound, surrounded by others, part of a community."

Kourtney Stack stares at the calloused, dirty hand being offered to her from one of the men on the flatbed, and she gets a little unnerved by the whole ceremony and starts backing away from the rig.

"Kourtney?!" the father calls from up on the flatbed. "Kourtney, what are you doing?"

All at once, Spencer-Lee sees several troubling developments presenting themselves, each requiring immediate attention. The girl is obviously hysterical. She turns and starts to flee in the direction of the distant woods. On the edge of the trees, a few dozen walkers have already appeared, snarling and drooling, drawn to the noise, lumbering this way. The father is screaming.

"KOURTNEY!"

The father pushes his way past the men on the truck, hops off the rear, and charges after the fleeing girl. Spencer-Lee races after the two of them, calling over his shoulder, "Stay with the other two! Be right back!"

Over the course of the next minute or so, the girl slips and falls, and the walkers surround her. The father howls with terror as he approaches. A few paces behind the father, Spencer-Lee Dryden sees this all happening in a kind of dreamy slow motion as he races toward the fallen girl, pulling a twelve-inch Randall knife from a sheath on his right thigh. Originally from Birmingham, Alabama, the former politician played left-side linebacker for the Crimson Tide during his freshman and sophomore years, and he still has explosive strength and speed in spite of the expanding spare tire around his waist.

The stench of death rolls in despite the rain and the wind. The awful smell engulfs the area as the chorus of mortified vocal cords rises above the downpour. Spencer-Lee fixes his gaze on the oncoming wave of reanimated cadavers. Most of them are male, older, garbed in the tattered sun-bleached dungarees of farmworkers. Some of their faces are caved in, the mortified flesh hanging off the corners of their skulls, their dead, opaque eyes like milky blisters in their eye sockets. One of the creatures is furry with moss, as though the very ecosystem that spawned them is now slowly assimilating them.

Spencer-Lee starts in on the monsters with the practiced nonchalance of a stockyard worker putting down cattle. The tip of the knife flashes and pistons into skull after skull, sending stringers of fluid through the rain, causing the ferocious creatures to collapse one at a time as though puppet strings have been severed. The last one goes down like a sack of dung, splatting in the mud, the rotting blood already mingling with the first rivulets of floodwater seeping into the wetlands along the Chattahoochee.

By this point, the father has knelt by his daughter and helped her up into a sitting position. He comforts her with soft reassurances, stroking her hair and wiping the rain off her filthy face. She starts to sob, burying her face in the man's jacket. "It's okay, sweetie," he says to her. "We're going to take this one step at a time."

"That's a good approach," Spencer-Lee says as he walks up to them, wiping the knife on his pants, the dark cerebral fluids making a black, oily stain on the fabric. He shoves the knife back into its sheath. His other hand fishes in his parka's pocket and wraps around a small leather-clad object some folks call a sap, others call a black-jack. The thing weighs over a pound and a half, and is as hard and unyielding as a stone.

The father gazes up at him and starts to say, "Sir, I appreciate your generosity, but I think my family and I are going to—"

The sap strikes the man hard just above his left ear, making a sound like a muffled snare drum being struck, sending the father's eyes rolling back in their sockets before his body goes slack. The man collapses just as the daughter starts to scream.

The scream is cut off by another impact of the sap striking skull.

Spencer-Lee Dryden signals for his men to come help carry the bodies. Meanwhile, seeing all this transpire from the vantage point of the truck, the mother and older sister have started to scream and yell, trying to wriggle out of their captors' grasps. Spencer-Lee makes his way through the rain back to the rear of the rig. He pauses, looks up at the hysterical females, and gives them a sad, empathetic, almost parental look. "I'm sorry you had to see that," he says softly. "It couldn't be avoided. But they'll be fine, trust me." He smiles that same congenial smile his men have been exhibiting. "It's for their own good. You'll see. It's for all of you. For your safety."

John Stack comes awake in the rear of the truck just as it's pulling around a hairpin turn and heading down a narrow farm road. The rain continues unabated, thumping off a canvas canopy above him, dripping on his face, cooling the feverish pain throbbing behind his eyes. Every few moments, the dull rumble of thunder rattles in the far distance.

At first, he blinks and coughs, trying to figure out where he is while ignoring the horrendous stabbing pain in his skull from the impact of the sap. His daughter Kourtney lies unconscious next to him, breathing normally, covered in a blanket. He checks her pulse, feels her forehead. She seems fine. He sits up and the pain shoots down his cervical vertebrae like a bolt of electricity.

"John?!" His wife's whisper is taut with nervous tension. "Are you okay?"

"I think so . . . did you get the license number of the truck that hit me?"

"We have to get out of here." She glances over her shoulder at the two men riding up front, near the cab, each perched on peach crates. They look like they're either playing cards or trading cigarettes back and forth. "This is not good."

John glances over at his eldest daughter. Kayla sits against the wheel well, her knees gathered up against her chest, holding herself as though she might crumble into pieces at any moment. Her slender face is slack, her eyes fixed on the middle distance as though glazed with catatonia. She has reached her limit, and has gone inward as though an internal circuit breaker has shut her down.

"Dad?!" Kourtney's voice draws John's attention to his other daughter. "Are we—?"

"Sssshhhhhh!" Jennifer Stack scoots over to her youngest, putting her arm around her, stroking the bruise that's already forming above her temple. The girl's eye is rimmed in dark, livid purple from the wallop of the sap. "It's okay, honey . . . ssshhhh. We're all okay. We just have to be quiet right now. We have to be quiet and bide our time and wait for the right moment to get the hell out of here."

This last sentence Jennifer directs at her husband with a withering look.

From a distance, it looks like a military outpost or mobile surgical unit from some third world war. A half dozen trucks are parked in a circle around the main camp, enclosed in razor wire, some of the vehicles with machine guns mounted on their cab roofs. In the middle of the camp, a massive conglomeration of mobile homes and old renovated school buses sit in a row, connected like train cars. The windows are painted black, the doors boarded up. At first glance it appears to be a kind of surreal mobile commune—like a crazy, ramshackle version of Noah's Ark—poised to transport the chosen people to the Promised Land.

Upon closer scrutiny, however, one might draw different conclusions—mostly due to the armed guards at either end of the convoy, the burglar bars on some of the windows, and the chicken wire nailed across many of the hatchways and doors. John Stack makes all these observations in a daze of confusion and pain, his back still burning between the shoulder blades from the impact of the rubber bullet. He tries to gather his thoughts as the flatbed truck pulls up to the compound's makeshift gate. A few inaudible words are exchanged with the guards, and then the rig pulls through the gap.

Spencer-Lee Dryden walks alongside the flatbed with the proud smile of a real estate agent showing a property. "You're safe now, folks!"

The rig backs up to the end of the train of campers and trailers. Air brakes hiss. Gears grind, and the rig shudders to a halt. The wind whips the rain in a minicyclone around the rear of the truck as guards hop off the running boards and go around to help the passengers off the flatbed. Pausing at the edge of the bed, John and Jennifer Stack share a loaded glance. Jennifer cocks her head at her husband as though waiting for him to make a move.

"Just go along with it," John whispers to her. "For now . . . just play along."

"Your new home awaits!" Spencer-Lee says as he comes around the rear of the truck and gives them a hand as they step off the flatbed. The guards help the girls off the truck's rear ledge—Kayla still semicatatonic, shuffling along as though drugged. The family is escorted across a small patch of sodden ground to a series of steps leading up to the rear of a modified Winnebago. Burglar bars are mounted across its back screen door. The odors of coffee and disinfectant waft around the door.

Spencer-Lee knocks twice on the corner of the trailer and calls out, "Got some newcomers, Sally! Open up!" The muffled sound of a bolt rattles, followed by a click. "Folks, this is Sally, my long-suffering better half." Spencer-Lee announces this with pride in his voice, neglecting to explain what the woman's function or purpose in this place happens to be.

The door squeaks open a few inches and the face of a middle-aged woman with a black scarf knotted tight around her head peers out. She wears an oversized olive-drab Dickies work shirt—the kind a janitor or a maintenance man might wear—with a name patch that says YOUR NAME HERE. "Sorry, Spence . . . had a kindergarten class going in the north wing." The woman grins. "So we got some new-bies?" Her eyes twinkle as she surveys the four disheveled members of the Stack family. "Welcome, friends. Looks like y'all have been through the mill."

"Um . . . yeah. Hello." John Stack glances at his wife and then back at the woman in the doorway. "I'm John." He points out the others. "This is Jennifer . . . Kayla, Kourtney." He notices a few of the men from the truck standing back a few feet behind Spencer-Lee, look-ing on, ever vigilant, with AR-15 assault rifles cradled up high against their chests like independent contractors in some Middle Eastern war. It feels wrong all of a sudden. It feels . . . all wrong. John Stack turns to the woman in the door and starts to say something else when the woman lets out a joyous chortle.

"Aren't you the sweetest things?" She claps her hands together and pushes the door open wider. "Come on in, take a load off and let's look at those boo-boos."

Reluctantly, nervously, John Stack leads his family into the long jury-rigged enclosure, the metal door slamming behind him. He doesn't hear the bolt locking, but his hackles instantly go up.

If asked to describe the feeling inside the long chain of camper-trailers and buses, the word *purgatory* would invariably bubble up from John Stack's imagination. Five or six individual families occupy the living quarters that stretch at least three hundred feet—the size of a modern cruise ship—spanning thirteen individual vehicles connected in the style of train cars. Most of the interiors are exceedingly tidy, with floors clean enough to eat off of. Some of the inhabitants, mostly children under the age of twelve, smile and nod at the Stacks as they pass. These young residents of the convoy wear similar secondhand work shirts in various sizes and shades of beige and brown, looking strangely like Hitler Youth or members of an Orwellian work crew as they push brooms around the open floor space. Some of the shirts have pocket patches emblazoned with the names of previous owners—Chuck, Stan, Fred, Dick, Hank—none of which corresponds to the current wearer. The air smells of cleanser and Sterno and soap. Long tendrils of houseplants dangle from many of the ceiling vents, and most of the windows are barred or draped. *Work farm* and *cult compound* are phrases that also bounce around John Stack's mind as Sally, the official welcome wagon lady, leads the Stacks to an empty trailer near the front of the chain.

"I guess y'all can bunk here for the time being," she says cheerfully, indicating a narrow chamber of white-sheeted cots, cabinets, small sofas, and a tiny kitchenette. John takes in all the disturbing little details: the rose tattoo on Sally Dryden's wrist, the canned peaches on the kitchen counter, the little caddy of ancient, dusty magazines on the floor by the cot.

"I know it's a big adjustment," the woman in the baggy work shirt assures them. "But believe me, you're gonna love it here." She claps her hands again. "You got fresh towels in the pantry over there, clean shirts and pants, a first aid kit under the sink. Anything else y'all need—anything whatsoever—you just let me know. Now I'm gonna let y'all settle in, get your bearings, and I'll be back in an hour or so to answer any questions you might have."

She turns and walks out the inner door, which leads to the adjacent trailer.

The Stacks just stand there for a moment, dripping on the floor like wet rats, looking around the airless little camper with its ancient canned goods and old issues of *Us Weekly*. Outside, the rain drones on, hammering on the enclosure's roof. Back still aching, John rubs the bump on his head as Jennifer leads her oldest daughter over to a cot by the draped window, carefully lowering the girl to the bed, careful not to bang her head on the low shelf. The girl lies back, still staring emptily. Jennifer goes to the pantry for towels.

Across the room, Kourtney says, "I'm sorry but *what the fuck*?"

John looks at her, not responding but turning things over and over in his mind. He takes a towel from his wife and starts to dry off, still marveling at this bizarre turn of events. Less than thirty minutes ago, they were homeless, adrift in the most dangerous, walker-infested countryside in the South, and now they're in a place with houseplants. Part of him wants to wait and see what happens next, but another part of him wants to run screaming from this place.

"You know what this place is?" Jennifer's voice cuts through his thoughts and tugs at his attention. She stands next to him, a grave look on her face. "It's a goddamn prison."

Before John can respond, a voice comes from the inner doorway.

"We prefer to think of it as protective custody." Spencer-Lee Dryden stands in the archway, watching them with a convivial smile on his face and a twinkle in his eye. He stands next to his wife, holding her hand, the two of them looking like a sinister couple at the top of a sinister wedding cake. "Look. You folks are exhausted. Who wouldn't be? Why don't you make yourselves at home, we'll have a good talk later."

He gives a nod, as though the subject is closed, and then turns and ushers Sally back the way they came, closing the door behind them, the lock making a loud, resounding, final click . . . locking the Stack family in their new home.

Not long after the Drydens have made their departure, John Stack hears the muffled sounds of another family in the trailer in front of them, and curiosity gets the better of him. He squeezes past a stack of supply crates and peers through a narrow window in the front of his enclosure—a firewall that used to be a bunk window—and he sees three children and one adult.

At first, nothing about these people strikes John as extraordinary, most of them dressed in those odd work shirts and uniform pants that look like they were cribbed from a bowling team or a school for budding repairmen. The children all appear to be middle-school age, and mostly content, maybe even drugged, it's hard to tell. They sit languidly reading books or drawing with crayons. But then John's gaze falls on the lone adult sitting off by herself on the floor in the corner of the trailer.

Something about the way the woman is sitting there is troubling to John but he can't quite put his finger on it. Rawboned, lanky, with a swimmer's physique, she sits Indian-style in her work uniform, her legs interlaced, head down, brow furrowed in thought. She has short, dark, razor-cut hair, and a patrician face that conjures images of Ivy League schools and East Coast money.

But the way she sits there, tapping a spoon on the floor, deep in thought, her intelligent eyes shifting around the chamber, tells John Stack there is a lot more going on here than a mother of three trying to decide what to cook for dinner tonight.

Turning back to his own family, John Stack feels his skull throbbing with pain, his stomach clenching with panic. He sees his wife sitting on the edge of Kayla's cot, pressing a cold rag to the injured girl's head. He sees his youngest daughter over by the window, gazing out like a caged animal. He realizes not a single one of them has made a move toward the clean clothes or the cooler or the water dispenser on the counter or any of the amenities.

John Stack can feel the tension twisting in his gut. He knows this feeling well. He has felt it many times over the past few years. It is the genetic memory stewing in him that some call fight or flight— that silent warning going off inside a person when danger is on the horizon. He feels it now in his gorge like a fist. Something terrible is about to happen.

He turns back to the narrow window, gazes down at the woman

in the first trailer, and wonders if she has anything to do with these feelings.

Hunkered down on the trailer's floor, reviewing her plan over and over, trying to ferret out the flaws, the stumbling blocks, the ways things could go wrong, Ashley Lynn Duart watches her adopted kids out of the corner of her eyes. The children seem docile enough tonight. Little do they know what is in store for them. They are the weakest links in her plan, but there is nothing Ash can do about that now.

She rises to her full height—nearly six feet—and brushes the top of her head against the trailer's ceiling. Clad in an XXL Dickies shirt, cinched at the waist with a leather belt, the name GARY stitched on its pocket, she puts on a happy face for the children and announces, "Think I'm gonna make us some macaroni and cheese for dinner tonight."

They all think this is a pretty good idea, so Ash starts pulling out the camp stove and pots from their storage cabinets. She pours the water and drops the pasta and lights the Sterno can under the saucepan, silently reviewing her plan, agonizing over every detail. She secretly reaches under the counter and feels for the road flare she has hidden there, the twelve-inch-long stick taped to the underside of the tiny sink. She brushes her fingertips across it, reassuring herself, girding herself.

It was the only item even remotely close to a weapon that Ash had been able to smuggle into the prison camp when her and Quinn's kids had been kidnapped from the fields outside Haralson last month. She had hidden the twelve-inch stick of potassium nitrate, sulfur, sawdust, and wax down the back of her pants, and now she knows it represents her only chance of escape from this madhouse.

Her one last card to play.

Tonight.

THREE

Lilly Caul works throughout the afternoon and early evening, her head pounding, her joints aching.

With Tommy Dupree at her side, she hauls two portable generators down from the second floor and loads them onto the back of a modified pickup truck. The front end of the rig has been severed off at the windshield, the greasy, exposed chassis in front now acting as braces for a team of two horses. Lilly and Tommy will go it alone in this Frankenstein's monster of a conveyance. After pleading, cajoling, threatening, and bargaining with the others, Lilly failed to convince anybody else to join her. Now she has no choice but to go ahead and take off without them. It's still a free country, and with Tommy's help she believes she can make it back to Woodbury and start over. The plan is to return for the children when the town is rendered safe.

All of which is fueling her with adrenaline right now as she fills the pickup's cargo bay with treasures from the store. Over the next hour, they bring down cartons of freeze-dried entrees from the cafeteria, solar cell lamps, kitchen utensils, cartons of granola, blankets, outdoor solar showers, garden implements, seed packets, lightbulbs, storage boxes, portable grills, charcoal briquettes, lighter fluid, potted plants, growing soil, juice boxes, jars of pickled vegetables, batteries, battery chargers, pillows, backpacks, and half a dozen shrink-wrapped cartons of bottled water.

By midnight, the makeshift horse-wagon is so laden with weight the rear tires have practically flattened out against the cement deck of the parking garage. Lilly and Tommy secure the cargo with bungee cords and rope, and then go fetch the horses.

The group's official horse wrangler, Burt Stankowski, grew up on a farm in Virginia. A year ago, he acquired two sturdy draft horses in trade for his ailing eighteen-wheeler, and a few months later, he picked up a stallion and a mare from an abandoned dairy farm outside of Macon. The mare has already had two foals and is expected to have more. In addition to these six horses, they have the three that Musolino and Boone brought in when they joined the group.

Now all the animals hunker together in the makeshift stable at one end of the garage, shuffling through the shredded paper that doubles as hay, nickering nervously at the occasional volley of thunder that rattles the ground floor above them. Lilly and Tommy approach cautiously. The animals seem nervous. Lilly whispers, "Go easy, Tommy. Storm's got them a little jumpy."

They untie the two draft horses, and then lead them back across the cluttered garage.

"Holy shit," Tommy Dupree comments as he returns to the modified pickup. He comes to an abrupt halt, the horse tossing its head and whinnying. Tommy stares. He doesn't move.

Lilly pauses in front of the pickup, speechless, holding the horse by the lead and staring at the twelve figures gathered around the pickup wagon. "What's going on?" she asks them.

"We took a vote," Musolino tells her. Clad in an army surplus raincoat, a pair of ammo bandoliers slung over his broad shoulders, he glances at the others. Most of them are looking down at the floor with embarrassed smiles as if sharing a private joke. Norma Sutters just shakes her head with wry amusement and glances at Eve Betts, who grins at Boone, who grins at Stankowski. They're all dressed in rain gear. Some of them carry duffel bags. Even the children are bundled up in raincoats with their adorable little knapsacks slung across their backs. Musolino smiles at Lilly. "We decided life would be too boring without you around here to bust our balls."

Lilly looks at Tommy, and Tommy giggles. Lilly is about to say something else when she notices Sophie Leland standing in the back, holding the baby, looking earnest and brave. Three of the teenagers—Connie, Bradley, and Lyle—stand behind her, gun belts and bandoliers weighing down their emaciated bodies, causing their shoulders to stoop. Lilly sees all the downturned faces around her, feels the awkward silence, and instantly understands what's going on.

"None of you are wearing raincoats," Lilly says to the group huddling against the back wall. She speaks softly, deferentially.

The former prostitute smiles sadly but doesn't yet look up at Lilly. "Yeah . . . well." Then Sophie looks up through wet eyes. "I think me and Doe are gonna be safer staying behind. The kids will watch over us." She gestures toward the heavily armed teenagers. "When you get situated down there, and everything is cool, you can come back for us."

Lilly processes this for a moment. "Okay. Um. Are you sure about this?"

Sophie nods. "Yeah, actually, I am. I think this is the safest bet for the baby. We'll be fine. We got that whole walk-in full of freeze-dried food. And Connie and Brad have a wheelbarrow full of bullets."

"All right . . . I get what you're saying. I just want to make sure you're cool with this."

"I am. We got enough powdered milk to last Doe into her teens. And we can all stay on the third floor indefinitely. We'll be fine."

Lilly ponders the lithe little woman and her wan, slender face. Along one side of the woman's swan-like neck is a jailhouse tattoo of a spiderweb. A ropy scar of indeterminate origins winds down one arm like a seam in her flesh. The fingers of her left hand—the one currently holding the pacifier—are each adorned with a letter, together spelling the word *L-I-V-E*. Along the inside of one forearm is the phrase *Don't Judge Me*.

Right then, Lilly realizes all the hard miles that this waiflike former streetwalker has traveled, and she concludes if there's anybody who could survive in this place with a baby, a gaggle of unruly teenagers, and a million square feet of home furnishings, it's Sophie Leland.

At last, Lilly gives Sophie a forlorn smile and says, "If you're absolutely sure this is what you want to do."

"I am, Lilly. Don't worry about us. Doe will take care of all of us."

Lilly grins. "I believe she will." Lilly pulls the woman and the baby into a warm embrace, gently stroking the child's silky hair. Lilly can smell that unmistakable powdery fragrance of baby, and it makes her eyes water with emotion. She steps back. "Good luck, sweetie."

"Thanks." Sophie takes a deep breath. "Same back at you."

With a nod, Lilly turns and looks at the group of stalwart friends standing before her with earnest expressions. The tears well up in her eyes. She wipes them. "Never a dull moment with you people," she finally says.

That night, out in the rain-lashed farmland, in a warren of interconnected trailers occupying a backwoods meadow, a big man reclines on a sofa in the largest trailer, a gaggle of children snuggled around him, some of them sucking their thumbs, others beginning to drift off as the man's baritone voice renders an O. Henry story from memory. "And the beautiful young bride presents the handsome young husband with the gorgeous watch chain," Spencer-Lee Dryden softly utters, "for which she sold her lovely blond hair."

He speaks in the rolling drawl of down-water Louisiana, stretching the words into *luhhhv-lee blahhhhnd hayyyyahh*, which only adds to the hypnotic quality of his voice. Lying back on a heap of feather pillows, his shirt unbuttoned to reveal his graying chest hair, he resembles a land baron or a king lounging in his castle, surrounded by his tiny subjects, his heirs. He has a faint smile on his boyish face, warm and cozy in the knowledge that his palace guards are, at this very moment, out in the rain, patrolling the borders of his encampment, keeping the wolves at bay. And King Spencer-Lee the First is free to revel in his happy place, his passion, his obsession: *family*.

Spencer-Lee grew up in Slidell, helping his dad deliver kegs of Dixie beer to bars and taverns across the bayous and backwaters. He learned the hardscrabble wholesale liquor business with his bare fists and street sense, which ultimately landed him in the wild and woolly world of Georgia politics. But it was the loss of his entire family in a terrible house fire when he was away at school in Alabama that truly shaped him as a person. He had rushed home the day after and had to identify the bodies at the city morgue in Montgomery. Seeing those woeful, charred remains of his dear mother, his pop, and his brother Willy laid out on those slabs changed him. He would suffer the invisible scars of that day the rest of his life.

That autumn he met his sweet Sally, then a coed at the U of A, and married her the following spring, and he never looked back. Even when he and his wife were told they could never have children, he went on secretly believing that his family would one day blossom.

"And the handsome young husband presents a beautiful golden comb to the young bride," he goes on in his honey-sweet basso profundo purr. "For which he sold his watch. But neither useless gift could match the love they had for each other, for God, for country, and for the most important thing of all: *family.*"

This last part he completely invents on the spot, punctuating the final sentence of his tale with a kiss on each downy-soft head of each child. Sally materializes in the shadows near the door, as if on cue, and Spencer-Lee gently lifts the slumbering children—one at a time—from his sofa, handing them over to the matriarch. With a wink and a little grin, she carries each child back down the long corridor of trailers to their respective quarters.

Spencer-Lee washes up, brushes his teeth, and retires to his private bedroom. He peers through the slatted blinds at the rain-scourged woods outside. In the intermittent lightning, he can see his men surrounding a moving corpse on the edge of the forest. It's a large male with some age on it, its innards hanging out of its ruptured midsection. The light flickers again and Spencer-Lee sees one of the guards drive a crowbar through the creature's skull.

The body is dragged away and disposed of, and the quiet drone of rain returns.

The big man lies back on his bed, clad only in his boxer shorts. He turns off the oil lantern and lets his mind wander. The sound of the rain on the trailers' rooftops is calming. He is about to drift off when the faint voice of his wife stirs him. "I love that story," she says, climbing into bed with him, still garbed in her work shirt. "The way they each sell the very thing the other one is accessorizing."

They kiss. Spencer-Lee chuckles. "'Accessorizing' . . . I like that."

Her hand goes down to his groin, awakening him further, their mouths opening, tongues exploring and flicking. They begin to make love, longtime partners, each with an intimate knowledge of the other's zones and quirks. Sally's shirt falls open as she lies on her back. Spencer-Lee pulls the shirt off her and tosses it on the floor, the strange pocket patch—YOUR NAME HERE—still visible in the low light.

The work shirts had been Spencer-Lee's idea. A couple years ago, he found an entire warehouse full of them, and he realized they would help him keep track of the inhabitants of his symbolic ark. The "guests" in his little hermetically sealed compound would wear the frumpy, utilitarian uniforms as a sort of nod to community, to family, to democratic ideals. The guards would be better able to identify residents in the event of an emergency, and the *uniformity* of it all would lend a kind of utopian quality to the place. Sure, at times, the work clothes can give off an air of the penitentiary, and the irony of false name patches on the breast pockets of plague refugees is not lost on Spencer-Lee. But on the whole, the Dickies cast-offs have worked out well.

Now, Spencer-Lee and Sally build up a rhythm, faster and faster.

They are about to climax when the shadow of a third figure crosses the room.

It happens so fast, neither Sally nor Spencer-Lee notices the shadow moving to the bedside table and grasping the leather sap before it's too late. The sap comes down hard on the back of Spencer-

Lee's skull. It makes a sound like a broken bell in his ears, a shooting star of pain flashing across his field of vision.

He flops backward onto the floor, and begins to gag on his own saliva.

The passage of time seems to slow down as Spencer-Lee wavers in and out of consciousness. He can barely see the tall, feminine figure slamming the sap down on Sally's head, knocking her unconscious, then tying her wrists to the headboard, gagging her with a length of fabric. Then, in a flickering burst of lightning, he sees the assailant's face. At first, he doesn't recognize the woman. But then, in a second flash of ambient light, he realizes it's the Ashley Duart woman—better known as Ash—the stuck-up blueblood from Haralson.

Dressed in a black sleeveless blouse and jeans, her arms sinewy with muscle, she turns to apply the restraints to Spencer-Lee when the man lunges at her.

For a moment, the two figures collide into a violent bear hug, slamming each other against the opposite wall of the trailer, knocking a shelf full of wineglasses and knickknacks to the floor. Sally comes to across the room, tied to the headboard, her eyes bugging wide and hot with terror.

On the other side of the room, each combatant goes for the other's throat, a primal move on each of their parts. The woman is ferocious. She's a lot stronger than Spencer-Lee would expect, and in the darkness of the room, in the heat of the fight, he almost forgets she's a lady. Finally, he backhands her hard—as hard as he can—and she lurches backward, tripping over her own feet, and sprawling to the floor.

Spencer-Lee pounces on her. His head throbs with agony, concussed by the impact of the blackjack. He strangles her. "Fucking goddamn bitch whore," he growls as he squeezes the life out of her.

All at once, like a magic trick, she produces a blinding corona of light in her hands.

At first, Spencer-Lee doesn't see that she has ignited a road flare.

He only sees the sunburst of brilliant pink light in his face, causing his head to whiplash backward. The air sizzles as the searing pain shoots through his skull. His hands slip off her throat as she jabs the flaming tip of the flare at him, grazing his face, again and again, the luminous bloom of sparks finally going into his mouth, the glowing tip thrust so deep it lodges in his throat.

A strangled noise—part shriek of agony, part psychotic howl of rage—erupts out of him as he collapses backward with the flare still stuck in his throat. He lands hard, knocking over another shelf, clawing at the terrible fire choking him, sending molten hot bits of spittle and burning flesh through the air. Sally convulses on the bed, her muffled screams like hyena howls across the room.

Meanwhile, Ash has recovered enough to rise back to her feet and snatch the man's keys and .38-caliber pistol off the bedside table. Spencer-Lee flails on the floor. He claws at the source of agony lodged in his throat. He can't breathe. His hair crackles and catches fire.

In another flash of lightning, out of the corner of his eye, he can see his assailant lunging across the trailer and bursting out the door. It makes a sound that he is only dimly aware of—like a muffled, distant volley of thunder in his brain—which throbs in his ringing ears. He finally manages to roll onto his hands and knees, and then somehow dislodges the flaming tip of the road flare from his throat.

He collapses onto his side, coughing bloody sparks and clutching at a corner of the bedspread. He finally manages to douse the flames with the blankets, covering his head, the stabbing, hot pain unlike anything he's ever felt. He lets out a honking, pathetic sob. He rolls onto his back and stares at the ceiling tiles.

The smell of burning flesh and the haze of noxious smoke trigger memories of the conflagration that took his mom and dad. And for one terrible moment, he flashes back to that horrible day during his sophomore year at the U of A when he had to identify their bodies in the Montgomery morgue, their faces barely recognizable, so scorched and burned they looked like plastic mannequins that had melted into the stainless steel surfaces of the cadaver drawers.

At last, mercifully, the memory fades and unconsciousness rolls over Spencer-Lee Dryden like a tide, taking him down into its cold, black depths.

Ashley Lynn Duart creeps through the rainy darkness, stumbling and slipping on the slimy-wet weeds outside the Drydens' trailer as she thumbs back the hammer on Spencer-Lee's police special, her heart thundering in her chest, her eyesight heightened by the adrenaline coursing through her. She must act quickly, decisively, and without mercy if she wants to get out of here alive with the others. She can see the shadowy figures of guards—obviously roused by muffled noises coming from the Drydens' trailer—coming toward her from two separate directions.

"Hey!" The first one, an older man known as Fitz, sees her in the rain. "What the hell are you—?!"

She has already raised the pistol with both hands, taken aim, and squeezed off a single shot. The blast strikes the man named Fitz in the neck, causing him to whiplash, his feet slipping out from under him, his AR-15 assault rifle flying out of his hands. He lands on his back, splashing in the muck—his wound fatal—his lifeblood draining out with the speed of a slaughtered hog.

The other guard slips behind a tree, pulls the cocking lever, and fires off a fusillade that sounds like a drumroll in the droning storm. Ash manages to drop to her belly at the last possible moment, the bullets zinging over her head, sending a chain of noisy ricochets ringing and sparking across the underbelly of the second trailer. Ash scoots under its chassis.

She crawls out the other side, gets back to her feet, lurches toward an opening between two of the trailers, and finds the second guard in her sight, the man darting wildly toward the trailers. Before the man can fire, Ash sends three rounds into his gut. The man collapses with his finger frozen on the trigger, sending a volley of gunfire into the sky. The noise mingles with the rumbling thunder.

Ash hears other guards coming from the far corners of the

encampment now, lights snapping on inside windows—some of them on generators, some oil lamps—the muffled sounds of prisoners panicking behind the boarded windows. Ash fumbles for the keys. She knows she has mere seconds to get everybody out of their enclosures.

The first door sticks, the key jamming in the rusty, congealed bolt. She digs the key into it and shakes it furiously. The door finally gives, and Ash opens it to find four faces huddling in the shadows—two little kids, a father and a mother—gaping out at her with feverish expressions of terror.

"What in God's name are you doing?" the father demands to know in a hoarse, sleepy voice. A skinny, pale-skinned former grocery store manager from Augusta, Ronnie Nesbit was snatched along with his wife and two grade-school-aged children from a derelict shopping mall outside Atlanta six months ago. He now wears the customary work uniform of the Dryden cult and has the whipped-dog stare of the brainwashed.

"We're getting outta here!" Ash hears the other guards coming around the far corner of the convoy. "Leave everything but the clothes on your back, anything you can use as a weapon, and . . . and your family!"

It takes a fraction of a second for Ronnie Nesbit to snap out of his daze. He looks at his wife Dina, and she gives him a nod, and then they help their two kids—a boy and a girl—out of the trailer into the wind and the rain.

Ash goes to the next door, unlocks it, and finds the Stack family huddling together in their brown work uniforms. At first, John Stack looks reticent, panicky, confused. "What are you—?" he starts to say but then sees the look on her face. Something clicks behind his eyes. Maybe he remembers seeing her coiled on the floor of her trailer like a caged animal. He gives her a quick nod and starts to say, "Do you have any other weapons we can—"

All at once, a series of noises cuts off his words and all heads turn toward the Drydens' trailer. The force of the fire has blown out one of the windows. The glass explodes, and flames curl through the rain, filaments of sparks and debris shooting up into the wind. A woman's scream mingles with the crackling noise of the fire.

Two more guards come around the corner and try to tear open the Drydens' door.

Ash fires her last two rounds at the guards, one of the bullets grazing one of them in the shoulder, the other blast going wide and high, ricocheting off the Drydens' roof vent. Fortunately, the gunfire slows the guards down enough for Ash to turn to John Stack and say, "Grab that guy's assault rifle while I get my kids!"

In all the confusion, with the fire in the Drydens' trailer, the guards coming from all directions, and all the shooting as well as the window blowing out, Ash is able to safely and quickly extract her own kids from the last trailer at the same time John Stack is able to procure the AR-15 off the body of the fallen guard. John is also fortunate enough to find an extra ammo magazine on the dead man with twenty rounds tucked into its chambers. Nowadays—a good four years into the plague—virgin ammunition is just about as rare as gasoline. But apparently, Spencer-Lee and his men have been able to plunder enough of their clients' original habitats to stockpile an impressive arsenal. Now, kneeling by the dead man, John Stack works quickly, pulling the man's pants off him. He springs to his feet and steps into the pants, then stuffs the mag into the belt and quickly searches the corpse for anything else that might be of value. He's looking for edged weapons, handguns, a lighter, a canteen, or whatever, when the corpse's eyelids flutter open to reveal opaque white corneas the size and shape of marbles.

John rears back with a start as the dead guard snarls and bites at the air, its blackened lips peeling away from its exposed incisors.

Reacting almost involuntarily, John Stack slams the barrel of the assault rifle down into the mouth of the reanimated cadaver, and then twists it up through the nasal passages and into the optic nerve.

The muzzle breaks through the dura mater and protrudes out the top of the biter's scalp like a horn, gushing blood around the rifle's muzzle.

Springing back to his feet, John pulls the rifle free of the skull, sending runnels of cerebrospinal fluid into the flooded weeds.

He hears Ash calling out for them to get their asses in gear and get moving, and he rushes to her side, joining his family and the others as they plunge into the adjacent woods, enveloped in darkness, lashed by the wet winds and unrelenting rain.

The rain eventually lifts, the storm finally moving through the area, leaving behind an eerie stillness as they make their way into the deeper woods. All ambient light from behind them gets squeezed out of the margins, and the darkness sets in like a black pudding. It seems to dampen all sound. The air has a washed-out, crystalline quality now, as well as a troubling scent—smoke, rot, and wet animal fur. Ash hears only her own breathing, and the muffled, wet crunch of footsteps on her flanks. Tandem shadows of children and adults move alongside her and flicker in her peripheral vision.

The noise of the Drydens' encampment has completely faded away behind them. Now there are only the sounds of their footsteps, the huffing of their breaths, and the thumping of their hearts.

"Stay close," Ash whispers, and brushes her fingertips across the grip of her pistol. She puts a gentle hand on the shoulders of Quinn's kids. The darkness has become so dense now that she can only see the outlines of their faces, bobbing along like shadow puppets on either side of her. Most of them have shed the ridiculous janitor uniforms and now wear clothes they managed to grab at the last minute. Bobby, the oldest, a tough little nine-year-old cuss with a thatch of unruly black hair, wears faded overalls. His two younger sisters—Chelsea, eight, and Trudy, seven—each have Quinn's trademark dark eyes and olive skin, and each wears an identical dirty pink sweatshirt.

Ash would die for these kids, but right now, that's not an option.

"I'm tired," Chelsea Quinn complains. "My foot hurts."

"Mine does, too," Trudy pipes. "How far do we have to go?"

"Shut up," Bobby barks at them.

"Sssssshhhhhh!" Ash glances over her shoulder and sees only a wall of darkness. No flashlights, no dogs, no figures, no walkers . . . *yet*. "As soon as we can stop, I promise I'll make it all better, but right now we have to play the little game I taught you."

Trudy looks up. "The runaway game?"

Ash smiles despite her nerves. "Exactly, honey—yes, that's the one. Do you remember the first rule?"

"Keep moving?"

"You got it. And the second rule?"

Trudy thinks and thinks, and finally Chelsea chimes in, "Be really quiet?"

"*Exactly.*"

Bobby grumbles, "So that means you can go ahead and shut your traps now."

"Bobby—" Ash starts to admonish the boy when a flashlight snaps on to her immediate right. Ash flinches at the light. "Turn that off!"

Ten feet away, Ronnie Nesbit, still clad in his Dickies work shirt with KEN on the pocket, fumbles with the switch on his small battery-operated flashlight. "Sorry, sorry." He finally extinguishes the light. "Just thought we might be able to—"

"It's okay," Ash cuts him off, ushering the children down a gentle slope of pine needles and animal droppings, the odor of which braces her like smelling salts. The trees have grown thicker, and the smell of fish off in the distance tells her they are approaching a creek or maybe even a tributary of the Flint River, which is most likely swollen with floodwaters at the moment.

Ash whispers to the adults, "I just don't want to give away our position . . . to whomever . . . you know . . . best to use the cover of darkness."

"Plus, the last thing we want to do is have the walkers see us," Bobby Quinn adds with his half-baked nine-year-old swagger,

which thinly veils his terror. "That happens, we're screwed and tattooed."

"Yeah, Bobby's right, because they can see light, too," little Cindy
Nesbit agrees.

Another young voice from the darkness: "And if they find *uth*
they'll eat *uth* all up." This comes from the youngest child, Teddy
Nesbit, a precocious six-year-old. "And then we'll all be like dead
and then we'll all like turn into them things!"

"Hey!" Ash addresses all of them in a loud whisper. "What is it
about being quiet that you kids don't understand? Please. I'm asking you to not talk until I say it's okay. Just stay close and keep really
quiet."

Now the silence settles back in as they descend the mossy slope.

Ash shivers. In spite of the low, overcast night sky and complete
lack of moonlight—the rain still dripping in the high boughs, filter-
ing down through the black network of branches—Ash can see a
faint glint of water in the middle distance. It floats behind the
skeins of foliage like rough-hewn diamonds in the darkness, and
Ash uses that glimmer as a point of reference, a destination toward
which she now leads the group. She has a vague idea of their location. Judging from the movements of the Dryden clan, as well as the
chaotic events following Ash's kidnapping, she knows they are at
least forty miles or so south of Atlanta, and at least ten to twenty
miles east of Haralson, maybe somewhere near Zebulon or Wil-
liamson. One thing she knows for sure: in this part of Georgia, all
creeks and tributaries run toward the Flint River. If Ash can get
them to the Flint, then she can navigate by that serpentine body of
water.

Eventually, of course, Ash wants to get back to Haralson, where
Quinn, the children's father, and others are most likely tearing their
hair out trying to figure out what happened to Ash and the kids. But
for now, just being able to locate their position will not only help
them escape the threat of a Dryden search party, it will also aid their
efforts to get home.

Ash sees the creek materializing through a break in the trees. Her eyes have adjusted to the darkness enough now that she can see that the flooding is worse than she thought. Timbers and debris and fallen leaves float in the moonless dark along the banks of the stream where a sidewalk used to be. Many trees appear to be submerged up to their middle branches, and a lazy drizzle still pocks the surface with intermittent raindrops.

She signals for the group to follow her along the snaking shoreline of the creek. Morning is still a good four hours off but if she can get the children to travel through the night, or at least for another hour or so, she'll be able to put enough miles between her and Spencer-Lee to at least be able to pause for a few hours of sleep.

Moments later, the moon peers out from behind the thinning, dwindling storm clouds. The pale light seems as bright as a streetlamp to Ash as she follows the twists and convolutions of the flooded creek bed southward. She believes that the Flint is only a few miles away. And once they locate the river, they are halfway home. All at once, she feels better, emboldened, stronger. She smiles at her adopted kids, and they smile back at her. "We're gonna make it," Bobby Quinn says to her.

Ash gives him a nod, completely unaware that she's leading the group directly into one of the largest multitudes of the dead that has yet to randomly coalesce in the Georgia farmlands.

FOUR

The next morning, well before dawn, Lilly and company light out from Ikea.

They start out with four modified horse-wagons—a team of two horses on each conveyance—as well as Musolino's battered Escalade SUV with its .50-caliber machine gun mounted on a tripod on its rear cargo deck, the ventilated barrel sticking out of the rear hatch window. They have a grand total of forty gallons of gasoline left in four separate ten-gallon containers—more than enough to get them to Woodbury, with many gallons left over to run the emergency generators. They also bring along two battery-operated toy walkie-talkies that someone found in the bargain bin of the Ikea children's department. Lilly decides that she and Musolino will communicate via the toy two-ways. The audio quality of the cheap, plastic devices is inferior but they have no other options.

At exactly 5:11 A.M., Eastern Daylight Time, the caravan makes its exit through the south ramp of Ikea's underground parking garage. Tommy and Musolino have ignited two large dumpsters at opposite corners of the street in order to draw the walker population away from the open garage door and create a gap through which they can slip into the city. The procession emerges from the bowels of the building one contraption at a time.

First comes Lilly and Tommy in their deconstructed pickup, the skeleton of its front half-braced between the two trusty draft horses, each animal frothing at the bit. The two younger Dupree kids—Bethany and Lucas—ride in the rear, nestled in between the spoils from Ikea. Next out is Burt Stankowski, seated in the cab of an old panel van sans its front engine, front wheels, and windshield. The old truck driver is in his element, chewing on a cigar and snapping the reins of another pair of economy-sized workhorses. Four of the children ride in the van's payload area, tucked among piles of bedding and pillows, accompanied by a stack of board games and a thermos full of Kool-Aid.

Then comes Eve Betts at the reins of a railroad flatcar pulled by yet another brace of horses. Boone stands on the flatbed behind her, an assault rifle slung over his shoulder, a pair of ski goggles making him resemble a member of the Rat Patrol. Lilly had discovered the train car a few blocks away from Ikea, capsized in a ditch along the defunct tracks of the Western and Atlantic Railroad. The car is now stacked ten feet high with plastic storage bins, each brimming with treasures, lashed together with rope and strapping material, making the horse-drawn monstrosity look like something out of a Dr. Seuss book.

A massive tow truck with no front wheels or engine—also pulled by workhorses—emerges after that, Norma Sutters at the reins, a do-rag wrapped around her head, a long machete thrust down the side of a belt made from an Ikea curtain sash, all of which gives her the look of a female pirate. Behind the tow truck booms Musolino's heavily armed Escalade, bringing up the rear of the ragtag convoy, the SUV roaring up the ramp in a cloud of exhaust.

They make their way down a flooded Northside Drive, which swims in the ashen predawn light, the wreckage and human remains floating like bloated doll parts on the random currents of the floodwaters. This part of the city was hit hard by the deluge, most of the streets now underwater, the gutters and open manholes still gushing silently under the surface of the muck. The sewers have vomited their contents, both animate and inanimate, creating a stew-like quagmire of waterlogged carnage the likes of which Lilly and her people have never seen. The air reeks of putrid, moldy decay. The sense of desecration is so palpable that Lilly can feel it on her skin like a thin layer of slime.

"Musolino, you copy?" Lilly lifts her thumb off the Talk button.

Through the crackling static, a faint male voice says, "I can barely hear you but go ahead."

Lilly thumbs the button, keeping a tight grip on the reins with the other hand. From the backs of the animals' regal, tapered heads, the horses look nervous, skittish, spooked by the floating abattoir around them. The bridles and leads are all homemade, jury-rigged by Norma with Ikea sewing machines. Lilly says into the toy device, "Water's already up to the horses' hocks."

Through the crackle: "I know, looks like it's almost two feet deep."

Lilly presses the switch. "If it gets any deeper, we can try the freeway."

The voice replies: "The Abernathy's fairly clear, and much of it's raised on viaducts. We'd have to go a little out of our way to the west."

Lilly thinks about it, and then thumbs the switch. "Okay, we'll take I-20 to Bowdon Junction, then head south on 27 through Newman. Keep your eyes open for swimmers."

Crackling, fizzing static: "Copy that."

Lilly drops the toy onto the seat between her and Tommy and keeps the horses moving through the brackish, hellish soup. They pass the ruins of the Georgia Dome, one side of the great cupola caved in by weather and winds, the sides of the structure black with overgrowth, dead kudzu, and opportunistic vines. The vast reaches of the parking lot lie under three or four feet of water—it's hard to tell the exact depth at this distance. Some of the rusted-out carcasses of cars now drift upside down like capsized turtles. The wan, early-morning light has dawned enough for the human eye to see count-less objects the size of small buoys skimming the surface of the floodwater. Lilly does a double take when she realizes that these are the heads of walkers aimlessly trudging through the mire.

She notices Tommy staring at the surreal sight, shivering in the clammy predawn air. He murmurs something that she can't quite decipher.

"What was that, Tommy?"

"Are those . . . the rooftops of houses?" Tommy points out beyond the heads at the floodplain half a mile away, the roof pitches sticking out of the water like icebergs, the road they're on vanishing into its depths. The morning sun has just begun to peek over the horizon, sending cold motes of sunlight through the low-lying mists enrobing the drowning neighborhoods. The wind whips the surface of the floodwater as it whistles around street signs, telephone poles, train trestles, and viaducts.

Lilly grabs her walkie-talkie. "Musolino, we got a situation."

Through the static: "Copy that, I see it, and so do the others. What do you want to do?"

Lilly glances out at the cracked side mirror and sees Burt Stankowski behind her, tugging on his reins, slowing his team to a stop in the stagnant water of the wreckage-strewn highway. The others yank their horses to a standstill behind him. Lilly pulls her team to a stop. Within seconds, the entire caravan has abruptly halted.

"What now, d'ya think?" Tommy keeps his eyes on the periphery, nervously making sure none of those drifting heads comes too close to the side of their conveyance. He puts a hand on the hilt of his machete. He can hear the lapping burble of water against the pickup's undercarriage, and wonders, *What if the horses get bit?*

Lilly mulls it over for a moment. She glances over her shoulder, remembering coming down here for barbeque years ago when she lived with Megan. She thumbs the Talk button on the toy two-way. "Mus, there's a road we just passed, Fairburn Road I think is the name of it."

She lifts her thumb off the button and hears the faint voice cut through the crackle: "Yep . . . copy that, I remember it. Doesn't it eventually cross the Chattahoochee?"

Lilly thumbs the switch. "If I remember correctly, it crosses 154 about two miles from here. Should take us around this mess."

"Copy that."

Lilly leans out her open window and signals to the others that they're turning around.

Then she gives the horses a yank to the right, and the entire make-shift carriage creaks and moans as the team executes 180-degree turn, pulling the contraption back in the direction from which it had come.

Ash is the first one to see the throngs pressing in through the trees, and at first she thinks she's hallucinating. Whether it's the stress, the lack of sleep, the exhaustion from trudging through the woods the better part of the night, or the injuries sustained in her violent confrontation with Spencer-Lee, she very well might be seeing things. She comes to a sudden stop and raises her hand. "Sssshhhhh . . . ssshhhhhh!" She glances over her shoulder and whispers, "Every-body stop, and be very still. Don't move a muscle."

For a moment, both the children and adults abruptly freeze, standing motionless side by side in the clear morning light, as though playing a game of musical chairs, and the music has just ended and there are no more chairs. For most of that previous night, they have been feeling their way across wooded hills and defunct tobacco farms in full darkness, pausing only when one of the children has had to pee, and now they stand in a narrow clearing shot through with luminous beams of sunlight. The morning sky, partially visible through the chimney of pines, is a crystal-clear cerulean blue for the first time in weeks, the dust motes and insects drifting through brilliant rays of light, giving the clearing an almost primeval cast.

Over the next few seconds, each person in the clearing almost unconsciously huddles closer together, the adults gently pressing in around the children, forming a human barrier. And over the course of those tense, surreal moments—during which time Ash still thinks they can play possum and silently wait out the passing of this unprecedented number of dead—the true nature of the horde reveals itself. Ash stares at it, mesmerized.

About fifty yards away, behind layers of thick woods, the leading edge of the herd comes toward them like an inebriated marching band, each walker intermittently rubbing against its neighbor, clawing at the air, groaning and drooling with feral hunger. They move with relentless slowness, dragging through the carpet of leaves and humus—scores of them, maybe hundreds—awkwardly yet steadily moving in a southerly direction. It's impossible to see the length and breadth of the full herd due to the trees, but the sense Ash has is that it's immense, vast, perhaps even a thousand strong.

"Ash!" The sound of Ronnie Nesbit's whisper tears her attention back to the group.

Most of them have crouched down now, their eyes as wide as silver dollars, their hot gazes shimmering with terror. Ronnie Nesbit has his arms around his two children as well as his wife, Dina, who trembles convulsively. The others huddle together mere inches away, the Quinn kids, the Stack family. Ash moves to them, puts her hand on Bobby Quinn's shoulder, softly shushing the group. The boy feels hot to the touch, feverish, sick with fear. Terror has etched itself on every face.

Ronnie whispers, "We have to turn back, there's too many of them."

"We can't turn back," Ash informs him, trying to keep her voice down, the hairs on her neck bristling at the terrible noise rising in her ears. It's that otherworldly chorus of rusty growling and moaning and shuffling feet drawing closer and closer. The air has begun to waft with greasy, black death-stench. Ash tries to ignore the chills rushing down her back. "We'll run into Dryden for sure."

"I'd rather run into a million Drydens than this parade of shit."

"We'll go around them."

"Around them?" Ronnie Nesbit chews the inside of his cheek as he considers this, gazing through the trees at the oncoming mob of reanimated dead. Ash quickly surveys the surrounding woods for a suitable route around the multitude of walkers. She eyeballs the distance between the clearing and the crest of a neighboring hill, and while she's doing this, she's too preoccupied to notice the profound exchange occurring behind her.

At first, the signals between John Stack and his wife Jennifer are all nonverbal. He looks at her, and he looks at his children, and then he gazes through the trees at the throng. Jennifer Stack glances over her shoulder and sees the herd expanding around them. Like an immense amoeba splitting and multiplying, absorbing every cell in its path, the sides of the herd have separated off in opposite directions, surrounding the clearing.

Now there are countless walking cadavers pressing in on either flank, close enough for Stacks to see their ruined faces, their frosted glass eyes, their wormy mouths working constantly, chewing ceaselessly, driven by insatiable electric hunger. The noise and smell rise to unbearable levels. John Stack takes one last look at his children, and then his face does something remarkable. It falls for a moment, a look of resignation crossing his features. Then his expression softens, and he touches his wife's cheek. He smiles warmly, a look of pure devotion. He softly says to her, "I love you. Always remember that, baby. You're my one and only."

Jennifer Stack stiffens, her eyes welling up with terror and tears. Behind her, the kids remain frozen with bug-eyed awe on their faces. Jennifer starts to shake. "John, don't. Whatever it is you're thinking. I'm begging you. Don't do it!"

By this point, Ash has noticed the exchange, and she slowly rises to her feet. She sees the look in John Stack's eyes, and she immediately recognizes the import of it. She knows that look. She knows it well. She's seen it on the faces of people who have come to terms with oblivion, people at the end of their tether. "John, what are you doing? We're going around—"

"*You're* going around them," John Stack corrects her, straightening up to his full height. He begins to back toward the edge of the clearing, smiling that beatific smile. He picks up a stick. He bangs it on a tree. "Go ahead. Go on. GO! GO NOW!"

Jennifer cries out, "John, don't do this . . . goddamn it . . . DON'T DO THIS!"

Kayla and Kourtney Stack have both begun to softly cry, almost in unison, each knowing exactly what's happening but not knowing why.

John Stack bangs on the tree and howls: "COME AND GET IT!! SOUP'S ON!! FRESH MEAT!!"

Now things start happening very quickly, so fast that it's hard for Ash to keep track of it all. Out of the corner of her eye, she sees the closest walkers reacting to the sound of the raised voices, the banging noises; a row of older males with mutilated faces and skin like rancid bread dough start staggering toward the noise. At the same time, the children have begun to whimper and struggle to run away, Dina Nesbit holding them tightly. Jennifer Stack is screaming, Ronnie Nesbit holding *her* now, keeping her from running into the fray. Some of the kids are sobbing into Dina Nesbit's blouse. Ash realizes they have mere seconds to make their move or they will all become fodder for the throngs.

"This way!" Ash calls out, and grabs the clammy little hand of Bobby Quinn, who is stunned silent, clutching his sister's hand.

Ash yanks the children across the southeast corner of the clearing, through a gap in the trees, and up a gentle incline of rocky earth.

The others follow—terrified and sheepish—trying not to look back at the man on the far side of the clearing who is, at this moment, distracting the horde, yelling profanities, lashing out at the dead with his knife, swinging the woefully insufficient weapon at all the gruesome faces and milky shark eyes descending upon him. Most of the humans fleeing the scene look away when the first set of rotten teeth embed themselves into the fleshy part of John Stack's neck.

In a fountain of blood, John collapses. He hits the ground hard, rolls, and tries to climb back to his feet. But the bite wound has opened his jugular. He falls to his belly and coughs and gasps for breath in a warm pool of his own blood spreading across the leaves. He tries to crawl away but the cold spreads through him and steals his strength. More of the creatures pounce on him and sink their teeth into his thighs, his torso, and the nape of his neck. He lets out a caterwaul that sounds more animal than human. The pain is so enormous that he wavers in and out of consciousness but somehow manages to keep his eyes open.

In his last moments of life, he sees the faint shadows of his family climbing the adjacent hill, hurrying after Ash, following her to safety. He smiles that serene, reverential smile one last time, and he thinks of saying one last thing to the walkers: "Fuck you . . . we won this one."

The caravan is halfway across a bridge above the swollen Chattahoochee River when the horses that are pulling Norma's modified tow truck get mired in ten inches of soupy mud. For a moment, Norma just stares in morbid awe from her perch on the truck's bench seat as the animals slip and slide in the muck. They toss their heads and snort in frustration for several moments, their shoes sliding backward on the slime.

Norma finally waves at the others, each of which has pulled to a stop midway across the bridge, Lilly sticking her head out of her pickup's open window and gazing back at the mess, assessing the problem. She says something on her two-way to Musolino.

"I got this!" Norma calls out, and motivates her weary bones to climb out of the cab. Her joints complain and creak as she steps off the truck's corrugated foot rail, hopping into the brackish standing water with a splash.

Norma Sutters comes from a family of rheumatics, and she has inherited a smorgasbord of late-life ailments. Her father, a Baptist minister from Jacksonville, had terrible gout and arthritis, and her mother's side featured osteoporosis and diabetes. Since she turned forty a few years back, Norma has enjoyed back pain, tendinitis, flat feet, bursitis, and major rheumatoid arthritis. For a while, regular ibuprofen and swigs of whiskey from her trusty flask kept her relatively pain free, but since the outbreak, meds are harder to come by, and any alcohol worth drinking has already been drunk.

Now she wades through the ankle-deep water, trying to ignore the twinges of pain as she approaches the threshold of the overpass. The biblical rains of recent days have flooded the Chattahoochee to the point of washing out most adjacent roads and bridges. This one is nearly impassable, the water coming right up to the span, seeping up through the seams in the timbers. The entry points on either side have been reduced to mushy sinkholes in which the tow truck's team of beefy, seal-brown draft horses now wallow noisily, slipping and fidgeting, unable to get any traction.

"Easy does it, big boy," Norma murmurs, her rubber boots sinking into six inches of muck as she waddles up to the larger animal. The horse whinnies nervously. Norma gently strokes and pats the animal's flank, clucking her tongue and trying to figure out how she's going to pull a thousand-pound beast free of the mire. "Don't you fret, Tiger. Gonna get you right out of this nasty shit hole."

A muscular specimen with a spotted coat and huge withers rising up at least five feet tall, the horse nickers nervously, tossing its head and bugging its eyes out as prominently as two enormous marbles. The other horse seems spooked as well, and Norma just figures it's the loss of traction in the mud patch that's got them so jittery. She doesn't yet realize the horses are spooked by the movement in the woods on the periphery of Valley Hill Road. She also doesn't hear Musolino's frantic voice calling her name.

"Okay, here's what we're going to do," she informs the animals as though they comprise a work crew and she's the foreperson. She sees a flat outcropping of stone to her immediate left running along the crest of the riverbank. It looks like a former sidewalk that has cracked into fragments and sunken slightly due to weather and age. If she can steer the animals onto that flagstone walkway, then they should be able to extract themselves as well as the truck from the quagmire.

"NORMA!"

Musolino's booming voice pierces the wind, and Norma glances over her shoulder at the Escalade, idling about twenty-five yards away. She can see the big man bursting out of his driver's-side door with his AR-15 bouncing on his shoulder, and she just figures he's coming to help her. The big Portuguese muscle man is a gentle giant on whom Norma has developed a secret crush. Late at night, alone in her bedroom suite, she sometimes fantasizes about him visiting her, wrapping those big, muscular arms around her. She has never told anybody this, and doesn't plan to. In fact, right now, she's a little embarrassed that he thinks she can't get these horses back on track herself.

"It's okay, I got it," she calls back to him with a dismissive wave. She turns back to the horses and grabs the big one's bridle. She clicks her tongue and says to the beast, "C'mon, big guy."

Norma doesn't see the walkers emerging from the ocean of darkness behind the adjacent trees. The sun has risen to a point at which the shadows beneath the thick pine boughs completely mask the moving corpses until they are right on top of the road, pushing their way out into open daylight. She doesn't see Musolino trip on a greasy patch of mud as he races hell-bent toward her, frantically trying to warn her and protect her from the oncoming swarm. She doesn't notice him sprawling to the flooded pavement, his gun flying out of his arms and splashing into the standing water. More importantly, Norma doesn't smell the rancid, meaty death-odors until she has pulled the two horses out of the mud pit and led them across the side of the road to the sunken walkway.

At that moment, she freezes only inches from the ledge running along the flooded river, still holding the horse team by the traces. Her senses immediately fill up with troubling details all piling up on each other—the sound of Bethany Dupree's scream, the horrible stench of dead flesh, Musolino hollering at her, telling her something about walkers coming, other voices, the cab doors on other horse-wagons shrieking open, other voices crying out. Shots are fired, the air crackling with bullets. All of it jumbles up into an amorphous blob of panic coursing down her midsection like a cold electric current.

For a moment, Norma stands thunderstruck, clutching the horses' lead, paralyzed with confusion. The animals are so large that they block Norma's view of the approaching horde. She can smell them, and she can hear them, and she can hear the gunfire whizzing back and forth. But she doesn't see anything but shadows closing in on the other side of the horses until it's too late.

The smaller horse lets out a keening shriek as the first set of putrid teeth sink into its hindquarters, the larger horse rearing up and kicking its forelegs wildly. The sudden jerking movement yanks the reins out of Norma's grasp. She sees the walkers now on the other side of the horses, and she realizes all at once why Bethany is screaming, and why Musolino was coming to save her when he slipped and fell, and why the horns are honking and the guns are blazing and the air is filling up with blue haze and rot.

None of this, though, prevents her from then making a fatal misstep.

She pivots toward Musolino, and she takes her first leaping stride toward him when she misjudges how close she is to the deeper water's edge. Her left foot, clad in the same lumberjack-style work boot that she has worn since the plague broke out, slips off the edge of the mossy, ruined stones of the sidewalk.

She plunges into the water, sliding down the slimy slope of the bank that was once dry land.

FIVE

"No, no, no—*shit*—no, no—*fuck*—NORMA!—fuck-fuck-fuck—FUCK!" Bound up in the indigo smoke, weaving through the grisly remains of fallen walkers, Lilly shuffles sideways along the water's edge. She has her .22 still gripped in both hands, madly searching the agitated currents and windblown eddies of the Chattahoochee River. She scans the distant waters for any sign of her friend. The heavyset woman has simply vanished. Only a few tangled pieces of wreckage and deadfall logs now drift quietly and quickly away, coursing downriver on the flood currents.

Like a streak of lightning zapping across her midbrain, a fleeting memory flickers through the back of Lilly's panicky thoughts.

Norma Sutters had always joked about being accident prone, uncoordinated, the first to step on a banana peel. According to her, she was traditionally the last girl picked for softball teams, and seemed to have a perpetual series of casts and splints on her arms and legs throughout high school. She was a disaster on the dance floor, and at graduation she could barely make it up the risers to the dais to receive her degree without doing a comic pratfall into the front row of mortified dignitaries. All of this streams through Lilly's brain, making her struggle with an overwhelming urge to dive into the flooded Chattahoochee and expend every last iota of her strength searching the muddy river for the former choir director who had become Lilly's foil, her voice of reason, her loyal opposition. She steps up to the threshold of the deeper water, coiling herself, preparing to jump in, when she jerks at a loud and sudden noise.

The air behind Lilly erupts with gunfire as Boone, Eve, Tommy, and Musolino wipe out the remaining members of the swarm that only moments ago had come out of the woods like a nest full of tarantulas. Musolino has already completed the tragic task of euthanizing the tow truck's team of horses, each round fired point-blank into an animal's elegant head, and now he's in no mood for heroics as he rushes up to Lilly and grabs her by the arm. "Hey, hey! C'mere, Lilly, c'mere!"

The big man pulls her aside, ushering her behind the Escalade for privacy.

Lilly wriggles out of his grasp. "I'm fine. I'm good, okay?"

"Tell me you weren't about to jump in."

"She's my friend. Okay? I had to do something to—"

"She's *everybody's* friend, Lilly, but you cannot do stupid shit like that."

"Mus, we can't lose another—"

"We can't lose *you*!" He jabs his finger at her. "Do you understand?"

"Yes." She stares at him, her emotions working their way up her gut, up her gorge. Her eyes burn. She stares at Musolino's dark, chiseled face, his whiskers just starting to prematurely gray. His T-shirt clings to his burly chest, damp with sweat and stress. Lilly's eyes well up. "I understand. Okay?"

"Look. Norma's gone. It sucks. It kills me. But we don't have the luxury to commemorate it. Or we're *all* gonna be gone. Do you understand what I'm saying?"

"Yes."

"We just have to deal with it and move on. Especially you, Lilly. You're the honcho. You're fucking Moses. You're leading the exodus."

"I get it." She sniffs back the emotions. "I'm just trying to—"

Lilly abruptly falls silent when a voice behind her interrupts.

"Lilly?" Tommy Dupree has come around the opposite end of

the Escalade and now stands there, nervously stroking the stock of his 12-gauge shotgun, compulsively licking his lips. "Is everything okay?"

Over the past few months, since the upheavals in Woodbury have plunged Tommy and his siblings into bedlam, the boy has developed a nervous habit of licking his lower lip. He does it so much now that his chin has chapped and turned bright red from the irritation. Every time Lilly notices this sore patch of skin under his lip, it breaks her heart.

"We're good, Tommy, everything's okay," she tells the boy and then realizes her eyes are welling up. "No it isn't." She lowers her head and the sorrow courses through her. Her tears drip to the sodden ground at her feet. "Everything's not okay."

Tommy comes over, and Musolino fidgets uncomfortably, looking down, looking anywhere but at Lilly. Lilly realizes he's never seen her cry. All he has seen is the badass warrior chick that Lilly has become. And the truth is, there *was* a time in her life when she would have been embarrassed by this pitiful display. Not anymore. She doesn't care *who* sees *what*.

Another volley of small-arms fire rings out, making Lilly and the others jump. The protein-rich stench of rotting flesh accompanies the gunfire and sends a jolt of adrenaline down Lilly's veins. She wipes her face. She looks up and says, "Let's get the fuck outta here."

For a single instant that seems to last for ten eternities, Norma Sutters careens through the cold, empty blackness, her body seized with chills, her sinuses and ears and mouth filling up with greasy fluid. She tries to hold her breath and kick, or maybe paddle against the current, but she can barely move. All she can do is drift, and drift. She has slipped off the spindle of her sanity. She has no idea which way is up or down. All she knows is that she's going to die. She is going to meet her maker. Finally. She's going to Glory and will touch the hem of His garment, praise Jesus! Hallelujah, she's going home! Glory, glory, glory be to Jesus . . . *but wait.*

Wait.

Lord, what is this? An object registers in her peripheral vision, at first as faint as watercolors swirling above her, glimpsed through layers of silt as her lungs heave and burn with their final dwindling storehouses of oxygen. Something floats above her in the void, at first too milky and diffuse to make out. At this depth, it looks solid, but it's hard to know for sure. The flow and distortion of the currents disguise it as simply a bruise of color in an otherwise colorless ocean of darkness. Lord, is it an angel? Is this the archangel Michael come to usher her to paradise?

She feels contradictory impulses tearing at her, the irresistible force of the currents tugging her now, yanking her around the serpentine bends of the river, lulling her into a death trance. The feeling is almost inexorable, like tow chains hooked to her, pulling her down, down . . . down to her watery grave. But at the same time, the rectangular object above her is shimmering there, maybe ten feet away, beckoning to her with its liquid brilliance. Through the muddy, rheumy medium of the river, she sees that the thing is a mossy shade of orange, bobbing on the surface, speckled with the muted, golden dollops of sunlight that now stipple the land above her. *Lord, if this is Thy will, then so it shall be*, she thinks as she begins to paddle with her last shreds of energy.

In a matter of moments she will pass out from oxygen starvation, and her lungs will fill up, and she will sink like a stone, dead by the time the currents decide to deposit her on the river bottom. But the Lord is with her now. He wants her to reach that solid rusty object hovering overhead. Galvanized by the spirit, she feels a bolt of energy flow through her, even as her lungs explode with agonizing, searing pain. She opens her mouth, gasping an involuntary gasp of air, and she inhales water. Her body convulses, the shock of the cold, greasy water almost sinking her. But without even being aware of it, her arms and legs have been paddling and flailing and kicking with every last scintilla of strength for the past sixty seconds.

The object looms closer, only inches away now, the grain of its planks revealing itself to be a wooden door or a piece of a houseboat's exterior floating along the floodwaters. Beams of daylight penetrate the upper layers of the flooded river in sharp angles. She reaches for the door with everything she has left.

Her hand slips off the corner. She sinks. Her silent scream accompanies a second attempt, issuing plumes of bubbles. Paddling, scissor-kicking, she manages to grab the corner of the object, and the thing dips and bobs with Norma's substantial weight, but it remains buoyant on the surface. Her last burst of energy enables her to pull herself headfirst out of the water and onto the wreckage.

She sucks in a gargantuan, heaving breath of air and roars vomit all over the surface of the floating door, expelling mostly filthy water mixed with bile. She coughs and coughs, and for a moment she feels as though she might actually cough herself off the raft and back into death's embrace. But somehow, amid all the heaving and rasping and shuddering, Norma manages to hold tight to the floating door, at first not even aware of how fast she's drifting along on the swollen Chattahoochee.

For decades, NASA astronauts have reported the strange phenomenon of walking in space at orbital speeds. Although they are traveling at around seventeen thousand miles per hour, the space walkers feel as though they're leaving the house for a lazy walk in the park. Since their spaceship is traveling at the same speed, they are relatively "standing still." Norma Sutters experiences this same surreal feeling right at this moment as she floats along the fast-moving currents of the flooded river. It feels as though she's barely moving. She doesn't even notice the landscape rushing past her on either side of the Chattahoochee, the trestle bridges passing overhead. Human remains float all around her, scraping the side of the door, occasionally bumping the front of the makeshift raft.

It takes a while for Norma to get her bearings. Like a soaked rat, she pulls herself toward the center of the door and collapses onto her belly, the wind and sun in her face. The air hangs heavy with fishy, rancid death-rot. The woods on either side of the river form dense ramparts of foliage and tangled overgrowth, all of which filter the sunlight and cast the river in an eerie green light. As Norma's mind begins to clear, she starts to notice other things as well. The door on which she now floats, thank you Jesus, has the word GALLEY embossed at one end of the burnished surface.

The river brims with bloated carnage—mostly undead, Norma reckons—much of which continually brushes up against the sides of the raft. At this location, the Chattahoochee is only about forty yards across, some areas so rife with bodies and body parts that it would appear a person could walk from one side to another without ever touching the water. Norma swallows the burning taste of bile in her throat as a rasping noise pierces her thoughts. It sounds like a beehive is floating by the raft.

When Norma glances over the edge of the door at the water's surface, she sees the source of the noise and vomits a second time.

A severed head floats past the raft, faceup, its eyes wide open like tiny lightbulbs, filmed with waxy white cataracts. Its mouth works busily around rotten teeth, emitting a buzzing sound like a filing metal. Its sharklike eyes scan the sky as though cosmic answers lurk up there somewhere.

The raft passes the gruesome head, and Norma watches it recede into the currents behind her until it fades out of sight like a tiny bobber abandoned by a fisherman. Norma cannot take her eyes off it. The notion begins to form inside her that this is the end of the end—the final chapter, the last gasp of humanity—and she is drifting through this timeless purgatory because she's a sinner. The Good Lord has deposited her here to bake in the sun on this pitiful raft until her flesh cracks away and her bones bleach to powder and she crumbles away into dust. She lowers her head to the slimy surface of the door, her tears mingling with the metallic water of the river.

Over the course of the next hour, Norma drifts southward several miles, too weak to paddle to shore, too exhausted to care. She was never very good at geography in school, and now she wonders if the great Chattahoochee River ultimately empties into the Gulf of Mexico, or maybe the Land of Oz. It doesn't matter. She has no drinking water, no food, no weapons, no hope. She will be dead by the following morning.

It's almost comforting to know that one's time is drawing to a close. The best part is that Norma's conscience is clear. God knows she's not perfect. She has sinned as much as the next person, but she has no regrets. She doesn't fear death. She knows that the Good Lord will do with her what is righteous and just. She has unshakable faith in His mysterious ways. Thinking about this, she coughs up blood, her head so heavy she can barely lift it off the raft.

She lies on her side and prays that He will take her into His arms soon.

The river widens, the vegetation becoming increasingly wild and untamed. It's as though the woods have gone insane, the skeletal roots of massive live oaks reaching out from the flooded riverbanks, plunging into the water like petrified serpents. Chandeliers of Spanish moss hang down so low they brush the floodwaters, and the chaotic growth of kudzu has sent snarled, knotted vines across every surface, every trunk of every tree, every stone and deadfall log, creating a sort of endless verdant tapestry. The water crawls with pathetic scraps and partial human remains still twitching with the cursed energy of the plague. Hands still attached to severed arms float past Norma clenching and unclenching furiously as though their bloated, pasty fingers might grasp the ungraspable. Disembodied human feet bounce along the surface, baring a grisly resemblance to fishing bobbers.

The farther south she drifts, the more she notices that the buoyant heads seem to be floating *upright*, staring straight ahead, almost as though they're craning birdlike out of the water. Chills suddenly spider down Norma's back when she realizes that the heads are connected to *bodies*. They are not severed and miraculously floating upright; they are whole, intact walkers dragging along the river bottom. It makes sense, too, since Norma remembers from childhood fishing trips that the depth of the Chattahoochee gets notoriously shallow around these parts. This gets Norma up and motivated.

She fishes a floating branch out of the water, breaks it in half, and makes a weapon.

A moment later, one of the submerged walkers gets close enough to Norma's raft for the thing to register her presence. It starts reaching for her, its blackened nails clawing the edges of the raft. It's a larger specimen that's been in the water so long its gender has been erased by bloat and decay, now taking on the ghastly appearance of a gigantic baby with razor sharp teeth, currently biting the air with the fury of a snapping turtle.

Norma drives the sharp end of the branch into the thing's eye with such force, the stick penetrates the gelatinous material of the eye and the prefrontal lobe behind it with the gruesome sound of a kitchen knife plunging into a head of lettuce. She pulls the stick free, causing a gush of dark cerebral fluids to pour out of the breached eye socket and darken the water around the figure as it abruptly sinks out of sight.

Despite her humility in the face of death, and her love and devotion to the Lord, and her deep faith in an afterlife, and her respect for all living and nonliving things, she spits at the spot on the water where the bubbles still froth.

Ashley Lynn Duart and her flock of children and parents have trekked less than a mile into Coweta County when the walking dead attack from all sides, the megaswarm infiltrating the deepest part of the woods in a blur of ragged, dead figures stumbling out of the primordial shadows. Pandemonium erupts. Little girls squeal with terror while adults grunt with effort as they lash out at the monsters.

The sound of a keening howl rings out behind Ash, and she spins and sees Ronnie Nesbit sandwiched between two large male walkers. They tear into his neck with the fervor of pigs rooting and digging a truffle from the stubborn ground. Blood already has started to fountain from poor Ronnie, his wife Dina horror-struck twenty feet away, fighting off two females with a two-by-four. She drops the board and shrieks.

Ash grabs the closest child—Chelsea Quinn—and calls out to the others. "DON'T, LOOK!—Bobby! Kourtney! Everybody—don't look! Follow me! This way—Jennifer, you too! C'mon, if you want to live, come this way! AND DON'T LOOK BACK!"

With one last glance over her shoulder, Ash sees both Ronnie and Dina Nesbit being mauled by the dead. Ronnie has already lost consciousness, and now lies twitching in his death throes as monsters devour what's left of him in an orgy of glistening entrails and hemorrhaging blood. Dina struggles on the ground next to him, holding off one walker while a half dozen others come at her from all sides. Her final gasp of a scream is the last thing Ash hears before turning away and leading the surviving children as well as a catatonic Jennifer Stack away from the horrors of the forest toward the clearing and the vast, flat soybean fields beyond it . . . unaware she's leading them to their doom.

SIX

Lilly snaps the reins and leads her horse team down a winding farm road toward the Coweta County line. She can hear the pounding of the other horse-wagons behind her and can feel the thumping impact of the hooves making the very ground around her tremble. Each wagon is now overloaded with additional cargo taken from Norma's abandoned tow truck.

The floodwaters have receded in this area to the point of leaving the dirt access roads relatively dry and clear, nothing but a few puddles here and there, some minor washouts in the lower areas. Meriwether County, home of Lilly's beloved Woodbury, lies only twenty-some miles away. With a little luck, they'll make it in a couple hours.

Lilly feels the cauldron of emotions burning in her belly, the loss of her friend still pressing down on her, but the ever-looming proximity of her town and her imminent homecoming making her pulse quicken.

In the distance, she can see the heart of Coweta County spanning the horizon, thousands and thousands of acres of tangled soybeans and weeds and rain-softened earth broken only by the occasional split-rail fence or crumbling access road. From this vantage point, it looks like a green Mojave Desert of overgrown farm fields. A sun-baked asphalt two-lane runs down its center like a petrified spinal column. The road appears to be virtually free of wreckage, and only a few scattered walkers dot the pavement or mill about the adjacent gullies and ditches.

"Almost home," Lilly mutters, her voice drowned by the drumming of the hooves as she whips the reins and steers the contraption toward that main artery of asphalt.

Tommy sits beside her, gazing out at the immense flatlands. He nervously fingers the stock of his shotgun, scanning the horizon. "Wait!" The boy points at the horizon, about half a mile away, the landscape wavering and swimming in the heat rays of the late-afternoon sun. "What the hell is that?"

"Where?" Lilly squints to see through the glare of the sun. "What are you looking at?"

"People!"

"Living people?"

"Yeah, look—straight ahead—between those two fences. See 'em?"

Lilly finally spots the cluster of human souls so far away they look like specks floating through the sun. But the more she scrutinizes those specks, the more she recognizes the fact that Tommy Dupree is correct. The specks are adults and children, running in a single-file line across the scabrous field. "I see them," Lilly finally says. "Looks like a large family maybe, with kids."

The modified pickup rattles faster and faster down the slope as Lilly urges the team on, snapping the reins, clucking her tongue, and steering the contraption toward the fleeing adults and children. Soon, Lilly has gotten close enough to see that there are two women running alongside a gaggle of children. As a whole, the group runs with a haphazard, handicapped quality, as though some of them are traumatized or injured.

"You're not going to believe this," Lilly announces to Tommy. "But the woman leading the group actually looks familiar."

"The short one?"

Lilly stares at the adults. "No, the tall one, the one with the dark hair."

"Is that—?" Now Tommy seems transfixed by the taller female who seems to be leading the bunch.

"No, it couldn't be." Lilly hastens the horses across a wide inter-section, and then down the central two-lane blacktop cutting through the fields. They raise twin spumes of water as they careen through run-off puddles, closing in on the fleeing group of survivors. "It couldn't be. Tommy, tell me I'm crazy but that looks like—"

The walkie-talkie crackles, interrupting her words. Musolino's voice pierces the static. "Lilly, what's going on? Why are we trying to set a fucking land-speed record all of a sudden?"

Lilly grabs the toy device and thumbs the button. "You're not going to believe this, Mus, but I think—"

"Oh my God!" Tommy now recognizes the tall, slender, swim-mer's physique of the woman leading the group across the field. "You're right! I see her!"

Lilly shoots a glance at Tommy. "I'm not crazy, it's her, isn't it?"

They've drawn to within fifty yards of the fleeing humans. They can see their old friend from Haralson leading a group of seven children and one adult female across the leprous, soggy ground.

"Pull alongside them!" Tommy leans out his side window and yells at the top of his lungs. "ASH!"

The woman leading the group doesn't react at first, perhaps leery of mysterious convoys thundering up to her in broad daylight. She just keeps running, shouting something at her brood of children, her expression—even from a distance of thirty yards—knitted with ter-ror. Lilly nudges the horses to come as close to the cluster of children as possible without endangering any of them.

"ASH!" Lilly calls out this time, pulling parallel to the tall woman.

At this close proximity, maybe fifteen feet away, it becomes clear that the woman is spooked beyond anything Lilly has ever seen on the face of a fellow human being. This is no longer the Ashley Duart of the three-martini veranda and quiet nights on the cape in her hus-band's schooner. The tall woman now appears to be soaked from head to toe, either from the rains of the previous night or sweat or both, her lean arms tracked with wounds where trees and thorns have clawed her flesh. Her hair stands up as though from electrocu-tion, and dark circles rim her eyes. She glances up at the sound of

Lilly's voice as though poked with a stick, flinching, nearly stumbling, her stride thrown off by the shock of a familiar voice calling out.

Lilly yanks back on the reins, and the horses scuttle to a sudden and violent stop in a spray of filthy water.

Behind her, the closest horse-wagon—Burt Stankowski's chopped-down panel van—nearly tips over when its team is wrenched to an abrupt stop in order to avoid slamming into the back of Lilly's pickup. The other contraptions thunder to a stop behind Burt in a chain of snorting, frothing horses and hydroplaning tires.

Meanwhile, Ash has staggered to a stop herself, nearly passing out from hyperventilating so rapidly. The kids and Jennifer Stack gather around her, a motley-looking group in their tattered, soiled clothes and wind-burned faces. Some of them are spattered with layers of blood, while others are gasping for breath and looking as though they're about to go into cardiac arrest.

"Oh my God, Ash!" Lilly climbs out of the pickup's front seat, hops to the wet earth, and then lurches across the bean field toward her friend. "Ash!"

Ash is bent over, trying to catch her breath, hands on her knees, murmuring, "Thank God . . . thank God." She looks up, a weary, pained, cockeyed grin on her face. "Where did you come from?"

The two women hug each other, a desperate, sweaty embrace, all their collective fear and rage and grief leeching tears from their eyes.

For a moment, neither says a word to the other, they just hold each other in that sunbaked patch of soybeans as the others gather around them. Some of the younger children are crying, clinging to their older siblings. The teenage Stack girls stand on either side of their mother, each holding one of Jennifer Stack's hands. Bobby Quinn tries to be grown-up but can't hold off his own tears, a sister on either side of him, clutching the boy's shirt.

Lilly's people approach and keep a respectable distance, occasionally glancing over their shoulders, keeping tabs on the outer edges of the swarm, making sure no stragglers lumber too close. Burt Stankowski pivots in a 360, scanning the trees with his 9-millimeter pistol out, muzzle down, at his side, ready for anything. The four children from the van huddle behind Burt, the Slocum twins each sucking a thumb, the Coogans trying to be cool but revealing the jittery tension in their eyes.

Ash looks into Lilly's eyes and grins that trademark crooked grin of hers and mutters, "I thought I'd never see you again."

Lilly inspects Ash's wounds, looks at the others. "What the hell happened to you? Where's Quinn?"

Ash lets out a miserable, exhausted sigh. "Long story, I don't even know where to start."

Behind Lilly, Eve Betts comes up and stands next to Burt, her cut-down 12-gauge cradled in her arms, her eyes scanning the deserted fields to the north and the adjacent road to the south for any sign of the dead. Boone circles around behind Eve, taking off his goggles, looking flummoxed by the whole tearful reunion.

"Are you okay?" Lilly asks Ash.

"I'm hanging in there."

"What happened?"

"We got snatched by a crazy fuck, Lilly, kidnapped, me and Quinn's kids."

Lilly feels a fist clenching her guts. The wind blows the smell of walkers across the fields, the acrid stench making her eyes water. Across the clearing, the horses fidget and nicker. Lilly looks off at the distant clouds above the Chattahoochee. "Not again . . . Jesus. What is happening to us?" Lilly doesn't elaborate. By "us" she means humankind. The human race. People in general.

"It wasn't what you think. We got put on ice."

"Ice?"

"Like a prison, Lilly. It was insane. This maniac thought he was . . . keeping us safe. These poor kids, they've been through hell."

Lilly shakes her head, letting out a sigh, trying to wrap her mind around this concept. The sound of Musolino's Escalade roaring up pierces her thoughts.

The vehicle comes to skidding halt on the shoulder of the two-lane, the driver's door creaking open. The big man climbs out, grabbing his M16 rifle from beneath the front seat. In the low after-noon sun, he looks like an olive-skinned monolith, muscles bulging under his dago T, his sculpted Portuguese face and dark eyes alert and vigilant as he marches over to the two women, the rifle on his shoulder. "What's going on?" He furrows his brow. "Not crazy about stopping here, middle of nowhere, being this exposed. Tried to reach you on that piece o' shit two-way." He stops himself, notic-ing all the kids. "Oh. Sorry. Pardon my language."

"Johnny Musolino," Lilly says, making a grand gesture toward the larger-than-life man in the sleeveless T, "meet Ashley Duart."

Ash smiles at the man and shakes his hand. "Otherwise known as Ash."

Musolino gives her a polite nod and smile. "My pleasure, Ash."

Lilly turns and indicates the others, introducing them one at a time. "This is Tommy, Boone, Eve, Burt . . . and those little ones are Tyler, Jenny, Tiff, and Mercy. And those little munchkins in the back of the pickup pretending you can't see them right now. That's Beth-any and Lucas." Lilly turns to Ash's group. "Looks like we got enough kids for a baseball team with all of yours."

Ash turns and starts introducing all of her people when a strange sound interrupts, a muffled snapping noise, like a mousetrap springing underwater.

Lilly executes a quick pivot to her right—whirling toward the sound—just as a spattering of blood hits the side of her face. Muso-lino jerks forward as though shoved by an invisible hand, an exit wound blossoming almost magically just below his Adam's apple, sending a puff of blood mist and bone fragments out the front of his neck like a champagne cork popping.

This is followed by the echoing boom of a high-powered rifle, the sound emanating from the hills several hundred yards to the north.

PART 2

Welcome to the Terrordome

Now go and strike Amalek and devote to destruction
all that they have. Do not spare them, but kill both man
and woman, child and infant.

—Samuel 15:3

SEVEN

Sidearms such as .38-caliber revolvers, .22-caliber pistols, and 9-millimeter semiautos have muzzle velocities well below the speed of sound. But large-caliber sniper rifles—such as the one fired at Lilly Caul's group from the trees above Calister Hill on the northern edge of Coweta County—send their fully jacketed rounds spiraling through the air at speeds almost twice the rate of sound waves. All of which is why the bullet seemed to reach its target—the huge one in the sleeveless wifebeater—well before the thunderous blast of the M1 carbine even reached the ears of those standing around him.

The shooter keeps his eye—the only part of his face not heavily bandaged—pressed against the scope for several minutes after hitting the target, the air around him surprisingly still as he watches the silent chaos unfold in the bean field four hundred yards away. All that can be heard around the shooter now are the buzz of gnats and the sound of his own thick, mucusy breathing through the nose holes of his bandages.

Through the scope, he can see all of the adults almost involuntarily diving to the ground, crawling for cover. Then a few of them, mostly the women, realize the children are just standing there like silhouettes in a shooting gallery—sobbing, sucking their thumbs, gaping in terror. The ladies spring into action, climbing to their feet and lunging toward the kids. Heroically, they shield the young bodies with their own as they shove everybody back toward the cover of their modified horse-wagons.

All of this takes about sixty seconds to transpire, although the sniper is fairly certain that the span of that time probably seems much longer to those scrambling for cover down in the soybeans. In the crosshairs of the scope, the shooter can see the miniature people clamoring back on board their makeshift horse-wagons and modified vehicles, frantically securing their younger passengers in the rear compartments and cargo bays for safekeeping. Some of the adults attempt to return fire, the small florettes of light from their guns visible for one split second before their bullets zing impotently through the trees a mile away, the resulting reports echoing across the sky.

One of the women—a tough little thing in an auburn ponytail and ripped jeans—drags the victim's body back to the rear of her cut-down pickup, enlisting the aid of her teenage accomplice. The victim twitches, clinging to life, as he is lifted by the twosome into the payload area. The gate is slammed, and then the woman and kid hurry back around to the front of the cab, staying low, hyperaware of the threat from the hills now. The restless horses toss their heads as the woman flops down on the bench and snaps the reins, the modified pickup lurching into sudden movement.

The sniper then pans the scope's field of view over to the tall amazon nicknamed Ash, who is just now throwing open the door of the Escalade, piling her kids in the back, and lunging behind the wheel. Hatred burns in the shooter's guts for this horrible ingrate, this arrogant snob. Resentment and disgust and even a small amount of pity stir in him for this misguided, narcissistic soul. Full name, Ashley Lynn Duart: the sound of it reverberates in his brain like the echo of a scream, like a nail scraping across Sheetrock. He hates her and pities her in equal measures. He will teach her a lesson if it's the last thing he does.

Spencer-Lee Dryden exhales and lowers the scope from his eye, backing away from his shooting position. He kneels, bracing himself against the mossy boulder to his left and letting out a sigh. The faint pounding of his burns and facial injuries thrum in his nerve endings like distant, muffled summer thunder. He has anesthetized himself with enough drugs and antibiotics to soothe a hippopotamus, but his rage prickles in his nervous system, touching off fireworks of agony in his skull. He hadn't planned on his escapees being rescued like this. For the love of God, all he had wanted to do was hunt down the woman who assaulted him, kill her, and take back the children. He hadn't anticipated interference by a third party, but so be it.

He glances over his shoulder, peering through the branches of spruce trees. Fifty yards away, his convoy of six medium-duty trucks of different makes and models—some of them scorched and smoke damaged—sit idling, revving their engines, awaiting further orders in the humid air of a Georgia afternoon.

A little farther down the hill, parked along the shoulder of a crumbling blacktop access road, the modified mobile homes sit in the shade of ancient pines. Some of them are so badly fire damaged, they're missing entire sections of their bulwark, the soot-stained interiors visible through gaping holes. Others merely exhibit streaks of smoke stains rising off the windows and the lintels and the tops of doors. Each trailer has been secured to the one in front of it with a makeshift coupler in the style of a small train, the entire chain pulled by a massive Kenworth cab-over with an enormous power plant, which also now idles in a low, basso profundo rumble, every few seconds belching a puff of black smoke out of its stack. Sally Dryden sits behind the wheel of the Kenworth, garbed in her work shirt—a prototype from the Dickies catalogue, YOUR NAME HERE on one breast pocket, YOUR BUSINESS NAME HERE on the other—a fashionable scarf tied around her graying hair. Her face is a map of rage, as though a mask has been removed, revealing the true personality underneath.

Spencer-Lee takes all this in as he rises to his full six-foot-plus height, shaded by the tall trees lining the scenic turnoff. A lifelong hunter, he was taught to shoot by his daddy while hunting pheasant in the hills north of Talladega National Forest. Now he slings the rifle over his shoulder and carefully descends the sloping road, his line of vision dramatically cut down by the thick, Betadine-stained bandage covering 90 percent of his head. The burns he sustained from Ashley Duart's attack now throb constantly, a low simmer of agony, which in a strange way, he appreciates. It keeps him sharp, alert, focused. It's a tricky business being a patriarch. One can't allow anger issues to cloud one's judgment. One must not let one's fury pour out, as it used to do in Spencer-Lee's drinking days. One has to be fair but at the same time ruthless in one's acts of discipline. Adults sometimes have to be taught a lesson in the same manner as children.

"Foxes are on the run, boys!" he bellows to his crew as he approaches the circle of trucks. He climbs into the cab of a gray Ford F250 crew cab connected to an armored Airstream Flying Cloud trailer, giving the man behind the wheel a nod. Spencer-Lee gazes at the gleaming trailer in the side mirror. Pocked with rust spots, much of it ravaged by fire damage, the retro-futuristic camper has become Spencer-Lee's sanctum, and now, it shall be his command post in this dangerous but necessary mission.

In a thunderhead of exhaust and noise, the caravan of scorched vehicles booms out of that scenic area and starts down the winding road that leads into the vast, fecund flatlands of Coweta County.

Five miles to the east, just outside the ghost town once known as Newnan, Georgia, lay the ruins of a massive cloverleaf connecting Highway 85 with rural routes 34 and 127. Much of the overpass has caved in on itself, the upper tiers now lying in great fragments of mossy, crumbling cement across the intersection below. What remains is a single fragment of the overpass, broken off midspan, sticking out over the ruins of the cloverleaf like a balcony, terminating in tentacles of rusty, exposed rebar.

Right now, three heavily armed men stand at the edge of this outcropping, noticing something strange in the hazy distance.

"What do you make of *this*?" one of the men inquires somewhat rhetorically, peering through his binoculars at a distant row of vehicles—too far away to identify—picking up speed as they move across the horizon. The youngest of the three onlookers, his long, raven-black hair gathered into a ponytail, a bandolier of bullets across the breast of his denim shirt, the young man tightens his grip on the binocs. "You don't think this has something to do with . . . ?"

The question is posed with world-weary fatigue creasing the young face of the dark-haired, dark-eyed man. Lean to the point of emaciation, sunburned and weathered by endless days of combing the entire southern half of the state, Jamie Quinn has been searching for his woman and his children for so long now he almost can't bring himself to speak the names aloud. He lowers the binoculars.

"Ash and the kids?" The man standing to his immediate right completes the sentence. A fifty-something former landscaper from Arkansas, Frank Steuben is built like a German sedan—all round and sturdy and practical—with a huge belly jutting over his jeans and arms as thick as tree trunks from lifting fifty-pound bags of peat moss all his life. "I don't know." He wipes his thick, leathery neck with a handkerchief. "We're running on fumes already, and that's a long way away."

"It does seem weird, though," the third man comments. "Folks burning that much fuel, traveling that fast." A skinny, wiry little man with a .45 pistol holstered on each hip, Caleb Washburn is a former life insurance agent from Louisville and has the jittery-eyed look of a ferret. "Something's going down out there, that's for sure."

Quinn raises the binoculars to his eyes again. He watches the far-away drama unfolding, the distant players in the silent race—both horse-drawn and motorized—moving faster and faster in a southerly direction, kicking up larger and larger clouds of dust, water, and debris. It's hard to tell from this far-flung vantage point, but Quinn starts to see little indicators that suggest it's not necessarily a *race* as much as a *chase*. He can see two distinct clusters of conveyances—the one in the lead mostly horse-drawn, the one pursuing them mostly motorized—and even from this great distance it's obvious the vehicles with engines are gaining on the ones pulled by animals.

Again, Quinn lowers the binoculars and looks at the man on his right. "How far away is that little fracas, do you think?"

Frank Steuben lets out a long, weary sigh and purses his lips. "I don't know . . . maybe a mile and a half, two miles at the most."

Caleb says, "Quinn, you want to go check it out, just give us the word."

Quinn shrugs. "We've come all this way, seems crazy not to."

Frank Steuben shakes his head skeptically. "Hate to be devil's advocate here, but we have no clue what kind of wasps' nest we'd be stumbling into out there."

Caleb starts to object. "Frank—"

"Plus, I ain't even sure we got enough gas to get back to Haralson," Steuben adds. "Let alone go off on some cockamamie wild-goose chase."

"Frank, c'mon." Caleb's voice is hoarse, scalded by stress and exhaustion. "These are Quinn's kids we're talking about here."

"I'm aware of that fact, Caleb. I'm just saying, we ain't gonna do anybody any favors by—"

He stops abruptly when the distant clap of a high-powered rifle pierces the afternoon stillness, making all three men start, Quinn jerking nervously. They look at each other. The sonic boom of the distant gunfire seems to take forever to fade into the wind.

Quinn turns and hurriedly starts to climb down the service ladder embedded in the stone overpass.

For one brief instant, the other two men remain at the crest of that ruined cloverleaf, looking at each other, momentarily dumbstruck.

Finally, giving Frank a sidelong glance, Caleb turns to leave. "Looks like you're overruled, brother."

Another volley of gunfire crackles through the air, one of the high-powered rounds blowing a three-inch hole in the pickup's side mirror as the modified horse carriage careens toward a distant forest preserve.

The impact makes Lilly twitch at the reins. She blinks as though waking up. Up until this moment, she has been lost in a daze of panic, confusion, and grief—reeling from the horrors of Musolino's shooting. It happened so quickly—the man she has secretly been admiring from afar, thinking about late at night, fantasizing about romantic scenarios that she knows will never come to fruition—now ravaged without warning by the impact of a large-caliber slug slamming through his neck.

Since the early days of the plague's outbreak, Lilly Caul has seen too many loved ones go down in similarly tragic, nightmarish circumstances. She has seen her father, Everett, devoured by the dead as he tried to squeeze his way on board a bus. She has witnessed her lover and protector, Josh Hamilton, shot in the back of the head by one of the Governor's psychotic disciples. She has seen her best friend, Megan, hanging from the end of a rope, a suicide committed in the wake of the Governor's evil. She has watched in mortified terror as her boyfriend Austin was sacrificed to the horde outside a prison. And she has shared Bob Stookey's final moments on earth, cradling the old medic in her arms, close enough to hear the whisper of his death rattle. Each one of these deaths took another chunk of her soul—to the point at which she was starting to wonder if she had any soul left. But today, in the aftermath of Musolino's fall, she experienced a strange and sudden disconnect. Her mind has gone inward, snapping, plunging into a catatonic state of shock—a disassociation as palpable as a television losing its signal.

The horses gallop full tilt a few feet in front of her, their saliva frothing into the wind, spraying back in Lilly's face, their hooves kicking up clods of wet earth. The modified pickup bounces and slams over the corrugated terrain.

In the broken side mirror, now punctured by the 7.62mm armor-piercing round, she can see a blurry reflection of the armada bearing down on her. In that narrow slice of cracked mirror, the assailants look almost like a futuristic band of pirates with their makeshift gun turrets like crows' nests on the rooftops of their trucks, and the ramshackle chain of trailers like Spanish galleons bringing up the rear to plunder and pillage.

There was a day when Lilly Caul would have wondered why in God's name such a motley assortment of people would be expending this much energy, blood, and treasure. Why go to such lengths to kill Ash, take her children back, and destroy any person, place, or thing that gets in their way? There was a time when Lilly would have tried to communicate with these people, negotiate with them, and work something out that would benefit all. But the days of communicating, negotiating, and talking through problems in order to avoid bloodshed are long gone.

"I can't stop the bleeding!" Tommy Dupree's voice comes from the burrow of crates and boxes in the cargo bay. Lilly glances over her shoulder.

Through a small doorway cut into the rear of the cab—no bigger than a hatch one might find on a submarine—Lilly can see the chaos unfolding in the open cargo area, illuminated ironically by the warm, serene, sharply angled rays of late-afternoon sunlight. Musolino lies supine on the hard iron floor, convulsing, as Tommy Dupree huddles over him in a crouch, holding a towel on the wound. Blood flows around Tommy's cloth in rivulets, the cargo bay floor already swimming in the big man's blood.

The two younger children—profoundly callous and hardened by witnessing many similarly grisly sights over the last four years—sit off to the side and watch sullenly, the wind tossing their cherubic hair. Lucas compulsively sucks his thumb, a pathological habit even for a seven-year-old. Bethany plays nervously with a strand of her hair, staring at the gruesome proceedings with the casual ennui of a child waiting in the cafeteria line.

"Keep the pressure on it!" Lilly's voice sounds distant and warbly in her own ears, as if underwater. "Press down really hard!"

"I'm pressing as hard as I can, the blood's still gushing out!"

"Just keep pressing down!"

Lilly hears another salvo of gunfire from the .50-caliber machine guns coming up swiftly on her left flank—an unmistakable noise which sounds like chains rattling, the links snapping apart—which draws Lilly's attention to the fractured side mirror.

In the spiderwebbed reflection, she sees Burt Stankowski in his chopped-down panel van about five car lengths back, weaving wildly while the .50-cal bullets strafe the ground by his tires. Burt makes feeble attempts to return fire by squeezing off random rounds with his 9 millimeter out his side window as the marauders close the distance and increase the rate and frequency of their fire. Lilly makes a frantic mental note—a checklist—ticking off which vehicle is carrying which children. The Quinn kids and the Nesbits are in the Escalade with Ash. Kayla, Kourtney, and Jennifer Stack are with Burt. The Coogan kids and the Slocum twins are riding on the enormous flatcar with Eve and Boone.

Lilly swallows her fear. She focuses on the team of horses. She snaps the reins, stirring them up as fast as they can run, and she sinks into the seat.

The stocky fireplug of a man sits at the wheel of the tricked-out Chevy Kodiak truck, 250 horses of turbo engine roaring beneath him, guzzling biodiesel as the rig thunders across the scabrous fields, closing the distance on the fleeing mongrels in their cut-down horse buggies to about a quarter mile. The Kodiak's second passenger is only partially visible overhead, through the makeshift sunroof, manning the Browning.

The driver, his right arm bandaged from third-degree burns stretching almost from his wrist to his shoulder, sniffs at another twinge of deep pain itching under his dressings. He wants so badly to wreak havoc upon the skinny bitch who started the fires. But he will wait for the signal from the Big Guy. That's what the driver does best. He does what he's told.

Formerly a janitor in the Georgia state capitol building, his bald, scabby pate like a missile sitting on the launchpad of his thick neck, Barret Deems had learned to listen closely to the great Spencer-Lee Dryden. When Mother Nature went insane, and the plague broke out, it was only natural that Deems would become Spencer-Lee's right-hand man, part bodyguard, part all-purpose muscle.

Now he can see the four modified vehicles in the middle distance—maybe five hundred yards away, three of them easy pickings with their broken-down horse teams—and he can taste the revenge on his tongue like a bittersweet liqueur. He wants so badly to see that skinny chick Ash burn to *real* ashes, afterward maybe feed her scorched bones to the walkers. Every twinge of pain, every phantom flame that still licks up Deems's arm feeds his hunger for revenge.

He sniffs back the agony and tightens his grip on the steering wheel, altering his course slightly toward the Escalade that is now bringing up the rear of the mongrel caravan. A few torrents of .50-cal rain will fix that bitch once and for all.

Without warning, the two-way clipped to the dash crackles with a voice. "Barret, what are you doing? I told you she's mine."

Deems grabs the walkie, thumbs the switch, and says, "Sorry, Spence, I thought—"

"Don't think!" The voice cuts through the static with brittle anger. "Just do what I say."

"Of course," Deems says into the mic. "What do you want us to do?"

Through the speaker, Spencer-Lee Dryden explains the attack formation, the importance of sparing the lives of the children, and the absolute necessity of doing all this quickly and decisively. Deems listens closely, then signs off and swerves to the east.

Lilly urges the team to the west, swerving past an obstruction looming directly ahead of her—a pile of deadfall logs—when she sees something terrible unfolding in the side mirror's reflection. She's about to deal with it when a voice pierces her chaotic thoughts.

"Lilly!" Tommy calls from the rear. "Lilly, I—I think he's—!"

"We got a situation up here, Tommy!" Lilly's mind swims with panic, overloading with information streaming in from all quarters. "Just keep pressure on it!"

In the mirror, she can see enemy trucks closing in on both sides, roaring in diagonal vectors toward her pitifully slow horse-drawn contraption. She bullwhips the reins but the horses are already running at a high gallop, and Lilly's not too sure how long they can keep *that* up. She wants to give Tommy the reins and go to Musolino's side, try and save the man, do anything she can for him. But she also sees the troubling development in her side mirror.

She yells at Tommy: "Just keep pressing down on the wound!"

In the cracked reflection to her immediate left, Lilly can see the Escalade about a hundred and fifty yards back, several car lengths behind Eve and Boone's enormous horse-drawn flatcar. Something silvery looms behind Ash and the SUV like a lunatic valkyrie, the blinding sun shining off its dull finish. Lilly has no idea who's in that retro-futuristic camper, but whoever it is, they're on a collision course with the Escalade, fifty yards behind it and closing. Forty . . . thirty . . . twenty . . . until Lilly is certain the camper's front cab is about to ram into the SUV's rear end.

Then Lilly remembers the chintzy walkie-talkie. She grabs it off the unoccupied seat next to her and thumbs the Talk button. "Ash! It's Lilly! Pick up that piece o' shit walkie-talkie! Pick it up now! Can you hear me?! Ash! Pick that fucking walkie-talkie up and talk to me! ASH!? ASH, CAN YOU—?"

Through crackling static: "Lilly? What is it? What's going on?"

Lilly thumbs the button, gaping at the side mirror and the Airstream rig hurling toward the Escalade. "MAKE A SHARP LEFT! RIGHT NOW!—A SHARP LEFT!!"

In the reflection, the Escalade swerves just in time, the Airstream's cab plunging toward it, missing its rear hatch by inches. The barrel of an assault rifle protrudes suddenly from the Airstream's front crew cab. Silver magnesium fire spits from the muzzle, accompanying a salvo of high-caliber rounds, which puncture a string of holes in the Escalade's left rear quarter panel.

"You still there, Ash? You still with me?" Lilly hollers into the walkie-talkie. "Bastards got your tank, I can see the fuel leaking!"

Through the static: "Fuck—FUCK! They just missed one of the kids by inches!"

"Listen to me, Ash. Put the hammer down. Go as fast as you can, try to make it to my wagon!"

Static. "Okay . . . will do. Got the pedal floored. On our way."

"Lilly!" From the cargo bed of the pickup comes Tommy's frenzied voice. "I can't stop the—!"

"What is it? What's wrong?" She throws a quick glance over her shoulder, and sees the boy huddled over the twitching, jerking body of John Musolino. "Tommy, what's going on? Are you keeping pressure on the wound?"

"I can't stop the bleeding!"

Lilly can only take her eyes off the horses for a few moments at a time. Otherwise, they could easily slam into one of the split-rail fences that occasionally loom in their path. Adding to the difficulty is the fact that the rearview mirror was removed in the process of cutting the front end off the truck's body, so there's no way to see into the back other than looking over one's shoulder. Which she does right now.

What she sees sends chills down her spine. Beneath Tommy, Musolino lies faceup on the floor, convulsing and shuddering, soaked in his own blood. Tommy presses his blood-sodden hand down on the neck wound, valiantly stanching the blood loss, but it looks grave for Musolino. His face is a blood-marbled death mask. His mouth gapes, strangled like a fish wrenched from life and tossed on the dry deck of a boat.

Now Tommy presses both hands down on the exit wound with all his might, leaning into it, pressing down hard. "He's not breathing anymore." Tommy looks up, mortified, eyes wide and blazing. "Lilly, what do I do? He's not breathing!"

"Do you know CPR?"

"Do I know *who*?"

"C-P-R!-C-P-R!—it's something you learn in swim class!"

"Like when somebody drowns?"

"Yes! YES!"

"I think so, I mean, I think I remember learning it at the Y!"

"Okay, so—!"

Gunfire off their left flank makes Lilly start, jerking her attention back to the horses.

The animals look as though they're about to burst blood vessels, their muscular necks like massive pistons firing, their haunches churning as their hooves thunder over sodden, weathered earth. Lilly can feel the land very gradually begin to descend into a valley.

In the far distance, to the east and to the west, under a high, cloudless blue sky, clusters of dark ragged figures materialize like cockroaches emerging from the woods and from the ruins of old barns and from the empty shells of farmhouses, drawn to the noise and chaos of the chase coming their way. Lilly makes a series of instant calculations.

The flatlands ahead of them will be overrun in a matter of minutes, and the heart of this megaherd will be directly in their path. There is no escape, no way out. To the east the woods are too thick to navigate with the horses, the trees too densely packed. To the west, it's the same story. The pines are so profuse now with postplague overgrowth, the daylight turns to night behind the first row, the old-growth treetops scraping the sky.

Lilly's pulse rate shifts into a higher gear, the realization dawning on her that the only mode of escape is to eliminate the threat, obliterate the enemy by any means necessary. She has been in tight situations before, has looked disaster in the eyes, but nothing like this. Over the span of a single instant, which seems to unfurl with glacial slowness, she thinks of her precious children and the delicacy of their lives, *and the absolute imperative of their survival.* As the assailants close in on both sides, the thunder of large-caliber gunfire crackling in the sky, Lilly Caul goes down into that cold, dark, silent place—that primordial, ancient, limbic part of the brain.

An idea occurs to her there, in that cobra calm, in the eye of the storm.

She knows now exactly what she's going to do.

EIGHT

"Lilly!—LILLY!!—What do you want me to do?!" Tommy's voice rips Lilly's attention back to the cargo bay, where Musolino lies still now, barely a tic or a twitch left in him, as the two younger children look on, their brother trying to maintain pressure on the oozing, mortal wound that has already run its course.

"Okay, so, forget the wound." Lilly's voice sounds almost serene in her own ears, a voice coming from someone else. "Tie the cloth around his throat! Not too tight, just enough to stanch any more bleeding!"

Tommy wraps the bloody cloth around the throat. "Okay, now what?"

"Okay, so, push down on the center of his chest, hard, with one hand over the other, hard and fast—and do it over and over."

Tommy starts to palpate the sternum. "How many times should I do it?"

"At least thirty!"

"Then what?"

"Tilt his head back and—"

A bullet sparks off the roof of the pickup, making Lilly jump.

She sees in her side mirror the pattern and formation of the assailants changing. A Kodiak flatbed truck barrels directly toward her on her left flank, a machine-gun turret on his roof, an operator firing controlled bursts at her pickup. They seem to be going for her tires, but the rough ground keeps throwing off the gunner's aim. Lilly sees the Escalade coming up fast on her flank, passing Burt's van and Eve's trailer.

The sinister Airstream can be seen careening after the Escalade, a gun barrel protruding from the side of the cab, the muzzle flashing intermittently, bullets sparking and ricocheting off the ground behind the SUV. Another pair of trucks box in Burt Stankowski's van, the attackers coming to within inches on either side. Automatic gunfire sizzles on either side. The van fishtails, bullet holes puncturing its quarter panels. The van's rear doors suddenly snap, flapping open in the wind. Lilly sees cartons and boxes sliding off the edge, all their treasures from Ikea tumbling out of Burt's van—the lamps and boxes of cereal and bags of charcoal and portable grills—scattering across the sodden field. Some of the trucks swerve to avoid the surprise obstructions. One of the marauders skids out of control, his stake truck going into a violent roll, the massive chassis coming apart at the seams.

Turning her attention back to Tommy, she cries out, "You have to clear the airway! Tilt his chin up, Tommy! Do it now!" For a frantic moment, Lilly glances over her shoulder and sees the boy tilting the bodybuilder's head back. Lilly nods. "Now pinch his nose shut and breathe into his mouth. Do it, Tommy!"

Tommy takes a deep breath, pinches the dead man's nose, and blows air into his mouth.

"Now listen to see if he's breathing, listen close to his mouth."

Tommy does as he's told while a salvo of gunfire draws Lilly's attention back to the churning, galloping, sweaty horse team in front of her. In the whirlwind, bullets are strafing the front corner of the pickup, sparking into the back draft. They're aiming for the horses. Lilly grabs one of her Rugers off the seat, thumbs the hammer, and fires a series of .22-caliber responses out her side window. Then she yanks the right rein, and the horses split off from the caravan, hurling off to the west.

This buys her enough time to glance once again over her shoulder. Through the gaping hatchway, she can see Tommy looking crestfallen, eyes wet, shaking his head as he hovers over the lifeless body-builder. "Tommy?" She sees the boy lick his lips and reach for his Buck knife. "Tommy!" The boy draws the blade from its sheath on his thigh. "TOMMY!" Lilly screams at him. "DON'T DO IT!!"

"I have to," he murmurs. "For Musolino." He grips the knife with both hands now, raising it over the dead man's skull. "He would have done the same thing for me." And the boy is about to drive the tip of the knife down through the man's cranium when Lilly's voice pierces the boy's trancelike misery.

"Goddamn it, Tommy, listen to me! DO NOT DESTROY HIS HEAD!!"

Tommy looks up suddenly, the knife still poised in his hands, his siblings gaping in shock on the other side of the cargo bay. The boy stares at Lilly. For a moment, the knife just stays like that—poised in midair, inches above the big man's bloodless face—as though Tommy's internal workings have seized up. "What?"

"Listen to me! Do you understand what I'm telling you? I'm telling you to *not* destroy his brain! Nod if you understand me!"

The boy drops the knife, the blade clattering noisily to the truck's metal deck. Tommy's head droops, and he starts to tremble, shuddering with tears. "We have to do it—we can't just let him—"

"Tommy! Snap out of it! Come take the reins! You hear me? COME TAKE THE GODDAMN REINS, TOMMY—NOW!"

The boy finally wakes up from his momentary stupor of grief. "Okay, okay, okay. . . ." He starts climbing through the hatch.

She who hesitates is lost. The nattering refrain echoes incessantly in Lilly's head as she hurriedly climbs through the hatchway into the cluttered rear cargo bay. Meanwhile, Tommy has taken the reins from her and now snaps them furiously, keeping the sweaty horses at full steam. Over the last few seconds, the Kodiak truck has loomed closer and closer on their left side, the machine gun about to roar again.

Lilly does not hesitate. In the windy, vibrating cargo area, she crawls over to where Musolino's remains lie in a bloody heap, his limbs akimbo, one leg folded under the other. His skin is the color of wet cement. His eyes are still open. Lilly reaches down and tenderly pushes his eyelids shut. Then she unwraps the cloth from his neck. She twists the fabric into a ropy segment and turns it into gag, wedging it into his mouth and tying it off in a neat little bow behind his head. The bow is critical.

Out of the corner of her eye, she can sense the two younger children transfixed by all this gruesome minutiae, as though they're watching a ritual of some sort, which perhaps they are. Lilly lifts Musolino's remains into a sitting position against a stack of boxes. His head lolls as the pickup swerves.

Lilly looks at the children cowering in a cubbyhole between two boxes. Eleven-year-old Bethany Dupree—a former wallflower, reborn in this plague world as hard and brave as a miniature Navy SEAL—holds her little seven-year-old brother, Lucas, tightly in her arms. Both kids stare glassy-eyed and silent.

"He was a good man," Lilly assures them, keeping close tabs on the dead man's eyes. "And we already miss him. But I promise you. His death will not be meaningless."

Both children nod and say nothing.

Lilly gives them a hard look. "Do you both know what I mean by that?"

They nod again.

"Good," she says. "Now I want you both to be brave, no matter what happens. Just like Mr. Musolino. He was always brave."

They nod.

The thing that was once John Musolino opens its eyes to reveal the pale corneas like white sparrow eggs nested in the sockets.

"TOMMY!" Lilly calls over her shoulder, moving between the monster and the children. "GET AS CLOSE TO THE FLATBED TRUCK AS YOU CAN—RIGHT NOW!"

The Chevy Kodiak closes in on the pickup's left side, cutting the distance to twenty yards, now fifteen, now ten. The gunner, up top, strapped to the firewall with mountain climbing gear, gets inspired, and aims the Browning's muzzle at the horses. In that brief, tumultuous moment before squeezing the trigger, the man lets out a hysterical guffaw—half laugh, half war cry—which sounds more like a bark or a yelp. What was he thinking, shooting at the fucking tires?

A lanky, tall, sinewy former convict with a knife scar down one side of his neck, a barbed-wire tattoo down the other, Antoine Spanic grips the cocking lever with his Carnaby-gloved hand and yanks it quickly, charging the weapon, injecting a round in the chamber. He can see very clearly now the boxes and crates—many of them with the yellow Ikea logo—stacked ten feet high in the pickup's rear hold, straining the integrity of their restraint straps with each bump. He believes passengers lurk back there, hidden by the payload, but the smart move right now is to go for the animals.

Those horses get waxed, and it's game over for these motherfuckers.

Spanic yells down at Barret Deems, the stocky little man at the wheel: "BEAR! Get me as close as you can!"

"Will do!" the gravelly voice below replies with a bellowing yell, the sound of it barely audible above the din of engines and horses and wheels on bumpy ground.

The truck roars and drifts closer, and the gunner centers the crosshairs on the closest horse. Over the pounding noise of the steel-belted radials and the wind whistling across the open windows in the cab below, Spanic can hear the rhythmic grunts and snorts of the draft horses, and the noises touch off a deep well of rage and resentment in Antoine Spanic. The very sights and sounds of these majestic animals, their sweat-shiny coats churning underneath with the massive peristalsis of their muscles, stir something profoundly ugly in Antoine Spanic—his lost childhood, his days on the work farm, the smell of cow shit and moldy hay, the beatings, getting molested by the warden—and he begins to squeeze off the killing shot when something in his peripheral vision catches his eye.

The teenager at the reins has yanked the left rein with all his might, causing the team to rear up midgallop and swerve sharply to the left.

All at once, Spanic sees the entire contraption that was formerly a pickup truck lurch toward the Kodiak, the horses howling and tossing their heads. Spanic realizes that the thing is going to ram the side of the flatbed. He tries to squeeze off a volley of gunfire but before he can pull the trigger, the side of the pickup slams into the Kodiak, whiplashing Spanic sideways and breaking his harness. Something moves behind the Ikea boxes.

Spanic freezes as the boxes suddenly topple apart, someone pushing them aside. A huge male figure appears behind them, teetering, standing upright on the edge of the pickup's cargo bay.

It transpires in that dreamy time-lapse motion like a film developing in Spanic's mind. For the briefest instant, the thing that was once John Musolino stands there, gagged, pale as alabaster, black drool flagging in the wind, eyes like white pilot lights, teeth gnashing as it snarls at Spanic from the rear of that hurling pickup. At first, the gunner doesn't see the woman named Lilly Caul standing behind the creature, holding the monster up as though helping an inebriated friend get home. She steadies the thing in the wind, gripping the knot behind the gag as the creature reaches for Spanic.

Then, Lilly Caul heaves the massive walker onto the rear of the Kodiak.

The Browning submachine gun slips from Spanic's grasp, the long muzzle of the .50-cal tilting skyward, spinning on its greased tripod. Barret Deems yells something from below but all Antoine Spanic can do now is stagger backward, horror-struck, as the enormous walker lands on its belly only inches from him on the Kodiak's flatbed. Spanic tries to spin away but the thing that once spoke fluent Portuguese and entertained the Dupree children with impressions of Muppet characters now reaches out with its grappling hook fingernails and catches a corner of Spanic's denim shirt.

Antoine Spanic manages to get his hand around the grip of the Taurus 380 snub nose wedged behind his belt, but before he can raise the muzzle and fire at the thing's skull, a bolt of enormous agony explodes in his leg. The Musolino-Thing has already sunk its teeth into the fabric of Spanic's jeans a few inches above the knee—in the meaty part of the thigh. The dead teeth penetrate the flesh beneath the fabric and sink into the gunner's femoral artery. A geyser of blood fountains into the wind and atomizes into a fine mist.

In his convulsive pain, Spanic drops the pistol and almost instinctively tries to roll away across the flatbed. But the monster has both hands now dug into the gunner's waist, hooked into that belt, holding him in place. Spanic shrieks. The Musolino-Thing feeds, tearing up the gunner's leg, gobbling denim, and rooting down into the flesh of his groin. Spanic's scream rises an octave, sounding almost like a baby being born, as the creature's incisors sink down into Spanic's genitals.

Gun blasts ring out from the cab, the firewall sprouting holes from Barret Deems's .357 revolver, the Kodiak swerving. The pair of figures roll in a death-lock-embrace across the deck, slamming into the opposite bulwark. The monster gets hit in three places—shoulder, ribs, and hip—none of which has any effect.

Convulsing under the weight of the massive creature, Spanic gasps for air, flailing, losing blood by the pint, but somehow he marshals enough strength to reach up and make a valiant attempt to hold the head of the Musolino-Thing in place. It's like wrestling with an industrial-sized wood chipper, and it is Antoine Spanic's last conscious act on this earth. The creature bites into the gunner's fingers as nonchalantly as if he were sucking the meat off a barbequed rib, and the pain is so massive, so all consuming, that Spanic passes out.

At that point, the merciful darkness claims Antoine Spanic for eternity.

More gunshots bark up front, more holes dimpling the Kodiak's steel partition. The truck weaves and swerves wildly now, drifting away from Lilly Caul's horse-drawn contraption.

In the Kodiak's cab, behind the wheel, Barret Deems frantically twists around in a futile attempt to aim the gun at the monster. He empties the rest of the cylinder in a flurry of firecracker pops, then struggles to reload with a speed cartridge. His stubby hands are slick with panic-sweat, greasy on the steering wheel, his stocky body soaked with perspiration. The noise of the creature snarling and growling rises, reaching his ears like a death knell. He twists around to his right, then to his left, but he sees nothing through the narrow rear window, which is stained with the aerosol of the gunner's blood. But where the fuck is that giant biter?

Deems's hands fumble with the speed loader, which gets stuck, then slips from his grasp, spilling bullets all over the floor mats. He can smell the deathly rancid stench filling the cab, and he can hear the low droning growl of the creature, but still he can't see a god-damn thing.

He leans down and tries to scoop up one of the bullets, most of which are rolling around on the floor. And in that horrible instant, the ridiculous quality of his doom registers somewhere deep in his midbrain. All the shame, guilt, insecurity, and self-loathing flood his awareness. In one single split-second, he is back at his job sweeping up the capitol building after hours, trying to prove himself to big Spencer-Lee Dryden.

He looks up at the windshield and his eyes practically pop out of his skull.

The massive tangle of deadwood and old, fallen timbers from a storm-lashed fence loom directly in his path, and all he has time to do is cry out and yank the steering wheel. He gets sucked into the centripetal force of the turn, and he holds on, bracing himself for a tip-over. Somehow the truck manages to stay on two wheels for a moment, then slams down onto the other two. He holds his breath as he pulls the truck out of its skid. The rear wheels fishtail, and then dig in, regaining their traction.

Barret Deems is letting out a deep sigh of relief when the dead hand reaches in the side window and grabs a hank of his shirt.

"Holy shit—HOLY SHIT!" Tommy Dupree has the horses charging in a wide, arcing turn to the right, whipping the reins as hard as he can, the froth and sweat from the team blowing back in his face, when he hears a scream rising above the din behind the pickup. He shoots a look at his side mirror and sees the closest vehicle, the Kodiak flatbed, fish-tailing wildly. Then Tommy sees the huge, ragged creature that was formerly John Musolino climbing into the Kodiak's cab and devouring the driver, the inside of its windshield running red with blood. At this distance, it's hard to discern any details but it looks as though the creature is eating the face off the man behind the wheel.

"Oh my god, oh-my-god-oh-my-god!" Tommy sees the Kodiak going into another wild spin. "Lilly—LILLY!"

Over the space of the next few seconds, the dominoes tumble in a violent chain reaction that neither Tommy nor Lilly can do anything to stop. The Kodiak has listed to the side, tipping onto two wheels, the g-forces sending the truck into a roll. The Browning is ripped off its tripod and launched through space, and the eviscerated body of the gunner is catapulted into the air, coming apart at the seams in a bloody display. What remains of the truck lands on its roof, smashing the two figures in the cab into pulp.

Coming up fast behind the Kodiak is Burt Stankowski's chopped and channeled van, his horses rearing up with alarm as they swerve to avoid the wreckage. The van goes into a wild spin. Burt tries to pull out of the skid through sheer brute strength, madly tugging on the reins, when the entire van suddenly tips, yanking the horses off their feet and slamming the modified vehicle down on its side. The contraption as well as the horses slide fifty yards on the wet turf, throwing Burt a hundred feet across the field, slamming him into a tangled deadfall, the impact killing him instantly.

Two other vehicles make futile attempts to swerve away from the overturned Kodiak and the ruined van. The first one, a small moving truck with a machine gun placed on its roof, sideswipes the Kodiak, then goes into a spin, the driver overcompensating, sending the entire truck into a roll that rips two of its wheels off, crushes the occupants, and deposits the battered remains in an adjacent dry creek bed. The second collision involves a huge Chevy Silverado occupied by three gunmen, the driver of which panics and locks up the brakes, sending the vehicle fishtailing out of control. The Chevy careens sideways across a flooded patch of soybeans, slams through a fence, and throws each of its passengers through the air to their doom. The truck finally comes to rest in a crumpled, smoking heap, upside down in a stand of tall weeds, its wheels still wobbling furiously.

Simultaneously, three other vehicles involved in the chase narrowly avoid disaster. On one flank, the Escalade, with Ash at the wheel and five children huddled in the backseats, manages to swerve wide enough to skim past the hurling, out-of-control trucks and vans. On the opposite flank, nearly three hundred yards to the east, the souped-up Airstream—pulled by the massive crew cab— swings wide enough to hurl across a dirt road and narrowly circumvent the disastrous chain reaction.

The third conveyance to survive the chain reaction is the huge horse-drawn flatcar commandeered by Eve Betts, with Boone on the running board, and four children cowering in the rear, shielded by boxes and holding on to each other. Unfortunately, despite the fact that Eve is able to veer to the east quickly enough to elude danger, the sudden lurching motion sends most of the Ikea treasures lashed to the trailer's rear deck hurling off the ledge. Packaged foods, solar appliances, bedding, rakes, shovels, bags of potting soil, small generators, and various and sundry lamps and fixtures go tumbling across the sodden field, scattering the landscape with the remnants of Lilly's hopes and dreams for a civilized future.

In the chaotic seconds that follow, Lilly pushes her way through the modified pickup's hatch and takes her place on the bench seat next to Tommy, her pulse racing as she sees what they're up against now. She has no time to experience the shock of losing another close friend, Burt Stankowski, in the blink of an eye. She can't spend one second absorbing the trauma of seeing Burt's van collapse, doubtlessly crushing and instantly killing the Stack women who were riding in the rear. Lilly doesn't have the luxury of pausing for one moment to grieve or cry or scream in anger or express any emotion whatsoever. All she can do now is tamp down her panic and remain in that zone of hyperfocus as she gazes at the rapidly disintegrating path ahead of her.

The sight of the megaherd is almost spellbinding, a wave of dead from the east, and a wave from the west, converging in the open field like opposing tides of oily black ocean crashing up against each other. At this distance, the nuances of each walker are a blur, the figures as small as tin soldiers lumbering drunkenly into a reenactment of some forgotten, archaic battle. But the closer the pickup gets, the more Lilly can see the infinite variations. She can see the older ones with their peeling, mottled flesh, their sunken faces and tattered Sunday go-to-meeting suits. She can see the ones snatched from their youth, many of them missing a limb or a portion of their face, their iridescent eyes like reflectors in the sun. The air streaming past the pickup's open cab reeks of death-stench and rot and ammonia. It smells like the end of the world, and Lilly tries to drive it from her senses.

She turns to Tommy and starts to give him his next order when she hears the tiny walkie-talkie crackling noisily. Through bursts of static, the voice of Ash can be heard, screaming something barely decipherable through the noise like, "Lilly!—you got—on the—look out—it's going for—!!"

Meanwhile, Tommy Dupree is gripping the reins, steering the horses directly toward the multitudes with white-knuckle intensity, his eyes huge with terror. "Lilly, what's the plan? What do we do now?!"

"Stay on course until I tell you otherwise!" Lilly hears Ash's voice garbled and drowned by static but can't find the walkie-talkie. She can hear the squawking but doesn't see it on the seat. She searches the floor. Her hand brushes a plastic device under the seat. The toy two-way must have fallen there during the tumult of the last few minutes, and now Lilly scoops it up and presses the button. "Ash, say again! I did not copy that!"

Static crackles. "Lilly, you got a walker on your pickup!"

"What?—What do you mean?!"

Through the static: "You! Have! A! Walker! On! The! Back! Of—!!"

There's no need for her to finish. The cold, pale, palsied hand of a large male corpse has already thrust its way into the cab through Lilly's open window. Lilly rears back but not before the blackened, greasy, untrimmed fingernails hook themselves onto her Georgia Tech T-shirt.

NINE

For generations, urban legends have maintained that human hair and fingernails continue to grow after death. Images of crone-like ghouls with dagger-sized nails have populated horror movies for years, but the truth is, the human body does not produce more hair or nails after expiring. Perhaps the myth began because pathologists have long studied the phenomenon of "apparent growth" through desiccation. In the hours following death, the skin loses moisture and recedes, exposing more hair and making nails seem longer.

The young male walker that has managed to latch on to the rear of the horse-drawn pickup—and now, somehow, has managed to inch along the ledge of the cargo bay in the wind and the shifting gravitational forces of the chase—is recently deceased. Maybe only days have passed since the thing turned. Its long hair is still fairly shiny, its flesh fairly smooth and intact, its beard still dark. From the looks of its denim vest and gang insignias, it was formerly a member of some biker gang. Its nails are so long—the edges as sharp as pruning shears—that Lilly accidentally tears half her T-shirt off in the process of jerking away.

She gets her hands on the Ruger just as the large male goes for her jugular. She kicks out at the thing, driving it back toward the open window. Yellow teeth snap at the air centimeters from her ankle. She raises the gun and squeezes off a shot.

The pistol just clicks impotently. Wrong gun! The words blaze in neon in Lilly's brain as she strikes at the creature now with the empty pistol, using the steel barrel as a bludgeon, slamming it repeatedly into the thing's skull. Her anger fuels the force of the blows. But this walker is fresh, its bones and membranes still sturdy enough to withstand the impacts of the blunt edge. It claws at her, engulfing her in its black stench.

"MOVE!"

Tommy's voice gets her attention, and she ducks down just as the boy fires a single blast from the loaded Ruger. The thing's head snaps back, the entry wound drilling a hole above the left brow, sending a bloom of pink mist out the exit wound in its scalp, the blood and fluids aerating in the wind.

The thing plummets into the slipstream, tumbling back into the wind and oblivion.

Once again, Tommy has taken his eyes off the path ahead at the most inopportune time, and now, just as he turns back to the team of horses, he sees the dark object looming to his immediate left and lets out a yelp that sounds more like an animal than a human vocalization. Lilly sees what he sees, and she grabs the gun from his grasp. She aims it at the horses, and she starts shooting. But unbeknown to her, the die has already been cast. It's already too late to save the animals.

"Oh Jesus!" Ashley Lynn Duart, behind the wheel of the careering Escalade, sees at least four moving cadavers latching on to Lilly's flailing horse team. The creatures have almost accidentally fastened themselves onto the horse team, their dead limbs tangling up in the bridle and lead lines, each monster swept up by the inertia of the moving contraption. Now the creatures have begun to feed—even while the stalwart animals continue pulling the modified pickup—all of which deteriorates into a frenzy of blood and fur and screams melding into one horrible moving nightmare.

"Lilly, there's a bridge up ahead! I know this area!" Ash howls into the walkie-talkie. "Try to make it before the horses are lost! Can you hear me?!"

Ash listens to the static, no reply. She sees Lilly up ahead in the passenger seat of the pickup, firing futilely at the attackers. "Lilly!" Ash tries again, yelling into the plastic device. "Can you hear me?" No response. "Lilly! Grab the radio!" Only static crackles out of the cheap piece of Japanese manufacturing. "Goddamn it!"

She throws the walkie on the seat next to her. In her rearview she can see her five passengers in back like little nesting dolls squeezed into the cavities between the boxes—Bobby, Chelsea, and Trudy Quinn, and the two Nesbit kids, Cindy and Teddy—all crouched down in defensive postures, a few of them in the jump-seat area way in back, a few on the floor of the second row. Most of them appear petrified, bug-eyed by the turmoil of the chase. In a weird compartment of Ashley Duart's memory, they remind her of the "duck and cover" training films of the Cold War era. She remembers those cheesy movies in which the futility of guarding against a nuclear attack is ignored in favor of ridiculous safeguards such as children quickly scurrying under their school desks.

"Kids, listen to me," Ash says to them. The Escalade has gained ground, pulling up to within a car length of Lilly's pickup, which is now faltering, slowing down at an alarming rate. "I'm going to need your help, all of you, do you understand?"

The children all nod, and then look at each other, and then look back at Ash.

Ash sees that Lilly's pickup has gotten bogged down even further in the soggy earth, her horses faltering, the walkers like giant leeches on the animals' backs, the blood spurting and swirling up into the wind from the feeding frenzy. The horses toss their heads and emit horrible noises in their death throes, somehow continuing to drag the pickup along, albeit slower and slower.

Ash hollers back at the kids, "I'm going to need all of you to start throwing boxes out through the back window! Go ahead! Throw it all out! All the boxes! Quickly, kids, DO IT NOW!!"

Nine-year-old Bobby Quinn, his little freckled face furrowed with intensity and emotion, starts heaving crates out the Escalade's open tailgate window, the other children taking his cue and starting to form a sort of bucket brigade, handing the older boy box after box after box. In her side mirror, Ash can see the payload tumbling out now, scattering across the earth behind the moving SUV in clouds of dust and soggy debris.

Ash turns back to the windshield and sees Lilly, off to the left, firing wildly at the creatures swarming her team, taking one of them down. The remaining three keep burrowing into the horse flesh like gigantic ticks, bringing about an ignominious end to the faithful, steadfast team of draft horses.

In her side mirror, Ash sees the madman in the Airstream's front crew cab coming up fast behind Eve Betts, the blunt barrel of what looks like an Uzi protruding out the crew cab's passenger window. Boone, riding on the flatbed with the other children, rises up every few seconds behind the cover of cargo pallets and intermittently squeezes off volleys of high-caliber rounds from his AR-15, some of the bullets ricocheting in great florettes of sparks off the top corners of the Airstream, making the silver beast swerve wildly.

For just an instant, Ash notices the massive interconnected chain of trailers about a quarter mile behind the Airstream. Something's wrong with the driver of the massive Kenworth cab pulling the trailers—even from this distance, it's fairly obvious there's a problem—the entire train of vehicles weaving wildly now for no apparent reason, the Kenworth's exhaust stack issuing huge plumes of black fumes into the air.

Ash scoops up the walkie-talkie and presses the button. "Lilly, can you hear me?"

Through the hissing noise of static a series of garbled words and phrases: "Fuck!—Tommy!—Close the hatch!—Go ahead, Ash!"

"Lilly, I'm going try to get close enough for you to transfer the kids over to the Escalade!"

Through the speaker, Lilly's voice says, "Okay, fine, whatever, but you better fucking hurry, because we're gonna be hip-deep in walkers in about ten seconds."

"Stand by!"

Ash swerves toward the hobbling pickup, the feeding frenzy on the horses now attracting more walkers, the megaherd pressing in from all sides. The scent of the kill, the dwindling shrieks of the animals as they expire, the river of blood now flowing in immense sheets across the soggy turf around the gruesome orgy—all of it sends out a beacon to the throngs of undead. The entire megaherd seems to be shifting toward the stalled pickup like a storm front moving in.

The Escalade roars up to the powerless truck, slamming into the mob of walkers swarming the remains of dead horses. The impact catapults half a dozen walkers, torsos and limbs and decapitated heads hurling through the air, careening into the oncoming horde, knocking over dozens more like dominoes.

Eve Betts—behind the reins of her massive flatcar trailer—approaches the pickup and the Escalade far too quickly to stop.

The flatbed goes into a skid on the grease of the blood-soaked, flooded Georgia clay.

Everything starts happening all at once, too fast for Eve to delineate or react in her frantic state. She hears the rumbling engine of the Ford F250 pulling the Airstream trailer coming up fast behind her, the collective din of the dead rising like a lunatic chorus from every direction. She sees the vast soybean fields ahead of her darkening with so many walkers of so many shapes and sizes and degrees of mortification that the very landscape itself looks as though it's sick with the plague.

Overreacting, Eve Betts yanks the reins a little too sharply in the opposite direction of the skid, and the horses lunge suddenly, making a virtual ninety-degree turn. The abrupt shift in gravity sends the entire flatbed hurling onto its side.

Eve is lifted out of her seat and slammed against the ground so hard she instantly loses consciousness. The remaining stacks of crates and boxes lashed to the deck have also broken free and now spill across ten square acres of untilled land.

At the same time, Martin Haywood Boone, Eve's faithful tail gunner and de facto boyfriend, is also thrown clear of the wreck. He soars thirty feet through the air, his gun flying out of his grasp, his arms pinwheeling wildly, his body arcing out over the hordes.

He lands hard on a leprous patch of bare ground, hard enough to crack his skull open on a mossy stone. The closest walkers descend on him immediately, digging into him with the fervor of gigantic army ants. The man's last conscious thought—a fact that will soon come into play on this tumultuous afternoon—is a strange kind of gratitude, a thankfulness for a life well lived, and relief that his final act before his death may very possibly save the lives of the children huddled still on the rear deck of that overturned flatbed. Boone's eyes close for the last time as the monsters feast on his midsection.

The man dies at peace with the fact that he had enough foresight to make sure that each and every one of those kids was strapped securely to U-bolts embedded in that deck.

Sally Dryden has lost most of her eyesight, can't hear much with her left ear, and finds her thoughts jumbled up into a knot of regrets and inarticulate rage, but somehow she manages to stay semiupright, slumped behind the steering wheel of the massive Kenworth power plant pulling the chain of campers. The hollow-point bullet that plinked through her windshield almost by mistake fifteen minutes ago—a shot meant for the marauding truck in front of her—had stung her just above her sternum.

She had gasped as though slapped, and then had glanced down at the tiny coin of blood, a scarlet tear tracking down her cleavage and soaking the prototype patches on each pocket, as if she were outside of her own body. There was very little pain considering the fact that the bullet had lodged itself in her chest cavity not far from her heart. It merely felt as though she had to cough and couldn't muster one, her breathing a little labored, her ribs panging a bit as she sucked in air. She had reached for the two-way immediately, at first meaning to contact Spencer-Lee and tell him the bad news, but something had stopped her.

She loathes delivering bad news to Spencer-Lee. He is so busy now, trying to retrieve his extended family from the clutches of these mongrels. How could she bother him with something so trivial in the grand scheme of things? It's a minor injury. She'll most likely be fine. Most likely. No need to mention it.

So she goes on driving, roaring along behind the Airstream, pulling the remaining families still in protective custody, all of them adults, no children left, the Weimann couple in the second trailer, their elderly grandparents in the third, the Fordhams in the last trailer. Even after her vision has started to blur. She goes on. Even after the dizziness has coursed over her, and her arms have gone numb, and her ears have started to ring . . . she keeps the pedal floored, keeps the big Kenworth cab booming along.

Now she realizes she probably should have said something because the throbbing pain in her chest is enormous, like a sledgehammer slamming into her ribs with the regularity of a metronome. She reaches for the two-way radio but it's not on the seat next to her. The seat next to her is soaked with her blood.

With clumsy fingers, Sally Dryden searches the sticky upholstery, her vision going in and out of focus. She can't find the damn radio. What did she do with it? She must contact Spencer-Lee immediately. She can't breathe anymore. Her lungs have caught fire. She coughs and heaves and coughs some more, her bloody spittle stippling the dashboard. She tries to see through the windshield, and everything slows down in her failing vision.

She starts to lose consciousness, losing control of her hands, the steering wheel beginning to turn on its own. How is that possible? The steering wheel is spinning, and the massive Kenworth cab-over has transformed into a carnival ride like those teacups that used to delight Sally as a child, spinning and spinning, lifting her above the twinkling night lights of the Georgia state fair.

The gravitational tug now yanks her toward the far door, the weight of her injury pressing her down into the blood-sodden seat.

The sound of wrenching metal drowns the sudden keening wail of her scream.

If viewed from a godlike aerial perspective ten thousand feet above the soybean fields, the next fifteen seconds would resemble a tantrum visited on the scene by an angry child of a giant. It all happens so spontaneously, so violently, so quickly, that it would only be possible from this height to comprehend or parse exactly what is happening. When the massive chain of campers—repurposed by the Drydens as a benevolent mobile prison—finally jackknifes and tips, the world for those on the ground literally shudders at the force of the impact.

The very earth itself seems to quake with off-the-charts seismic vibrations as the tangled chain of vehicles rams into the ruins of Eve Betts's overturned flatcar, fracturing the enormous conveyance into three pieces, causing a chain reaction of collisions as the careening campers break apart, each hurling piece of metal slamming into the next object or vehicle in line.

One of the campers slams into the Airstream trailer, sending the silver beast and its cab into a wild 360-degree spin, mowing down split-rail fences, and chewing through hundreds of walking dead with the bloody efficiency of a runaway harvester.

The final impact sends the Escalade tumbling onto its side.

The SUV then violently slides across fifty yards of wet turf before coming to rest in the sudden, jarring, hazy miasma of silence.

Lilly lies there for a second or two, her back screaming in pain. She feels an unidentified body pressing down on her but at the moment she can't move her neck to see who it is. In the shell-shocked silence, she realizes several things, each of them dawning on her one at a time.

First and foremost, the kids appear to be all in one piece, knocked around a bit, but generally unharmed. Some of them—the younger ones—softly whimper, while others, like Bobby Quinn and Bethany Dupree, shift their feverish gazes around the sideways vehicle trying to wrap their minds around what just happened.

Second, it becomes clear that there are two people lying on top of Lilly in tangled heaps—Tommy and Ash—each trying to extricate their limbs from the pileup. At last, Ash pulls her arm out from under Lilly and says, "Lilly, darling, do you think you could possibly remove your knee from my ass?"

Lilly starts to formulate a wisecrack response when she is stricken with her third realization.

The vehicle is moving. Just slightly. Not in a straight line, though—its wheels are facing sideways, and still squeaking and turning uselessly. But every few moments, a tremor passes through the bones of the Escalade as though nudged by someone. Then it grows still again. Then comes another shudder, accompanied by a muffled scraping noise, which builds and blends into more sounds of objects brushing past the SUV, making it tremble and creak.

Lilly smells the thick pall of death-stench, as acrid and rotten as a compost heap. She hears the low, grinding, baritone vocalizations coming from all around the car, a slow, dissonant, Gregorian chant of growling, which in the past has reminded Lilly of a warning sound way in the back of a dog's throat when violence is imminent, when the animal is cornered and threatened. She tries to see through the Escalade's windshield.

Auto-glass does not break in great chunks like a window pane or a drinking glass. It crumbles uniformly upon impact, and usually stays somewhat intact, like a sheet of diamonds. Lilly gazes through this fractured prism now and sees the multitudes of dead congregating around the Escalade. In the distorted shadow-play of geometric fragments, she sees tall ones, short ones, portly ones, emaciated ones, some that are little more than skeletons draped in moldering flesh, all of them drawn to the wrecked SUV. Lilly's heart practically stops. She sees no escape. No way out. In a matter of minutes, the Escalade will be completely engulfed. It will be a challenge to give this situation a positive spin for the children. Lilly has faced impossible odds before but nothing like this.

Flinching at another tremor traveling through the chassis, she turns to the children. "Sssshhhhhhhhh," she whispers softly to them. "Everybody stay really, really quiet." She gently slides out from under Ash. "Everything's going to be okay." She manages a pained smile. Her back twinges, the pang taking her breath away. "We're gonna be fine . . . if you just . . . if you promise to stay very, very quiet . . . and . . . and stay inside this car. Let me see everybody nod their head."

Most of them nod robotically, fidgeting, squeezed against each other in the narrow vertical seats. Lilly notices Tommy, a few inches to her left, curled into a fetal position, gazing horror-struck through a corner of the windshield at the swarm. The atonal chorus of growls has risen to such a level that it's becoming hard to hear each other. "Tommy, are you okay? Tommy?"

He doesn't respond. He's spellbound. Lilly notices Ash carefully moving her body out from under the boy, reaching for Musolino's AK-47. She checks it, very carefully pulling back its charging lever, making as little noise as possible.

Lilly looks at her. "We still got eight shells left in Tommy's Mossberg."

"I got twelve rounds left in the banana clip." Ash feels along her right leg for the leather sheath. "I got the Randall knife as well."

The SUV jerks, one of the children in back mewling softly with terror. More and more creatures scud up against the undercarriage, scraping along the sides, looking for weak spots. The sideways vehicle teeters, the upholstered interior closing in on Lilly like a luxurious coffin, claustrophobic and airless, as more and more creatures engulf it. She nods at Ash. "There's an axe inside this crate somewhere, Musolino kept it handy. Look under the seat."

Ash twists into an awkward crouch, reaching under the vertical seat. She gets her hand around a brand-new, spotless, three-foot-long Ikea garden axe. "This'll do nicely," she murmurs more to herself than to Lilly. "We gotta keep things as quiet as possible."

Lilly checks her .22 pistol. "Still got a full magazine for the Ruger—"

"Good!" Tommy's voice penetrates the tension like an ice pick. "That ought to be just enough bullets to shoot each one of us in the head!"

"Tommy!" Lilly hisses at him, not exactly angry, just buzzing with adrenaline and emotion, and maybe even a little annoyed because she knows he's right. There's no narrative in which they fight their way out of this. "Keep it to yourself, okay?"

He shakes his head. "Whatever." He looks at her, his eyes shiny. "I'm sorry. I'm being a dick." A tear gathers in the corner of his eye. "To be honest . . . I don't really want to die right now."

She reaches up and dabs the tear, wiping it off his face. "Neither do I, kiddo. That's why we're going to make sure we don't."

"You're a terrible liar," he says with his patented crooked grin.

Ash looks at Lilly. "One thing's for sure." She reaches down and tenderly wipes a tear off *Lilly's* cheek. "If we die, we're going to do it together, and we're going to do it in style."

Lilly looks at her. "And we're gonna take as many of these mother-fuckers down with us as we can."

Ash gives her a nod, and looks at Tommy, who has gone stone-cold calm. The young man nods back at Ash, and then looks at Lilly.

"You guys ready?" she says. "We'll go out through the sunroof."

The other two nervously nod not even remotely ready.

TEN

It feels like diving into a slaughterhouse, the air dank and sticky, the coppery odors of blood and offal pressing down on them. Lilly shimmies through the sunroof, hitting the ground and rolling for several feet, clotheslining a half dozen unsuspecting walkers, knocking them over like bowling pins. Ash follows, diving and shoulder-rolling in the other direction. Tommy lunges out behind them, letting out a garbled war cry, instantly climbing to his feet and lashing out with his machete.

Lilly starts in on the closest row of upright corpses, backhanding the skull of the first one with her eleven-inch Buck knife, slicing a deep divot through cranial bone and dura and brain matter, sending streams of gore through the air. She spins and forehands the knife into another one, and another one, and yet another. Very quickly she gets stippled and splashed and spattered, and starts losing track of her comrades. Her eyes take on the slimy red cast of blood, as though a filter has drawn down over her field of vision. Her spine burns, the stabbing pain taking her breath away. There are so many creatures pressing in on her now from all sides, she starts executing a controlled spin, stabbing skull after skull. The bodies stagger and fall, one after another, causing brackish splashes of muddy bodily fluids and long, ropy ejaculate of cerebral fluids swirling through the air.

In her peripheral vision, Lilly gets only blurry glimpses of Ash and Tommy on opposite flanks, stabbing and slashing and thrusting.

For one glorious moment, it feels to Lilly as though they might actually beat the odds and fight their way out of this mind-numbing mob of dead. But the waves keep coming, and coming, and coming, increasing in size and intensity.

Without warning, Lilly finds herself suddenly surrounded by two dozen larger males in some kind of random formation, closing in on her with ferocious, snarling bloodlust. Some of the older ones sport burial suits still clinging to their decomposing flesh, their cadaverous faces full of rotted dentures and jagged, yellowed incisors that gleam in the late-afternoon sun. Some of the younger ones wear gouged and tattered leathers with indecipherable patches from forgotten motorcycle clubs.

Tommy and Ash have made progress on the opposite side of the clearing, cutting a swath at least fifteen yards wide through the onslaught, but now the twosome gets into trouble, boxed in by an unexpected salvo of creatures from the other side of the wrecked SUV. That's when Lilly hears the children screaming.

She glances over her shoulder. Just for a single instant. Just long enough to see the blitzkrieg of dead surrounding the Escalade, countless numbers of them, all stages of deterioration, some eviscerated, some mangled beyond recognition of what one might call human, some clawing stupidly at the broken windshield and side windows, a large portion of them pushing up against the vehicle with enough collective pressure to make it start to teeter on its side. Lilly is too far away to do anything about it, and the recognition of that fact, as well as the momentary pause in her slashing motions, throws her balance off just enough to cause her to trip over her own feet.

Tumbling to the ground, striking the tender part of the small of her back on an exposed root, Lilly lets out an involuntary cry of agony. Sharp, scalding pain shoots up her spine and takes her breath away. The knife slips from her gasp, the weapon skittering across the ground. She madly claws for it but she loses it in the sun.

Warning alarms go off in her midbrain. She blinks, her vision bleary now, only barely registering the indistinct, blurry figures looming above her. She fumbles for her gun. Something presses down on one leg, and she realizes all at once that she's being mauled. One of the creatures—on its hands and knees now, hunching down on Lilly's left leg—bends down to take a bite out of the fleshy part her thigh.

In that fraction of a second before the thing can sink its teeth into Lilly's femoral artery, she grabs it by both sides of its head.

Call it survival instinct, or call it genetic memory, but whatever the source, Lilly ignores the astronomical odds stacked against her at that moment and continues to keep that iron grip on the creature's head, paying little attention to the other ragged cadavers now descending on her. She disregards the overpowering odor engulfing her, the rancid, black, greasy stench of rotten meat. In fact, she doesn't give a single thought to the fact that she will be devoured in a matter of seconds.

Right then, in that terrible instant before the rest of the creatures dig into her, she focuses solely on those two milky-white pupils staring down at her from deep within a pair of hollowed-out eye sockets. Her gaze remains unyielding, steady as a rock. She stares into those empty, uncomprehending, feral eyes with almost serene defiance. *You will never stop us*, she says with that stare. *I am just one of many.*

The thought echoes in her mind as she closes her eyes and waits to die.

The thunder of a single high-powered rifle blast gets lost in Lilly's final reverie. But when the cold, wet spatter of blood sprays her face, she opens her eyes.

At first, she doesn't trust what she's seeing. The mind plays all manner of games when the tether has broken, when death is imminent. Forget the light at the end of the tunnel. At the end, the brain will produce vivid hallucinations. All of which is why Lilly can't believe that the very head she has been holding in a vise grip between her two sweaty palms has literally erupted.

A vertical geyser of blood jets from an exit wound two inches above the bridge of the creature's nose, the thing's body stiffening suddenly with that strange phantom electric current. Lilly still holds on to the creature's head as the rest of it goes limp in her grasp. Stricken, transfixed by the almost peaceful expression passing over the monster's face, Lilly finally lets go.

The attacker collapses to the ground at Lilly's side in a pool of spreading fluids. More shots ring out. Lilly sits up. Getting her bearings back in stages, still woozy from the near-death event of a minute earlier, she sees dreamlike images of heads snapping back in momentary slow motion, spurting with plumes of pink mist all around her. Bodies tip, and fall, and flop to the ground in heaps. The leather-clad cadavers, the former old men in ragged, gouged pinstripes, the bloated, drowned females, the casualties of the floods, the teenage girls missing pieces of their torsos, their midsections spilling streamers of intestines as though caught in the ribbons of maypoles—each and every one of them are now collapsing in awkward piles.

By this point, Lilly has risen to her feet, and has regained enough of her senses to see the source of their high-caliber savior.

"ASH!" The voice booms a hundred yards to the north, emanating from a dark-haired man standing on the rear bench seat of a dusty Jeep Wrangler. Parked in a clearing beside a mangled, flood-damaged barn, the Jeep sits idling in a cloud of its own exhaust and fumes. Its two other passengers stand on opposite sides of the vehicle, each perched on a running board, one with a Remington 700, the other with an M24 tactical rifle. Each man fires at will, taking down creature after creature, gradually clearing the square acre surrounding the Escalade.

In the Jeep's rear seat, Jamie Quinn takes his eye off the scope of his AR10 semiauto rifle for just one moment. He has nine rounds left in the magazine and no time to spare. Right now, though, he has to squint against the setting sun in order to see if his eyes are playing tricks on him.

Even from this distance, he easily recognizes the woman on the ground just now pushing the limp cadaver off her and struggling to her feet—the dishwater auburn hair, the ponytail, the beads and ripped jeans. It's Lilly Caul, alive and still kicking. Thank God. But Jamie Quinn also sees the unmistakable figure of a statuesque woman on the other side of the walker-infested clearing. She wears a tattered black sleeveless blouse and bloodstained denims, wailing with her Randall knife, dispatching monster after monster. He can see her trademark swimmer's physique and the sinew of her long arms.

"ASH!" he bellows once again, his voice lost in the winds. "ASH!— ASH!"

He puts the scope back to his eye, sees another cluster of creatures closing in on Lilly, and opens fire. Six consecutive booming reports, the shells flinging out the port, ringing and clanging to the ground. More walkers go down behind the crosshairs, one after another tipping over like bottles falling, corks popping, blood mist fizzing like pink champagne bubbles. But where are the children? Where are his babies—Trudy, Chelsea, and little badass Bobby? Where the fuck are they?

"Does anybody see the kids?!" Quinn hollers to his cohorts without taking his eye from the cup. "You think they're in that ditched Escalade?"

"I don't know, maybe." Frank Steuben snaps the cocking mechanism on his Remington. "Right now we got more walkers coming at the boy—nine o'clock—on the left. See 'em? Just behind Ash!"

The three shooters unleash another volley of hellfire on the clearing a hundred yards away, Quinn emptying the remaining rounds in his magazine. The thunderous barrage from the rifles of the other men continues unabated while Quinn ejects the spent cartridge, pulls a fresh mag from his belt, and slams it home into the receptacle under the stock. He yanks the charging lever and fires off another half dozen rounds, eye to the scope, holding his breath, watching the distant creatures whiplash, spin, and fall in halos of pink mist made radiant by the dusky angle of the sun.

In the narrow visual field of the scope, Quinn can see the situation with Ash and the others changing rapidly. The blood-drenched clearing, bound in thick blue smoke and motes of particulate shimmering in the sunbeams, is virtually cleansed of reanimated dead— at least for the moment—the second wave still emerging from the adjacent forest over a quarter mile away. And now it looks as though Ash has finally recognized the source of the friendly fire, or at least latched her attention on to it. She stands very still for a moment, staring straight ahead, her expression knitted with confusion, looking directly into the crosshairs.

Quinn's gut clenches with emotion when he sees her waving, her face brightening with the revelation that her man has returned. He hears her distant call, her voice so beautiful, honey-thick and smoky-rich. "OH MY GOD, QUINN?! QUINN!! IS THAT—?!"

Behind her, the boy—Quinn can't quite remember if his name is Tommy or Timmy—has turned and rushed back to the Escalade with Lilly. The two of them begin to furiously rock the entire sideways monstrosity back and forth, as hard and fast as they can, in a frantic attempt to roll the thing back over onto its wheels. Quinn lowers the scope and waves back at her wildly. "YES!—ASH!—IT'S ME! STAY THERE, WE'RE COMING!!"

Quinn's excitement has distracted all three men to the point that nobody hears the rumblings of walkers emerging from the deeper woods behind them, at least twenty-five large adult creatures, drawn to all the gunfire. As the men climb back into the Jeep, not a single one of them notices the two former farmhands—now decomposed into shriveled, desiccated corpses in filthy, threadbare denim overalls—lurching toward the Jeep just as it roars into motion, its rear wheels spraying sludge into the air.

The larger of the two creatures manages to clasp its bony claw of a hand around Caleb Washburn's ankle. The forward momentum of the Jeep instantly hauls the walker off its feet, carrying it away with the vehicle. Caleb lets out a yelp that sounds almost canine, a burst of involuntary shock that makes him kick wildly with his right leg as he goes for his gun.

The monster latches on to Caleb's foot with its teeth. Rotting incisors penetrate the leather welt of Caleb's work boot. Quinn sees all this unfolding and tries to swerve in an attempt to throw the creature off the Jeep. But all this does is send Caleb Washburn slipping off the edge of his seat and over the ledge of the running board, sprawling to the ground behind the Jeep, the walker still attached to him.

Quinn makes a tight turn and roars back toward Caleb and the walker, throwing a wake of soggy humus off the rear wheels, while Frank Steuben squeezes off four quick blasts from his .44 Taurus revolver at the two figures on the ground thirty feet away. Jostled by the fishtailing Jeep, Frank's aim gets thrown off, the bullets missing their mark by only inches, ripping through the attacker's shoulder and ribs, doing very little to slow it down.

Meanwhile, beneath the creature, Caleb wriggles and fights as the monster goes for his neck, tearing into him with ferocious hunger. Finally Caleb gets his Glock 9 millimeter in his right hand and presses the muzzle to the side of the beast's skull. A single shot spews brain matter out the opposite side of the thing's head, making it sag instantly, collapsing onto Caleb, then slipping off him onto the ground.

Standing amid the battlefield of contorted, disfigured walker remains, her pulse racing, her body like a tuning fork vibrating with adrenaline, Ashley Lynn Duart gets so excited by the appearance of Quinn that she loses track of her surroundings. She barely registers the fact that Tommy and Lilly are right next to her, madly rocking the Escalade, trying with all their might to tip it back onto its wheels. All Ash can perceive is Quinn's Jeep hurling toward them, coming across the field, closing the distant with each passing second.

Ash doesn't even notice the second wave of walkers coming from the long shadows of the scabrous orchards to the west. Nor does she notice the injured man in Quinn's Jeep as it approaches, the poor soul now writhing in pain in the rear, his left foot, left leg, and lower abdomen bleeding profusely from the walker attack. Nor does Ash notice Frank Steuben trying valiantly to stanch Caleb's bleeding with a piece of his shirttail serving as a makeshift tourniquet. But these are trivial developments compared with the most important thing that Ash misses.

She doesn't see the battered, hobbling Ford crew cab coming toward the Escalade from the north, pulling a rust-pocked silver Airstream trailer, mowing down row after row of walking dead.

"Slow down, Daniel, please . . . slow *way* down." The man leaning out of the jagged, broken passenger window of the crew cab speaks with an eerie calm behind the stained gauze of his facial bandages, despite the fact that his brain blazes with rage and sorrow and pain. His wife of thirty-two years is dead, their dreams of a better world—a safe place to live, children nurtured well, tranquil days—all of it literally gone up in smoke. His compound has been destroyed. All his children and extended family are either dead or kidnapped. His body and soul have been blighted by an evil woman—the same one now visible in the distant heat waves and waning sunlight struggling to turn a sideways SUV over onto its wheels before the next regiment of the dead moves in.

Spencer-Lee Dryden gets very calm as the cab and trailer grinds to a halt, sending ripples across a flooded dirt road fifty yards from the Escalade—surprisingly calm, considering the ceaseless agony radiating outward from his third-degree facial burns under his bandages. He turns to the driver and says, "Keep it running, Daniel."

"Wait, um . . . yeah but . . . what about . . . ?" Daniel Klouse nervously slams the Ford's stick into Park and glances over his shoulder at the shifting population of dead creeping across a square mile of matted weeds, withered crops, and flooded farmland. A gnarled, gangly ex-con garbed in sleeveless flannel and Oakley sunglasses, a cornucopia of tattoos adorning his gristly musculature, Klouse used to play chess in the joint. He remembers being taught by one of the best—an old, grizzled arsonist—who kept hammering the primary directive of great chess masters into Klouse's head: always imagine at least four moves ahead of your opponent. Which is why Klouse can't stop thinking right now that they should get the fuck out of here immediately.

Four moves ahead of the current one will likely involve Klouse and every other human within a mile radius becoming dinner for the outrageously huge second swarm that is just now coming out of the ravines and gulches of the surrounding wetlands.

"This won't take long," Spencer-Lee informs him, gazing out the windshield. He reaches down to a long, rectangular lockbox between the seats. The stencil says APD SWAT TACTICAL ONLY and the lock displays evidence of tampering. Up until this moment, Spencer-Lee was not able to use the weapon in the box due to the chances of endangering the children. He would rather die than jeopardize the lives of his precious, sweet, innocent young brood. They are everything to Spencer-Lee. They are all that he has left.

Inside the battered metal lid, Spencer-Lee finds the oiled, shiny weapon nestled in its felt concavity. It was procured years ago—right around the start of the outbreak—from the SWAT team's tactical storeroom in Spencer-Lee's congressional district. His congressman owed him a big favor, and had traded the keys to that warehouse for the lives of the congressman's family.

Now he quickly pulls the thing out, assembles the tailpiece, and loads a projectile. Klouse watches with morbid interest. He's seen these things in movies but never in real life.

Meanwhile, Spencer-Lee opens the cab door and climbs out with the heavy, bulky weapon on his shoulder like a yoke. He splashes through the standing water.

He sees the Jeep coming—still maybe forty or fifty yards away—and he lowers himself to one knee. He carefully aims the RPG, leading the Jeep ever so slightly in the crosshairs.

ELEVEN

Quinn and his men are still a good thirty yards away from the Escalade, circling around a patch of flooded ground—Ash giggling with the giddy emotions of a teenager—when the rocket-propelled grenade is launched a little over fifty yards to the north.

Off a nearby log, a flock of crows erupts into flight at the boom of the RPG—an inkblot spreading poisonously upward across the pastels of the setting sun—heralding the flight of a decidedly more dangerous man-made projectile.

The blur of the shark-finned rocket tracing through the humid air, spiraling toward the Jeep, looks almost surreal as it seeks its moving target. It happens so quickly and unexpectedly that Ash just stands there, her waving hand still raised but now paralyzed, motionless. The Jeep explodes twenty-five yards away from the Escalade.

The force of the blast levitates the entire vehicle ten feet straight up into the air, the sonic boom shaking the earth. The secondary explosion follows as the gas tank goes up, the fireball immolating the Jeep, as well as the remains of all walkers lying strewn across the ground within a radius of fifty yards.

The shock wave lifts Ash off the ground and catapults her backward twenty feet before depositing her in a flooded, swampy patch. The spongy wet ground probably saves her life; had she hit something hard she would have certainly been killed. At the same time, that violent surge of energy cashes into the underbelly of the Escalade, ironically pushing the SUV over onto its wheels—right side up—as Lilly and Tommy dive out of the way of the debris, shrapnel, and particles flying in all directions.

Twisted metal, shards of molten hot plastic, and a supernova of shattered glass hurl through the air, some of it strafing the sides of the Airstream fifty yards away with the force of a vertical storm. The backdraft throws Spencer-Lee Dryden to the ground, a jagged piece of the Jeep's transaxle, shaped like a spear, crashing through the crew cab's windshield.

Daniel Krouse attempts to duck but is not fast enough, and the pointed end of the iron scrap impales his head, fixing it to the fire-wall behind the seats.

A moment later, the air sizzles with the aftermath of the explosion. Ears ringing, pain throbbing in her spine, Lilly Caul rolls onto her lower back and gapes up at the heavens as though shell-shocked by the eerie colors painted across the darkening sky. The ringing in her ears seems to drown out all other ambient sound for a moment. She sits up and notices the Escalade is upright now, on its four wheels, and she starts to regain her bearings. She can see the kids in the back rows moving, peering out the windows, apparently unharmed. Where is Tommy? In her deafened ears, a faint, high-pitched whistling rises above the ringing noise.

Out of the corner of her eye, she sees the boy on his hands and knees about twenty feet away from her. He looks as though he's been vomiting, his pale face partially powder burned, his gaze down-turned and fixed on the swampy grass. She manages to rise to her feet, dizziness threatening to knock her over. That's when she sees the Airstream rig fifty yards away behind a deadfall pile, sitting still, blood swathed across the inside of its crew cab's windshield. She assumes both men in the cab have bitten the dust, but just before turning away she catches a glimpse of a large, middle-aged man behind the Airstream, lying supine on the ground, writhing in pain, dazed by the percussive blast of the RPG, his face covered in bandages.

This gets her moving. She rushes over to the boy, grabs him, and yanks him to his feet. Her hearing still impeded by the traumatic aftereffects of the blast, her ears still ringing incessantly, she sees the boy's lips moving but can't hear a word. All she hears is that high-pitched whistling rising above the tinnitus like a teakettle boiling over. She yanks Tommy toward the SUV. "Get in! Quick! We have to get outta here! NOW!"

Lilly can barely hear her own voice but she sees Tommy staggering toward the front passenger door, clawing at the handle, getting it open, and climbing in. The door slams shut but Lilly hears only that thin, falsetto shrieking noise that seems to be coming from the rear of the Escalade. With great effort, her spine stiff and panging, she steadies herself on the Escalade's quarter panel and hurriedly makes her way around the rear of the vehicle.

Ash is on her knees behind the SUV, shoulders slumped, her face a mask of agony, her eyes locked on the smoldering wreckage across the clearing. She is screaming. Lilly goes to her and puts a hand on her shoulder. "Ash! We have to go! Now! ASH! ASH!"

In all the miserable, tragic events that have transpired between humans throughout the years of the plague—and that includes grand larceny, starvation, torture, kidnappings, rape, mass murder, guerilla warfare, and all manner of brutality—Lilly Caul has yet to hear a person shriek in this manner. Ash's scream is a scream of existential horror—a naked, unbridled, primal cry of loss—her eyes so wet with tears and agony they look almost luminous. Her tears track down her face. Her shriek finally deteriorates into strangled, convulsive sobbing.

Lilly, her hearing partially restored, pulls on Ash's sleeveless blouse and says, "Ash, listen to me. Listen. If we don't get out of here right now—and I mean *right now*—the children will most likely die."

"Leave me. Fuck it . . . leave me." Ash looks up at Lilly with heartbreaking grief sweeping over her face. Her voice crumbles. "Leave me here, I don't want to go anywhere, it's over, it's useless and it's over, the plague won, who gives a shit. . . ."

In her peripheral vision, Lilly can see the next wave of the horde—hundreds, maybe thousands in number—coming this way from the lengthening shadows of surrounding forest preserves and ruined homesteads. The dusk has almost given over to evening, the sky now the color of a wound, pink and salmon with streaks of crimson. In the far distance, the horizon flickers with spangles of heat lightning, as though the storms of recent days are refusing to leave quietly, a vast engine continuing to diesel after being turned off. Darkness is closing in.

Lilly's pulse quickens, her focus narrowing, and that steel enclosure clamping down on her emotions. She slaps Ash across the cheek—nothing vicious in it, just sharp enough to cut through the trauma. "Goddamn it I'm not leaving you here, and it's not over! You're gonna get your shit together for the kids! You understand? Nod! If you understand what I'm telling you, nod your fucking head. Look at me, Ash! Look at me! I SAID NOD YOUR FUCKING HEAD!"

Ash looks up as though her head weighs a thousand pounds and she nods, swallows thickly, and nods again and swallows again, hard. She nods a third time. Her voice changes, flattens out, all emotion leeched out: "Let's go."

Lilly drives. Tommy sits in the front passenger seat with his shotgun between his legs, his gaze shifting nervously to the side mirror. Ash sits in the second row between Bobby and Chelsea Quinn, holding the kids as they softly struggle to keep from crying. The other kids are squeezed like nesting dolls into the second and third rows of bench seats, nine tiny people clinging to each other, crammed together in sweaty catatonia, the fear keeping them still.

Nobody speaks for the longest time. It's as if their hearts and minds are readjusting to the loss, the new dynamic in Musolino's

Escalade. The children have witnessed everything—every violent episode over the last several hours—through that narrow tailgate window. Even when they had fallen sideways, stacked on top of each other, they saw every exchange of gunfire, every kill, every edged weapon going into every skull. Now their agonizing silence is troubling to Lilly. She keeps glancing in the rearview, watching them watch her. Most of their little soiled faces are bloodless and blanched with exhaustion and trauma. Some of them have dirty streaks snaking down their cheeks where the tears have dried; others suck their thumbs obsessively and compulsively. They all seem to have fallen into a collective daze, as though the terror and uncertainty have finally blown fuses within them.

Lilly finds a shit-strip of leprous dirt that once served as an access road for tobacco farmers, and she takes it slowly and steadily in a westerly direction, away from the most concentrated portions of the megaherd, away from the invisible fog bank of death-stench, away from the continuous grinding chorus that sounds even from a distance, even under the noise of an engine, like a dissonant symphony of chainsaws. She keeps her speed at around thirty-five to forty miles an hour—radio off, A/C off, headlights off—in order to conserve fuel. The gauge says they're almost empty. They have plugged the bullet hole in the tank with cloth, but they will need to properly patch it and find fuel soon.

Darkness is closing in, the sky turning the color of black lung disease, the air cooling down, the thickening forest to the north falling into dense shadows, as opaque as velvet drapes.

Lilly Caul knows this sprawling rural area south of Atlanta better than anyone but even *she* will not be sure exactly where they are until they come upon a road sign or landmark. She thinks the chase has led them astray of Woodbury by many miles. She estimates that they are at least halfway to the Alabama border, if not farther. They have to at least be west of Luthersville, but maybe be even west of LaGrange, and that will present both advantages and disadvantages. She vaguely remembers a Love's Travel Stop somewhere around here, if she can find the ruins of what used to be Highway 85.

Next to her, Tommy keeps shooting glances at that side mirror. Lilly can see what he's looking at: the vast, walker-riddled farmlands behind them, the smoking wreckage of Quinn's Jeep, and that battered Airstream rig receding into the distance and gathering darkness. She's keeping an eye on that silver camper and its crew cab as well, but not for the same reasons as Tommy. She has her own reasons, and she plans to reveal them to the others in due time.

Five minutes later, they come upon the crumbling remains of what once was a major transportation artery along the Georgia–Alabama border. Now, in the moonlit darkness, the four-lane divided interstate looks like some obscure ancient ruins one might find listed in the back pages of a Roman guidebook—the Lost Portico of Cement, perhaps, or the Concrete Coliseum of Pine Valley—stretching into the night in either direction as far as the eye can see. Some of the overpasses have been washed away or have collapsed out of neglect, and now all that remains are desecrated support columns rising up against the sky like snuffed-out candles. Old wreckage and carcasses of vehicles weathered beyond recognition.

Lilly pulls onto the road and heads north, toward the ghost towns of Hogansville and Franklin, and the wilderness of the Chattahoochee River delta beyond them. She drives for another mile or so, weaving between the overturned, rusted-out shells of abandoned cars and the kudzu-carpeted viaducts, when she suddenly, without any warning to the others, pulls over and stops.

Ash has already begun looking around the gloomy interchange with confusion. Tommy also glances over his shoulder at a bullet-riddled road sign that says COLUMBUS 57 MI, a frown creasing his brow.

"Isn't Woodbury in the other direction?" he asks, looking at Lilly.

"We can't go there right now. Not yet. We need to find fuel somewhere, and there's something I need to do first before we head back home."

Ash speaks up. "What's going on?" Her voice is hoarse and spent. "What are you talking about? What are you up to, Lilly?"

"Give me a second," she says, digging her Ruger pistol out of the map case, pulling back the slide, checking the breach. "I promise I'll explain everything." She opens the door, pauses, and looks back at the kids. "Everybody cover your ears, there's gonna be a bang."

She steps outside the car, aims into the night sky, and squeezes off a single round. The muzzle barks and sends a flicker of silver light up into the clouds, the report echoing over the Chattahoochee.

She gets back into the car, slams the door. She slams it loudly.

Tommy gives her a look. "You want to explain what the hell is going on?"

Ash pipes up: "Lilly, I don't know if you're keeping score but we left one man alive back there. The walkers are not the only ones gonna be drawn to the sound of that gunshot."

"I know, I know, and that's exactly why—"

"No, I don't think you *do* know! I don't think you have the first inkling what we're dealing with here. This man is bug-fuck crazy."

Little Teddy Nesbit slams his tiny hands over his ears and cries out, "Stop cursing!"

Next to him, Tiffany Slocum starts to whimper softly, tears welling up in her enormous blue eyes. This starts an epidemic of sniffling and mewling across two rows of seats. Mercy Slocum starts to sob, and thumbs go into the mouths of many of them.

"Okay. Okay. Everybody calm down." Lilly twists around and gazes at all the owlish faces in the green glow of the dashboard light, the looks of reticence, trauma, bone-deep weariness, and debilitating shock. She gently puts a hand on little Teddy's knee. "I promise we'll refrain from cursing." She looks at the others. "I'm going to get you all back to Woodbury safe and in one piece. You have my word on that. All in good time." She looks at Ash. "The thing is, I *wanted* this silly man to hear that noisy old gunshot."

Ash stares at her. "And why, Auntie Lilly, would you do something as . . . *silly* as that?"

"Because I want to . . . draw him into a little game, I guess you could say."

Tommy gapes at her. "What are you talking about?"

After a long pause, racking her brain for another way to say it, she finally replies, "We're gonna kill him."

PART 3

The Sky Is Bleeding

For you have girded me with strength for battle.

—Psalms 18:39

TWELVE

The morning dawns brilliant and clear over the untamed border-
lands southwest of Atlanta. The sunlight drives away the wee-hour
mists that cling to the back roads and piney woods, cleansing the
floodplains with the impact of a cauterizing flame.

It has been mere days since the advent of the epochal floods. In
the absence of a National Weather Service, some local survivors have
named the tropical storm of the previous week Scarlett, as in Scarlett O'Hara, the archetypal petulant, spoiled, volatile southern
belle. But now, with the convivial, late-summer weather, many of
the swampy portions of the farmlands have already started to recede and many of the flooded patches of the roadways have less-
ened, or in some cases, have completely dried up. The only area that
remains in a state of virtual impassability is the long, 150-mile strip
of lowlands paralleling the serpentine twists and turns of the swollen Chattahoochee.

The wide, muddy, prehistoric river—which forms a natural
border between Georgia and Alabama—has become the little
sister to the Mississippi, a primordial main cable running like a
circuit through the American South. Starting its journey way up
in Blue Ridge Mountains, the Chattahoochee tumbles southward
all the way down into the festering coastal plains south of Talla-
hassee, where it ultimately empties into the Gulf. Along the way,

it widens intermittently into a string of narrow lakes, zigzagging somewhat maniacally on its way to the sea.

Historians believe that early Native Americans lived along these verdant, green deltas and berms that line the river's hundred-mile midsection as early at 2000 BC. Archeological evidence reveals that early societies believed the river had mystical powers—and not all of them benign. Nineteenth-century riverboat captains wrote in their journals of ghostly phenomena late at night in the shallows, apparitions of ancient shamans on makeshift rafts performing rituals and ceremonies. In 1828, the captain of the riverboat *Julia Swain* reported seeing an entire one-mile stretch of the river above Franklin turn deep crimson red, filling with the blood of past generations who have met violent ends along the ribbon of wormy-gray water. The twentieth century generated its share of folklore as well, from alleged body dump sites up and down the river to celebrated sunken treasures from the Civil War era being dredged up on a regular basis.

That morning, along the fetid tidal swamps and flooded deltas of the Chattahoochee's north branch, that same intense sun shines down on a modified VW Beetle being pulled by a draft horse through the standing water of a two-lane. The crumbling road weaves its way southward along the flooded landscape, most of its pavement dry enough now to be passable. At the moment, the two occupants of the makeshift horse-cart are idly chatting—despite their language barrier—about the discoveries they've made over the last twenty-four hours. They have seen disturbing things—the remains of thousands of bodies, most of them walkers, littering the farmlands, as well as human casualties, partially devoured horses, and dozens of wrecked vehicles—as though a battle in a larger war had occurred in these parts very recently.

Now these two friends move south at a slow but steady pace, their horse exhausted, foaming at the bit, drenched in sweat and steaming from five straight days of travel.

At length, the man behind the reins breaks the momentary silence, speaking in a measured tone as he gazes out at the flooded banks of the river. "Guess we'll never know for sure what happened back there."

"You saw something, though, did you not?" the younger man says in a heavy accent, his complexion as dark and rough as tree bark from days upon days spent in exile. He is not an unattractive man—his dark eyes sparkle with intelligence, his boyish face creased with world-weary sadness—but even now, after days of camaraderie with the older man, compulsively crisscrossing the lower half of the state, he still gives off an air of the stranger, an alien in an alien land. "I saw it in your face."

The other man shrugs. "I don't know, it could be nothing, or it could be . . . *something*."

"What was it?"

The man at the reins doesn't answer straight away, instead just clucks his tongue pensively at the horse, worried about the animal's fitness. A man well into his sixties, David Stern wears a ratty silk roadie jacket, a Braves cap, and an iron-gray goatee. The burns along the side of his face, which interlace a series of severe scars, have faded, and he now gives off his default appearance, an aging college football coach. All of which masks his desperate loneliness and need to find his sweet Barbara. "Okay," he finally says. "For the longest time, I was convinced that Babs and the others had been taken to Atlanta. We heard the kidnappers talking about heading north, getting back to the city—I just figured they had a place up there. But after kicking around that hellish town for months, barely getting out with my skin intact, I came to believe I was wrong. They must have ended up somewhere else."

"But you don't feel that way anymore? You saw something back there that changed your mind?"

The dark-skinned young man looks tantalized by the possible clue left among the gruesome aftermath of the chase. Perpetually curious, Rafael Rodrigo Machado is a bundle of contradictions. At one time, a notorious drug runner playing two cartels against the middle, a hard-ass who took a prison sentence over snitching, Rafael also has a childlike way about him. In just five short days, he has practically become a surrogate son to David Stern. And Rafael is convinced the feeling is reciprocated by the older man.

"I saw a box," David Stern says at last. "In some of the wreckage."

"A box?"

The older man glances at the younger man. "You ever heard of Ikea?"

"What?"

"I-kee-uh. Furniture store. Scandinavian, I guess." He makes a gesture with his hands. "Big. Big place. All kinds of stuff. Cheap." He gestures again. "Affordable . . . for students, young couples. ¿Comprende?"

Rafael chuckles. "Yeah, I *comprende*. We have one in São Paulo. Fantastic for bookshelves."

David Stern laughs. "Right . . . right . . . and their meatballs are not too shabby either."

"You think this has something to do with your wife?"

David shrugs. "I don't know. It's like an onion, you start peeling it . . . I don't know. There's this big Ikea in the city. I can't remember if I passed it. The truth is, it just sounds like something Babs would appreciate. Something Lilly Caul would do."

"You mean go to an Ikea?"

"Not just *go* to it." David looks at him. "Think about it. They must have all kinds of goodies there, could sustain a group for years. Did you notice that stuff scattered across that field? Lamps, small generators . . . God knows what else. That kinda stuff could all be from Ikea."

"But how do you know it was your wife? How do you know it was them?"

A weary sigh escapes David Stern as he gazes thoughtfully across the fecund tide pools and mossy, contorted landmasses poking out of the floodwaters to the west as the horse splashes through six inches of standing water. The river crested a few days ago, sweeping up untold numbers of dead into the roiling currents and carrying them into deeper waters, where some flailed and sank in clusters, populating the river's depths like schools of bottom-feeding fish, while others collected in the shallows, water bound and stuck in the mire, snarling impotently at the dispassionate sky above them. Now curtains of gnats and water bugs swirl in glistening clouds above the waterlogged necropolis. For some reason, the sight of the hellish, walker-ridden waterway weighs on David Stern as they pass. It twists in his guts, and taunts him. "I don't know anything anymore," he grumbles. "Maybe the only thing I know for sure is that I'm gonna keep looking. She's out there somewhere."

In the sudden silence, Rafael nods, saying nothing, gazing out at the horizon to the south.

They have yet to explore this part of the state. They've been as far as Augusta to the east, and as far as the Florida border to the south, finding plenty of devastation, aimless swarms of the dead, and the ruins of once vibrant little towns. It appears as though the survivor settlements have dwindled, either through attrition or death, or perhaps folks being driven underground (in many cases *literally* underground). David's search parameters—in his typical anal-retentive style—have followed a very logical, grid-like pattern. They have swept three corners of the state without finding a trace of Barbara and the others, and now they are embarking on the last leg.

Now they ride south, mostly in silence, tracing the convolutions of the flooded river for nearly an hour. For most of that time, Rafael looks as though he's working something out in his mind, occasionally glancing over at David, then gazing out at the wasted landscape to the west. Rafael Machado has no girlfriend, his parents long ago deceased, no friends, no surviving family. At last, he says, "Tell me another one."

David Stern smiles to himself. "I never thought I'd run out of them." He purses his lips, snapping the reins and urging the horse through a washed-out patch of road. "Okay. Here's another one for ya." He takes a deep breath, the memory kindling in the back of his mind, warm and somehow reassuring. "We were just kids. This was way back in the prehistoric era when phones had dials and I had all my hair. We were both students at Vanderbilt, and we were going out occasionally. Nothing serious, mind you. She had another boyfriend,

I think. Can't remember his name." He shrugs. "Doesn't matter. Anyway, I wasn't sure about her. The jury was still out, to be honest."

"The jury was what?" Rafael asks, not really comprehending.

David chuckles. "Sorry, another American expression. Like a jury, I had not yet reached a verdict about Barbara. She was cute. No doubt about it. But I wasn't sure she dug me as much as I dug her. You know what I mean?"

Rafael nods. "Yes, absolutely."

"Anyway. One night we go out to a dive bar—a tavern in Nashville—and we get hammered. I mean plastered. We were so drunk we could barely walk outta there. So as we're leaving, I have to pee something awful. She says to me, 'Just go around back in the alley.' I thought it was a good idea, so I did. And I'm standing there in that dark alley, minding my own business, pissing on the wall, when this blue light starts flashing all around me. It was a cop car. And these two patrolmen corner me with their flashlight in my face, and they tell me they have to take me in for public indecency or whatever. I'm stunned. Dizzy. Confused. And I start to go with them when this voice calls out."

Rafael is smiling. "It is Barbara?"

"Bingo." David shakes his head at the memory. "Here she comes, coming down the alley toward us, drunk as a skunk, but keeping it together. And believe me when I tell you, she was a looker back then. Drop-dead gorgeous. In her peasant dress, her curves, her long blond curls and blue eyes—like a Michelangelo painting. And she says to the cops, 'Excuse me, but this is my date, and I have no way to get home without him, and by the way, this is utterly beneath you as law enforcement officers.'"

Rafael grins. "Very nice."

"Yeah, well . . . I cringed at first, thinking they're going to throw the book at me now. But then I see the two cops look at each other, and it was kind of magic. She got to them. Instantly. She won them over. They were shaking their heads, and had these little grins, as she goes on and says, 'And by the way, if I'm not mistaken, you two gentlemen are of the male persuasion, and you have probably urinated yourselves in the great out of doors more times than Carter has pills. If I'm wrong, please throw the book at this man. But if you have any conscience whatsoever, you'll let him off with a warning this time so that he can escort me back to my sorority house safely, which, as you know, is his duty as a gentleman regardless of his urination habits."

Laughing out loud, Rafael nods and says, "This is quite a woman, yes?"

David grins. "Yes indeed, this is quite a woman. In fact, I have to admit, on that night, at that moment, I realized I had fallen big-time for this girl. She was everything I had ever dreamed of. She was . . . my girl. From that point on."

Rafael nods and thinks about it, and they ride another few moments in silence.

At last, David Stern says softly, "She's still drop-dead gorgeous . . . you'll see."

By late afternoon, they've crossed nearly thirty miles of waterlogged roads and dirt paths winding along the flooded Chattahoochee River Valley. They have passed several little river towns along the way—West Point, Fort Valley, Hemdale—which have succumbed to the flooding, their little antebellum cottages and gazebos under twenty feet of water, their locks and dams either submerged or destroyed by the storms. David remembers this part of the river having a dam every mile or so, behind which, in a happier time, families enjoyed boating and fishing.

Now the day has turned as hot as a blast furnace, not a cloud in the pallid sky, the sun an angry god hurling righteous misery on the simmering tidal swamps, the straggling hordes of dead, and the derelict, storm-tossed fishing villages. Visibility is practically unlimited, which makes David Stern all the more nervous. As he pushes the poor draft horse long past its reserves of energy—the animal wheezing and snorting now with each twist in the two-lane—his shifting gaze alternates between the muddy river to his right, and the vast ramshackle farms and shanties of the rural lowlands to his left.

"David!" The sound of Rafael's taut cry gets the older man's attention. "Look! Out on the water—see it? Is that a—?"

David Stern yanks the reins and pulls the sweaty workhorse to a stop. "Son of a bitch, you're right!" The older man twists around and fishes through a rucksack on the backseat, looking for a small pair of field glasses. He finds them, digs them out, and looks through the narrow eyecups. "I'll be a monkey's asshole. . . ."

In the narrow oval field of view, David can just make out a person floating slowly southward on a large scrap of wood, lying on their stomach, head down, motionless, drifting on the lazy currents. At this point in the river, the water line has widened out to almost a thousand feet from shore to shore, the waterborne walkers thinning out as well (David's not certain but this may be one of the many inner lakes that connect the river like a series of baubles on a vast necklace). David can see that the raft is fringed with sticks and trash and weeds that have apparently adhered to it over the course of God knows how long. The person on the raft does not appear to be moving. From this distance, David can't tell if they are simply unconscious or dead.

Rafael speaks up. "Think they're still alive?"

"Can't tell. But if they're dead, they probably would have come back at some point." David fiddles with the focus dial. His stomach clenches with excitement. "Jesus Christ, it can't be . . . it can't be."

"What's wrong? Can't be what? Do you recognize the person, David?"

David can see that it's an adult female sprawled on that ramshackle raft, which looks as though it's been through hell and back. The woman is black, portly, with a bandanna wrapped around her head. Her brown skin is ashen and sunburned, and her big feet—still clad in their trademark clodhopper boots—hang off the end of the raft, the toes partially dragging in the water. David murmurs softly, nervously, with his eyes still pressed to the tiny cups, "Goddamn right I recognize the person!"

David whips the reins. The horse lurches into a gallop. Both men sink into the Bug's seats as the animal pulls the contraption into a headlong charge around a bend in the road. The wheels cobble over roadkill and splash through the muck, the VW rattling so severely it sounds as though it's falling apart. David yells over the noise. "See if you can find that nylon rope—the one we use to hitch the horse to trees at night! I think it's in that green rucksack! Quick, Rafael, quick as you can!"

While Rafael maneuvers himself between the seats and into the cluttered rear compartment, David maintains the horse's speed with regular snaps of the reins while simultaneously keeping tabs on the raft floating along the filthy surface of the river. It may be his imagination, but it seems as though the raft is subtly picking up speed as it nears the south end of the lake.

David sees the road ahead split off to the left, and he yanks the reins accordingly.

"We need to get ahead of her, as far ahead of her as we can!" He hollers this over the noise of the hooves drumming on the wet gravel road and the cargo rattling in the VW's rear seats.

He steers the animal down the cracked, weedy, crumbling Main Street of another small town. It seems as though there are a million of these little river rat nests along the endless serpentines and alcoves of the muddy river. Now David barely notices the modest little houseboats and bait shops passing in a blur. In the heat of midday, the air has an inimitable fishy odor to it—a foul blend of mold, river rot, and walker-stench.

"Is this it?" Rafael has returned from digging in the rear seats. He holds up a large coil of nylon mountaineering-style rope.

"Yes—great—thanks—now look for that second bridle that we rigged for the horse!"

"The one made of belts?"

"Yep—that's the one. Quickly. We're coming up on Lake Harding!"

Rafael gives a nervous nod, and he doesn't ask what the hell Lake Harding has to do with anything, and he doesn't pry into the identity of the mysterious lone passenger on that raft. He simply drops the coil of rope on his seat, turns, and dives back into the warren of crates, supplies, and firearms stashed in the VW's rear seats.

Meanwhile, David urges the galloping horse around a tight corner and down a narrow side road, splashing through deeper water. He can see the distant horizon over the rooftops of half-submerged boat shacks, a bridge maybe half a mile away, and just beyond it, the entire world plunging into the uppermost mouth of skinny Lake Harding. His blood pumps faster and faster as he frantically searches for a way to physically get close to the center of the waterway before the raft reaches that far horizon.

He is approximately a quarter mile ahead of the woman on the raft now.

He fixes his sights on the bridge, and snaps the reins, hastening the horse.

His timing will have to be close to perfect if he is to save Norma Sutters's life.

It's known in geological circles as the Fall Line, a sort of miniature continental divide that runs across Georgia from Augusta to Columbus. Symbolically, it serves as an interstate line of demarcation, a Mason-Dixon-like border between the new south of Atlanta and the old, piquant, badass deep of Valdosta peanut farms and haunted old plantation homes. It is also a physical dividing line where the red clay earth gives way to sandier, grittier soil, and the rivers and streams "fall" from higher to lower elevations.

None of this registers to the woman on the raft, despite the fact that she is still semiconscious as she drifts closer and closer to the threshold of that narrow, earthen-brown lake. Not a single memory of her middle school geography class in Jacksonville flickers across her mind, the lessons of which included topographical features of the south such as the Fall Line and its impact on the farms of the Florida panhandle. Nothing even remotely like panic kindles inside the woman as she floats faster and faster on the muddy currents toward her inexorable destiny.

Dehydrated, flirting with sunstroke from prolonged exposure, soaked to the bone with sweat, vomit, and river water, nearly paralyzed with septic shock, she can hardly lift her head. Even her eyelids feel as though they weigh a ton. Lying tummy-down, her breathing shallow and wheezy, her ribs panging with agony, Norma Sutters feels as though the side of her face is glued to the slimy burnished boat door to which she has clung for over thirty-six hours. She has drifted down more than twenty-three miles of flood-swollen river, come dangerously close to getting devoured more than once, and tried unsuccessfully three separate times to paddle to the shore and climb out of this watery grave. She has prayed . . . talked to herself . . . cried . . . recited the 23rd Psalm countless times both silently and aloud . . . cursed the walkers with language that would bring a blush to the face of a longshoreman . . . sung "Oh What a Friend We Have in Jesus" so many times it made her throw up (twice) . . . spoke aloud the Lord's Prayer forward and backward . . . screamed for help . . . tried to drink river water . . . vomited again . . . hallucinated synchronized swimming mermaids from an old Busby Berkeley movie, including the great Esther Williams, circling her raft . . . cried some more . . . and also, much to her surprise and delight, experienced moments of stunning clarity and soul-stirring serenity.

Up until these last thirty-six hours, Norma had been operating under the assumption that all the beauty had been wrung out of the world with the advent of the plague. The universe, she had thought, had turned bone-stick ugly, and it would remain that way—it had seemed to her—for the rest of her days, which now seem numbered, in fact countable on one finger.

But she was wrong.

Over the last day and a half, when she least expected it, she would see or smell or hear something heartachingly beautiful. Around Bush Head Shoals, the first night, she floated through a cloud of fireflies. Later, she rolled onto her back and counted the stars in the crystalline night sky, engulfed in the scent of gardenias. Her mother had worn a corsage of gardenias to church every Sunday, and the perfumed breezes on the river that night had calmed Norma and given her peace in the face of death. Later, around the mouth of West Point Lake, she had tried to paddle ashore and got cornered by a pack of grotesque, bloated, bog-dwelling walkers. Something distracted them, though, at the last moment, something like a scream, which had allowed Norma to paddle back out into the open water. Minutes later, she realized it was the screech of barn owls that had misdirected the monsters. She floated away thinking of fate, luck, the beauty of an owl, and the Good Lord working in mysterious ways. Not long after that, in the wee-hour darkness, fading in and out of a restless slumber, she heard the distant sound of a deep baritone voice singing a hymn. She believed it was "A Closer Walk with Thee" coming from somewhere over the trees, and it was perhaps the most beautiful thing Norma had ever heard. Or maybe she had imagined it. But that doesn't matter anymore. What really matters is that the water had become her refuge, her prison, and now her grave.

Right then, she manages to crane her neck slightly—she still can't lift her head—and sees that she's approaching a bridge.

Just beyond the bridge she can see the water's edge, maybe a hundred yards away, as straight as a chalk line. At first, she thinks she's hallucinating. How could the horizon line ahead of her be that uniform, that level, that flat? It reminds her of one of those infinity pools she saw years ago on *Lifestyles of the Rich and Famous with Robin Leach.* In the episode, Robin chats idly with George Hamilton on the veranda of Hamilton's lavish Brentwood estate. Norma remembers being fascinated by Hamilton's enormous pool, which seemed to jut out over the San Gabriel Mountains, a magical, heavenly isthmus in the sky. It appeared as though one could literally jump off the diving board into a cloud.

But just as quickly as the memory of that pool flicked across her mind, it disintegrates like a snowflake melting, replaced by another memory. She recalls the lessons from her geography class.

She remembers the church picnics to Ocawallee State Park south of Augusta, and the hikes into the hills, and the babbling brooks careening down the slopes in narrow white-water rapids. She remembers the Ocawallee Falls most of all, her granddad explaining the Fall Line to her. Now her skin crawls as she recognizes the Lake Harding lock and dam—dead ahead of her—one of the largest waterfalls she has ever seen. It's no Niagara, but it's big enough to send her to Glory. Send her to that muddy river in the sky.

Realizing this, she prepares to die. Her soul contracts into a tiny seed inside her, and she clenches her fists, and she closes her eyes. In her mind, she shuts out the world and prays. She speaks to her Lord and Savior, and she asks Him to welcome her as a guest, and to anoint her head with oil. She tells Him that her cup overflows with blessings. And she silently rejoices that His goodness and unfailing love will pursue her all the days of her life, and she will live in His house forever.

Amen.

A voice calls out to her, penetrating her thoughts and piercing the darkness of her last rites.

"Norma!"

At first, she ignores it, passing it off as an auditory hallucination. She doesn't even open her eyes. She's been hearing things for the last twenty-four hours, strange and wonderful and horrifying things. Why wouldn't she hear her own name as she's about to enter the house the Lord? Maybe it's Saint Peter calling out to her, maybe an angel welcoming her to paradise.

"NORMA!"

She opens her eyes. She blinks as though coming awake from a dream.

The raft is just now drifting under a massive, rusty, iron girder bridge. She manages to gaze up into the cobweb-clogged rafters as she passes under it. She sees the graffiti of many generations tracing up the great, mossy pillars rising out of the muddy depths. The raft continues drifting, threading through the middle columns. The soft burble of water lapping against the buttresses, echoing, the raft drifting, drifting . . . drifting toward the opening on the other side of the bridge, a tranquil moment before the death plunge.

"NORMA!—IT'S DAVID!"

This is no hallucination. This is no voice in her head. This is real, a man shouting down at her from the far edge of the bridge, his voice echoing, bouncing around the iron trestles—a real voice, a real person.

In one great, heaving paroxysm, Norma is yanked back into the here and now. *David Fucking Stern?!* All at once she wants to see this guy's gray, goateed face leaning over the ledge. She wants to live another day to see this old curmudgeon with his silk roadie jacket and bad jokes and Yiddish sayings. She wants to go back in time, rewind the tape, rip the page off, and start over with a fresh one!

As the raft approaches the opening, a tangle of dark-brown straps drops down from the sky as if pulled from a magician's hat.

"GRAB THE STRAPS!!" The bellowing call of David Stern reverberates around the iron echo chamber. Norma manages to raise her head. She sees the knotted bundle of leather belts hanging on a tether of rope ten feet away and closing, swaying in the wind, almost within reach. "GRAB THE STRAPS, NORMA!—GRAB 'EM AND HOLD ON!—GRAB 'EM NOW!!"

Norma lifts herself up on one knee, the raft teetering and listing suddenly. She has one chance. She fixes her gaze on that pendulum of straps looming closer and closer. The light shines in her eyes as the raft clears the opening. She reaches up.

She grabs for the bundle of belts, her hand greasy with sweat.

Either due to the force of the current, her exhaustion, her sweat-slick palms, or the awkward and severe tilting of the raft, Norma feels the loop of leather slipping out of her hands as soon as she gets a good grasp on it.

She loses her balance, the raft tips over, and she plunges into the cold, filthy rapids.

THIRTEEN

If she were looking back on it—perhaps writing in a journal, or reporting her impressions and experiences for posterity—she would be hard-pressed to remember just exactly what it was like to careen over the edge of that waterfall. She would recall very few details of sliding across fifteen feet of mossy, slippery rocks, or the subsequent twenty-five-foot drop through chaotic, churning torrents, landing blind and ass-first in the boiling vortex of white water at the base of the falls. She probably would remember only the eerie sound of dropping through that jet-engine din and then plunging into the deep, dark silence.

Suddenly weightless and virtually insensate, she falls through the void for the longest moment. Her leaden body paralyzed with shock, numb, hypothermic, she sinks like a stone. Her eyes remain open and yet sightless, absorbing only the bubbling murk that swirls and enrobes her like a nimbus on her way down.

She begins to see blurry shapes moving around her—dark, brittle, and tattered like bare diseased trees swaying in the eldritch underwater breezes—as she approaches the silt on the floor of Lake Harding.

Landing in the thick, gelatinous mire, she starts to scream. There is no logic to the act—opening her mouth this deep underwater is a suicidal enterprise—but Norma can't help it. She is taken by surprise, the daylight from the surface penetrating the depths just enough to cast the lake bottom in a greenish glow, illuminating something the likes of which she has never seen.

An eruption of bubbles and a strangled, muffled, atonal shriek pours out of her.

She finds herself surrounded by the most lurid, atrocious, ghastly versions of the walking dead she has ever seen—and that's saying something, since the woman has an uncanny gift for observation and has been dodging all manner of undead for the last four years. These creatures have either fallen or wandered into the deeper water over the course of many, many months—years, even—some of them former children, some former adults, and some senior citizens who must have died in the recent floods, all of them oblivious to the eternal prison enclosing them on the floor of the man-made lake. Their bodies have little substance or buoyancy, their flesh blanched of color, much of it eaten away by the fish, leaving behind skeletal remains with barely a suggestion of skin. They are inhuman cairn, as cold and ruined as cancerous, moving shipwrecks. Their emaciated, bony extremities flail and claw in constant slow motion, as though attempting to paddle their way toward food. In some ways, they look like spindly underwater fauna, aquatic plants with blighted leaves and bare limbs oscillating in the languid currents. Only their eyes, many of them rotted away down to the gristle of the sockets, reveal the pathos of the waterlogged human remains. The maggoty white concavities still covet, still implore, still long for something they will never see, never comprehend. Some of them brush their needle-nosed digits against the cold flesh of Norma Sutters's leg, intensifying her terror, making her paddle frantically with little or no oxygen left in her bloodstream, no air left in her lungs, which now begin to fill up with water. The creatures surround her like a school of gruesome, prehistoric, deep-sea denizens with slimy fangs sharpened by the ceaseless flow of currents.

Norma starts to falter, sinking in and out of consciousness, writhing in the jaundiced light, choking on the weight of her own flooded lungs, kicking at the monsters, falling to her back in syrupy, suspended animation as though weightless on some far-flung outer planet. She barely notices the flicker of silver light all around her, the roar of a fully automatic assault rifle sending round after round into the lake from somewhere up above. Norma can't see any of the bullets or their trajectories—she's not even sure that's the source of the sudden introduction of noise and light—but she can see flash after flash, like lightning, accompanied by a muffled thrumming rattle behind the gathering throngs of underwater walkers.

The commotion draws the monsters' attention away from their human prey.

A new shape appears above Norma—that same angelic presence, perhaps, that materialized above the bridge—now looming closer and closer, a celestial being in the green medium of the lake coming to usher her to heaven. Norma heaves and chokes, drowning now as she lies on her back, witnessing the miracle above her. The strangest part is that the angel coming for her has no halo, no cherubs holding its heavenly cape, no golden breastplate of holy armor. This angel is of the earth, visible even in the murky light as it comes for her. Old, gray, gangly, weathered, suntanned, and wearing a very familiar tattered jacket of silver silk.

David Stern grabs Norma by the nape, lifting her off the lake's bottom as though lifting a cat from its napping place. Norma goes limp in the man's arms, not breathing anymore, so cold and numb that she can hardly sense being hauled upward through the layers of drift and cold and filth, upward toward the brilliant green light, upward toward . . . heaven.

Norma blacks out just as she reaches the surface and feels the wind on her face.

She jolts awake, head pounding, lying on her back on the high ground above the access road, smelling pine needles and somebody's atrocious pipe tobacco. She's also coughing convulsively.

She's never coughed this furiously in her life, a combination of hacking and vomiting. Her eyesight is blurry, obscured by tears, but she can sense a man hovering over her, pressing down on her chest between her breasts. She upchucks again as more water is forced out of her lungs.

The man lowers his graying face to hers, and he presses his lips over hers, blowing air into her lungs. She pushes him away, making a yawping noise of protest—a cross between a bark and a squeal—not remembering much of anything other than the waking nightmare of being underwater with demons and angels.

She rolls onto her side and vomits again, a yellow, viscous mixture of stomach bile and river water. She has not eaten in forty-eight hours.

An excruciating moment later, she finally catches her breath.

She rolls back onto her back, slowly coming to her senses. She recognizes the man hovering over her now but she can't quite formulate a greeting yet. She remembers floating on that hideous piece of varnished wood and thinking she was going to die when David Stern had shown up.

Meanwhile, the man in the soaked roadie jacket leans down to blow more air into her windpipe.

"That's enough!" she croaks at him, pushing him away. "You're a married man!"

David grins, tears in his eyes, strands of wet gray hair dangling down in his face. "Thank God, thank God." He strokes her brow. He pulls a canteen from his belt, thumbs it open, and carefully touches it to her chapped, cracked lips. She chokes the water down. She coughs some of it up but keeps most of it down. She looks up and sees David giving her a stupid grin. "You're back," he marvels. "You're back and just as obstinate as ever!"

"It's good to see you, too." Her voice is raspy. She tries unsuccessfully to sit up. Her midsection feels as though it's filled with rusty nails. Her flesh radiates heat from exposure and sunburn. She lies back down, head throbbing. She coughs and lets out a hysterical laugh. "But you try and French kiss me again I'll kick you in the family jewels!"

"Very funny." David shakes his head. His eyes burn with urgency. "Did you find Barbara? Is she okay?"

"Long story. Who's your buddy here?" Norma says, avoiding the question. She notices a second man—younger, dark complexioned, dressed in a hoodie and jeans—standing behind David, looking on nervously, wringing his hands.

"That's Rafael. He's a good man. You'd like him. He's stubborn like you."

Norma nods and takes a deep breath, her lungs and left side panging. She may or may not have cracked a rib going over the falls. "Nice to meet ya, Rafael. I'm Norma Sutters. How'd you hook up with this old fart?"

Rafael Machado steps forward, looking down with a deferential expression. "We met on the road, I guess you could say."

David sighs with exasperation. "The man is being modest again. He saved my life down by Thomaston. I was about to become ko- sher lunch for a convention of roamers, and this man comes out of nowhere with an arsenal, makes the A-Team look like the junior league." His eyes narrow. "Where's Barbara, Norma? Is she all right?"

Norma looks at David. "Help me up." David gently raises her into a sitting position. She coughs and wipes her mouth, and then ges- tures at the canteen. "Mind if I wet my whistle again?" He hands it to her and she drinks. She exhales breathlessly, wiping her mouth, catching her breath. Her eyes are still watering. She takes a girding breath. "I'll tell you one thing, I didn't think there was any way in hell I'd make it out of there." She looks at David. "Miracle you found me."

David licks his lips, kneeling next to her. His eyes blaze with fear. He's a bundle of emotion now. "Did you or did you *not* find Babs? Answer me, Norma!"

"Lilly found her," she says, her voice softening as she studies Da- vid's face. "She was with the kids. They were being kept in an old hospital. Some crazy-ass doctor was using the kids for research purposes. You believe that? They were using the blood of children to find a damn antidote."

"Barbara's alive, though . . . right? She's okay . . . right? Norma . . . ?"

For a long, agonizing moment, Norma looks at the man, and searches for the proper words. She wants to explain everything. She wants to tell David how heroically Barbara Stern had died, how she had always put the kids first, how she was a badass broad whom everybody—even the bad guys—respected if not loved. But before Norma can utter another sound she notices the look on David Stern's face. He has already figured out the truth. From his body language, it's clear he knows that his wife is gone.

He turns away, looks at the ground, his expression starting to collapse as though all the air has gone out of him. He thrusts his hands in his pockets. His shoulders slump, and he purses his lips as if trying to solve a mathematical problem.

Norma looks away. She speaks softly as she studies the stony earth. "Lilly told me how it happened. The hospital got overrun. Barbara fought to the bitter end, even tried to save some of the dudes that had kidnapped her. She was a very special lady. She was good through and through. She was also a fighter."

David nods and keeps staring at the ground and chewing the inside of his cheek. His clothes drip with lake water, his eyes misting over with agony.

Rafael looks on sheepishly, desperate to assist in some fashion. He has a ratty towel in one hand, and he decides to offer it to the man. He approaches cautiously, taps David on the shoulder, and hands him the towel.

David Stern looks at the towel in his hands as though he's holding a dog turd. "I don't need this." He throws it on the ground. "Did I ask you for a towel?" He fixes his cauterizing stare on poor Rafael. "I don't need a fucking towel right now! Okay?" His expression crumbles suddenly with grief and exhaustion, and he looks down, the tears coming. He starts to sob.

Norma lets out a long, anguished sigh. There is nothing left to say or do. She looks down and waits for the worst of it to pass.

"They could be anywhere." Norma sits on the passenger side of the VW Beetle horse-cart, wrapped in a blanket, sipping a cup of instant soup that David whipped up with his trusty acetylene torch and bottled water. "But my guess is, they're back at Woodbury. At least that's where they were headed when I pulled off my graceful stunt of falling into the damned Chattahoochee."

"There's nothing there." David glumly puffs his pipe, the stale cherry tobacco wafting. The Beetle sits motionless on a high ledge overlooking the piney woods west of the river, the horse grazing in the traces. David's voice is hoarse from crying, his eyes red. But somehow, he seems to have worked through the initial shock. He has the vacant stare now of a soldier who has seen too much active duty. "Woodbury's a shell of a town—like everything else in this world. People, families, life in general . . . they're all fucking shells of their former selves."

From outside the driver's window, casually whittling a small branch with his Buck knife, Rafael speaks up. "How far away is this Woodbury?"

David shrugs. "I don't know . . . maybe twenty miles, maybe less. Fifteen, maybe. But why bother going to Woodbury when there's plenty of nothing to be found out *here*."

It's Rafael's turn to shrug. "I'm just thinking . . . what could it hurt to go back? See whether or not your friends have returned?"

David puffs his pipe ruefully. "The way I left the place, it's probably crawling with dead by now. The barricade along Folk Avenue is gone, burned down with the rest of the train yard."

Norma sips her soup. "What about the tunnels? The sewer system?"

David shakes his head. "Part of the underground has completely collapsed into itself. At the end of Main Street. There's this crater, looks like a bomb was dropped. Like a little mini Hiroshima."

"What happened?"

"The fire did it. I guess. Maybe due to all the activity down there, trying to build a home in those tunnels. Maybe it weakened the original structure. All I can tell you is, for the most part, the underground is now either caved in or overrun with walkers." He looks like he may break down again. He wipes his eyes, sniffs back the pain, and gives them a cockeyed, mirthless smile. "Other than that, it's a perfect place to raise a family."

Norma sighs. She takes another sip and shivers. She feels hot one moment, cold the next. She may be running a fever. Her side pangs with each breath. "Is there *any* part of town that's still in one piece? Still livable?"

David Stern shakes his head, skeptically puffing his pipe. "There's a part of Flat Shoals Road, some of the row houses are still standing. But that part of town's been picked clean. It's pretty grim, Norma."

"What about the crops, all that work we did on the speedway? Lilly told us some of the corn crop could come back."

"Burned to the ground." He takes the pipe out of his mouth and spits. "Nothing's coming back, Norma."

"And Lilly's public gardens? All the plantings we did on the square?"

"All gone. Basically scorched earth. Completely razed. It was the only way to keep the hop heads and the crazies from taking it over."

Norma finishes her soup, wipes her mouth, and stuffs the cup into a knapsack at her side. She takes a deep breath and thinks about Woodbury for a moment. "You know, the truth is, for all we know, Lilly and them might have already been there and gone by now."

David looks at her. "You think they might have gone back to Ikea?"

Norma lets out a sigh. "No sir, I don't think that's a possibility."

"Why?"

Norma thinks about it. "Because Ikea was just a temporary fix for Lilly."

"What do you mean?"

"It just isn't Woodbury."

David smokes and processes. "Yeah, I know what you mean. She has a major thing for that little Podunk town. Doesn't she?"

"That's an understatement," Norma says with a dry little chuckle.

"Babs and I thought she was crazy at first. We'd been through so much, been there since the Governor took over. God, how long ago was that? Three years, three and a half years now?" He swallows the melancholy pang, staring wistfully into the middle distance as if the memories live there. He shakes off the sorrow and spits again. "I'll tell you one thing, though, something about that little town sunk a hook into Lilly. Like it came to mean something more than just a place to wall yourself off from the walkers."

"Tell me about it," Norma says softly. "For the last few months, ever since she saw the ruins, she would talk about the town like it was this magical place, this Shangri-la that had to be brought back from the ashes. Lord knows, I tried to reason with her. Tried to talk her out of going back there. But she'd get this gleam in her eye anytime anybody mentioned the place."

"So I take it you would have preferred to stay back at Ikea?"

"We had it *made* there, David. We had food, we had electricity, shelter, and we were on an upper floor. We were safe up there."

David Stern taps his pipe on the side of the horse-cart, thinking about it. "How long would that have lasted, though? Think about it."

"Look. Nothing lasts, nowadays. I'll give you that. But you find a place like that, you hold on to it for as long as you can."

David looks at her. "Then why the hell did you come with her?"

Norma sighs. "Lilly Caul has a way of . . . winning a person over."

"That she does."

"I ain't ashamed of the fact that I trust her, I believe in her. You gotta believe in something. Besides, I guess I kinda see her point about Ikea being sort of a prison. On the other hand, a small town, if you can make it work"—she pauses, looks at David, thinks about it, shrugs—"you can breathe, you can feel almost normal."

David looks at the woman, really looks at her, maybe for the first time since they reunited. "Maybe she's right, Norma. Who are we to say?"

Norma shrugs again. "This day and age, you could live in a lot worse places than Woodbury."

David shoves his pipe in his pocket. Something changes in his expression. The change is subtle at first, but the grief seems to mutate. The furrowed brow narrows into something more like determination. He studies Norma. "We'd be starting from scratch essentially."

"Where else are we gonna go?"

"It'd be dangerous as hell, Norma. We don't know what we're going to find there."

"What am I gonna do? Build another raft and float down to the Gulf of Mexico?"

"It would be backbreaking work, and we'd be exposed for a long time, really exposed to all manner of shit from the wastelands."

"It's worth the risk, you ask me."

"The barricades alone would take us weeks to repair, and we'd have to find a hell of a lot more fuel than we got in that storage bin."

Norma dismissively waves her plump hand. "I've been in far tougher situations. You try living alone in the choir loft of your church for eighteen months when the rest of your congregation wants to feast on your damn guts."

David exhales a pained sigh, turns, and ambles over to the edge of the hill. Thinking it over, he gazes out through a gap in the foliage at the verdant river deltas drying in the sun. The flood levels have already receded significantly, leaving behind tangled knots of old growth deadfall, human remains, pockets of roamers, and ground cover growing so profusely one can almost see it spreading into the nooks and crannies of the landscape. The air has an almost pleasant smell of fishy decay and fecund earth. David looks down and murmurs so softly his voice is barely audible. "I suppose Babs would have wanted us to go back."

Across the clearing, sitting in the Beetle, Norma smiles to herself.

Tommy Dupree doesn't see the shiny object through the trees until he passes out of earshot of the others. Ostensibly, he has wandered away from their encampment to look for a stream or perhaps signs of an underground spring. They are down to their last drops of drinking water, and Lilly worries about consuming water from the stagnant tide pools. During normal times, dysentery is a horrible ordeal, but if somebody comes down with the trots out here, it's a death sentence. Dehydration can be deadly, bringing on seizures and, ultimately, heart failure. They are also completely out of fuel, despite the fact that they have properly patched the bullet hole and conserved the last ounces in the tank. Their plan will be useless if they can't locate any more fuel. The vehicle is the lynchpin—pivotal to their plot to draw Spencer-Lee Dryden into a trap and remove him from the earth. All of which is why Tommy now moves so quickly and stealthily through the thick foliage, snaking his way down a gradual slope toward a dry riverbed.

Shirtless, a bandanna around his head, his flesh sunburned and scarred with scratches—both new and old—he bats at the thicker branches with his rusty machete as he moves toward the natural trench cut through the sandy earth fifty yards away. He carries a spare Ruger .22-caliber pistol—on loan from Lilly, its silencer screwed on to avoid attracting attention—tucked into the back of his belt, safety off, mag chock-full.

The day has turned muggy, blistering hot in the sun, the air in the forests along the Chattahoochee sultry and hectic with gnats and cottonwood fluff. The motes drift lazily through rays of sunlight, which filter in radiant beams down through the high oak boughs, making Tommy itch and slap at mosquitos. Filmed in a layer of sweat and grime, he worries about the noise attracting walkers. He saw a few about a hundred yards back, burrowing into the carcass of a deer, gorging on entrails, too distracted to hear or smell him. Now he moves as quietly as possible through a narrow space between two needle palms.

That's when he sees the silver metal gleaming through a break in the foliage twenty-five yards away.

He freezes. He crouches down. His hand goes instinctively back to the beavertail grip of the .22 in his belt. He stares. His throat goes dry with panic. The foliage is too thick for him to be sure, but the rust-pocked silver metal peeking through the netting of branches just beyond the other side of the dry creek bed looks so familiar, so specific, it makes his heart pulse in his ears, a snare drum beating out a syncopated rhythm to his thoughts.

For a moment, he remains crouched in that cloud of gnats, paralyzed with indecision, staring at that shiny metallic harbinger silently screaming at him through the trees. He squints and tries to see the front end of the thing, or perhaps the red taillights of the rear end, but all that's visible is that small patch of battered silver metal, slightly curved, ridged, and riveted along the seams.

He hesitates, his arms and legs seized up with paralysis. His mind swims with an internal debate: Should he finish this whole drama himself right now—maybe becoming a hero—or should he go tell Lilly about it like a pussy? What would Lilly do?

Right then, Tommy Dupree realizes what he has to do—the smart play, the grown-up thing—and he pulls the pistol. This is the only way. That son of a bitch is probably resting right now inside that beat-up trailer, secure in the knowledge that he's hidden behind the cover of trees and vegetation. If Tommy hesitates or takes the time to go get help, the silver monster could be gone. If he gets too close, Dryden could hear him.

No, the only way to be sure is to attack right now, from this vantage point. That's what Tommy's dad would have done. That's what Bob Stookey and Musolino and Burt Stankowski and Eve Betts would have done. He kneels behind a fallen pile of timber and pulls back the slide, making sure a bullet is seated properly in the chamber. He picks up a small stone and tosses it at the thing. The rock hits the silver bulwark with a metallic thunk. He raises the gun, steadying himself against the hollow log, waiting for a door to burst open.

Nothing happens. He aims at that silver metal peeking out of that wall of undergrowth, holds his breath, and squeezes the trigger.

Once, twice, three times he fires—just to be sure—the recoil jamming his upper arm into the socket of the shoulder. Each blast makes a muffled bang, not much louder than a large twig snapping. He can see through the blue haze the silver metal trailer twenty-five yards away punctured in three spots, something pouring out of each bullet hole. Is it blood?

He cautiously approaches the target, hopping over the dry streambed, scaling the other side, and then weaving through the thick foliage with his gun in both hands, ready to fire at a moment's notice. He sees dark liquid pouring out of the holes in the silver metal. Pushing his way through the wall of scrub and spindly branches, he emerges into a small clearing of bare earth.

He gapes at the massive silver thing leaking fluids where the bullets have punctured it.

"Oh my God," he utters under his breath, staring and staring.

FOURTEEN

Lilly Caul is opening the last can of peaches that survived the pandemonium in the soybean fields when she hears a commotion coming from the woods. Instinctively, she springs to her feet, the faint ache in her lower back panging. She had found a bottle of Advil in the Escalade's glove box earlier that day and swallowed four of the tablets, which has stanched the worst of the pain, but it still simmers. She grabs the AR-15, swings the gun toward the noise, and calls over her shoulder to Ash and the children, who all sit on a semicircle of stumps and deadfall logs arranged around the clearing. "Everybody, stand up, grab the hand of the person next to you, and head back to the car very quietly, very quickly."

Some of the children look up, their attention yanked away from digging in their rucksacks, looking for the last morsels of food. Others, tending to their bumps and scrapes, glance up with a start. The clearing is a square acre of bald earth, sandy and sunbaked, bordered on all sides by a natural barrier of densely packed sugar maples and white oaks. The Escalade is parked along one side, camouflaged with palm fronds and large, leafy branches. Bethany Dupree, the oldest in the group, stands up and blurts, "Is it walkers?"

Ash has already risen off her perch, grabbed the Mossberg 12-gauge, and aimed the muzzle at the figure bursting out of the trees. "Is that—?"

"Wait, hold on." Lilly sees the scrawny, shirtless figure coming toward them, waving excitedly. "False alarm, gang, sorry, everybody relax." The relief in Lilly's tense voice is all too apparent to her own ears.

The stress of the past twenty-four hours, playing cat and mouse with Spencer-Lee Dryden, has taken its toll. The mixture of exasperation, rage, sheer terror, and bone-deep frustration has dogged Lilly at every turn, every false sighting, every failed attempt at luring the lunatic into a trap. Initially, the plan had involved trundling through the ruined, flooded back roads of Whitewater Estates, during which time she would squeeze off regular blasts of the AR-15 in order to draw the madman in, but Lilly soon realized she was merely wasting bullets. Later, she had tried circling back toward the main artery of Highway 85, thinking Dryden would stick to the four lanes whenever possible. But the divided highway proved to be practically impassable, a virtual junkyard of mossy, weed-whiskered, fossilized carapaces of wrecked cars. Now Lilly has shifted her strategy a third time, attempting to stay put, pitch camp, and bait the trap with the odor of campfire smoke and the intermittent revving of the Escalade's enormous engine, which, so far, has yielded little results other than wasting fuel and drawing walkers.

Every once in a while they hear a large vehicle somewhere nearby, drifting on the breeze—more than likely Dryden's battered crew cab and trailer—and they all spring into action, taking their places and preparing to ambush the man. But the noise invariably drifts away like a ghost on the wind. But somehow, for some reason, Lilly knows that Dryden has not given up the search for them. His malignant presence is pervasive, just out of sight, just beyond the horizon, as powerful as the smell of walkers on the breeze. The others know this as well. It is unspoken, a vein of anxiety running through every conversation, every attempt to make long-range plans. They know Dryden must be destroyed, he must be surgically removed from the earth like a cancerous tumor.

All of which is why Lilly feels so jumpy as Tommy Dupree approaches the campsite, breathlessly coming up to Lilly, stammering,

"I thought he was here, I thought it was him, I was sure of it, I saw the silver metal, I saw it through the trees and I fired at it, but I was, I was—"

"Okay, slow down, Tommy." Lilly turns to Ash. "Ash, take the kids back to the SUV for a second." She turns back to Tommy. "C'mere." She takes him aside, leading him behind a small stand of oaks. "Take a breath, tell me exactly what happened."

Tommy swallows air, trying to get his bearings and calm down enough to make sense. His shirttail is ripped in several places. "You won't believe what I found. I thought for sure it was that silver trailer he was driving. But it wasn't a trailer at all."

"You said you fired at it? What was it?"

He looks up at her, still trying to catch his breath. "It's not far from here, let me show you." He turns and starts toward the woods. "C'mon, it's not far."

"Wait a second, hold on!" She grabs his arm, pulls him back. "Where are you taking me? What did you shoot at? What are you up to?"

He gives her a strange grin. "Hint—we should probably bring a few of those plastic gas containers we got under the back deck."

The boarded, slumped buildings sit at the end of a dirt road, their opposite walls connected to a weathered, gray dock protruding out across the brackish water of a large inlet. The inlet's scummy surface—still swollen and high from the floods—buzzes with dragonflies and water bugs. But it's not the ruins of a deserted pier on which Lilly now latches her awed gaze.

"Holy fucking shit," she marvels under her breath as she circles the massive storage tank now punctured with three fresh bullet holes. Pieces of Tommy's shirttails are visible stuffed into the holes.

The boy proudly leads Lilly around the metal monolith with that weird, crooked grin on his face. "You gotta admit, from a distance it looks a lot like that shitty silver trailer. But check this out." He goes over to the storage tank and pulls one of the cloth plugs.

Yellow liquid shoots out of the hole, and he catches a few drops in his palm.

Lilly takes a closer look, smells the liquid, and detects the sweet, delicious, life-affirming fragrance of high-test gasoline. She looks at the boy. "Oh my God, you did it. You just put us back in action." She drops her container, grabs the boy, and pulls him into a tight, loving embrace. "Great work, Junior."

"Thanks," the boy says softly, his voice muffled by her shoulder pressed against his face. He hugs her back with reciprocal emotion. He closes his eyes, soaking in the human contact, the love, the protectiveness, the longing to have a family again. He loves this woman unconditionally. He would walk into hell for her.

"C'mon," she says, finally releasing him from her embrace. "Let's get as much as we can into these babies."

She grabs the container, unscrews the cap, and then holds it up under the spewing fuel. Tommy does the same, pulling a second piece of cloth from a second bullet hole, the nectar spurting profusely. Gas flows into both containers—each holding five gallons— until the level reaches the brim and bubbles over.

Lilly puts her container down, replaces the cap, and then thumps the side of the massive tank with her knuckles. "Sounds like the damn thing is almost full. How the hell did this end up untouched for so many years?"

"I know, right?" Tommy fills his container and sets it down, screwing the cap back on. "Too bad we can't take all of it with us."

"I'm thinking there's another way." Lilly looks around the boat dock, a dragonfly buzzing past her. The drone of crickets is almost jet-engine loud, the sun hot on the back of her neck. "We could camo the hell outta this thing, draw a map, and come back to this place in the future." She surveys the neighboring foliage. "C'mon, gimme a hand."

She starts gathering up branches, palm fronds, old timber, fence wire, and anything else she can drape over the huge storage tank. Tommy finds a soggy piece of canvas that was once stretched over a boat, designed to winterize watercraft. He drags it over and throws it across one side of the silver beast.

They work for another fifteen minutes or so, disguising the storage tank as best they can, when Lilly hears something weird drifting over the treetops to the east. She stops. Putting her finger to her lips, she shushes Tommy and cocks her head and listens closely to the noise.

"Is that somebody screaming?" Tommy asks nervously, glancing up at the colorless sky.

"Yeah, I think it is." Lilly listens to the echoing shrieks. They echo for a moment over the river, then fade. They sound as though they're coming from a great distance, maybe miles away. "Could be somebody getting swarmed out there."

The screams start up again, horrible keening sounds that set Lilly's teeth on edge.

Tommy frowns. "Usually, somebody getting swarmed, the screams will stop for good. You know what I mean? Because the person is getting . . . you know."

"I guess I follow you, yeah."

"What I'm saying is, you don't hear them start up again like this."

In the time it has taken to complete this last exchange, the screams have stopped and started again, and now the noise deteriorates into garbled, watery sobbing, praying, begging.

Lilly listens closely to this for a second. She looks at Tommy and says, "You definitely don't hear people begging walkers to stop." She grabs her container. "It's gotta have something to do with—"

"*Dryden?*" Tommy utters the words as though they're a curse. He grabs his container. He looks at Lilly.

"Oh my God, do you think it's—?"

Lilly has already started back down the embankment toward the creek bed. "We gotta warn the others," she calls over her shoulder. "This might be our only chance."

Tommy hurries after her, lugging at least thirty pounds of fuel. They're going to need it.

By all normal laws of physics and biology, Frank Steuben should be dead by now. The human body simply isn't equipped to withstand the kind of trauma inflicted upon Steuben's squat, muscular frame in the explosion that rocked Jamie Quinn's Jeep. The secondary fireball that erupted after the initial impact of Spencer-Lee's RPG—instantly killing Quinn and Caleb Washburn—had catapulted Frank Steuben out the rear of the vehicle on a wave of concussive fire, slamming him into a fence post, and then tossing him to the ground in a flaming heap.

Somehow, Steuben had managed to roll several yards until the fire had snuffed itself out, and there he lay for countless agonizing minutes, his spine fractured in two places, his left thigh impaled on a two-foot shard of wood. One leg and a large portion of his left side had been seared by third-degree burns, and his blood loss was significant. But Frank Steuben is a tank, a human Humvee. Gripped in shock and paralysis, he lay there, helpless, while a swarm of biters passed him on either side like distracted commuters brushing past a homeless man on a train platform. Through some quirk of fate or random act of God, the walkers left Steuben alone. Maybe they thought he was already dead and turned. Regardless of the reasons, though, the former landscaper from Arkansas with the huge belly and ham-hock arms managed to survive long enough to be saved by the tall man in the face bandage.

Twenty-four hours of dreamlike floating followed—with cycles of mind-numbing pain followed by narcotic relief—as Steuben lay in the rear seats of the beat-to-hell crew cab driven by this two-bit Phantom of the Opera with the weird mummified face. The man behind the wheel exhibited the scars of old burns as well as fresh ones as he chased after Ash and Lilly Caul and the others, murmuring insane nonsense and singsong diatribes.

In his twilight state, Steuben had difficulty hearing just exactly what this southern-fried Phantom was mumbling about, his psychotic ramblings muffled by the bloody face bandages. But one thing was clear. The man wanted to keep Steuben alive as long as possible as the pursuit of the women and children dragged on into the next day. Every hour or so, the bandaged man would pull over, bring the crew cab to a stop, dig in his huge doctor's bag, and administer another injection to Steuben's left arm. The substance in the hypodermic—whatever it was—had both a painkilling effect as well as a hypnotic aspect. The cool numbing agent would course through Steuben like mother's milk, lulling him into a woozy state of dislocation and confusion. But at least the pain would momentarily be stanched.

Then, something changed in the driver's mercurial demeanor.

Early this morning, frantically searching the Chattahoochee River Valley along the deserted, ramshackle backwaters of Franklin and Whitewater Estates, the man behind the wheel had stopped administering the drug. The pain had crept back into Frank Steuben's consciousness like a wild dog returning to its bone, gnawing at the wound in his leg with more and more fervor. Pain can come in a startling array of flavors, textures, and colors. Some comes in low, throbbing, purple aches. Other pain pinches and shoots like fireworks behind the eyes, sharp and metallic. The pain in Steuben's leg—where the massive splinter of fence wood still protruded like a signpost—had begun to scream a dissonant high soprano of agony.

Somewhere, deep down in his flailing consciousness, Frank knew he only had a little while longer to live. He had been around heavy machinery enough to know an injury as catastrophic as this would almost instantly lead to shock, hypovolemia, and sepsis, all of which were now taking him down the long tube toward the permanent dark. But somehow, in some miracle of stubborn bullish strength, as well as the cocktail of whatever this lunatic had been pumping into him, he still clung to semiconsciousness, his vision blurry, fixed on light at the end of the tunnel that was quickly closing around him.

Now Frank is dimly aware that the bandaged man has stopped the crew cab on a low stretch of bare earth along a ditch and has come around to the side door where he can get better leverage on Steuben's mangled leg.

"Gonna have another little talk, you and I," the man had said only moments ago in a voice that was suddenly crystal clear behind the gauze. "Gonna ask you a few questions. No big deal. Just some background information." He had paused then for dramatic effect. "If you answer honestly—and I'll know if you're lying, believe me, I'm good at that part—then I'll give you relief." He had held up the hypodermic at that point, its needle dripping a pearl of blessed nectar. "But if you don't comply, I will bring you pain the likes of which you have never dreamt."

At that point, Spencer-Lee Dryden grasped the end of the wood sticking out of Steuben's leg and wrenched it backward hard like a lever.

The shriek that had burst out of the stocky, muscular, tattooed former landscaper at that point could have easily been mistaken for the caterwaul of an animal being skinned alive—a high, razor-sharp squeal—which issued spontaneously from deep within Frank Steuben's lungs. The pain slammed through Steuben with all the garish hues of a kaleidoscope in his brain, stealing his breath, sending his testicles retracting up into his groin and causing him to shit his pants.

A series of calls and responses followed. Spencer-Lee would holler out a question, and Steuben would attempt to answer it as sincerely and completely as possible with his breathless stammer. Spencer-Lee asked the name of the woman with Ash—the alpha girl with the auburn hair pulled back in a ponytail—and Steuben told him it was Lilly Caul. At certain points, the pain would get the best of Steuben, and he would stumble over his answer, and Spencer-Lee would yank back on the wood again, eliciting another series of screeching yelps and garbled pleas for mercy.

Most of the answers Frank had learned from either Ash or Quinn over the last two years of living in Haralson. He knows Lilly Caul casually—he had worked with her on the railroad restoration project the previous year—and he likes her. She's a no-nonsense kind of gal, a natural leader with a soft touch that Frank Steuben can appreciate. He had run his landscaping company in Little Rock in a similar manner. He was tough but fair with his employees. He sees that same integrity in Lilly. But the truth is, he owes the woman nothing. Extreme pain will do that to a person. It denatures heroism into pure expediency. It purifies intent into simple survival instinct.

Now Frank Steuben struggles to hear the current question through the noise of his agony. His vision has blurred. He sees only a ghostly figure in a mask of white gauze hovering over him. He can't see the man's lips, and can only hear the muffled words faintly through the breathing hole in the Betadine-stained face bandages. "P-p-please . . . s-s-say it again," Steuben begs. It is now almost impossible for Steuben to decipher that nasally, disembodied voice. "I . . . c-can't . . . un-der-s-s-stand . . . the . . . *question*."

"Oh for chrissakes!" The tall man reaches up to his face and picks at the corner of the bandages. It takes him a second or two but he finally manages to carefully peel back the multiple layers of gauze that have adhered to his burns over the last few days, now pulling on the thing with enough force to remove it. The bandage comes off with a sticky, gluey crackling sound. He tosses the grotesque wad of gauze away with the ease of a snake shedding its own skin. "There! You happy now?"

The face looking down at Steuben is straight out of a nightmare. Much of it scorched beyond recognition, with flesh the consistency of axle grease, it stares through bloodshot eyes set deep in singed craters. Much of Dryden's hair is burned off, the rest reduced to the bristles of a hog's hide. One corner of his mouth has been burned away by the fire, leaving behind a row of exposed yellow teeth gleaming in a perpetual grimace.

He aims the hypodermic at one side of his face, and plunges the needle into his own jaw, injecting enough of the agent to numb any residual pain. "Okay," he says. "One last time." His words are clear now and yet slightly impeded by the mangled corner of his mouth. "I'll ask you where the girl named Lilly is originally from—the name of the town or the settlement where she's been living—the place they're probably heading back to as we speak. What is it?"

Steuben feels himself sinking into the folds of the backseats. He knows the answer, but his reflexes are slow now, his bodily functions failing. He can feel the warmth of his bladder emptying in his pants. He tries to pronounce the name of that little village plopped down smack-dab in the middle of nowhere about seventy-five miles south of Atlanta but can only make a faint, breathy noise that sounds more like, "Wwwwuhd . . . wwwuh . . . wwhh."

Spencer-Lee Dryden leans down so closely that Steuben, even in his debilitated state, can smell the pus and cheesy odors of infection radiating off the scorched face. The smell of Spencer-Lee's breath is caustic, sulfurous. "You can do it now, Bubba," Spencer-Lee urges softly. "Tell me the name of the town where this woman is from . . . that's all I need you to do. No big deal."

"Wwwwwuhhhd . . . wwwuh."

Spencer-Lee grasps the end of the wooden sliver and prepares to once again yank the thing.

"Wwwwoodbury!—W-w-woodbury!—The n-name of the t-town is Www-w-woodbury!"

Spencer-Lee lets go of the splinter and gives the dying man a satisfied nod. "There ya go, Bubba! That wasn't so hard, now was it?"

Steuben feels himself sinking into the seat, which has become almost liquid, the light fading to black all around him as though the day is on a rheostat and some godlike being is dialing it down. In his imagination, Frank Steuben sinks through the upholstery, down through the chassis, into the ground, sinking, sinking into the cold abyss of the earth. He doesn't even register the fact that Spencer-Lee Dryden has drawn a small 9-millimeter pistol from a hip holster. Steuben can barely feel the cool, oily touch of the gun's muzzle on his temple. He can hardly make out the sight of a burned face looming over him, twisting into an expression of sympathy.

"Good night, sweet prince," the face says, the voice almost tender.

The blast makes a popping sound, a single bullet penetrating

Frank Steuben's skull, turning the dial, once and for all, mercifully, to Off.

It takes a minute or two for Spencer-Lee to hear the unexpected noise echoing over the wetlands to the west.

At first, he's too busy disposing of Frank Steuben's remains, dragging the body from the rear of the crew cab and dumping it in the marshlands behind the truck. He stands there for a moment, wiping his hands on a towel, watching the portly body slowly sink into the mire, the oily bubbles punctuating the end of the man's existence on this earth.

Before the plague, Spencer-Lee Dryden had testified in several grand jury hearings involving local mafiosi and hometown hoodlums who had tried to muscle the Atlanta city council. He had studied transcripts of evil deeds, bodies being dumped, assassinations of rival gang leaders, and various and sundry instances of intimidation, violence, and blackmail. He had become obsessed with protecting his constituency from these bad elements. He grew to see the voters in his district as family, and when it came to protecting his family, Spencer-Lee was relentless. He would do anything—short of murder—to shield his people from the wicked and the immoral. And if he were honest with himself, he probably could be pushed to commit atrocities, including homicide, if it meant protecting the ones he loved. Nevertheless, Spencer-Lee doesn't see the death of Frank Steuben as murder. The man was suffering horribly. The head shot was an act of mercy. Now, Spencer-Lee returns to the crew cab, flips open the map case, pulls out a dog-eared road map of Georgia, and spreads it open on the middle seat.

He remembers passing through the little town of Woodbury a few times when he was younger, taking shortcuts through the deep country while on business trips and vacations to Panama City, Florida. He recalls very little about the place—the village was nothing special to a big-shot politician from the city, pretty much just a wide spot in the road—and now he sees on the map why nobody really ever talked much about it. There's no main interstate within miles of the town, and many of the railroads that once intersected in the train yards of the little hamlet have now long since gone the way of the dinosaurs.

Perhaps this is why Woodbury—postplague—has become the best-kept secret among the survivor class. Maybe the remote, middle-of-nowhere quality is what makes the place so secure. The very thought of finding a gem of a place that could be a fortress against the swarms and the bandits and all the misfortunes of the plague-ridden tobacco fields touches something deep within Spencer-Lee. His eyes well up as he thinks of his sweet Sally, gone now, perished in such a meaningless, incomprehensible way. He thinks of the children—his extended family—out there somewhere. They have to be close. They may have already gone to Woodbury. Spencer-Lee has always been a deeply intuitive family man—despite the fact that he and Sally never had any children of their own. He always had a sixth sense when he came to his loved ones. He could feel their presence—even when they were out of his reach, out of his sight.

He is thinking about this psychic connection when he hears the faint echo of a revving engine.

At first, he thinks he's imagining it. The noise wavers and warbles, drifting on the breeze. He turns and cocks his head toward the west. He listens more closely, and sure enough, the unmistakable sound of an engine—a large one—can be heard on the wind, revving and revving, over and over, as though stuck. It makes the hair on the back of Spencer-Lee's neck stand at attention. Ashley Duart and her arrogant accomplice, Lilly Caul, had fled the accident scene in a Caddy—an SUV—perhaps an Escalade.

This sounds like just such a vehicle stuck in the mud a mile or so away.

Spencer-Lee climbs behind the wheel, fires up the engine, shifts it into gear, and carefully maneuvers the crew cab across the swampy, flood-swollen deltas, heading in the general direction of the noise.

FIFTEEN

Tommy Dupree crouches in the tangled undergrowth on the edge of the encampment with the gnats and the centipedes, his hands sweaty with nervous tension. His heart pounds. His legs cramp. His stomach roils. He grips the stock of the Winchester Model 70—the barrel of which rests on an adjacent log—clutching it so tightly his knuckles are bloodless. In his mind, he goes over Lilly's plan again and again. He will not let her down. This is his chance to prove himself once and for all.

Through a narrow gap in the foliage, he can see the Escalade—about twenty-five yards away, on the opposite side of the clearing—parked on a marshy patch of ground that runs along a weedy, neglected access road. Gouts of carbon monoxide cough out of the tailpipe as Ash guns it repeatedly. It took many anxious minutes to switch the vehicle over to RWD and jack up the rear, rigging the lift apparatus so that it would blend in with the weeds. The elevated rear end and disengaged wheels now create the illusion that the SUV is stuck, the rear tires spinning wildly in the mud, throwing miniature wakes of brackish muck into the air.

The rest of the plan relies on a theory deeply held by Ash as well as Tommy's marksmanship.

"There are more variables here than I would like, sport," Lilly had cautioned the boy only moments ago. "The thing could go to hell quickly, it could deteriorate instantly. The man is bug-fuck crazy."

Tommy nodded. "So he's the most unpredictable of all the variables?"

"Ash is highly confident that he would never harm a child, so this is our best shot."

"I'll take him down, Lilly, don't worry," Tommy had assured her then. "I'll make it count."

"Just don't forget, you're gonna be all by your lonesome at the sniper position—you got no backup."

"I'll get the job done."

This conversation had taken place only moments ago, but now Tommy feels as though he has been crouching in this incessant cloud of insects for days. His knees and upper thighs throb painfully. He's reminded of the era he played catcher on his little team, and how much he hated it. He loathed the constant squatting. It killed his knees. He tries to clear his mind and focus on the shot. He holds the rifle the way Bob Stookey had taught him—breathing deeply through his nose, body as relaxed as possible, both eyes open, one eye defocused, one eye peering through the scope.

In the telescopic realm of the crosshairs, he can see the Escalade on the edge of the road, gleaming in the sun, Ash hunched at the wheel, her jaw set and tense as she pretends to struggle with the supposedly stuck rear wheels. The ruse is working. Tommy can hear a second car coming up the winding delta road. He can't see it yet but can sense it coming at a slow, steady, discreet speed. *He thinks he's sneaking up on us,* Tommy marvels silently. *He thinks he's going to surprise us.* Through the scope Tommy studies Ash.

He can't imagine how much she hates this guy. This asshole took the life of her boyfriend—the father of her adopted children—and kept her prisoner for months. In fact, ever since the RPG had wasted Jamie Quinn, Tommy has been waiting for Ash to have a full-blown mental breakdown. But the woman is tough. She has remained strong for the kids. Tommy thought for sure that *she* would be the one to kill this creep. But now it's up to Tommy. It's all up to him. The weight of responsibility presses down on him now.

The smell of rotting fish drifts on the breeze, mingling with the mossy odors of the woods. Tommy keeps wondering what point Lilly was making when she had warned Tommy that he would be "all by his lonesome" once he took his position. But now, squatting in the thick odors of decay and ground-rot, he thinks he knows what she meant. The feeling of being exposed courses through the boy on a wave of gooseflesh. Nobody's watching his back, and it makes the skin on his nape prickle with terror.

The presence of the dead is always pervasive—ever-present outdoors—but right now the sensation of danger looming behind him is almost overwhelming. Tommy can hear strange noises in the deeper woods back there. He can smell rancid meat. Since the weather has changed, and the floodwaters have greatly receded, Tommy has noticed odd noises coming from the forests and gulleys along the Chattahoochee: dripping, snapping, crackling, shifting noises, as though the entire valley is settling, rearranging itself. Like a haunted house. Tommy can remember trying to ignore the bloated darkness behind his open closet door in his childhood bedroom as he slept alone at night. The more he tried to ignore that darkness, the more terrifying that half-open sliding door—and the unknown shadows behind it—would become. He feels that way right now, as the rumble of a heavy-duty pickup truck draws closer and closer.

He presses his brow into the scope's eyecup and concentrates on the far end of the access road. The road ends at a hairpin turn, which plunges down into the adjacent farm fields. A huge weeping willow has grown wild and contorted above the hairpin, shading the area with deep shadows. The blur of an oncoming vehicle can be seen, a slow-moving shape through the trees.

Tommy pushes his finger into the trigger guard. He applies light pressure to the trigger pad. He breathes regularly. He waits. He hears the crew cab approaching, and then hears it creak to a stop. He adjusts the eyepiece, panning the scope a few centimeters to the left, and he sees the truck standing still behind the trees.

For the longest time, the driver just sits there, perhaps debating what to do.

Lilly whispers, "You ready, sweetheart?"

The little girl crouched in the shadows behind a massive live oak trembles as she whispers, "Am I supposed to say anything?"

"No, honey . . . just look scared. Remember it's like a play." Lilly looks at the others. "Remember, all of you, just stand behind us and look really, really scared."

Bethany Dupree speaks up in her patented snarky adolescent snarl. "That won't be a problem."

Lilly nods, finding no humor in this comment. She swallows hard and gives them all a nod. "Okay, here we go. Remember to look really, really frightened."

Right then, Lilly Caul steps out from behind the tree, her heart pounding.

She yanks Trudy Quinn, the youngest little girl, out into the open first. Lilly clutches the child by the shoulder strap of her filthy little denim jumper. The child's cornflower-blue eyes are huge with horror. Her lips quiver. She doesn't have to act.

"DRYDEN!"

Lilly's voice booms, making the other children jump as they crowd in behind little Trudy. Lilly presses the muzzle of her Ruger .22-caliber pistol hard against the downy-soft head of the seven-year-old. "GET OUT OF THE TRUCK! UNARMED! HANDS WHERE I CAN SEE THEM! OR I WILL PUT THIS CHILD OUT OF HER MISERY!"

The timbre of Lilly's voice—the coarse, frantic texture of it—is truly terrifying. Drenched in madness, desperation, and soul-searing rage, it is so fearsome, in fact, that some of the younger kids start to cry—for real—and Lilly has a momentary thought: *so be it.* The crying will help sell the routine.

"SHE'S GOING TO BE TRAUMATIZED FOR LIFE BECAUSE OF YOUR SICK SHIT! I'LL BE DOING HER A FAVOR, PUTTING HER

DOWN!! GET OUT OF THAT FUCKING TRUCK OR THE CHILD DIES!"

Earlier that day, Ash had cautioned Lilly that Spencer-Lee Dryden is many things—mentally ill at the top of the list—but one thing he *isn't* is stupid. He would likely see through the ploy the moment Lilly started threatening the kids. But Lilly was privy to a little-known fact about such things. She knew that the angst that lives in all human hearts can spill out at a moment's notice. There's no need to coax the desperation and insanity from the imagination. In these plague times, the thin veneers of self-control, civility, rational thought, and basic humanity can easily snap—whether consciously or unconsciously—resulting in mayhem, madness, and acts such as child murder. For Lilly, the trick here is to not let things go too far.

Even now, with her back to the other kids, her heart hammering in her chest, she feels her tether stretching to its breaking point. "YOU HAVE TEN FUCKING SECONDS! GET OUT OF THAT VEHICLE NOW!!"

Something twists and contorts within Lilly. Her hand tightens on the girl's jumper. Her right index finger tingles on the Ruger's trigger. Her stomach clenches. Her brain swims with contrary emotions, fragments of past trauma, painful memories, a dust devil rising off a prison yard, a stainless steel speculum stippled with her vaginal blood, a bleary memory of losing her only chance to have a baby in a makeshift infirmary beneath the Veterans Memorial Speedway of Woodbury, Georgia, dissolving into machete blades cracking open rotting skulls, and the self-loathing, the disgust, the blinding rage and gut-wrenching guilt after inadvertently shooting a mother and child on the grounds of that same prison, and finally, like a coda to a dissonant symphony, Lilly sees in her imagination an assault rifle in her hands, the back-sight rising to her eye, the trigger closing down, the boom, and the lurid spectacle of a bullet smashing through the skull of a man named Philip Blake.

Right then Lilly makes a critical error, changing the dynamics of the standoff in the spark of a single cerebral synapse firing.

She makes the mistake of looking down at the poor little girl who is attempting to play her role to the hilt. Lilly can see the genuine terror on that tiny angelic face, the miniature tulip lips shivering with fear. The girl's flaxen curls are matted with blood. Her forehead has deep abrasions from the rollover accident, and her chin is bruised. The sight of it cuts through Lilly's rhino-thick skin, her angst, her memories of human travesties that she uses to bolster her courage. The pathos of that tiny face penetrates Lilly down to the deepest core of her being. She can't do this to this innocent little creature, this gift to the world from God. She simply can't put this poor child through this ordeal anymore. She looks down at Trudy Quinn and winks.

The little girl looks up, picks up on the signal, and manages to return Lilly's wink with a tepid smile.

The sound of a truck door bursting open makes Lilly jerk with a start.

Maybe Spencer-Lee Dryden saw the subtle transaction between woman and child. Perhaps he had been peering through the foliage with binoculars, and he caught the exchange, the reassuring wink and the little grin from the girl. Whatever it was that changed his mind, it now propels him out of that crew cab on a wave of madness and rage, a 12-gauge, pistol-grip shotgun in one hand like a grotesque magic wand. He bats away the branches with the hog leg of a gun as he emerges from the undergrowth, his attitude as fearsome as a golem rising out of the mystical mud. His face comes into view, his exposed teeth shimmering in the mossy green light of the clearing. It is the face of a demonic entity, the gruesome mask of a death skull. "I AM COMPLYING WITH YOUR DEMANDS!" he booms. He holds the shotgun above his head. Slowly, carefully, like a coiled snake, he lowers it to the ground, leaving it there. He holds his empty hands up palms open.

Lilly can plainly see that he has a second firearm tucked inside his belt.

"Let them children be." He speaks in the voice of a mad pilgrim, nasally, the consonants buzzing in the back of his scorched throat.

He slowly approaches with righteous, Old Testament swagger. He walks with a limp, which makes his ghastly appearance all the more imposing. "Listen to me now—them babies ain't bargaining chips. You got no right negotiating with them."

From her position in the shadows of a live oak fifty feet away, Lilly can clearly tell he is reaching around for the sidearm.

Several things happen then, all at once, as though choreographed to accompany the burned man and his tirade. The droning insects fall silent. Ash ducks down beneath the level of the Escalade's dashboard. Lilly grabs the little girl and dives to the ground, protecting the child's head.

The other kids scramble for cover, bracing for the kill shot to ring out.

At that moment, Tommy Dupree—crouching apelike behind drapes of willow branches and layers of foliage—is unaware of the shadow behind him closing in. He is focused only on the single head shot that will solve the Spencer-Lee Dryden problem. Tommy doesn't hear the garbled vocalizations or smell the thickening stew of death-rot. He is concentrating solely on what Bob Stookey and Lilly Caul taught him on the makeshift shooting range behind Woodbury's speedway.

He holds his breath, eye pressed against the cup, and centers the man's head in the nucleus of the miniscule circle at the intersection of the crosshairs. He pulls the trigger at the precise moment the lurker pounces on him.

The rifle barks as the ragged creature rams into Tommy, a rusty growl accompanying the blast, the impact of the corpse causing the gun's barrel to waver a just a hair sideways. The fully jacketed armor-piercing 7.62mm round rips through the humid atmosphere, striking the ground at Spencer-Lee Dryden's feet, sending a puff of debris up into the air. The tall man reels, unhurt, instinctively discharging his own weapon.

That second blast goes into the sky, hitting nothing, echoing over the treetops, as Tommy rolls across the matted pine needles and kudzu with a reanimated cadaver latched on to his legs.

Kicking and swinging the rifle as a bludgeon, Tommy tries to beat the thing off him. The creature—a withered, leathery female in tattered farmwife attire, with slimy black teeth and eyes like dull gray opals sunken into its face—absorbs the blows with robotic resilience. It tries to get its rancid teeth into the meaty part of Tommy's thigh but Tommy is too quick for the thing and connects a hard blow of the gun's barrel to the monster's forehead.

The sharp end of the muzzle cracks through the skull and embeds itself in the pulpy matter of the frontal lobe, gushing black fluids down across the cadaver's gaunt features. The creature folds, landing on Tommy's legs, a surprising amount of weight that precipitates a spontaneous grunt from Tommy as he tries to pulls himself clear.

He can see other creatures emerging from the deeper foliage to his right, a couple of males with bloated, waterlogged flesh, and a large female—formerly obese, but now a sack of soggy flesh-folds jiggling off the corners of a waddling, reanimated skeleton. These ragged creatures lock their sights on Tommy as the boy struggles to extricate himself from the weight of the former farmwife.

Finally pulling his legs free, Tommy rolls toward the other side of the thicket.

He barely has time to get his legs under him, rise up, and launch into a dead run before the oncoming creatures swarm him and cut off his egress.

He bursts through a wall of foliage and finds a narrow footpath. Racing down the serpentine trail, he searches for the rendezvous point.

Across the clearing, the dynamic shifts. Spooked by the near miss of the sniper's bullet, Spencer-Lee almost instinctively retreats, whirling around, and hurling back into the shadows of the undergrowth. He lurches around the side of his crew cab, claws open the door, throws the weapon in, and climbs behind the wheel.

His engine howls to life, a cloud of exhaust visible in the upper limbs of the woods.

On the other side of the clearing, Lilly simultaneously gathers the children together. "Everybody, make a chain!" she hollers at them. "Older kids, take the younger kids' hands!—Put the little ones between you!—Quick-quick-quick!—C'mon, stay low and follow me! C'mon! No talking—C'MON!!"

Meanwhile, Ash has shifted the Escalade into Park and flipped the transmission back into 4WD. She quickly climbs out, stays low, and trundles around to the rear end. She kicks the jack out from under the car. Twigs and leaves and debris fly as the rear wheels slam down on the ground. She hurries back to the cab, climbs in, yanks it into Reverse, and floors it.

The SUV screams backward, the gravitational force slamming Ash against the dashboard. Lilly and the kids are waiting near a grove of spindly maples.

"Hurry!—Hurry!—Hurry, everybody! Pile in!" Lilly ushers the children, one after another, into the rear compartment of the massive SUV. As she does this, she gazes out across the clearing, searching the far copse of spindly trees. The crew cab has vanished. Lilly surveys the wooded area on either side of the road. Dryden is gone. Only the thin, dissipating cloud of carbon monoxide remains. Lilly climbs in behind the children, pulling her pistol from her belt. "Okay, let's go! Let's go! We gotta find Tommy before Dryden does!"

Ash puts it in gear and slams the foot-feed down to the floor.

Spencer-Lee gets halfway down the access road when he catches a blurry glimpse of the shooter running behind the trees down a parallel trail.

At first, through the damaged glass of the cab's windshield, the figure appears to be merely a blur of filthy denim scurrying through the woods. But soon, Spencer-Lee identifies the sniper as a child—the poor, mixed-up teenage boy whom Ash had joined back at the outset of the chase—and now Spencer-Lee yanks the steering wheel. The crew cab careens wildly off-road.

For a moment, Spencer-Lee considers calling out to the child. Maybe he can save this kid, teach him a more noble approach to survival. Unfortunately, the forest floor is so bumpy, and the foliage so thick—relentlessly scraping the sides of the vehicle, bullwhipping across the shattered windshield—that Spencer-Lee realizes in one frenzied instant that the kid will never hear him. There's only one way Spencer-Lee is going to save this misguided, abused waif of a kid.

Spencer-Lee makes a sharp turn to the left, the massive grill of the crew cab mowing down a cluster of aimless walkers coming up from the river, drawn to the gunshot and commotion. Bodily fluids and rancid matter spray across the steaming hood, washing up against the windshield and streaming across the cab's bonnet. Spencer-Lee flips on the wipers and ignores the distraction of bloody teeth like kernels of rotten corn gathering in the gutters of the hood.

The land west of the clearing is uneven, primordial, a verdant river valley with untrimmed dirt roads that snake around small kudzu-blanketed hills before plunging down short slopes into quagmires of tide pools, sulfurous, walker-ridden inlets, and Byzantine, oddly shaped coves. Some of the tributaries of the Chattahoochee have flooded to the point of forming tiny ponds and marshes that didn't even exist a week ago, and now many of the pathways appear to vanish without warning, abruptly sinking into the mire. To add to the virtually impassable environment, the fierce afternoon sun has turned the area into a vaporous gumbo pot of low-lying mist and banks of methane so thick, the crew cab's windshield is fogging up. Spencer-Lee reaches up and wipes the condensation from the inside of the glass.

Without warning, a skinny male figure darts across the road directly in front of the crew cab.

Spencer-Lee lets out a shocked gasp and slams his boot down on the brake pedal, the truck's rear wheels immediately locking up, going into a skid on the soupy surface of the road. The boy dives out of the way. The cab spins out of control. Spencer-Lee wrestles the steering wheel. The landscape spins in a deep-green blur, as the boy—glimpsed for one more fleeting moment in Spencer-Lee's peripheral vision—leaps over a parallel ledge.

The truck comes to a sudden stop angled sideways across the road.

Spencer-Lee sits behind the wheel for a moment, breathing hard, sweating, the heat making his mutilated, scorched face prickle. He jacks the driver's-side door open and gets out. He rushes over to the edge of the hill and sees a short, sloping bank leading down to the water's edge. The boy has vanished. He is nowhere in sight. There is hardly a ripple in the marsh, only a ghostly haze of methane adding to the illusion that the boy has performed some kind of diabolical magic trick.

The sound of a large engine approaches from the east—the Escalade, most likely—which instantly gets Spencer-Lee's hackles up.

He takes one last glance down at the marshy cove, and then peers into the distant thicket of trees and creeping vines along the bank, the overgrowth stretching to the north and to the south as far as he can see. The flood level has receded somewhat in this part of the wetlands but the water is still so high that the trees are half-submerged, the great ancient cypresses with their gnarled roots like petrified tentacles probing out into the brackish stew.

He gets an idea. Face twitching, tingling with phantom pain, Spencer-Lee glances over his shoulder at the dense pine forest blanketing the convolutions of the vast, ramshackle river valley—the run-down, derelict bait shops to the south, the pulverized docks, the useless power lines stitching through the high trees to the north, the flooded roads, the beached, demolished houseboats and sunken dinghies.

The noise of the Escalade wavers in the middle distance, the echo of the motor bouncing off the trees. From this vantage point, it's difficult to tell if it's coming this way or leaving the area.

Spencer-Lee goes back to the crew cab and climbs in, flipping open the glove box. He searches through the jumble of owner's manuals, stale packs of cigarettes, old service invoices, and receipts. He finds an old folded state map. He takes it out and spreads it open on the passenger seat. He traces his thumbnail across the farmland to the east, across old Highway 85, past Highway 27, coming to rest on a tiny pinpoint of a dot.

The dot sits in the middle of nowhere.

SIXTEEN

"I'm staying here until hell freezes over or Tommy shows up, whichever comes first." Lilly gazes through the side window at the unforgiving shadows behind the trees, and then nods, more to herself than the others. Her spine twinges for a moment, her nervous system crosswired between her simmering pain and the insidious, debilitating doubt creeping back into her thoughts. Sometimes people disappear in this environment and they stay disappeared. Sometimes they come back and you wish they hadn't. "He'll be here. Trust me. He'll find us. I know he will."

Sitting behind the wheel of the Escalade, she speaks to herself as much as to the others, scanning the impenetrable forest on either side of the rendezvous point. She feels scoured out, hollowed by all the violence and loss. The children hunker in the rear two rows behind her, so silent that their breathing is the only thing heard above the monotonous droning of insects and frogs in the humid air.

"Looks like we got another one, heard us, sensed us, whatever . . . coming up on the right." Ash grips the machete's handle tightly, palm sweaty, gaze fixed on the creature. "Hide your eyes, kids."

Nobody hides their eyes—even the youngest of the children—they just stare through the windows as another ragged male adult stumbles out of the adjacent woods and shambles toward the SUV. This one drags its left leg along like deadwood, the cue-ball-shaped top of the femur bone sticking out of a knotted mess of bloody tendons.

Its upper body is clad in a gouged and torn work shirt—most likely the attire of a former dockworker—its pallid face mutilated and hanging in shreds. Only its milky white eyes and yellow teeth fix themselves on the passengers huddling inside the parked Escalade.

When the creature reaches the front quarter panel, Ash lowers her window, clucks her tongue as though herding chickens, and waits almost nonchalantly for the thing to lunge at her. She thrusts her blade though the opening in a hard, quick, sideways arc, the weapon embedding itself in the thing's scalp. The fluids bubble as the creature starts to collapse.

Ash quickly extracts the machete and wipes the blood-coated blade on the thing's arm before it tumbles to the ground.

Lilly looks over her shoulder at the kids. Some of the younger ones just stare blankly with their thumbs in their mouths, appearing almost catatonic. Others take in the gruesome proceedings with a sort of grim ennui, their eyes glassy and far away, as though witnessing the completion of a household chore, the extermination of a roach or the swatting of a mosquito. The corruption of these innocent little people—or maybe *desensitization* is the better word for it—has taken years but it seems to have completely set in. Lilly can see it in their body language, their eyes.

The process started in earnest over four years ago when the outbreak turned the world upside down for surviving children. It began with the nightmares. Lilly remembers trying to read comforting bedtime stories to the children of Woodbury during the Governor's regime. Nothing helped. Some of the parents had tried to shield young eyes from the horrors of the walking dead, and worse, the brutality of fellow survivors. It hadn't worked. The children—as they always do, eventually—see everything. They internalize it. They absorb it, and dream it, and mutate it into private, personal, nightmare angst that stunts their personalities and makes them sullen and withdrawn.

Now, these eleven children have looked into the face of a *human* monster named Spencer-Lee Dryden, and the sight of those burning red eyes peering out from that devastated black monster-mask of a face has pushed most of these kids over the edge. But somehow, right now, strangely, glancing from face to face, Lilly sees a change in most of them—even the youngest ones—that maybe she should have seen coming all along. It's a change that now comes over little Lucas Dupree in the way-back seats.

"Lilly?" he says softly, aware of the need to stay quiet in order to avoid drawing more walkers. His huge blue eyes blaze with some unnamable emotion.

"Yeah, Luke?"

"Shouldn't we go back?"

"Back where?"

"To kill the burned man."

Lilly takes a deep breath. "We will, Luke. As soon as Tommy gets here. We will. I promise. We're gonna get it done once and for all."

"I'll do it," Chelsea Quinn says from the corner of the middle seat, her tiny chin jutting with courage. She has on a soiled pinafore dress over a filthy Pokemon T-shirt, and for the longest time Lilly had found that little corduroy coverall heartbreakingly adorable. But now, oddly, it looks to Lilly like body armor.

Tyler Coogan gives Chelsea a withering glare. "How are *you* gonna kill some crazy dude? You couldn't kill a fly with its wings torn off."

"Yes I could!" Chelsea's chin juts even more prominently. "I would just stomp on the fly and squash it."

"So that's what you have in mind for this Dryden dude? You're gonna squash him?" At ten years old, Tyler Coogan has just recently entered the prepubescent sarcasm zone, in which every statement seems to come with air quotes. "Oh, that's like totally brilliant, yeah, that'll work."

"Tyler, leave her alone," Jenny Coogan admonishes her brother, her nine-year-old eyes aglow with righteous indignation behind her horn-rimmed eyeglasses.

Chelsea crosses her little arms ruefully. "What if I dropped a boulder on him? Huh? Huh? I'm pretty sure that would squash him real good!"

"Keep it down! You're gonna wake up more walkers." Bethany, the voice of reason from the other side of the back row. "And nobody's gonna squash the burned dude."

A feeble voice, faint and yet firm in its conviction, comes from Tiffany Slocum. "We're gonna shoot him in the head . . . like a walker . . . right?"

Her twin sister nods fervently. "Yep. Tommy's got more bullets. He's gonna do it."

Bobby Quinn chimes in. "And if that doesn't work, I'm gonna do it."

Cindy Nesbit says, "You don't even have a gun, Bobby. How are you gonna shoot him?"

"I'm gonna stab him in the chest with my knife. Then I'm gonna twist it back and forth so it'll tear up all his heart and lungs and stuff."

"That's a good idea," Trudy Quinn comments, contemplating her big brother's plan. "Then he won't be able to kill anybody else like he did our dad."

Lilly has been listening to this strange discourse, fascinated, but now she glances at Ash, who sits in the passenger seat, head down, a tear like a single pearl dangling off her nose. The tear drops in Ash's lap. Lilly feels a pang of empathy for her friend, for the loss of Ash's partner and mate and father of her children. But something deeper within Lilly overrides this twinge of sympathy. Lilly has lost many friends of her own over the last couple of years, including her father and every man she ever loved. The pain is a living thing inside her, metastasizing, spreading, malignant. But now the pain has transformed into something new—an existential savagery not unlike the cold expressions passing among the children. Lilly will happily assist little Bobby Quinn in the twisting of that fucking knife.

Behind Lilly, pressed against the side window, Trudy Quinn begs to differ. "You have to stab him in the head, though, if you don't want him to kill anybody else . . . right? If you don't stab him in the head, he'll turn. Aren't you going to stab him in the head, Bobby?"

Bobby shrugs. "I hope he does turn."

"Why?"

"Because then I can cut his head off and hang it in a tree forever and ever, and he'll have to spend the rest of ever and ever staring down at the world, like a . . . like a . . . bobble head . . . and he won't have any arms or legs, or any way to hurt anybody else ever again, but he'll be in hell because he can never die."

Silence grips the car for a moment. Lilly reaches out and puts a gentle hand on Ash's shoulder. No words are spoken between the two women. But the glance that's exchanged is loaded with portents.

Ash looks down into her lap. "This is all my fault."

"That's ridiculous . . . what are you talking about?" Lilly strokes her shoulder. "This is all the fault of one homicidal maniac."

"I'm the one, got caught . . . I'm the one, trashed his compound, killed his men, got Quinn killed." She thinks about it for a moment. The kids are riveted to her words. "I'm the one turned him into monster."

"Ash, listen to me. He already *was* a monster. And by the way . . . Quinn saved our lives. He died a hero. Quinn was an amazing man. He lived a great life—a full life. He died well, Ash. He did. He died well."

For a moment, Lilly lets the words hang there in the silent vehicle. She glances over her shoulder and sees the faces of children ruminating on her words, her message of heroism, love, and courage.

"Lilly?" Mercy Slocum says at last, her pear-shaped little face all furrowed with thought.

"Yeah, sweetie?"

"What's 'dying well' mean?"

Lilly gives her sad smile and says, "That's an excellent question. Put it this way . . ."

Pausing for a second, Lilly gazes out the shattered side widow at the densely packed rows of sugar maples growing riotous against the taller trees, the massive trunks of ancient live oaks like scabrous behemoths reaching their contorted bones to the sky in immortal tableau, all of it cloaked in thick cables of kudzu and creeping vines.

The dirt macadam on which they sit and wait for a young man who may never arrive—a pair of intersecting paths shrouded by foliage, veiled by undergrowth—looks as though it tunnels through the shadows of the underworld. A dilapidated, weathered sign along the shoulder says LOWER GLASS BRIDGE ROAD 1 MI. The rendezvous point, chosen for its hidden quality, and hastily mapped out on pages torn from an old yellowed Rand McNally atlas, now worries Lilly. Maybe the place is so hidden, even Tommy Dupree can't find it. Lilly's father used to say, "Never tempt fate, darlin'." But maybe that's exactly what Lilly has done by talking about dying well. Tommy Dupree might be doing just that at this very moment somewhere out in the wilderness.

A shiver of dread travels down Lilly's spine, and she looks at Mercy Slocum and finishes her thought. "I guess it means being a hero."

"Like Superman?"

"Yeah . . . but it's even better than that. You die well, you're better than Superman."

"Why?"

"Because Superman has supernatural powers. Your daddy was human, and he died like Superman. A person should be proud of that."

Mercy silently chews on this concept for a moment. "But my daddy can't be proud of nothin' no more 'cause he got hisself dead."

Lilly has no answer.

There is no answer.

An hour passes. The kids get restless, fidgeting in the rear rows, occasionally shoving each other or bickering, the seams in their nervous systems beginning to show. The Escalade's interior turns into an oven—the open windows not helping much, the late-afternoon heat pressing down on them—and Lilly starts running the engine and AC intermittently in order to conserve fuel. They all share the meager supply of drinking water. The car smells of BO and stress and mold. Little Teddy Nesbit falls asleep on his sister's shoulder, the girl squirming and pushing him away. Lilly and Ash keep gently chastising the children to keep quiet and sit still but it doesn't help much.

Lilly hears a noise, looks up at the rearview, and sees a pair of withered, skeletal creatures—apparently once an aging couple in some nursing facility, their emaciated faces sunken like rotted gourds—emerging from the woods and trundling up from the shadows behind the vehicle.

The tattered, moldering creatures are most likely a former couple, still linked by muscle memory—the male in dungarees, the female in a threadbare robe so worn and darkened by the elements it looks like a layer of tar paper—dragging side by side up to the Escalade's hatchback. None of the kids notices them, but Ash sees them right away and reaches for the passenger door handle. Lilly stops her, gets an idea, turns the key, starts the engine, and then flips on the rear wiper blade.

In the rearview Lilly can see the two creatures pausing, mesmerized by the back-and-forth motion of the wiper. Their glassy pale eyes fix on the blur of that rubber blade, and their heads swing mechanically, as though on spindles—back and forth, back and forth—in synchronized motion like two people watching a tennis match. Lilly wrenches the shift lever into Reverse and gives the SUV some gas.

The two former senior citizens instantly flop out of sight. The sound of brittle, desiccated bones crunching under the Escalade's massive rear wheels is faintly audible above the rumble of the engine. The car shudders slightly as it backs over the obstructions. Then Lilly pumps the breaks and brings it to a stop. The freshly mangled and flattened remains lie in the road among all the other bodies put out of commission in the last hour.

Lilly puts the SUV in Park, turns the engine off, and sits there for a moment. She notices Ash gazing around the shadow-veiled crossroad at all the carnage. Lilly sees the extent of it—there must be twenty or more bodies—some stacked up like casualties on a macabre battlefield. Ash wipes her eyes. Has she been crying again? Lilly isn't sure. Ash's stoic exterior has now completely corroded away. But what's left? This is troubling to Lilly on many levels. Lilly needs Ash to be sharp, lucid, and ready to rock at a moment's notice. But more importantly, so do the kids. The kids need her now more than ever.

"You okay?" Lilly asks softly, studying her friend. The bruises, scrapes, burns, and cuts crisscrossing Ash's elegant features— some old, some new—belie her seething inner pain, her loss. Lilly's been there, she knows the look. "Ash?"

"I'm fine." Ash looks up at her. "Lilly, we can't stay here forever."

"Nobody said anything about staying here forever, we're just gonna stay until Tommy gets here."

"Lilly—"

"Don't even start, Ash. I'm not leaving without Tommy. Period. End of discussion."

"We've been sitting here for hours."

"And we'll continue to sit here until—"

"I know, I know," Ash interrupts. Her eyes glitter with anguish and tension. "We'll sit here until hell freezes over, but you know what's going to happen before that—before hell freezes over? We're going to get . . ." She stops herself and glances over her shoulder at the children. Most of the kids display vacant, distracted expressions on their faces. Ash lowers her voice. "We're gonna get *swarmed*, Lilly. Which kinda defeats the purpose. Wouldn't you say?"

Lilly breathes in, tries to control her rage. "You want to take the kids, that's fine. I'll stay here and wait. We'll meet back—"

"Would you stop! We're not splitting up. Tommy will be okay . . . wherever he is. He knows where to find us. C'mon, Lilly. Please."

Lilly looks down. Her stomach clenches. She can't leave. She can't abandon Tommy. But she also knows that Ash is right. They can't sit here waiting much longer. If the walkers don't swarm up on them soon, it'll be Dryden who finds them. She is convinced the madman is still combing the area for them. Tommy is resourceful, strong, smart. At last, Lilly says, "I can't do it, Ash. He's as much my adopted child as the Quinn kids are yours. I can't leave him behind."

Ash burns her gaze into Lilly. "Listen to me. Logic. Think about it. You're not doing Tommy any favors staying here. There's a good chance we're going to be dead meat long before he gets here."

"I don't care. Take the kids. Go. Leave me the pistols and some water."

"No! Negative. We're not going to do that. We get back to Woodbury, we can send out a search party. But we're not splitting up."

Lilly glances out at the wall of trees, the thick skeins of undergrowth and kudzu like tendrils of cancer choking the life out of the forest. The shadows behind the deeper woods swim and dance. Is it the wind tossing the treetops? Or more walkers gathering, sniffing them out? The day is moving toward dusk.

Ash is right. If they stay there much longer it will be too late for all of them. Logic dictates you don't let the safety of one compromise the lives of thirteen others. But Lilly can't bring herself to leave. Her heart feels as though it's sinking down into her gut. She has heard the stories over the years. The sheer terror of losing a child in a shopping mall or a busy street corner is one of the most terrifying things a parent can experience. But this situation is a shopping mall times a billion. Lilly doesn't even know if Tommy was able to escape with his sniper rifle. He had an extra few rounds with him, but no supplies, no water or food. And Dryden fled at the same time Lilly peeled out of the clearing. She's not sure what direction either of them took.

Lilly breathes deeply, trying to come up with the words that will convince Ash to keep waiting, when a small familiar voice rings out from the rear seats.

"Lilly, it's okay."

Gazing over her shoulder, Lilly sees Bethany Dupree staring at her with a heartbreaking expression on her face—a mixture of sorrow, sympathy, and hope. A sturdy little eleven-year-old with saffron-colored hair and a tomboy's direct no-nonsense manner,

Tommy's younger sister now speaks with the clarity of a lawyer making a closing argument. "Tommy has gotten lost many times, and he's always found his way home. He'll make it back to Woodbury. Believe me, Lilly. You don't have to stay."

Lilly ponders the freckled little girl. "Okay, sweetie. Okay. Fine." Lilly reaches down to the shift lever and snaps it into Drive. "You win."

The Escalade roars as the rear wheels dig into the sodden road, launching the vehicle into motion in a cloud of exhaust and debris.

SEVENTEEN

The purple shadows of dusk unfurl across the tobacco fields of eastern Georgia, softening the light and cooling the air. Lilly decides to take Owens Road for the last leg of the journey to Woodbury. The crumbling serpentine of asphalt wends its way through the pine forests of Meriwether County, through rugged granite passes, past desolate crossroads and long-abandoned farms, and ultimately eastward across the outskirts of Woodbury's defunct train yards.

Through the windshield, straight ahead, Lilly sees the first signs of the town's outskirts. Her pulse quickens, the rest of the passengers gazing out their windows in silent awe. Some of the children have never even seen the place but have certainly *heard* of it. Lilly talks about it constantly, the way a person speaks of a former lover, past glories, the heydays of high school, all the agonies and ecstasies of growing up. In a psychological sense, Lilly *did* grow up in this town. She faced loss, personal demons, and unadulterated evil in the form of Philip Blake. But now, as she drives into town from the west, she wonders if Blake was indeed pure evil.

After all the water under the bridge, all the violence in the name of protecting her people, hasn't Lilly done the same thing as Blake?

A bullet-riddled sign looms. SPEED ZONE AHEAD. Highway 109 curves to the left, and then the road narrows and turns into Main Street, the macadam appearing to be strewn with more and more storm debris, more and more unidentifiable human remains lying in morasses of dried blood, petrifying in the unforgiving sun.

Another sign looms, this one broken and hanging on its side: WOODBURY BAPTIST CHURCH WELCOMES YOU. The irony is not lost on Lilly. She remembers the first time she laid eyes on Woodbury: It was night, it was snowing, and a man named Martinez escorted her and Josh Hamilton into a militarized version of an iconic small town. It had been Mayberry by way of Beirut, a place of walls and concertina wire and gun turrets and flaming trash barrels. Now, the once-charming little hamlet—originally a place of low-slung Americana; quaint little feed stores and taverns; nineteenth-century gazebos and railroad switchyards; and manicured lawns with jockeys and bird feeders and bathtub madonnas—has been reduced to a gothic vision of hell on earth.

The Escalade slows as it passes the old Chevron Station, now a blackened ruin with gaping, cavernous holes in the ground filled with storm waters, swimming with the bobbing heads of the undead. This is Bosch's underworld, the ninth circle. The telephone wires have all broken off their poles and now skitter across the ground, snapping in the wind like bullwhips. Streetlight poles lie on their sides, blankets of broken glass glittering diamond-like in the waning light. More and more ragged, soulless figures—the damned, the revenants of the town's former inhabitants—come out from behind fallen awnings and mangled billboards. Much of the barricade surrounding the central safe zone has fallen, some sections burned, others trampled. The massive eighteen-wheeler that originally served as a movable entrance gate now lies on its side, a blackened shell.

The Escalade passes the old watering hole at which Bob Stookey was a regular—Smitty's Cafe—now a gaping wound of a building, the roof blown off, the exposed rebar and wiring like the ribs of a fallen dinosaur. Lilly starts getting a bad feeling as they slowly roll past the tumbledown storefronts of the old U-Save-It Pharmacy, Dilly-D's, and Carrol's Feed and Seed. It's nothing specific. It's merely a dull anxiety brought on by the palpable feeling of being watched.

She can see the town square in the distance, the ghostly gantries of the Veterans Speedway rising up against the darkening sky, the clouds now the color of port wine. She slows the vehicle to a crawl. She and Ash share a nervous glance.

The feeling grows. It's a little bit like being a child and coming home from school and finding something different about your bedroom. Maybe your mother has rearranged the stuffed animals, changed the water in the aquarium, turned off a light, or turned *on* a light. Something is different, and it has been changed recently. Is somebody hiding in your closet? Sleep will not come easy to you tonight when the wind blows the branches against your window.

Lilly keeps slowly driving toward the center of town. Something hums just beneath the drone of summer insects. An odor Lilly can't remember ever having detected drifts on the breeze, a metallic smell like burned circuits. The ruins of Woodbury's residential streets stretch into the distance to Lilly's left. Through the side window, her gaze lingers on one of the houses. Is that a light behind one of the windows? Is that a shadow that just darted across the backyard?

Bethany Dupree is first to break the excruciating silence, her voice coming from the backseats, hushed and awed. "What happened here, Lilly?"

"Good question."

"Do you think David Stern did this?"

"I don't know, sweetie. I have no idea why *anybody* would do this."

Ash mumbles something.

Lilly looks at her. "What was that?"

Ash stares out the window. "I said *scorched earth* . . . it looks like somebody decided it was best to take this whole place out rather than leave it for somebody else."

"Maybe . . . but that still doesn't the answer the question why."

Ash shrugs. "Maybe David Stern lost his mind."

"Yeah, well . . . who hasn't?"

The two women share another glance. Ash can't help but give Lilly a crooked smile. "Speak for yourself."

"Sorry, I was just thinking—"

"Hey! What's *that*?!"

Lilly shoots a glance up at the rearview and sees Bethany Dupree pointing at something off to the right. Lilly glances back at the windshield. She slams on the breaks. The vehicle skids to a stop. The g-forces throw Ash and the kids forward in their seats. Ash looks up, startled. "What the hell, Lilly?"

"Ash, check those two extra magazines." Lilly's voice has gone cold and colorless, her gaze locked on something floating in space, dead ahead, about three blocks away. "The 223 millimeter for the AR-15."

"What is it?" Ash peers through the cracked glass of the windshield, searching the middle distance. "What are you looking at?"

"Reach under your seat and see if you can find that extra box of .22-caliber rounds."

"What's all the—?" Ash goes still when she sees the thing hanging in midair about two hundred yards away, dangling from the massive boom of a construction crane. The crane sits in the ruins of an enormous parking lot in front of the saucer-shaped stadium once known as Veterans Memorial Speedway. The sight of the dark object dangling at the end of a cable, silhouetted against the mauve-colored clouds, causes Ash to straighten as though an electric current has bolted up her spine. She reaches down to the ammunition.

"That was not here last time, that's new." Lilly Caul utters the understatement of the year in a low, taut voice, pulling her Ruger .22 from its holster. She thumbs the hammer back without even looking at the gun, her gaze locked on the figure hanging in the distance.

"It could be anything," Ash murmurs. "Suicide . . . a message to prospective looters. There's no reason to believe we're in—"

"Why bother leaving a message, though? There's nothing here. There's nothing left to loot." She swallows hard. "No . . . I think this is meant for us."

"What?!"

From the rear seats, another tiny voice tinged with terror interjects. "I think we should go somewhere else."

Another child says, "Me, too. I think we should leave this place."

"Everybody stay calm." Lilly puts the vehicle in Drive and slowly proceeds along Main Street. "I won't let anything happen to you. We're just gonna take a closer look. No big deal."

In the rearview, most of the children appear skeptical, their little faces wrinkling and frowning incredulously, as though they know, deep down, this thing in the distance *is* about to become a big fucking deal.

They reach the central intersection of Dromedary and Main and slowly roll past the devastated town square and firebombed courthouse. The building's facade is literally burned off, exposing the charred bones and insulation of the first floor. The door hangs open, ash and cold embers still swirling across the vestibule on the breeze. The enormous copper dome on top has caved in on one side from the blaze, the lawn strewn with human remains, most facedown and scorched beyond recognition. The air smells of burned rubber, acrid smoke, and brimstone. The crickets and cicadas continue to drone, a low, sizzling white noise.

The silence in the Escalade's rear seats seems to deepen and intensify as they pass Lilly's public garden, which now looks as though an army has tromped through it, the vegetation either ground into the earth or blackened by the firestorm. To Lilly's ears, it sounds as though the children are holding their collective breath. In the distance to the north, massive solar panels litter the street, broken into pieces. To the south, the railroad buildings and newly constructed stables have been completely razed, demolished, burned to cinders.

Lilly blinks at the bracing horror of seeing at least a dozen scorched corpses of horses lying strewn across the desolate rail yard.

"Oh, Jesus." Ash's voice shatters the silence as she gapes up at the body dangling fifty feet above the abandoned construction site in front of the speedway. Upon closer scrutiny, it looks male, young, motionless, just swaying gently in the breeze, although it's hard to ascertain its age or gender with the shroud of dark fabric hastily tied over its head. Ash's voice is reduced to barely a whisper. "That's not a suicide, Lilly. Somebody did that recently."

Lilly pulls the SUV up to the speedway entrance, where a huge, weathered, bullet-riddled sign says VETERANS MEMORIAL SPEEDWAY— ESTABLISHED 1974—RACES EVERY SATURDAY NIGHT. She stops the vehicle, slips it into Park, and lets the engine idle. Her heart pounds. Her throat feels tight. The old fears start crawling up her gorge like cold centipedes as she scans the stadium's littered, weedy parking lot, the overturned construction equipment, the ransacked gardens, and the scattered heaps of unidentifiable remains.

The site of a dead man hanging from a cable as though lynched is only part of Lilly's dread.

The racetrack itself has become a potent symbol of Lilly's identity within the larger symbol of Woodbury. More than a petrified dirt oval surrounded by broken-down bleachers and miles of cyclone fencing, more than an iconic piece of southern leisure time, more than a place to grow crops and build wind turbines and have community meetings . . . the racetrack represents the Reformation, the Rebuilding, the Reclaiming of Civilization. Once upon a time, it was the site of Philip Blake's brutal gladiatorial games between humans and walkers. It was the place the Governor took alleged enemies of the state down into the cavernous warrens of underground service bays and offices to be questioned and tortured and raped. Miraculously, Lilly Caul had transformed all of that savagery and horror— albeit fleetingly—into a peaceful community center in which to share and generate resources.

Now she fixes her gaze through the fractured prism of the Escalade's windshield at the slender male corpse hanging by the neck from a construction crane. "How do we know for sure this is recent, Ash?"

"Look at him." Ash stares through the open side window at the body lazily turning in the breeze. "He's still . . . he hasn't turned yet."

"How do you know he's not . . . he hasn't been shot in the . . . you know what I'm saying?"

"Yeah. But. There's no blood. Right?" Ash glances over her shoulder at the kids, still reticent to utter aloud the graphic, grisly truth. "There would be blood. Wouldn't there?"

Lilly shrugs nervously. "It's a dark hood, and it's a long way off."

She looks up at the rearview. In the reflection, she sees the tightly packed seats, and the rapt faces staring as though caught in a dream from which they can't awaken. Some of the kids finally look away, chewing their nails, looking as though they're trying to *wish* the thing out of existence, as if ignoring it might actually make it go away.

Lilly draws her pistol and holds it at the ready, both hands cradling the grip, hammer back, finger on the trigger, safety off, one round in the chamber. In her peripheral vision, she catches glimpses of roamers on the edges of town, tattered silhouettes milling about the trees to the west and the east, coming across the access road. They're heading this way, drawn to the noise of the engine and the smell of living flesh. Lilly grasps the door handle, pauses, turns to Ash, and says, "I'm going to shoot him down."

"No, Lilly . . . wait. Don't do that."

"Why the hell not?"

"Because the noise of the—" Ash abruptly falls silent, her eyes widening as she gazes up at the dead body hanging in space.

Lilly looks up.

In the weakening light, the hanging man has started to twitch. The hooded head begins to loll and jerk. The man's fingers curl and clench and claw at the air, the body outlined in a halo of golden, dusky radiance.

The time it takes for a person to turn from death to the ravenous state of the walking dead varies greatly from individual to individual, and Lilly Caul has seen more people turn than she cares to even admit. She has seen it take mere minutes, and has seen one man lie in state for nearly an hour before the spasms of the plague shivered through him. She has almost grown inured to the process, the strange electrical impulses that seem to flick in the joints and the muscles at the outset, that ragged breathing that follows, the moment the eyes pop open to reveal wormy cataracts. But *this* time, in this bizarre context, in the fading light of the sunset, the change that comes over the hanging man seems alien, macabre . . . and just plain grotesque.

Lilly reaches for the driver's-side door and starts to say something else when the hooded shroud begins to slip off the hanging man's head. Nudged off-kilter by the convulsive, awkward clawing of the fingers, as well as the jerking movements of the body, the hood falls away and reveals the face underneath.

Lilly stares. Even from this distance, she can see that the victim was formerly a twenty-something young man, fit, dark complexioned, maybe Hispanic. She can see that he's slender and sinewy, his skin weathered and sunbaked. All of this gets very little in the way of a reaction, though, despite the fact that the gentleman was obviously executed against his will, very likely as some kind of statement.

The fact is, Lilly does not recognize this former prisoner of the Cuban government—this once brave, stalwart, loyal friend of David Stern. In his undead state, Rafael Machado has the same milky, lifeless, amphibious eyes as thousands and thousands—maybe *hundreds* of thousands—of walkers that have crossed Lilly's path.

But none of that matters right now because Lilly hears a familiar baritone voice calling out behind her, rising over the white noise of crickets.

"Ashley Lynn Duart?" The voice is calm, authoritative, in fact almost bored, like a state trooper asking for someone's license. "At this time, I would ask all of your people, as well as yourself, to kindly throw every last one of your weapons out the windows of your vehicle."

EIGHTEEN

People in the armed services—as well as law enforcement officers, hostage negotiators, and first responders—all agree that the most difficult kind of subject to neutralize is the one with a mental illness. When dealing with a sane adversary, one can operate on a set of reliable expectations. Past performance *does* guarantee a sort of predictable series of outcomes. The enemy will fight to survive . . . up to a point. They will take as few chances as possible, listen to reason, and generally exhibit behavior based on human nature and logic. But the insane will act on their scrambled, magical thinking, which makes encounters exceedingly problematic. Does one treat the crazy as one would treat a rabid dog? Put them down as fast and hard as possible? Or should one keep them talking, keep them distracted?

All of this crosses Lilly's mind in the flicker of an instant as she carefully looks out at the side mirror and registers the tableau reflecting back at her.

Across the street, on the roof of a rusty semitrailer, Spencer-Lee Dryden stands proudly in the waning blue glow of twilight, a 9-millimeter semiauto in each hand, his ruined face glistening grotesquely, his exposed rictus of teeth gleaming. He wears a Kevlar flak vest over his denim chambray shirt.

Two people kneel, gagged, hands tied behind their backs, in front of him—David Stern on the left, Norma Sutters on the right—the wind tossing their ragged, blood-soaked clothing. The sight of these battered hostages sends a momentary jolt of relief through Lilly. She had assumed that both of these people were dead. But her relief is instantly squelched by the 9-millimeter muzzle pressing against the back of each head. Their faces are bruised and lacerated, but their eyes—each pair glittering with tears—reveal their shame and rage in equal parts.

Every few seconds, David Stern shifts his gaze from the metal of the trailer's roof to the poor soul hanging from the cable across the street.

The horrific grief in David Stern's eyes is visible even from Lilly's vantage point fifty yards away. She can see the trail of a tear on his gray, grizzled face, absorbed by the cloth of his gag. Lilly has no idea who the young dark-skinned hanging man is—or *was*—but from the look of David's expression, the two of them had been friends.

This revelation is merely one in a series of synapses firing in Lilly's brain right now, a string of instantaneous reactions bombarding her mind. She turns to Ash and calmly says, "We're gonna do what he says."

Ash swallows. "You sure?"

From the backseat, Bethany Dupree says, "Lilly, I don't think we should—"

"No talking!" Lilly rolls down her window. "From this point on, do exactly what I say!" She slowly, carefully sticks her Ruger out the window, barrel pointed down. "Exactly what I say." She drops the weapon to the ground. In the dusty silence, the gun lands with a metallic thunk. "Trust me, it's the only way we're gonna get out of this alive." She speaks in a flat monotone. "Throw everything out . . . right now . . . everybody . . . knives, guns, everything."

Dryden's voice echoes like a pistol shot over the gantries: "That's an excellent start! Now, if we could see the rest of it, that would be great!"

The others roll down their windows and toss their weapons out of the car. The older children mostly have crowbars, machetes, and knives. Ash throws out the AR-15, a Glock, and a .38-caliber short-barrel. She also pitches her machete, a twelve-inch Randall knife, and even her extra carton of high-caliber ammo. The box hits the ground and spills bullets like marbles across the weeds.

"That's awesome!" the voice praises them from the roof of the semi. "Now, I'd like to ask you all to very slowly open all the doors, and I'd love it if you could all get out of the Caddy."

Nobody in the Escalade moves. Lilly glances over her shoulder and gives the children a nod. "It's going to be okay, I promise. I'll get us out of this. Right now, though, let's just do what he says." Sweat trickles down from her scalp and into her eye, and it burns. She wipes her face. She sniffs back the pain, bracing herself. "Nobody give him a reason to do anything aggressive. Don't make him mad, and we'll be okay. I promise."

Bethany looks at her. "What's gonna happen to us, Lilly?"

Ash chimes in: "Bethany, just do what Lilly says. It's going to be okay."

The friendly baritone voice from outside echoes off the clouds. "Excuse me, kids. I'm gonna need you all to do what I say. Now, let's all very carefully get out of the vehicle, okay? C'mon, gang. Let's all just calmly get out with our hands up."

Lilly's flesh crawls. She looks at the others. "I'm gonna figure it out." She clicks her door open. "I won't let him hurt you." She looks at them. "Cross my heart. C'mon, let's do what he says . . . everybody out."

"The thing to remember here is, I ain't fond of hurting people, and I never *was*, not even a little bit. That's the Lord's honest truth, folks. There's been far too much tragedy already, way too much death. We are steeped in death. We're soaking in it."

The tall man with the burned face speaks in a soft monotone as he leads the group of eleven children and four adults down the middle of the street, past the ruined buildings of Woodbury's long-abandoned business district, past the demolished George Washington elementary school and boarded storefronts of merchant row, toward some unknown destination. He walks behind the prisoners, a sawed-off shotgun in each hand. He has rigged the barrels to remain pointed at Norma and David—the muzzles pressed against the napes of their necks, held in place with rope and duct tape—to ensure that nobody does anything heroic.

The children trundle slowly along in a tight cluster, elbow to elbow, with Ash and Lilly on either side of the gaggle.

Lilly jerks at a noise to her left as a flock of bats takes flight from the gutters of the old cafe, the creatures spiraling up across the darkening sky like inkblots, then coursing out across the heavens in a billowing black carpet of specks. Night has begun to roll in, the sunset almost completely extinguished, the final glowing embers smoldering away to nothing behind the trees. The air smells of must and a cold front moving in, and the indigo light makes the rubble of the devastated buildings glow with an eerie luminous quality.

Lilly keeps limping along with her gaze forward, waiting for the right moment to strike, hyperalert and seeing everything all at once in her peripheral vision. The duct tape that was hastily wound around her sinewy wrists is starting to loosen from the pressure of her flexing. She pretends to obediently trudge along, but she is now working the tape down the length of her hand, flexing and relaxing, flexing and relaxing. She almost has it off, and she keeps trying to catch Ash's eye.

"Hell, I never dreamed I would lose my dear, sweet Sally," the burned man drones on behind her, the deep baritone breaking a little, the emotion choking him. "My Long Tall Sally . . . she meant the world to me, and now *look*. She's gone. A crying shame is what it is. She only wanted to be a mother in this life, a good caring mom, and the Good Lord denied her even that simple and profound pleasure. That's why she was such a good mother to all our kids, our babies, our big ol' extended family. Sally was a good mother to all them babies . . . and now she's gone . . . just . . . gone." He notices something important up ahead and gestures with a nod. "Y'all keep moving, now—through this intersection—it's not much farther. Almost there."

Without making a big deal out of it, Lilly finally slips her hands out of the duct tape shackle. She keeps her wrists behind her back as she walks along, keeps her hands together so nobody can see what she's done. She will go for the shotguns first. Her pulse quickens, her heart thumping painfully in her chest. She will spin around and nudge the barrel of the closest 12 gauge up away from David Stern and directly into the face of the tall man. A trickle of sweat runs down the right side of Lilly's face. She's drenched in perspiration and terrified that Dryden will notice. Her move will have to be quick and definitive—executed before the tall man can react—and it will all depend on Ash. If Lilly can catch Ash's eye, and coordinate a combined counterattack, then maybe, just maybe, they can get out of this alive.

"The world has gone over to the realm of darkness, my friends," Dryden is saying now, leading them along like a demented tour guide. "It is hell on earth. The thousand-year reign. Most folks, shoot, they just figure if you can't beat the devil, join him. You know what I'm saying? Wallow in it. Kill, kill, kill. Before somebody kills you. And if that's playing into Satan's hand, then so be it. But I don't believe that at all. Not at all. All I want to do is protect the children. Protect them at all costs. If that means locking them up, then, well . . . that's just what I'm gonna do . . . because you children are the only hope for us. You are the only future we got. And that's why I'm going to protect you young'uns by any means necessary."

Lilly notices a dull gleam of concertina wire in the darkness ahead of them, just past Dromedary Street, a ring of barbed wire about twenty-five feet in diameter in the middle of the street.

"Now, if that puts somebody diametrically opposed to that objective in the middle of my path," Dryden is saying, "I'm going to deal with them in a decisive manner. But the fact is, I never want *anybody* to get hurt. Even that young Mexican gentleman. Rafael was his name, I believe? I never wanted to do him any harm. Especially after what he did. Damn heroic of him, if I say so myself."

A few inches away from Dryden, yoked to the muzzle of a shotgun, David Stern looks down, his expression crumbling with sadness.

"This day and age," Dryden continues jabbering, "it's the hardest thing to do . . . to die well. But the Mexican did it. He did. No one can take that away from him. You understand? Consider what he did, folks, that's all I'm saying."

The big man pauses, as though for dramatic effect, and Lilly tries to ignore the tingling in the base of her spine, the tightness in her chest, the tension in her neck in the moments before she makes her play.

The superficial facts of how Rafael Rodrigo Machado died—his final thoughts, his willingness to sacrifice himself—would forever be lost to postplague history. But even in her heightened state, Lilly could read between the lines of Dryden's account. She had never met Rafael Machado, but she just knew intuitively by the forlorn expression on David's face that the two men had been friends, and perhaps that is why the Brazilian died the way he did.

Dryden tells the tale with clinical detachment. When he launched his surprise attack on the town, and the bullets started flying, Rafael and David accidentally got separated. Dryden went after the older man, chasing David through the narrow side streets and across the ruins of Woodbury's town square. With superior firepower and drug-fueled stamina, Dryden managed to corner the older man in the parking lot behind the courthouse. David was trapped, blocked off on three sides by the scorched wreckage of overturned trucks. Out of ammo, out of energy, and stubborn to the last, David fell to his knees and launched a salvo of obscenities at the invader. He knew his time was up. He knew he was about to die. But he refused to lie down.

Dryden took aim, when all at once, a loud crash and a scream surprised him off his left flank, and he spun around just in time to see a dark figure burst out of a boarded window in the rear of the courthouse. At first, Dryden thought it was a walker. He instinctively fired at the creature, the bullet barely missing its right leg, when he realized it was the Brazilian.

In a blur, Rafael hurtled across the lot to where David lay. Dryden emptied half his ammo magazine into the air around the two men as Rafael threw his body in front of David, shielding the older man, taking the brunt of the fusillade in his back. Half a dozen direct hits pierced his kidney and the lower part of his spine but he remained crouched in front of his friend, eyes locked, a strange sort of resolve crossing over his face.

Something was whispered between the two men that Dryden would never know.

"Pretty impressive way to go out, you ask me," Dryden is saying now as he leads the group toward the fencing of barbed wire in the middle of Dromedary Street. "I decided the old man should live in honor of his young buddy's final act. It was the least I could do."

In the deep blue twilight, Lilly gets a better view of the crater as they slowly approach.

A fence of razor wire has been haphazardly installed around the massive hole in the street like a barrier in a public garden. A lone chair—a battered old piece of lawn furniture—sits at one end of the fence. The mysterious crater plunges down into darkness as though a hydrogen bomb has been dropped on the town and this huge pit is what remains of ground zero.

"Truth is," the big man continues, "even before this whole mess started, I never wanted anybody in my district to suffer. Even the ones we had to deal with harshly, I didn't want them to be in pain for any longer than was necessary. And believe me, some of them boys deserved to be severely punished. I remember this one gentleman, member of the Chicago Outfit, came down to Atlanta to run the slots at the Riverboat Casino, open some new houses of ill repute, grab some vending machine action and such. I made it known that I would stay out of his way as long as his crimes were of a victimless nature. But then I caught wind he was snatchin' little girls off the street and putting them to work in the bawdy houses down on Piedmont Road. We're talking children no older than twelve or thirteen years old. What I wanted to do to that fella . . . well, there are children present here . . . so just suffice it to say, I went easy on him.

I made sure it was quick and painless." He sees that the children are approaching the edge of the crater, and he signals to them with a little whistle. "Okay, kids, that's far enough. Hold up for a second."

The group comes to an awkward stop at the edge of the pit, the gathering darkness drawing down on the town like a funeral shroud.

From this proximity, Lilly can see down into the pit. She can see the crater walls plunging at least forty feet down to the soggy earthen floor, and a stepladder jury-rigged to one side by bungee cords. Apparently formed by an immense cave-in following some great explosion, the walls are made up of huge stone fragments of pavement and slimy mortar chunks of sewer tunnel. The base of the pit spans a diameter of at least thirty feet, and somebody—Lilly's assuming it's Dryden—has unfurled an old rug across its floor and positioned a couple mattresses along one side.

Right then, Lilly and Ash exchange a fleeting glance. Lilly burns her gaze into Ash's eyes, just for a moment, just enough for a signal to pass between the two women. Ash goes very still, staring at Lilly. In a discreet, furtive shifting of her eyes, Lilly looks at the shotgun on the left, and then at the shotgun on the right. The nod that Ash gives Lilly is barely discernible to the naked eye but it carries much weight and import.

"It's only temporary, folks," Dryden announces from behind them, oblivious to the transaction that has just occurred. He has slowly begun to nudge Norma Sutters and David Stern around the side of the pit. Norma looks as though she is about to pass out, her bruised and battered face downturned, furrowed with pain and desolation. David moves like a robot, emotionless, dazed, somnambulant. "I promise you," Dryden goes on. "Just as soon as I can secure this place, I'm gonna go ahead and prepare better living quarters for y'all. You'll see. This'll be the safest little town in southern Georgia. But for now, you'll be safe down there, and I'll make sure you all get plenty of—"

Lilly makes her move, the sudden and violent explosion of movement cutting off Dryden's words with the abruptness of a film breaking in a projector.

Over the space of a single instant, which seems to stutter and jerk like a jump cut in a film, Lilly kicks one of the shotguns—the one pointing at David Stern—out of Dryden's grasp. The shotgun pinwheels through the air and clatters noisily to the pavement as Dryden rears back, letting out a hard, sharp breath, instinctively squeezing the trigger on the second shotgun.

Luckily, before the gun has even had a chance to discharge, Ash has rammed her shoulder into Dryden, causing the barrel to jerk to the left. The blast misses its mark, crackling in the sky, the heavy-grain shot ripping through the metal flashing along the eaves of an adjacent building. Most of the children instinctively duck, some of them going down on their tummies and covering their heads as though caught in an air raid.

Meanwhile, Lilly has moved in and grabbed the second gun, finding herself in a tug of war with Dryden, each of them trying to wrench the shotgun away from the other. Dryden is stronger than Lilly, and he easily yanks the gun out of her grasp. But by that point, Ash has lunged around behind him, her hands still tied behind her back. She executes a perfect knee block—a move that would not be out of place on a pro football field—knocking Dryden's legs out from under him.

Dryden topples to the pavement, dropping the shotgun. He rolls awkwardly.

Ash tries to kick him, but he rolls across the road to the far curb, banging into the cement barrier. Lilly makes a lunging dive for the shotgun, which has come to rest against the curb. She doesn't see Dryden pulling the small, heavy, leather sap from his back pocket.

Lilly scoops up the shotgun. She doesn't see the tall man springing to his feet with the blackjack gripped tightly in his hand. Lilly cocks the slide, injecting another shell, the sound of Dryden slamming the sap down on the back of Ashley Duart's skull ringing out like a rim shot on a drum. Ash drops to the deck as the big man spins toward Lilly.

Everything becomes a blur as Lilly raises the muzzle and prepares to fire off a shot when she sees the big, arcing swing of

Spencer-Lee Dryden's arm coming straight at her. The sap strikes her head between the eyes just above the bridge of her nose. The impact is like an ice pick plunging into her brain, the sudden stabbing agony an explosion that stiffens her spine and causes her to instantly drop the weapon and collapse. The leprous pavement of Main Street rises up and slams into the side of her face as she falls.

The dusk turns to midnight as the dark, silent void draws down over her.

NINETEEN

Silent, dreamless, empty time passes, Lilly floating, engulfed in eternal night. She floats and floats, as though entire generations are coming and going. Epochs are passing, glaciers cutting rivers, entire ecosystems springing to life, spanning the centuries, and then dying away. Through it all, Lilly continues drifting in a black vacuum. How did she get here? Where is *here* exactly?

In the wake of these questions, a spark of awareness kindles in her midbrain as the sound of a voice penetrates the endless night. "*. . . what was I saying . . . ?*" The voice is crackly, staticky, as though coming from a great distance, broadcasting on an ancient, malfunctioning shortwave. "*. . . oh yeah, I remember now, I was talking about keeping them children safe . . .*"

The words fade in and out of audible range, wavering and warbling in Lilly's ears as though underwater. She blinks and tries to identify the pale, diffuse blur of light hovering above her.

"*. . . I promise you this place is only temporary . . . once I secure the town, we can find a better residential facility . . . believe me . . . it'll be like a regular palace . . . but for now, this little hole in the ground is home sweet home . . . in fact, it's the safest place in the state of Georgia, if you want to get technical . . .*"

Lilly realizes she is lying on her back somewhere cool, dark, and fetid-smelling. She struggles to sit up but her body is encased in cement. It won't cooperate. She can't budge her hands or arms or legs.

She feels as though she's mummified. She can see a portion of the sky above her, and the early-morning sun canting down in brilliant, angelic rays of light. She coughs and gasps for breath. She feels like she's drowning.

"Easy does it, girlfriend," Norma Sutters whispers as she dabs Lilly's forehead with a cold hank of cloth. Lilly tries to focus on the plump, battered, brown face looming over her. "Gonna be okay, Lilly-girl, that head of yours is as hard as a rock."

The rest of the space around her comes into focus. She sees the damp rugs hastily unfurled across the stony floor, the mattresses along one side on which the kids now sit gnome-like with their knees pulled up against their little chests. A few items have been added to the massive hole in the ground, a couple tattered lawn chairs, a cooler, some bottled water sitting on the floor in the corner, and a Coleman lantern, which still burns faintly despite the sharp rays of morning sunlight angling down into the pit.

To her left, Lilly sees Ash sitting cross-legged on the floor, staring into space, her eyes glassy and distant, a makeshift cloth bandage wrapped around her head where the sap broke the skin. She looks like a dazed patient waiting for electroshock therapy.

Then Lilly sees David Stern kneeling next to the Slocum twins, ministering to their cuts and bruises with a damp rag. David looks up at her and says very softly, "Look who's back with the living." He gives Lilly a forlorn smile, ignoring the rambling soliloquy going on above them, echoing down from the lip of the pit. "Welcome home," David utters to Lilly, dabbing the child's scrapes. He smiles again at Lilly and mouths the words, *We missed you.*

Lilly manages to sit up, a ballpeen hammer pounding behind her right eye.

The voice continues droning from above. "Ain't no picnic protecting people . . . I'll tell ya that right now."

Lilly leans back against the scabrous cement wall and takes deep breaths, trying to get her bearings. Her sleeveless denim top is soaked in blood and sweat and unidentifiable fluids, making it feel as though it's glued to her skin. The events of the last few hours come back to her slowly, in flash frames, like the events of a drunken evening coming back to an alcoholic the next morning. The top of her forehead stings, and she reaches up to feel it. She looks at her fingertips and sees crusted, dried blood. Her throat is sore, the stabbing pain in her back returning with a vengeance. She looks up and sees the madman sitting on a lawn chair.

"You gotta be willing to be the one puts his foot down . . . the one ain't afraid to be feared by his people, by his children, feared and respected."

The sight of Dryden up there—his mangled, scorched features crestfallen, verging on tears, as he sits in morning sun in his battered aluminum folding chair—nauseates Lilly, makes her dizzy. He addresses his captives like a drunken father making a wedding speech. "There's gotta be one who protects, one who has the nerve, the stones to keep the bad element away from the innocent, away from the vulnerable and the weak. I ain't never won no popularity contests, not by a long shot, but I'll guarantee you one thing . . . I guard my precious ones with every last shred of my strength. I will gladly die in the service of guarding my beloved." He pauses, hitching in a breath, his voice crumbling with sorrow and grief. "My beloved . . . my beautiful Sally . . . in the end I guess I couldn't keep her safe . . . and I lost everything . . . everything I hold dear. I failed in my mission." He begins to sob. His ruined face creases with misery, his tears tracking down his scarred flesh, his voice demolished by grief. "I'm so sorry, Sally, I'm so sorry I failed ya." He cries a little bit more, and then his eyes seem to fix the people below him. Lilly can feel his glassy stare like the gaze of a dying animal. He sputters and chokes on his words. "This is all my fault . . . I can't control myself . . . I'm sorry, Ashley . . . Miss Caul, I'm so sorry . . . I never should have . . . I'm not . . . I didn't mean to—"

He stops and looks down at the kids, all eleven of them bunched up on the mattresses, the older ones holding and comforting the younger ones. Dryden wipes his eyes. He pulls a handkerchief from his shirt pocket and blows his nose. His permanent grimace of exposed teeth makes him look as though he's grinning mirthlessly.

Spencer-Lee stares at the kids as he says, "I'll never make these mistakes again . . . I promise you, my sweet babies . . . I will keep you safe by any means necessary." His eyes practically roll back in his skull as he cocks his head toward the sound of shuffling feet behind him. Lilly recognizes the telltale noise of walkers, coming from the east, drawn to the ceaseless babbling of the madman. Their stench wafts across the grounds, announcing their arrival. Dryden pulls a long machete from the sheath on his leg. "I will protect y'all from here on in," he says, almost as an afterthought.

He turns and quickly dispatches the three stray roamers, two males and a female, each with the filthy rags of former farmhands. The blade sinks into each skull, spilling rancid fluids and putting each creature out of its misery. Lilly sees the bodies fall behind the barbed-wire barrier, one after another, like cordwood.

Satisfied, Spencer-Lee Dryden turns back to his subjects in the pit and softly proclaims, "Y'all never have to be afraid ever again." The permanent rictus of a grin widens, his cracked blackened lips revealing more of his exposed, yellowed molars. "Daddy's home now."

TWENTY

The words reverberate with horrible implications over the next twelve hours. Lilly keeps hearing that terrible phrase—*Daddy's home*—echoing in her ears, and she keeps ruminating on the fact that she and her people may very well be trapped in this hideous pit for the rest of their lives. She doesn't verbalize this, or even hint to them that she's thinking it, but she can tell the others have drawn the same conclusion. She sees it in their body language and sullen expressions as the madman continues lecturing them, bringing them things, promising them that "Daddy" will never leave their side. Every few hours he lowers foraged food in buckets down to them, plastic containers with various and sundry canned goods, utensils, blankets, lantern oil, even board games that he must have found in some of the surviving homes along Flat Shoals Road. The air in the pit has a moldy, damp quality to it, probably due to the seepage of sewer water through the walls of the cave-in. The crater doesn't feel temporary to Lilly. It feels like a tomb. In fact, she decides to whisper this very thing to David Stern that afternoon during one of the brief respites during which Dryden has gone off to fetch something else—some other provision or necessary item for their comfort—an interval in which the inhabitants of the pit let down their guards and try to figure things out.

"I'm trying to look on the bright side," David grumbles as he combs eight-year-old Cindy Nesbit's hair with a plastic comb that he's kept in his back pocket since the Nixon administration. In her nearly catatonic silence and filthy blouse—stained with road grime and gore—the youngest Nesbit child looks as though she stepped out of the pages of a Charles Dickens tale of impoverished waifs and evil headmasters. David has taken a shine to the Nesbit kids. "It's a hell of a lot better than being out there on your own with all these kids."

"Is it . . . ?" Lilly somberly gazes up at the concertina wire and empty lawn chair at the edge of the hole. Her back is killing her. She can't believe she has returned to Woodbury as a prisoner. She can't fathom that the darkening sky she's currently gazing up at is the same sky that looked down on Woodbury all these years. She digs in her pocket for the bottle of Advil. She swallows another handful of painkillers. "You sure about that?"

David shrugs, continuing to carefully comb the matted hair of the little girl. "No . . . actually I don't believe a word of it." He looks at her. "But I keep telling myself it's true in order to keep myself from going as bat-shit crazy as 'Daddy.'" The way David says "Daddy" drips with hate and contempt and something troubling underneath these feelings—something like bloodlust.

"Point taken." Lilly glances across the pit and sees Norma checking Ash's bandages. The tall, stoic woman sustained a series of injuries in the rollover accident that hadn't revealed themselves until now—a contusion the size of an egg above her hairline, lacerations on the backs of her legs, bruises galore on her arms.

The kids have currently separated into groups according to family. The Slocum twins sit on opposing lawn chairs playing some modified version of patty-cake, their hearts not really in it. The Coogans are on the other side of the pit, sitting side by side, leaning against the wall, each reading a book thrown down to them earlier in the day by Dryden. For a lunatic, Spencer-Lee Dryden apparently has pretty good taste in middle-school-level literature. Ransacking what's left of the burned-out shell of a library, he chose a partially scorched *The Phantom Tollbooth* and *The Diary of a Young Girl* by Anne

Frank, the latter of which, in Lilly's mind, is doubly ironic in this strange context.

They are all Anne Frank now, hiding from ever more menacing layers of danger. In fact, Bethany and Lucas Dupree, who now sit cross-legged on the floor, facing each other, making a halfhearted attempt to play an old, dog-eared Monopoly game, appear to be signaling each other every few minutes with silent gestures, a nod here, a shake of the head there, a pointed finger, a frown, as if the slightest peep from them will tip the scales from this tenuous stalemate into death and disaster.

"I never told you how sorry I am about your friend from Cuba," Lilly says softly to David, wanting to keep him talking, wanting to fill the horrible awkward space with words and the pretense of normality. "How did you two hook up with each other, anyway?"

"He wasn't from Cuba," David says, combing and stroking the passive little girl's hair. "He was Brazilian, but he was in prison on an island just off the Cuban coast. He was a drug runner. He was also maybe the finest person next to Babs I ever met. He comes out of nowhere down by Thomaston, saves my life, and boom. We're brothers from that point on."

"How did—?"

"When Dryden showed up, we tried to fight back, and we got separated," David says, and then proceeds to tell her the whole story.

Lilly listens carefully, and when David reaches the end of the story, she says, "What did Rafael whisper to you? At the end?"

David looks down, sorrow twisting his face. "One word. He said, 'survive.' I thanked him, and I told him I'd give it my best shot."

Lilly looks down. "I'm sorry."

David shrugs. "It is what it is." He swallows the grief and then utters, "I'm still trying to get used to being a widower."

"She was the best of the best. Everybody misses her terribly."

David doesn't say anything then, just keeps combing the dirt from Cindy Nesbit's hair. Then he murmurs without looking up at her, "Sorry to hear about Tommy Dupree, he was a good kid."

Lilly looks at him. "Thank you. I appreciate it. But he's just missing, David, he's not necessarily gone." She pauses. "You mind if I ask you something else?"

"Give the man a break, Lilly-girl," Norma Sutters chimes in from across the pit. "We got plenty of time for catchin' up."

"No, that's okay." David waves off Norma's edict. "Go ahead."

"Why did you do it?"

"Do what?"

"Blow the town to smithereens." She gives him a look. "I understand it was a mess, and it was under siege . . . but why the scorched earth policy?"

David takes in a breath. He exhales softly before saying, "I'm not proud of what I did. But I was alone, and I was getting bombarded from all directions." He swallows back the bile and the bad memories. "After you left, the banditos moved in. Every skinhead, every juicer . . . every psycho cowboy this side of the Mississippi wanted to take this charming little place down. And that's the thing, they didn't just want to rob it clean and strip it to the ground, they wanted to destroy the place. Like it was an offense to their shitty lives. How dare someone try to make a beautiful place to live? They wanted to burn it to the ground because of all that it meant to them. It was something they could never build." Now David looks at her, a rueful, indignant glare, his eyes blazing with righteous anger. "Why did I do it, you ask?" He pauses. "I did it because they were going to do it anyway . . . and at least I could take that satisfaction away from them."

For a brief moment, Lilly stares at her old friend, taken aback by the intensity of his rage. Then she reaches out and puts a hand on his shoulder. She can feel his muscles seizing up with emotion, his upper body trembling. She gives him a tender squeeze. "I get it. It's okay. I'm sorry I pried."

David stops combing the child's hair. He reaches over and touches Lilly's cheek. "You're a good person, Lilly Caul . . . I don't care what anybody says."

She lets out a dry chuckle and starts to say, "It's all water under the—"

"Listen up, y'all!"

The baritone voice shatters the calm like a clap of thunder, cutting off Lilly's words. It sounds as though it comes from the heavens, the voice of an angry god, but as quickly as it insinuates itself into their little hermetically sealed universe, Lilly realizes that it comes from about thirty feet above them.

"I need y'all to pay attention because it's story time!" The burned man clumsily pulls the folding chair back into position at the gate cut into the barbed-wire enclosure. He sounds almost drunk, as though he tippled something during this supply run. But soon Lilly realizes that he's not inebriated at all. His speech is softened and slurred by a wave of tremendous sorrow coursing through him. He's grieving, and this pronouncement is more than likely part of the process. He flops down on the chair.

"This is for the children," he says, opening a large, shopworn leather folder. He holds his machete in his hand as he reads, ever aware of moving shadows behind the buildings, drawn to the sound of his voice. Lilly can't tell if he's reading published pages or his own insane scrawl. "It's for the children because I love them, and my mama used to read to me when I was just a little tyke, so here goes." He takes a deep breath. "Once upon a time, there was a beautiful queen who lived in a beautiful land."

Lilly looks around the basin of the crater as the others gaze upward in uneasy, silent awe. Some of the younger kids have taken seats on mattresses or against the wall, and are already sucking their thumbs, listening intently to the man they were prepared to kill only twenty-four hours earlier, as though the simple pleasure of a bedtime story overrides everything, and reverts them, heartbreakingly, to their default personalities.

"The countryside was green and lush and filled with beautiful flowers," the lunatic in the lawn chair above them is saying, reading from his worn-out portfolio. "There were flowers of all species, there was bougainvillea that climbed up the walls of every castle, and orchids dipped in every color of the rainbow, and daylilies of all shapes and varieties. The lovely tobacco fields to the south of the kingdom were sumptuous and healthy with crops that the people of the kingdom sold to buyers around the world."

Lilly sits down on one of the unoccupied lawn chairs and lets out a sigh. Her spine simmering with that relentless, dull ache, her brain battling the flood of contrary emotions—rage, desolation, disorientation, all touched off by Spencer-Lee Dryden's insane soliloquy—she finds herself wondering if this is the man's autobiography.

"In the heart of this kingdom, there was a dashing, handsome king who ran things with fairness and love, and the people of the kingdom were happy. The king made the kingdom run on time like a perfect, flawless watch, and he loved his fair queen with all his heart. But the queen was sad because she could not have children. She cried sometimes, late at night, alone in her bedchamber. But then, the great tribulations came. The scourge of a great plague spread across the land and infected the kingdom with a horrible sickness. The plague turned the ones who had passed away into demons, cannibals, flesh-eating monsters who—"

A thunderous boom cracks open the sky, making Lilly and everybody else in the pit jerk at the sudden roar.

Spencer-Lee Dryden lurches forward, midsentence, as though pushed by an invisible hand, as the front of his neck and chest erupt. His machete flies out of his hand and tumbles into the pit, landing at Lilly's feet. Like a valve on a pressure cooker busting off, Spencer-Lee's cartilage and bone fragments and blood jettison through the air over the pit. The pink spray rains down on the occupants of the crater. Lilly flinches at the blood spattering her face. But she doesn't look away. She can't take her eyes off the body thirty feet above her as it sags and collapses to the ground, its arms dangling over the ledge like dead vines.

"Lilly?"

The voice—weak, garbled, and yet familiar—sounds as though it's coming from somewhere above them, from across the street, or perhaps from a nearby rooftop, carrying on the breeze. Again, Lilly thinks she might be imagining it.

"Lilly!—You down there?!"

Now Lilly looks at the others, and she sees from their startled expressions that she's not imagining any of this. It's really happening, and that voice belongs to exactly whom she thinks.

TWENTY-ONE

At first, as the gangly fifteen-year-old appears above them, peering over the ledge next to the corpse, silhouetted against the setting sun, nobody notices anything unusual about Tommy Dupree, other than the fact that he's filthy, soaked in river water, and covered in mud and cockleburs from his long journey. Nobody sees anything out of the ordinary as the kid crouches there, near the lip of the crater, still clutching his Winchester. He looks down at the forlorn faces in the shadows of the pit. A series of gasps, sighs of relief, and even a few whispered prayers rise up to greet him. "Oh my God," he says, gaping. "What the fuck?"

"Watch your language," Lilly says with a grin, staring up at the boy. A surge of emotion rises in her, practically taking her breath away. She can't stop grinning. "Thank God . . . thank God you're still kicking. What the hell took you so long?"

Tommy emits a strange combination of a chuckle and a cough, his voice dry as flint, as he gazes down at his friends and siblings. He looks beyond exhausted. "Back off, lady . . . I got here as fast as I could. I got turned around near Mountville."

In the dusky light, his face furrows with cognitive dissonance as he tries to compute the madness he sees spread across the darkness of the pit. He sees the seamy mattresses, the makeshift latrine in the form of a galvanized tub in the corner, games and cards spread across the rugs, and blood spatters stippling the ground and the haggard faces staring back up at him. But mostly, he sees the hollow gazes, the beaten-down spirits.

In a soft, wheezing voice, he utters, "What the hell was this guy trying to prove?"

"Don't try and figure it out," Lilly says. "It's not worth it." She hardly notices the tears in her own eyes. The boy's silhouette has blurred above her, softened by the sunset and the wetness of her gaze. She wants to drop to her knees and thank God for sparing this beautiful young man. She wants to unleash a torrent of tears, but she refuses to lose control. Not yet. She stuffs it back down her throat. She knows that she doesn't have the luxury of expressing feelings right now. She allows herself one extra quick smile at Tommy. "God, it's good to see you."

He grins back at her. "It's good to be seen, believe me." Something in the boy's voice sets off an alarm in Lilly's brain. His words are slightly softened by fatigue, slurred around the corners just slightly. "I was wondering if I'd ever make it."

Norma Sutters stands off by herself, head bowed, plump hands clasped, softly reciting prayers of thanks.

David Stern stares at the boy. "I think you grew a foot since I last saw you."

Lilly chimes back in. "Listen, kiddo, we're all totally happy to see you, and we'll have a wonderful reunion, believe me, but right now we gotta get everybody out of here before that gunshot draws a crowd."

"I'm on it!"

Tommy rises slowly, laboriously. He wavers for a moment, as though drunk or sick, and then gets his bearings and vanishes back into the deepening shadows descending upon the town. Nobody notices the way he's favoring one arm, nor does anyone yet see the dark circles around his eyes or the flushed quality of his face.

Day is slipping into night, and the sky has turned the color of rust. For those in the pit, it's getting more and more difficult to see clearly. The sudden plunge back into silence spooks some of the younger kids. Seven-year-old Lucas Dupree takes a step forward, still clutching his sister's hand. "Is Tommy coming back?" he wants to know. "Is he leaving again? Where's he going?"

Lilly kneels in front of the boy and strokes the child's soiled cheek. "Your brother's not going away, Luke . . . he's just going go get something to help us get out of here." She kisses his forehead and smiles. "Your brother's an honest-to-goodness hero."

The child nods, still looking a little gun-shy and incredulous, intermittently gazing up at the ledge, pondering the heap of flesh that used to be Spencer-Lee Dryden. The body has stopped twitching and now lies stone still.

"Lord, lord, lord . . . what a world," Norma Sutters says, gazing at the body. "What kinda world we livin' in?"

David Stern keeps shaking his head, gazing up at Spencer-Lee Dryden's lifeless arms dangling over the ledge. They look strangely forlorn. David Stern can't seem to formulate any words for it. He just keeps shaking his head.

Tommy returns with a coil of rope in his arms. "I remember seeing this in the old train station building. It's a little scorched around the edges but it should work." He starts lowering the rope. "Tie it around your shoulders." He leans out over the ledge and gets dizzy—Lilly can see it on his face, in his body language—and for the first time since he arrived to rescue them, he looks terribly sick. "I'll lift each of you one at a time and—"

His knee slips on the grease of Spencer-Lee's blood, and he drops the rope.

Letting out a feeble little yelp, Tommy makes one desperate lunge to grab hold of the ledge but the surface is too slippery.

He plunges into the pit.

The boy lands hard on his side next to the piss tub. His breath knocked from his lungs, his body wracked with pain, Tommy turns over onto his back and gasps for air as though suffocating.

Lilly rushes to his side. She kneels, cradling his head and stroking his hair. "Tommy, you okay? Breathe! C'mon, breathe!"

The others gather behind Lilly, their horror-struck gazes fixed on the boy, as Tommy finally catches his breath and mutters, "So that happened."

"Can you sit up?" Lilly helps the boy rise up into an awkward sitting position against the crater wall. She brushes a matted strand of hair out of his eye. "It's okay, just breathe."

Tommy takes a few shallow breaths, looking around the pit, still disoriented. "God, I'm such a fuckup."

"Ssshhhhh." Lilly strokes his hair. He feels hot, feverish. "You saved us, kiddo."

He looks at her. "Should have taken that son of a bitch out at the clearing when I had a clean shot."

"Sshhhh, that's enough. You came through with flying colors. Everything's gonna be fine, we're gonna get out of this hole and . . . and . . . we're gonna be fine."

He nods and swallows the pain and tries to breathe as deeply as possible.

Lilly looks up at Ash, and the two women exchange grim, foreboding looks. Neither one of them is certain of anything anymore, especially something as farfetched as their escape from this tomb of a crater. Lilly glances at the sky a million miles above them. The daylight has faded even further. The heavens have now melted into deeper shades of red and gold, the edges of the clouds stained with deep scarlet as though the sky is bleeding.

Much worse than darkness, though, is the veil of death-stench rolling in now on the cool, clammy twilight, smelling of a desecrated slaughterhouse. Lilly can tell the horde is coming, drawn to the gunshot. She can hear the distant buzz like massive wasps marshaling for an attack. The sound puts a fine layer of gooseflesh on her back. The slow-moving shadows have already started to surround the edge of the pit. Lilly is about to look for weapons when she sees the cloth wrapped around Tommy's mud-spattered arm.

At first, Lilly hadn't put all the pieces of the puzzle together—his hoarse voice, his red-rimmed eyes, his cough, his lethargic movements—but now the realization trickles like ice water down Lilly's spine. She realizes why he felt so warm a minute ago. "What's this, Tommy?" She points to a tourniquet in the form of a torn, blood-soaked piece of his shirttail wrapped tightly around his left forearm with a stick just below the elbow.

He swallows hard. "I was gonna tell you." He flinches at a stabbing pain. It seems to take his breath away. "It happened just a few minutes ago."

"Oh God . . . okay."

"So ironic . . . got all that way here without getting bit, and then I get to Woodbury, and boom."

"Fuck."

"I was coming into town when this little one darted out from behind a tree." He winces again. "Got the jump on me. I didn't see it coming."

"Tommy, Jesus . . . why didn't you . . . ?" Lilly looks around the crater as though an answer lies in the shadows somewhere. She looks back at the boy. "Why didn't you say something?"

"I was gonna tell you when you got outta here." He coughs. "I fought that little thing off and managed to get my knife in through an ear but she nipped me. Got me just above the wrist." He nods at his left arm. "I got a tourniquet on it pretty quick, but it's not helping. I'm pretty much toast, Lilly."

"Stop it!" She springs to her feet. "We're gonna take care of it!" She hears the gnashing, grinding, shuffling drone of the horde pressing in on them. She looks up and sees the first ragged figures milling about the ledge of the crater, pressing in on the barbed wire, brushing up against Dryden's massive corpse. Two large males claw at the overturned lawn chair. "These motherfuckers will not beat us," Lilly hisses through clenched teeth. Then she addresses the dead directly. "YOU WILL NOT FUCKING TAKE HIM!"

"Lilly?" David Stern's hands are on Lilly's shoulders now, making her jump slightly. "Lilly, you know we can't—"

"No!" She shoves the older man away. She kneels next to Tommy, her eyes watering, her heart racing, her mouth dry with panic. She inspects the arm. "The tourniquet should hold off the infection long enough to—"

"No, Lilly, listen to me!" Tommy looks at her with old soul eyes, sad and full of horrible knowledge. "I'm cooked. It's over. I'm okay with it. I just need you to—"

"STOP SAYING THAT!"

Lilly's voice crumbles, the tears coming, her heart breaking, but she ignores it, wiping her eyes with the back of her hand, frantically looking around the pit for something to use on Timmy's infected limb. In her chaotic state, she doesn't notice the massive cadaver above her, the one that used to be Spencer-Lee Dryden, abruptly shuddering as though electricity were jolting through it. Lilly is too preoccupied with her frantic search of the pit to realize that the thing that once was Spencer-Lee is opening its eyes. Over a fraction of a second, its burned face creases in on itself, blackened lips retracting away from an enormous exposed rictus of teeth, a low guttural growl roaring out of it.

Most importantly, Lilly doesn't notice how close the huge, reanimated corpse is to the ledge overhanging the pit until it's too late. She doesn't see it slipping and flailing on the gore-slick precipice, sliding over the edge, until a scream rings out next to her.

"LOOK OUT!"

Lilly looks up and instantly jerks backward, the enormous figure plunging down into the pit, landing with a watery splat on the hard ground in front of her.

Breathing hard, gaping wide-eyed and thunderstruck, Lilly fumbles for the fallen machete. The creature sits up with the gravitational force of a catapult, driving it toward the closest warm, living flesh.

Before Lilly even has a chance to swing the machete, the big corpse has latched on to her left leg just above the ankle, its yellow teeth sinking through old denim and down into her tendons.

TWENTY-TWO

The machete flies out of Lilly's free hand, the pain is so enormous and sudden. She kicks the creature off her, scooting backward on her ass, and then springing to her feet. The searing pain jolts through her with the intensity of a deadly electrical shock. It sends her rearing backward, breathless, knocking over three of the children and slamming into the crater wall.

Now the thing that once was Spencer-Lee Dryden lurches toward the kids, drooling and snarling with feral hunger, arms outstretched, fingers transformed into frozen claws. A salvo of ear-piercing squeals bursts out of the younger children as Ash dives toward the creature, slamming into it as hard as she can, knocking it backward. The enormous dead man staggers but refuses to go down.

David Stern madly searches for the machete. It has vanished. Panicking, he vaults across the pit and slams into the creature, trying to knock it down. The creature grabs David and tries to gnaw on his neck but both of them lose traction on the filthy, blood-slick rug.

The enormous cadaver falls on top of David Stern, its full weight knocking the breath from the older man's lungs. David squirms and gasps and fights off the snapping jaws. Ash, Lilly, and Tommy are all on the other side of the pit, too far away to intercede immediately. David's strength falters. He lets out a moan as his arms cramp, and the scorched, grimacing Spencer-Lee-thing on top of him gets closer and closer to his jugular.

The sound of a large-edged weapon thwacking into the back of the monster's skull reaches David Stern's ears one instant before the body on top of him goes completely flaccid, as limp as a dead fish. The creature collapses on top of David Stern, practically suffocating him in its malodorous girth. David grunts with great effort as he pushes the immense human remains off him.

The body rolls onto its side next to David, and the older man gasps for air. He sees his savior standing on the other side of him, the little person still gripping the massive machete in both her hands. The blade drips blood and black fluids, and Bethany Dupree looks a little stunned by her own actions.

"Okay . . . all right," she utters, more to herself than anybody else. "I killed that thing pretty good."

David Stern stares at the little eleven-year-old woman-child for a moment, catching his breath, and then lets out a spontaneous, nervous, hysterical laugh. "Thank you, sweetheart . . . that was . . . yes . . . that was . . . pretty good indeed."

He rises up and pulls the girl into a desperate embrace, all his grief and pain and nervous energy and terror flowing out of him.

A moment later, Lilly Caul, on the other side of the pit, slides down the wall, collapsing in slow motion, holding her leg. The bite wound bleeds between her fingers. "Somebody get the machete," she croaks in a thin, papery voice as she lands on her ass and holds pressure on the injury, her eyes hot and wide, scanning the pit for the machete.

At the same time, Ash has grabbed a cardboard lid to one of the games, and she's now lunging across the floor to the spot where Lilly sits grimacing, holding pressure on her ankle. Ash crouches next to her. "Gonna tie it off," Ash says in her tense, flat, cold New England accent.

She tears her sleeveless blouse off, revealing her emaciated midriff and bra. Ripping the shirt in half, she quickly wraps the fabric around the wound as tightly as possible. She ties a knot, and then rolls the cardboard into a tube, which she slides under the knot.

In the meantime, Tommy rushes over to Spencer-Lee's remains and starts rifling through his pockets. Behind him, the other children back away, awed by Tommy's mettle and bravery in the face of his own imminent demise. Tommy finds a pocketknife, a crumpled pack of Marlboro Reds, a Bic lighter, a metal flask half-full of unidentified alcohol, and small .38-caliber pistol shoved down the back of the belt. Tommy turns to David Stern and hands over the lighter and the flask. Then Tommy opens the revolver's cylinder and looks in, his eyes widening, his pupils dilating with panic: one bullet remains tucked into a single chamber.

Tommy turns and scuttles over to where Lilly sits in a daze of pain on the crater floor as Ash works on her improvised field dressing. "You're gonna make it, Lilly," Tommy says.

"Tommy, not now!"

"You're gonna make it," he says to her again. "We're gonna get to your bite early enough." He shows her the gun. "There's one bullet left in this, though . . . which is gonna be for me."

"Tommy, please shut up!"

Ash has begun to rotate the cardboard under the knot of the bandage, tightening the fabric of the field tourniquet to the point of cutting off Lilly's circulation. Lilly grunts, wincing at the pressure.

Tommy watches. "You have to do me this one last favor, Lilly," he says, his tears tracking down his pale face like rivulets of scalding-hot mercury.

"Shut up!—SHUT UP!"

By this point, Norma has located the machete, and David has ordered the children to turn around again, and not look, and hold their hands over their ears. Gripping the flask of alcohol in one hand and the lighter in another, David tries to hold in his emotions. His voice has deteriorated, seething with terror. His words come out garbled as he tells the kids, "It'll all be over in a . . . in just a sec . . . don't worry . . . it's . . . it's gonna be okay."

Above them, night has fallen like a funeral pall pulled down over the crater. The cool evening air vibrates with the collective rasp of the swarm, hundreds of them emerging from every quarter, drawn by the noise and voices, their iridescent eyes like reflectors floating over the edges of the pit, some of them shoving, nudging others against the barbed-wire barrier.

Ash looks up at Norma, who approaches awkwardly, holding the machete. "I can't do it, Ash," Norma says, "I'm sorry, you gotta get somebody else to do it."

"Give it to me!" Ash grabs the machete out of Norma's hand. Breathing hard, swallowing her dread, Ash tightens her sweaty grip on the handle. With her free hand, she pulls Lilly's left leg toward her, exposing the wounded area. She clenches her teeth. She starts breathing harder and harder, as though she's about to hyperventilate. She looks at Lilly's sweat-slick face.

Lilly nods.

David moves in with the flask and a lantern, which he has kindled to life, the only light in the pit. The pale yellow radiance illuminates the wall of the crater like a footlight in a nightmarish stage show.

Ash just keeps breathing harder and harder until it begins to dawn on everyone that Ash is also having difficulty completing the procedure. Maybe it's the fact that it's Lilly Caul she's about to chop and quarter, their beloved de facto leader, their north star, their protector, their voice of reason.

"Do it, goddamn it!" Lilly's cry has a razor's edge of hysteria in it. "C'mon, do it—you're torturing me! JUST FUCKING DO IT!"

Tommy puts his arm around Lilly and says very softly, "I'll do it, Lilly." Their eyes meet, the flickering flame painting the boy's face with golden light. In a single heartbeat, something very profound—which nobody present that evening will ever be able to articulate—passes between the two of them. "I'll do it if you promise me one thing," he says. "You'll use that last bullet on me."

"God, no . . . Tommy, please . . . please don't ask me to do that." Lilly's moaning whisper is barely audible, her voice gone, her heart broken, dizziness washing over her. She puts her face into the soft part of Tommy's shoulder, and she lets out all of her pent-up sorrow, grief, and desolation. She sobs out loud, her voice taking on the quality of a wounded animal. She hugs her adopted son to her breast for what feels like the first time and the last time. "No . . . no, no, no . . . God no, no, no."

"I love you," he murmurs into her ear, softly, ensuring that she's the only one who will hear this one last word. "Mom."

In that one transcendent instant, Lilly knows in the deepest chambers of her heart that everything will be measured as either *before* or *after* this moment. "My sweet, sweet son," she utters almost inaudibly into Tommy's ear, as the waves of pain finally engulf her and drown her, pulling her down into a void of unconsciousness.

She collapses into a fetal ball next to the boy, her wounded leg still throbbing, still protruding awkwardly across the ground. She feels now as though she's coming apart at the seams, her temperature spiking, her spirit disconnecting from her body as a yolk might separate from the white, floating, drifting through a sea of agony, a wraith that has slipped free of its corporeal self.

She doesn't see Tommy Dupree painfully rise up and take the machete from Ash. She doesn't see him wobbling on weak knees, dizzy and faint as though drunk with sorrow, as he grips the machete with both hands. She doesn't see his tears shimmering on his porcelain face as he raises the blade. Nor does she hear his grunt of effort as he brings the machete down as hard and fast as possible.

The sonic boom of agony resonates through her body, sending her further into the vacuum of space. She stiffens as the ankle breaks—the snap of cartilage and bone, like a piece of her soul torn away by banshees—followed by the dousing of alcohol, cold and wet on her, the snap of a flint, and the eruption of cleansing fire. The inferno builds and chews through her marrow, a tidal wave of molten-hot pain crashing against her, sending her further into darkness. She can faintly smell the odor of her own burning flesh right before the black tide pours over her, and everything goes silent and dark.

TWENTY-THREE

Miraculously, some time later—minutes or maybe hours, she will never know for sure—her nervous system awakens with a start at the sound of a .38-caliber short-barreled pistol firing in the echo chamber of the crater.

The booming report sparks and spangles the darkness like Roman candles across the insides of Lilly's eyelids, illuminating the delicate radiant capillaries of her flesh like myriad rivers branching across miniature maps. She manages to peer through the slits of her lids and sees the woman named Ash hunched over the body of the boy, the gun smoke from a single blast a nimbus around their bodies, cocooning them in its steel-blue haze.

Lilly opens her mouth to scream but no sound comes out. She sinks back into the eternal, merciful darkness. Please, God . . . let it be a dream.

Later yet, in the wee-hour limbo, her eyelids flutter open again for a single instant to reveal the chaos in the pit, a syrupy slow-motion struggle unfolding before her, partially glimpsed in the flicker of lantern light.

From the darkness above them, the swarm has toppled the concertina-wire barrier inward to the breaking point. Now a single walker plunges into the pit. The stalwart, tenacious Ashley Duart— shirtless, in her bra—stabs the creature through the skull with the long-bladed machete. Then comes another, arms pinwheeling, plummeting into the hole, the machete instantly shutting it down. Then another corpse plunges, flailing, and then another, and another, and Ash greets them with a quick and decisive skewering. Norma and David and Bethany are each pitching in now, stabbing edged weapons into the crania of the monsters until the human remains begin to accumulate across the grimy floor of the pit like the aftermath of a battlefield.

Lilly tries to move, tries to crawl, tries to go and help them, but her body—wracked with agony, her entire left leg numb to the point of paralysis—will not function. Does she feel a phantom left foot? She gets a faint whiff of burned flesh. Or is it the death-stench of the mounting clutter of bodies?

Wavering in and out of consciousness, Lilly catches her last bleary glimpses of walkers tumbling into the hole, her people frantically putting them down in the fashion of a grisly assembly line. Off to the side, the children watch with stoical, empty expressions like the offspring of pig farmers observing the autumn slaughter.

The scene begins to fade, the noise diminishing. Lilly woozily glances to her right and sees the mangled, bloody remnants of her severed left foot. It lies nestled in a blood-soaked cloth, as pale as a marzipan mold. In her weakening state, semiconscious now, sliding back down the greased chute of oblivion, she finds morbid humor in the fact that even in the low flickering lantern light she can see the toes of her amputated appendage still have flaked and streaked evidence of the ineptly applied pink polish she put on back in Atlanta a few weeks ago in a vain attempt at normalcy.

Then she sees another object just beyond her pitiful disembodied foot, and her amusement evaporates. She stares at the slender body partially covered in a blanket as the shade slowly draws down on her vision. Tommy Dupree's remains lie on their side, his legs drawn up against his chest, his arms folded inward as though he is sleeping. The entrance wound in his head is barely visible, and he has a strangely tranquil expression on his face.

It's as though a fist has come out of the darkness and punched Lilly in the gut. She curls into a tight, helpless fetal position and silently sobs, her tears seeping down into the gritty, filthy rug beneath her as the world finally fades back to nothingness.

The rest of that night, the others sleep very little, engulfed in absolute darkness and the horrible stench of dead flesh, surrounded by countless ragged heaps of human remains. The children toss and turn, gripped in fragments of never-ending serial nightmares that have tormented them for the last four years. Ash sits slumped against one wall in her bra, a blanket draped over her shoulders, her head lolling every few moments as she drifts in and out of restless half-sleep.

David Stern lies next to Lilly, keeping an eye on her, intermittently thumbing the Bic lighter to check the makeshift dressing wrapped around the oozing stump where her foot used to be. He has nodded off a few times, snoring so loudly he wakes himself back up to once again flick the lighter on. In the dim yellow light, he sees Lilly's eyes moving fitfully back and forth under her eyelids. He figures she's having one doozy of a dream.

Norma Sutters, sitting against the wall on the other side of Lilly, is the only one who doesn't get a wink of sleep that night. She has an idea brewing in the back of her mind, and she wants to give it plenty of thought before she shares it with the others. Now, she waits for the ubiquitous droning chorus of gurgling, vibrating, dead vocal cords to fade away above her. The swarm has been dispersing for the last hour or so, the noise gradually dwindling. She can hear the awkward shuffling as the creatures lose interest in the contents of the pit and wander back toward the nooks and crannies from which they had come.

The sky starts to change as dawn approaches. Norma is the first to notice it. She's been gazing up at the stars all night, turning the idea over and over in her mind, and now she sees the first hint of the new day as the constellations begin to fade back into the hazy, ashy fabric of the night sky. She looks around the pit. The darkness has transformed ever so slightly like coffee with a hint of milk in it.

Her heart begins to beat faster. It's time to test the idea—perhaps their only chance of getting out of this godforsaken hole alive.

She goes over to Ash and nudges the woman awake. "Ash, honey, it's almost morning."

Ash sits forward with a jerk. She blinks, her eyes glittering with the residue of unspeakable violence. "What?!—fuck! Sorry."

"It's me, sweetie, it's Norma."

"What time is it?"

"Not sure but the light's coming up, it's gotta be four thirty, five . . . something like that."

"Jesus . . . for a second there I thought it was all a fucking dream."

"You and me both, girlfriend." The pale glow of predawn has risen enough now for Norma to see the younger woman's features. Her angular cheeks and patrician nose have seemingly aged many years in one night. Her dark hair looks as though it has turned gray, but Norma quickly realizes it's simply a trick of the light. "You and me both."

The day dawns gray and foggy, a cold front crashing up against the humidity and heat of the Georgia summer, making the sky vanish behind a ceiling of gunmetal haze and giving everything a dream-like cast. The occupants of the pit work in silence, careful not to attract any unwanted attention, while they gradually, laboriously transform the configuration of the objects strewn across the three hundred or so gruesome square feet of carnage.

The jostling shakes Lilly out of a near-catatonic stupor, the passage of time having become meaningless to her, the surreal narrative of her fever dreams deteriorating into lurid, cryptic imagery. As Ash and David gently lift her onto an improvised stretcher made from a collapsed lawn chair, she manages to open her eyes, just slightly, her eyelids feeling as though they weigh a thousand pounds apiece. She feels the stretcher tilt as they lift her onto the pile of human remains. She can't see the results of Norma and David's idea—piling up all those corpses by hand, one at a time, as though building an immense anthill of cadavers—nor can Lilly grasp the enormity of the accomplishment. But she *does* feel—even amidst the relentless, crippling pain radiating through her from the stump of her phantom left foot—the exhilaration of being resurrected from that massive tomb up a staircase made out of dead bodies.

For most of that morning, stacking one body at a time, they had built the mound of corpses. A couple of times the pile collapsed on them like a house of cards or a heap of charcoal briquettes toppling. A few of them vomited from the smell and the slime of rancid blood and fluids soaking their clothes. But they kept at it, kept tossing body after body on the pile, until the mound rose nearly thirty feet high.

Now they pull Lilly up and over the ledge, setting her down on the pavement of Main Street. The breeze blows through her damp, matted hair, stirring her, reaching down into her soul. That *breeze*— that patented magnolia-scented Woodbury breeze—it rouses her further. It feels like freedom, like hope, like wistful memories. Norma and the children stand around Lilly in a semicircle, clutching each other's hands as directed by Ash. Lilly tries to say something but hasn't the strength.

Out of the corner of her eye, she sees Ash and David lifting one last individual from the pit. They haul Tommy's body out on a second jury-rigged stretcher and give Norma a nod. The tears and the waves of pain obscure Lilly's vision, preventing her from seeing Bethany and Norma silently carrying the boy's body down Dromedary Street toward the speedway complex.

Lilly's tears blur the sight of the fogbound town as the group proceeds north, following Norma and Bethany toward the racetrack arena. They pass the bombed-out ruins of the old post office and the ancient live oak that sits like a mythical sentry in front of the burned-out shell of the old Baptist church. Their methodical movements, their careful, measured steps—even the way the children are not making a peep—give the procession an air of mourning, of ritual, of commemoration.

Closing her eyes Lilly tries to block out the pain, and think of

Tommy and his life force and his love. She can feel the presence of the horde lurking just out of sight, behind the derelict Piggly Wiggly, down in the gulleys and dry creek beds of Simmons' Woods, behind the billboards out near the highway, and within every shadow and underneath every rock in town. They mill about, aimlessly waiting, waiting for a signal, a scent, a sound.

Lilly concentrates on the smell of the breeze as they approach the safety of the speedway. Twenty yards left and they're home free. Twenty yards and Lilly will get medical attention. Twenty more yards and the children can breathe out again.

Fifteen . . .

Lilly focuses on that sweet, musky floral scent of the Woodbury wind.

Ten yards to go . . .

Lilly thinks of Tommy, and the fact that he will never smell this breeze again.

Five yards . . .

In her traumatized, tormented stream of consciousness, at that moment, Lilly imagines putting Tommy to bed, pulling the covers up to his chin, kissing him on the forehead, smelling the grassy, earthy scent of his hair, and telling him how much she loves him.

Then she imagines Tommy Dupree falling fast asleep . . . just as the town of Woodbury now slumbers in its deep, abiding silence.

Then, she and the others pass through the arena's portal, and into the shadowy warren of safe passageways and secure rooms.

Los Primeros Dias

A bridge of silver wings stretches from the dead ashes of an unforgiving nightmare to the jeweled vision of a life started anew.

—Aberjhani,
Journey Through the Power of the Rainbow

To this day, the airless, musty, subterranean room repurposed as a makeshift infirmary survives. Through the brutal reign of Major Gene Gavin and his National Guard henchmen . . . through the savage days of Philip Blake, aka the Governor . . . through the violent infiltration of Reverend Jeremiah Garlitz and his flock of zealots . . . and through countless invasions of the dead, attacks by roving bandits, and even David Stern's recent scorched earth conflagrations . . . Woodbury's sole medical clinic, lab, intensive care unit, and maternity ward remains essentially the same as it had been the day the irrepressible Doc Stevens first turned it into just such a facility. That was back when the plague had been young—only weeks after the first incident of the dead attacking the living—and people considered facilities such as this truly temporary. Now folks aren't so sure anymore. Nobody knows whether this nightmarish state of siege will *ever* end. All of which is why David Stern has become the unofficial head of the clinic, as well as self-taught practitioner, neophyte field surgeon, and amateur physical therapist.

"Give it a try," he urges Lilly while drying his hands on a towel. "If it feels weird, we'll adjust it again."

Lilly sits on the edge of a metal exam table on the far end of the cavernous tile room, a space situated directly under the east stands of the stadium. Once a service center office for stock car racers using the underground garages, the room features three halogen lights, two gurneys, a pair of emergency generators ventilated through an exhaust chimney, and metal shelving units stocked with pharmaceuticals, most of these items scavenged from the wastelands over the last four years. Some of the beakers and bottles lined up on the shelves—filled with everything from electrolytes to insulin—date back to the days of Bob Stookey's stewardship.

The room holds profound significance for Lilly Caul. It is the place that Rick Grimes lost his hand to the brutal tortures of the Governor. It is where Philip Blake was nursed back to health after Michonne had gotten her grotesque revenge. It is the private place where Lilly lost her baby, the very tiles lining the walls calling out to her now. She is a born survivor, and this room will see her go on, continuing to struggle, striving for an ordinary life. With this in mind, she pushes herself off the edge of the gurney and puts her full weight on the makeshift prosthetic that David has been working on for days.

"Ouch!" She sniffs back the pain and leans on her good leg, lifting up on the contraption belted and buckled to her stump.

"It's gonna take some getting used to," David comments, grabbing her shoulder and steadying her. "Feel free to use the crutches."

Lilly exhales painfully. Dressed in an old cardigan sweater, her hair pulled back in a tight ponytail, she looks like a woman twenty years older than her actual age, but there's also a glimmer of strength and resolve around the corners of her green eyes. She has cut the left leg of her faded jeans to accommodate the prosthetic, which looks like a horse's bridle has been buckled around her left ankle. The primitive-looking wooden foot, which David has hewn from a newel post, is currently hidden inside her boot. The stump is still tender, despite the fact that it's been healing fairly well.

For the last month, Lilly has been resting up in the infirmary, doing physical therapy, living on soup, antibiotics, and painkillers, and generally taking stock. She has lost twenty-five pounds and written hundreds of pages in her diary. She has grieved the loss of her adopted son, as well as many others who perished in the exodus from Ikea. But in the four weeks since the events in the pit changed the lives of all those who remain stalwart citizens of Woodbury, the only time she had shown her face outside of the speedway complex was to attend the memorial service for Tommy Dupree.

The boy was laid to rest under an oak tree on the edge of a town park next to the graves of Josh Hamilton and Austin Ballard. Lilly stood on two crutches that day, her stump bandaged, softly crying as the others backed away to let her say goodbye in peace.

"Maybe I'll use just one crutch," she says now, putting a little weight back on the prosthetic. "A little practice and I should be able to get around okay." She looks at David. "You do good work, Doc."

"You feel like taking a little walk?" He gives her a grin. "It's a beautiful day."

She smiles at him. "You got any more of those exquisite pain-killers?"

She emerges from the racetrack's north vestibule tentatively, along-side David, blinking at the brilliant sunlight, feeling like a vampire taking her first steps. It's a gorgeous Georgia afternoon, a warm, crystalline, dry Indian summer day. The cloudless sky is pure corn-flower blue, as genial and serene as skies ever get in these parts.

Norma, Ash, and Bethany are waiting for them at the exit gate. Both Norma and Ash have fresh flowers behind their backs and big grins on their faces. Bethany stares with awe on her innocent oval little face. They take turns hugging Lilly and telling her how good she looks. She calls them liars, and Bethany giggles with glee when Lilly shows her the wooden foot, which looks like an appendage off of Frankenstein's monster. Norma and Ash try to hide their moist-ening eyes.

They tour the town, walking slowly down Main Street, David and Norma pointing out all the restorations that are in progress.

Lilly falls into a syncopated rhythm with the single crutch, and soon she's moving along quite easily. She sees that they have begun to fill in the crater at the end of the street with gravel and concrete. They've also cleaned up much of the rubble caused by the firestorms.

Some portions of the building facades are in the process of being painted, and the barricades are back up along Dogwood and Pecan Street. Lilly sees the children now at the far end of the square, gathered in the furrowed dirt of a vegetable garden, fussing and planting handfuls of seeds. Tyler and Jenny Coogan stand at opposite ends of the garden, each cradling a rifle, each diligently keeping guard.

At the end of Jones Mill Road, Lilly and the others pause to rest and have some lunch. They sit at a picnic table at the crest of a small hill. Norma has filled a backpack with canned peaches, dandelion greens, beef jerky, and a horrible-tasting clear liquid that she claims is her latest batch of Georgia white lightning.

They eat and drink, and talk of the future, and at one point, Lilly gazes out across the patchwork grid of narrow streets, tiny buildings, and green public spaces—most of them enclosed behind the walls of the barricade—and she thinks to herself, *This time, maybe, just maybe, Woodbury will live on . . .*

. . . this stubborn, beautiful throwback, this place I will forever, from this day forward, call home.